THE
ANNIHILATION
PROTOCOL

ALSO BY MICHAEL LAURENCE

The Extinction Agenda

THE
ANNIHILATION
PROTOCOL

MICHAEL
LAURENCE

ST. MARTIN'S PRESS

NEW YORK

First published in the United States by St. Martin's Press, an imprint of St. Martin's
Publishing Group

This is a work of fiction. All of the characters, organizations, and events portrayed
in this novel are either products of the author's imagination or are used fictitiously.

www.stmartins.com

Designed By Omar Chapa

The Library of Congress Cataloging-in-Publication Data is available upon request.

ISBN 978-1-250-15851-2 (hardcover)
ISBN 978-1-250-15852-9 (ebook)

Our books may be purchased in bulk for promotional, educational, or business use.
Please contact your local bookseller or the Macmillan Corporate and Premium Sales
Department at 1-800-221-7945, extension 5442, or by email at
MacmillanSpecialMarkets@macmillan.com.

First Edition: 2020

10 9 8 7 6 5 4 3 2 1

For Dani

PROLOGUE

No enterprise is more likely to succeed than one concealed from the enemy until it is ripe for execution.

—Niccolò Machiavelli,
The Art of War (1520)

1

November 27

The man seated at the Macassar ebony desk was not accustomed to being made to wait. He wore a tie the color of honey to call attention to his amber eyes and had the silver hair and aquiline nose of his forebears, as evidenced by the gold-framed portraits hanging in the trompe l'oeil arches. The fireplace behind him cast a flickering glare upon the Gothic armchairs, bookshelves, and red stag heads staring down at him from their mounts. The velvet drapes were drawn, stranding shadows as dark as his mood in the far corners of the room.

He was known as Quintus, Latin for fifth, an honorific bequeathed to him by his father, although if everything went according to plan, he would soon assume the mantle of Quartus, if not higher. Even his esteemed great-grandfather had never aspired to such heights, and yet here he was on the cusp of elevating the status of his family name.

For the last hundred years, the members of Pantheon Maioris Tredecim—literally translated from Latin as Pantheon Majority Thirteen—had been content in their respective roles, largely because they had all been in agreement about their vision of the future. Despite their numeric rankings, their voices had been equal. Decisions affecting all of them had been made by the majority, and always after considerable debate. Technology had shrunk the world, though. Gone were the geographic boundaries that had once defined their empires, blurring borders that had been carefully negotiated and strictly enforced since the advent of the syndicate nearly three and a half centuries ago, allowing the more ambitious among them to discreetly enter industries formerly considered off-limits to all but the specific member who controlled them, causing fortunes to fluctuate and tensions to rise.

None of them had previously contested his ranking, as the wealth and power each honorific possessed had remained relatively constant. The path to ascension—rising in rank and stature—had been one that took decades, a combination of careful long-term planning by one house and a stroke of misfortune for another, and even then, Quintus was aware of it having happened only once every few generations. Time had changed that, however. Estates had diminished, members had grown complacent, and power had diffused through lineages that did nothing but squabble over it. Families were no longer satisfied with maintaining a seat at the table and conspired to rule it. While there had always been such men, none of them had ever attempted a coup d'état.

Until now.

Secundus had fired the first shot in a war that many of them believed had become inevitable. Although he'd vehemently denied it, his family, through subsequent generations, had patiently acquired solid minority holdings in critical resources outside of its designated sphere, resources that would increase exponentially in value after the coming cataclysm, the Great Culling, the time for which, they all agreed, was now at hand. While the other twelve argued over the ultimate mechanism by which they would thin the herd, he'd gambled on releasing one of his minion's engineered viruses—the profits from the fallout would have easily doubled his already considerable estate and elevated him to Primus—and lost. In doing so, he'd not only risked exposing the entire organization; he'd altered its dynamics by sowing the seeds of distrust and instigating what Quintus speculated would become a thirteen-way free-for-all for supremacy that each could blame one of the others for starting.

He'd spent his entire life preparing for this opportunity, though. As his father and grandfather had before him. And now, with Secundus's failure to unleash his pandemic, his position was ripe for the taking.

Tertius and Quartus were undoubtedly already implementing the machinations of their ascension and Quintus's rise was by no means guaranteed, which meant he needed to succeed where Secundus had failed, and his entire plan hinged upon the man who had already missed the prearranged starting time of their virtual meeting.

His laptop chimed to announce the arrival of an external user to his secure virtual conference room. The screen remained black for several moments before the shadowed form of a man drew contrast from the darkness. He wore a *sugegasa,* a conical Asian hat woven from straw. It was frayed around the brim and concealed the upper two-thirds of his face. Only the lobes of his ears, the tip of his nose, and his effeminate mouth and chin were visible above his slender neck and narrow shoulders.

"You're late," Quintus said.

The man made no reply. He rarely spoke, for reasons that were obvious to anyone who'd ever heard the sound of his voice.

"I trust you had no trouble relocating my cache."

The man offered a nearly imperceptible nod.

"Then I assume we're still on schedule."

Again, a slight dip of the chin.

"You know why I called this meeting. Are you prepared to commence?"

A faint shake of the head.

"Must I remind you that the remainder of your payment is contingent upon the successful demonstration of the efficacy of the product?"

The sound of breathing from the speakers became agitated. Quintus intuited the man's question.

"You want to know what happened to the team at the slaughterhouse."

The man nodded.

"Let's just say that no one who knew you were there is in any kind of condition to share that information."

The man made no appreciable movement.

"I've reviewed the forensics reports myself. The containment tanks were pulverized and buried under tons of burning rubble when the roof collapsed, and the gas chromatograph-mass spectrometer failed to detect the presence of any of the precursor chemicals. Everyone with working knowledge of the experimentation is dead. No one has any idea you were ever there."

The man's lips tightened.

"As far as the Thirteen are concerned, you were only there for your experience in bioengineering, to help incorporate that infernal bacterium into the Hoyl's virus. None of them has the slightest idea of what you were working on for me. Or what I intend to do with it. Trust me when I say that if they did, we'd both already be dead or spending what little time we have left on the run, like Secundus."

The man's facial expression remained unchanged.

Quintus felt a surge of anger. He was in charge. The man on the screen was his subordinate and in no position to dictate the direction of this meeting. The hardest part of his job was already done. Anyone could finish it from here for a fraction of the cost. He should just consider himself fortunate that Quintus hadn't already had him killed.

"The Hoyl is dead. His men are dead. Your lab was sanitized before the entire building was incinerated. Any residual traces of the chemicals burned off in the fire. The other twelve in the pantheon are oblivious. My assistant and I are the only two people alive who know what you were doing there."

A knock on his office door. There was only one person who would have dared to interrupt him. He pressed the button underneath his desktop and the lock disengaged.

The door opened inward and a hulking silhouette entered from the anteroom. While Marshall was technically his personal assistant, he hadn't been hired for his secretarial skills. The former U.S. Navy SEAL was the team leader of his personal security detail, which formed a veritable special ops team at his command, day and night. He stood close to seven feet tall and looked like he'd been chiseled from a mountain. His buzz cut was flat, his face angular, and his chest muscular enough to absorb a shotgun blast.

"This arrived at the gate." He carried a rectangular box in his massive hands. "The guy who dropped it off claimed he was given fifty dollars to deliver it to this address. He was told we'd be expecting it."

An unsettling smile appeared from the shadows beneath the brim of the man's triangular hat on the monitor. Quintus glanced up at his assistant, who confirmed his suspicion with a nod.

"What's in the box?" he asked.

The man's smile widened and revealed his teeth all the way back to his molars.

It appeared to be an ordinary cardboard box with Japanese characters scrawled on the top. Quintus recognized them. He knew exactly what they meant.

"I demand an answer," he said. "What's in the box?"

The man's smile didn't falter. He made a rolling gesture with his delicate hand.

Quintus nodded to Marshall, who grabbed the box and walked halfway across the room with it.

"Carefully," he said to Marshall.

His assistant removed a knife from beneath his jacket and slit the tape. Lifted an edge. Tried to see inside. Cautiously raised the opposite flap. He appeared genuinely confused until his eyes suddenly widened and locked onto his employer's.

"What is it?" Quintus asked.

Marshall reached inside, pulled out a gas mask, and let the box fall to the floor. The color drained from his face.

Quintus glanced at the empty box on the floor.

There wasn't a second mask.

"Give it to me!" he shouted. "Hurry!"

Marshall looked at the gas mask, then at Quintus, and then at the gas mask again.

The man on the screen started to laugh. It was a horrible sound, like a wet, rasping cough.

"I order you to give it to me!"

His most trusted confidant, the man who had sworn to protect his life, met his stare.

Marshall's free hand clenched into a fist. He bared his teeth and released a humming noise from deep in his chest. Took several deep breaths.

"I've seen what it does," he said. "How it kills. The pain. Jesus Christ. I can't . . . I'm sorry."

He quickly donned the gas mask.

"You can't do this to me!" Quintus shouted at the laptop monitor. "Do you have any idea who I am? The other twelve will scour the globe to find you. And when they do, you will be subjected to suffering beyond any the world has ever known. You and everyone you hold dear."

The man on the screen continued to make that awful laughing sound.

Marshall stiffened. Sputtered. His eyes widened. Filled with tears. His pupils shrank to pinpricks. He coughed. Grabbed his chest. Tore at his shirt. Vomited into the mask.

Quintus looked at the man on the computer screen, whose laughter abruptly ceased.

Marshall collapsed to the floor. Started to convulse. Flopped onto his back. Gasped. Choked. His entire body clenched, then went limp. He issued a hissing sound that freckled the inside of the visor with blood as his chest deflated.

It didn't rise again.

That had been the promised demonstration.

The Novichok agent had been inside the gas mask, presumably within the canister filter itself.

Less than thirty seconds. Start to finish.

Had Quintus opened the box, there was no doubt in his mind that he would have put on the gas mask. The man on the screen had gambled that his hired hand would betray him and, in doing so, eliminated the only other person who could connect either of them to the slaughterhouse.

When the man finally spoke, it was in a gravelly voice. His cadence was strange, halting. He had to take deep breaths between words.

"I trust . . . you . . . approve."

Quintus walked around his desk and stood over Marshall, whose blood and vomit concealed his face. Like the gas itself, they were completely contained inside the mask. The formerly imposing figure was now little more than a useless mound of flesh.

He was going to need a new assistant.

"Yes," he said. "I believe that will work just fine."

When he returned to the laptop, the man was already gone.

2

December 2

Special Agent James Mason struck off toward the distant police cordon, his FBI windbreaker flaring on the breeze, his sunglasses shielding his blue eyes from the winter sun. His hair had grown shaggy, but getting it cut was the furthest thing from his mind.

"Are you sure it's him?" he asked.

"The remains have been down there under all that mud, doing little more than breeding bacteria for the last week," Todd Locker said. He had a deep, melodic voice that sounded strange coming from someone who looked remarkably like a tall, skinny mole. "All I can say with any kind of certainty is that the decedent is definitively male and somewhere in the neighborhood of fifty years old."

"There should be some rather unmistakable characteristics."

"Gunshot wounds to both shoulders. Front to back, through and through. Exit wounds consistent with what one would expect from nine-millimeter rounds. He had fluid in his lungs, meaning he was still breathing when he went under. So unless you're telling me we're looking for more than one body matching that description, I'm fairly confident this is your guy, but that's why you're here, isn't it?"

Mason nodded. He'd given the assistant director of the Rocky Mountain Regional Forensic Laboratory explicit instructions to call him the moment the divers recovered the body from the bottom of the frozen lake. He needed to be sure this time. He'd already buried his former partner once.

Locker led him from the makeshift parking lot toward a line of skeletal aspens, which served as the framework for a cordon of yellow police tape. He wore his dark hair in a ponytail that bisected the letters CSRT emblazoned across the back of his windbreaker. Tiny round glasses perched on the tip of his nose. His neck was tattooed with a biomechanical design reminiscent of H. R. Giger's work on *Alien*. It was a carefully cultivated appearance intended to keep him out of the courtroom and in the field, where he could better utilize his skills.

Mason flashed his badge at the waiting officer, who controlled access to the site with a digital clipboard. Locker needed no introduction. He showed his ID as a courtesy, thanked the officer by his first name, and struck off through the tall weeds toward the distant lake.

Everything had changed since Mason was last here. Save for the drifts that lingered in the shade of the trees, all of the snow had melted, leaving the field muddy and choppy with the footprints of the crime-scene response team and police divers, who'd been out here dredging the lake for the past five days. Since it froze from the top down, only the surface had turned to ice. The twelve feet of water and twenty inches of sediment beneath it hadn't even been close. Of course, the task of recovering the body would have been a whole lot faster and easier had the weather been more accommodating and their manpower not been divided between four separate crime scenes, none of which was anything resembling textbook. Between the burned ruins of the slaughterhouse, this lake, the wreckage of the tram in the underground tunnel, and the Global Allied Biotechnology and Pharmaceuticals building at the former AgrAmerica complex, Locker had his hands more than full. Especially if Mason was right about the implications of the torn piece of paper he'd found.

And the chemical formula written on it.

He looked back over his shoulder to make sure he was out of earshot before speaking. Very few people involved with the investigation had been apprised of some of the more sensitive details, chief among them that the formula belonged to one of the Soviet Union's rumored Cold War–era Novichok agents, designed to both increase the efficacy of and stabilize the ordinarily volatile German nerve gas sarin, allowing it to persist exponentially longer in the environment in both liquid and gaseous forms.

"Have you found any evidence to suggest they were successfully able to produce any Novichok?"

"We've scoured what's left of the slaughterhouse with state-of-the-art carbon nanotube detectors and run thousands of soil and residue samples through the gas chromatograph-mass spectrometer, but we haven't found so much as a trace of a single precursor chemical. Chances are the fire would have consumed them anyway. Assuming they were even there in the first place."

"We can't afford to assume anything."

"You're telling me. I've got the DHS sniffing all around the periphery of this investigation."

Mason nodded his understanding. The Department of Homeland Security was a veritable army beholden only to the president and granted authority under the Patriot Act to do everything it deemed necessary to protect the citizens of the United States, including insinuating itself into any investigation with potential national security implications.

A gray shape appeared through the cattails, where a raft with an outboard motor had been dragged through the shallows and onto dry ground. The diver who'd recovered the remains sat on the side while he changed out of his neoprene wet suit. He glanced up at the sound of the men crashing toward him through the reeds.

"Can you give us a few minutes?" Locker asked.

The officer nodded, brushed past them, and headed back toward the cordon. He looked like he hadn't slept in days.

Locker climbed up onto the pontoon and leaned over the black body bag resting in the bottom of the boat. He unzipped it halfway and folded back the flap.

A horrible stench struck Mason. He covered his mouth and nose with his hand and stepped past Locker so he could better see the remains. The level of decomposition was more advanced than he'd anticipated. He slipped a nitrile glove onto his free hand, reached inside, and smeared the mud out of the dead man's eyes and mouth. The skin was pallid and gelatinous, distended with absorbed fluids that contorted the features, and yet there was no doubt in his mind that this was the man he'd driven all the way out here to identify.

He turned away and stared across the plains toward the distant Rocky Mountains, their sharp, snowcapped peaks forming a serrated blade against the horizon. His former partner had done the exact same thing before setting into motion the series of events culminating in him shooting the ice beneath his own feet and vanishing into the dark water.

"You know how this works," Locker said. "It's a simple answer to a simple question."

Mason remembered every detail of that night with perfect clarity. He'd sighted Kane down the barrel of his pistol as his former partner materialized from the blowing snow, his left arm hanging uselessly at his side, blood dripping from the gun clenched in his fist. They'd both known there was no way Mason could let him walk away, not after what he'd done, and yet he'd desperately attempted to justify his actions.

Everything I've done has been for my country!

His former partner had been part of a century-old plot to murder countless people with a genetically engineered flu virus. He'd conspired with Victor Thornton, Mason's egomaniacal brother-in-law, and a seemingly immortal monster with piercing blue eyes known as the Hoyl, to integrate a bacterium that accelerated the process of decomposition into the deadly microbe's viral envelope, preventing the threat of mutation and eliminating the need to dispose of the sheer quantity of bodies littering the streets in the wake of the resulting pandemic.

This is about survival. We're fighting a war, whether you choose to admit it or not. A war we're already losing.

Kane had helped track down the IRS agent who'd stumbled upon their financial trail during their plan's lone window of vulnerability and burned her alive to cover their tracks. In doing so, he'd stolen from Mason the one thing in his life that mattered, for that investigative officer was his wife, Angie.

Our entire species is poised on the brink of extinction. We need to act decisively before it's too late.

And he hated Kane for it. Equally, he hated him for drowning himself in the frigid water and taking the names of those who had pulled his strings to his grave with him. Men who hid behind their money and power, who believed themselves to be above the law.

I'm just a cog in the bigger machine. A machine that will continue to roll, with or without me. And there's nothing you can do to stop it.

A machine known as the Thirteen.

They hadn't just been experimenting with the Hoyl's virus inside that slaughterhouse, Mason now knew; they'd been at some unknown stage in the production of a nerve gas deadlier than any the world has ever known, a chemical weapon of mass destruction capable of wiping out entire cities in a matter of seconds, a Novichok agent that was potentially somewhere out there right now. And Mason's former partner had been the only man alive who could have led them to it.

"Is this the body of Special Agent Spencer Kane?" Locker asked.

Mason looked one last time at the distant horizon and started back toward his car.

"Make sure there's nothing left of him when you're done," he said. "Not even ashes."

3

DOWNTOWN DENVER

Mason pinned Kane's picture to the wall. It was still hard to believe his former partner had been able to fool him so completely. And not just him, either. He'd convinced everyone, including the FBI, state and local authorities, multiple teams of forensic investigators, and Rand Marchment, head of the Bradley Strike Force, who'd personally delivered the news of his death to Mason while he was still in the hospital, recovering from the injuries he'd sustained while trying to save his partner. Kane had even deceived his own wife, who'd stood over his grave with Mason and made him feel as though her husband's death was his fault, which he'd truly believed at the time.

He wrote "DECEASED" across the photo and stepped back to appraise his work. The picture of his dead partner was one of dozens he'd just finished posting on the wall. Together, they formed the foundation of his private investigation into the Thirteen. He'd painstakingly re-created the display Locker and his team had constructed in the conference room at division headquarters, including photographs from the various crime scenes associated with the deaths of his in-laws and the discovery of the remains of an estimated fifty undocumented im-migrants in the burned ruins of the slaughterhouse, only he'd expanded upon it to include additional information that even the forensics spe-cialists didn't have. He'd added photos of various people related to the Thirteen, most notably Special Agent Jared Trapp, who, like Kane, had been Mason's partner. Also like Kane, he was now dead, only by Ma-son's hand, not his own.

It had been an act from which Mason derived no pleasure, but, rather, a sick feeling in his stomach at the realization of just how deeply the FBI had been compromised. As long as he didn't know whom he could trust, his only option was to conduct his own investigation in parallel, not only to prevent tipping off other agents who might have been corrupted by the Thirteen but also to potentially expose the ele-ments of subterfuge within their ranks. His special agent in charge, Gabriel Christensen, was about the closest thing to an ally he had inside the Bureau, and even then their relationship was defined by an uneasy kind of trust. Under the circumstances, though, that was about as much as he could hope for.

While copying such sensitive imagery and displaying it in the house of a private citizen was a violation of any number of laws, he didn't see where he had much of a choice in the matter. His new place was still be-ing renovated to make it suitable for habitation by more than termites, and there were presumably construction workers coming and going throughout the day—although he'd yet to actually see any of them doing so—which was why he'd been forced to commandeer a spare room in his old friend Ramses Donovan's apartment. The sprawling suite en-compassed the top two floors of a forty-two-story skyscraper driven like an ebon stake into the heart of downtown Denver. His old friend had gutted both levels and transformed them into his own personal den of debauchery, complete with a private club illuminated by reptile terrariums, a bedroom that had at one time probably had a numbered-ticket dispenser mounted beside the door, and a vault stocked with an arsenal capable of withstanding a siege.

Mason had stripped the walls and proceeded to tack pictures to them, starting with what he believed to be the historical foundation of the Thirteen, including black-and-white photographs of Thomas Elliot

Richter and R. J. Mueller, infamous robber barons from the late nineteenth century, who'd collaborated with the previous incarnations of the Hoyl to release his vile diseases and profit from the sale of the cures. Their lines of financial inheritance had proved murky and convoluted, with money flowing through countless shell companies and offshore accounts, while their power had been distributed unevenly throughout subsequent generations.

His wife's family tree was heavily represented, too. Her great-grandfather had conspired with Richter to create the Spanish flu, which killed between fifty and a hundred million people at the end of World War I, so they could make billions from their patent on aspirin. Her father and brother had entered the biotechnology field and attempted a similar financial coup, one that had destroyed what little remained of the Thornton bloodline, which had come to an abrupt end with Angie.

Mason traced the contours of her face with his fingertips. He hadn't been able to bring himself to label her as deceased. It was an act of finality, one he wasn't certain he'd ever be able to perform, at least not while the Thirteen were still out there, and it was her memory that fanned the flames of his vengeance.

He heard a soft gasp behind him and glanced back. Alejandra Vigil stood in the doorway. She seemed to be looking straight through him, staring at the pictures of the crime scenes. The color had drained from her face, which made the scarred half appear more prominent. Gone was the flush of life he'd grown accustomed to seeing over the past week, replaced by the hardness of the woman who'd miraculously survived the horrors perpetrated at the locations hanging from the walls around her.

"I'm sure the last thing in the world you want is to be reminded of what happened," he said, "but it feels like—"

"We are missing something," she said, and slowly entered the room.

"Yeah, and whatever it is just might be the only thing that can help us find the people ultimately responsible for what happened to you."

Before enduring unspeakable atrocities at the hands of the Hoyl, she'd been with Cuerpo de Fuerzas Especiales. Had it not been for her training and an almost superhuman will to live, she never would have survived to lead Mason to the man who'd killed his wife. He hated making her relive the events, but there was simply no other way. She'd seen things that no one else had, which was part of the reason why she hadn't returned to Mexico and the special forces unit she'd abandoned to search for her missing sister; the other part being Ramses, who rarely let anyone get close to him, especially not whichever flavor of the month was currently sharing his bed.

Alejandra walked past photographs stolen straight from her worst nightmares. Mason had arranged them chronologically, starting with the burned remains of the barn and subterranean chambers at Fairacre Ranch, where she'd been taken after surviving the injection of the deadly virus and her subsequent trek across the Sonoran Desert. It was there that she'd been subjected to the decomposition bacterium that had caused her disfigurement, and there where she'd inflicted the same damage upon the Hoyl.

The internal setup of the structure was similar to that of the rock quarry his strike force had stumbled upon the previous year in Arizona, where undocumented immigrants who'd been exposed to various incarnations of the monster's virus had been strung up in wooden stalls and left to rot. He'd discovered the same carnage inside the slaughterhouse, officially classified as Crime Scene 1—CS1—at the southern end of a secret twenty-two-mile subterranean tunnel.

She hesitated near the detail photographs of the knocking pen that had once been used to immobilize and incapacitate cows being led to slaughter. The walls of the contraption had buckled beneath the weight of the fallen roof and its metal surfaces were scored with carbon from the fire that had consumed the building around it. Mason had found her inside of it, her arms drawn behind her back to hold the chain suspending a guillotinelike mechanism above her neck and a captive-bolt gun pressed to her forehead, the cord attached to its firing rod clenched between her teeth. Had she let go of either, he would have discovered her with her neck broken and a hole punched through her skull.

Alejandra surveyed pictures of the lake where they'd found Kane's body—CS2—and the wreckage of the tram—CS3—he'd used to escape the conflagration inside a three-story concrete building—CS4—on the AgrAmerica complex, the corporate headquarters of the Thornton family's agricultural empire, where Mason had killed the Hoyl. There were snapshots of mountains of scorched rubble and body bags containing the burned remains that had been dragged out from beneath it.

The final set of photographs had been taken inside the abandoned building near the old airport where Mason had lost nearly an entire SWAT team. They'd gone in with the intention of disrupting a deal for a biological weapon, only to find that not only were they too late but that they'd been expected. A trap Locker had called a "sophisticated self-cleansing gas chamber" had been set for them, using a burning lantern and a dense cloud of methane gas sealed inside a cubicle formed from airtight plastic sheeting. The moment they'd torn the opaque barrier, the concentration of methane had dropped to a combustible level and nearly incinerated them all.

"This place is different," she said, tapping the pictures.

Mason knew what she meant. While he was certain it was connected to the other crime scenes, it felt somehow separate.

"The Hoyl killed his victims in a clinical, dispassionate manner," he said. "This explosion was designed to inflict the most visceral damage possible, like the trap he set for you in the slaughterhouse. From a behavioral standpoint, it's a completely different MO."

"An emotional one."

"Exactly," he said. "It doesn't mesh with anything else we know about him."

"He hated me for what I did to him."

"I don't doubt that for a second, but if killing you were truly that important to him, why wouldn't he have done it himself? Why waste time rigging the knocking pen when the building was about to come down on his head?"

"Because he wanted me to know I was going to die," she whispered. She unconsciously placed her hand on her scarred cheek. "He wanted me to suffer."

Alejandra turned away from the pictures and tried to brush past him before he could see the glint of fear in her eye. She nearly bumped into Gunnar Backstrom as he entered the room. He'd shed his Caraceni suit jacket, loosened his tie, and rolled up his sleeves, ready to get down to business.

"The system's live," he said. "I'm ready whenever you are."

Ramses slipped in behind him and leaned against the back wall. His tight black V-neck revealed portions of the tattoos on his upper pecs, between which hung a Teutonic cross on a rawhide cord. As usual, he wore his jet-black hair slicked back and an unreadable expression on his face.

"What'd you do to upset Allie—?" he started to say, but stopped when he saw what Mason had done to the room. "The hell, man?"

"I did a little redecorating," Mason said.

"You don't see me coming into that roach motel of yours and putting holes in your walls. Not that you don't have enough already. Holes, I mean."

"Probably roaches, too," Gunnar said.

"Funny. You were saying . . . ?"

Gunnar smirked.

"Everything's logged in and ready to go. Time to cast out our bait and see if anything bites."

4

"Once we start down this road, there's no turning back," Ramses said. The computer setup in front of him was so advanced, it resembled the bridge of a starship. He spun around in his leather command chair and looked at each of them in turn. "We're about to take a deep dive into a dark hole with no bottom."

Mason fully understood the ramifications of what they were preparing to do. While he appreciated his old friend's concern, he'd passed the point of no return long ago. The moment the Thirteen murdered his wife, they'd declared a war that couldn't end without the complete annihilation of one side or the other.

"What choice do we have?" he asked. "We have no leads on the Thirteen and no way of knowing whether or not they were able to produce any quantity of Novichok A-234, a single drop of which would be enough to kill everyone in this room."

"I'm still not convinced this is the right approach, though," Gunnar said from his perch on the stool at the eating bar. The wavering blue reflections of the moonlight passing through the glass-bottomed swimming pool above him highlighted the scar running down his forehead, through his eyebrow, and over his cheekbone, a parting gift from the Hoyl. "This is like opening the Pandora's box of crazy."

Gunnar was brilliant in ways that defied comprehension. He possessed a preternatural understanding of high finance and the ability to bend technology to his will, skill sets he'd combined to re-create the secret website the Thirteen had used to both communicate and manipulate global financial events. Each of the nine monitors mounted to the wall above the computer displayed a different function, from stock indices and network feeds to satellite-positioning beacons and monitors upon which data and real-time conversations scrolled past so quickly that he'd been forced to write an NSA-style algorithm to pluck specific keywords and phrases out of the ether. Hidden somewhere within this torrent of information were the clues that would ultimately lead them to the members of the organization they were hunting.

"You know as well as I do that every conspiracy theory contains a seed of truth," Ramses said.

"True, but you're talking about cultivating the ones sown in fields of insanity."

"Even potentially unreliable sources are better than no sources at all," Mason said. "A single viable lead is all we need. We can't just sit around waiting for something else to happen. We need to get our message out there and hope to God we find the Novichok in time."

"Surely we are not the only ones who know of the Thirteen," Alejandra said. She padded across the tiled floor in her bare feet and grabbed a six-pack from a refrigerator filled almost exclusively with beer. "Someone will reply to us. It is up to us to decide if they can be trusted."

She offered a bottle to each of them, hopped up on the desk behind Ramses, and crossed her legs in front of her. He unconsciously stroked her calf with the back of his hand, an intimate display of affection Mason was unaccustomed to seeing from him.

"Then we need to agree right here and now that we don't act on any information until we're able to authenticate it," Gunnar said. "I don't like the idea of dealing with people who hide behind screen names."

"Speaking of which," Mason said, "are you sure none of this can be traced back to us? We don't want the Thirteen to see us coming until we're in a position to make our move. Considering they've infiltrated the FBI and however many other agencies, they have more than enough power to shut us down before we even get started."

"Trust me, this beast is cloaked in multiple layers of invisibility," Ramses said. Mason glanced at Gunnar, who confirmed as much with a nod. "Why'd you look at him? You think I don't have extensive experience conducting business online with total anonymity?"

Mason pretended not to hear him. While Ramses considered himself a purveyor of vices for clients of discriminating taste, there were aspects of his professional life that Mason would rather not know, largely because if his old friend ever fell from the legal tightrope he'd chosen to walk, Mason would have no choice but to take him down himself.

"Try it out," Gunnar said. "Let's see if Ramses is as good as he thinks he is."

"Prepare to have your minds blown," Ramses said, and offered Mason a wireless headset with an attached microphone. He switched the feed to the central monitor and brought up a program featuring six color-coded horizontal graphs labeled with different units of measurement for amplitude, all set against a constant axis of time, in milliseconds. It was an audiovisual biometrics program. Voiceprint analysis. "Of course, I did have a little help with some of the more intricate aspects of the programming."

"A little?" Gunnar said. He reached past Ramses and hit the mouse. The monitor beside the biometrics display showed Mason's face, as recorded by a camera that tracked his movements and superimposed a digital template composed of hundreds of dots connected by straight lines. Another click and a black mask with bloodred Xs for eyes appeared over his face. He turned from side to side and watched the mask re-form as though it were made from liquid. "There's no way of removing the mask. It combines with your existing features in such a way that the two become so hopelessly and inextricably entwined that even I couldn't separate them again."

"Testing," Mason said. "One, two, three."

A markedly different voice emerged from the speakers with a split-second delay, almost like the echo caused by a bad cell phone connection.

Jagged colored lines slashed across the graphs, followed in rapid succession by second, modified versions. His words appeared on the screen to the left of it in several columns at once, each containing a translation in a different language.

"The audiovisual modulator utilizes a randomizer function that alters both your voice and its behavioral tract, the combination of your unique voiceprint, inflection, and accent," Gunnar said. "It literally converts it into a completely different voice with a discrete spectrogram entirely distinct from your own."

"So there's no way anyone will be able to identify my voice?" Mason said.

"Not a chance."

"This bad boy's ready to go live over a dozen radio frequencies and Internet channels," Ramses said. "I'll set it to record and then repeat at irregular intervals. The words themselves will be posted on any number of message boards and inserted into virtual chats using the screen name XQtioner. We'll reach the right people, for sure, but it remains to be seen if any of them will reach back."

Mason nodded and looked from Ramses to Gunnar to Alejandra. The moment felt monumental, as though they stood at the precipice of a life-altering event. He could see it in their eyes. They recognized it, too.

He turned to face the whiteboard they'd mounted to the wall beside the monitors, the primitive predecessor of the photographic display he'd assembled down the hall, and focused on the stylized cross symbol drawn in the center.

And let the words flow.

"A shadow organization has insinuated itself into our midst. It has quietly infiltrated our governments and compromised our law-enforcement agencies in an effort to manipulate the course of world events from behind the scenes. This entity wields so much money and power that there's nothing beyond its reach. No goal it can't achieve. No group or individual it can't co-opt. And it's no longer content to sit back and allow its subtle machinations to run their course. The time has come for it to step out into the open and claim the entire world as its own, but to do so, it needs to cull the global population to a more manageable size, one that can be more effectively controlled, more efficiently ruled. One that views it as the savior of mankind, rather than its oppressor. One unwilling to rise in revolt against the agency of its enslavement, a cabal that calls itself the Thirteen."

Mason paused. He suddenly understood Ramses' concern. The conspiracy theorists they hoped to reach weren't the only ones hiding in the dark web. The monsters they were hunting were out there, too. Waiting. Watching. And they wouldn't take kindly to someone poking a stick into the shadows where they lurked.

"At this very moment," he continued, "they're preparing to unleash hell upon this Earth, to inflict widespread and indiscriminate suffering beyond our worst nightmares, and whether we like it or not, we're the only ones standing in their way. We have to stop them, and the only way to do so is by pooling our resources, starting with information. We need to know everything you've heard about them, no matter how anecdotal or inconsequential it might seem, if we're to have any chance of identifying them and drawing them out into the open. It's high time someone exposed them for what they truly are and put an end to their genocidal agenda, once and for all."

PART I

Human population growth is probably the single most serious long-term threat to survival. . . . If it isn't controlled voluntarily, it will be controlled involuntarily by an increase in disease, starvation and war.

—HRH Prince Philip, Duke of Edinburgh,
People magazine *(1981)*

5

GREELEY, COLORADO

December 25

Mason stood at the foot of his wife's grave, unable to raise his eyes from the yellowed patch of sod, which had yet to firmly take root. Soon enough, the grass would grow thick and green, and only the marble headstone would stand testament to the fact that Angela Thornton Mason had ever existed at all.

"Merry Christmas, Angie," he finally said, his frozen breath trailing back over his shoulder.

The wind whispered through the boughs of the spruces and rattled the skeletal branches of the poplars and elms. Dead leaves cartwheeled across the lawn and came to rest against the two adjacent mounds, which had been more recently filled and resodded. The proximity of the graves angered him, but at the same time, it was what she would have wanted. While the two men buried inside them—Paul and Victor Thornton—had been victims of their own insatiable greed, it didn't change the fact that they were her father and brother, or mitigate their respective roles in her death.

Angie had always seen the best in people, even those whose actions Mason found irredeemable. It had been one of the more glaring differences between them. His wife had viewed others as the products of their circumstances, gifted with the potential to rise above them, while through the course of his work he'd seen so many succumb to their violent animalistic natures that he was convinced mankind had commenced its devolution. Discovering the existence of men like the Thirteen had only compounded this belief. He was no longer able to see the good in people. Worse, he was unable to sense it within himself. All he felt was rage, the desire to lash out at those who had robbed him of the only person in his life who'd given it meaning. And it didn't help that their trail was growing colder by the minute while he searched for clues he was beginning to think he might never find.

Mason looked up into the blue sky to forestall the tears he could feel threatening to fall. A part of him resented it for its beauty, for without his wife in this world, it didn't seem right that the sun should ever shine again.

"I can't do this without you," he whispered.

He lowered his head and wiped his eyes with the back of his hand.

There was so much he wanted to say, but the words eluded him. Angie had always been able to read him like a book anyway. Wherever she was now, she probably knew better than he did what he was feeling. He had no doubt she'd forgiven him for not being there when she'd needed him the most; he just hoped she'd be able to forgive him for the things he feared he was going to have to do.

He walked carefully around the grave and placed a single red rose on top of her headstone, next to where the statue of a crying angel leaned over it, her cheek resting on her forearm, her cherubic features racked with sorrow. He wanted to lay his head down next to hers, but he knew that if he did, he'd never find the will to raise it again.

A hand settled gently onto his shoulder. He turned and found Ramses standing behind him. His old friend wore sunglasses to conceal whatever emotions he might have been experiencing. It was an unexpected gesture from a man Mason often forgot was more than a caricature, one who'd survived things so terrible, he hadn't even shared the details with his closest friends.

"She's in a better place," Ramses said.

"Do you really believe that?"

"Most of the time." He offered a half smile. "I'd hate to think the sacrifices good people make along the way don't matter, that their lives serve no purpose other than to protect and enrich men who grow fat from their suffering."

Mason nodded. He didn't know what had happened to Ramses in Afghanistan, only that he'd learned more about loss than any man should have to, which was why his old friend had practically dragged him out here today. Had he not done so, Lord only knew how long it would have taken Mason to summon the strength to visit his wife's grave on his own.

"I hope you're right," he said.

"When have I ever not been?"

The cell phone in the holster on Mason's left hip vibrated. It was an encrypted stealth model with anti-interception technology and location-spoofing features that made it impossible to trace or tap, and alerted him if anyone so much as tried. The only way to unlock it was by allowing it to simultaneously run fingerprint and facial-recognition scans to confirm his identity. If either failed, not only would the device go into permanent lockdown mode, it would erase every byte of data and corrupt the processor. He placed his thumb on the scanner and raised the pinhole camera to his face. The screen awakened and displayed a message box, inside of which were three words that caused his pulse to race.

SOMEONE REACHED BACK.

Ramses tipped the screen so he could see it. "It's about time."

Mason kissed his fingertips and pressed them against his wife's headstone.

"See you soon," he whispered, and struck off toward Ramses' car.

There were three numbers programmed into his stealth phone. He speed-dialed the first and waited for the call to connect. Gunnar answered on the first ring.

"You're not going to believe this," he said.

"Try me," Mason replied.

"I was just sitting here watching the monitors when a guy calling himself Anomaly—spelled using the Greek letters alpha and omega to replace the first A and the o, as in the beginning and end of all things—broke through the firewall using an algorithm the likes of which I've never seen before—high-end, military-grade stuff—and opened a chat window right in the middle of the screen. The entire exchange lasted less than fifteen seconds."

"What did he say?"

Mason opened the passenger door of Ramses' sleek black Jaguar F-Type and lowered himself into a seat that felt like it was mere inches above the asphalt. He put the call on speaker the moment Ramses climbed in and closed the door behind him.

"He said—and I quote—'Never again speak of the Thirteen.'"

"Did you reply?"

"Of course," Gunnar said. "I asked why not, to which he replied 'You are on their radar now. They will come for you and there is nothing you can do to stop them.'"

The way he said it made the hairs rise on the backs of Mason's arms.

"Let them come," Ramses said. "It'll save us the trouble of tracking them down."

"Did he give you anything we can use?" Mason asked.

"I told him we were looking for information that would lead us to them," Gunnar said. "He said—and again I quote—'Ask yourself why FEMA would trigger the level-two activation of its EOCs in the forty-eight contiguous states.' And then he terminated the connection."

The Federal Emergency Management Agency had established emergency operations centers in every state to help streamline its response to natural and man-made disasters. These EOCs coordinated with various national agencies and managed on-site operations of local medical, firefighting, and law-enforcement personnel. Level-two activation indicated there was the potential for an incident that necessitated the involvement of several of the agencies that formed the EOCs, requiring round-the-clock staffing to monitor a developing situation. A danger level that high was generally reserved for hurricanes or wildfires that promised significant casualties or actionable intel suggesting an impending terrorist attack, catastrophes that would require federal assistance if they failed in their efforts to control them, localized events generally confined by geography. Activation on a national scale implied they were dealing with a much larger threat, which also explained why the Department of Homeland Security, the federal branch responsible for the administration of FEMA, was hovering over Locker's investigation.

"Can you find out when the activation was triggered?" Mason asked.

"Give me a second," Gunnar said. His fingers buzzed across his keyboard. "November seventeenth."

"Nothing overly suspicious about that," Ramses said. "It's the day after we ended the threat of the flu virus."

"And the day the formal investigation commenced," Mason said. "I'll bet Anomaly knows all of this and he's just testing us."

"That was my theory, at least initially," Gunnar said. "But it doesn't explain why FEMA hasn't lowered the activation level."

"Do you think they know about the chemical formula I found?"

"They might by now, but they couldn't have learned about it until maybe three weeks ago, at the earliest. That leaves roughly two weeks during which they were actively monitoring a situation that had nothing to do with your discovery."

"They must have intelligence that we don't," Mason said. "Are they waiting for the flu virus to crop up somewhere else?"

"Everyone who had anything to do with that plot is dead," Ramses said.

"Not everyone," Mason said. "The man who commissioned the Hoyl to create the virus is still out there."

There was another explanation he'd been reluctant to consider until now. Perhaps they hadn't derailed the plan to launch the pandemic after all. The Hoyl was composed of a group of men who shared the same lineage, all of whom had taken up the mantle to perpetuate the illusion of immortality. Thus, only one could be active at any given time, regardless of how many were out there. A new version might appear following the death of his predecessor or merely rise to the forefront when called upon to fulfill his role in the extinction agenda of his masters. Each had a unique skill set when it came to engineering diseases, an unmistakable signature that separated him from the others, like warheads in the apocalyptic arsenal of the Thirteen.

They were identified using the biological abbreviation for filial generation, F, and their respective number in their bloodline. Mason had seen incontrovertible proof of the deaths of the early iterations known as F1 and F2, but the version immediately preceding the one he'd killed, the father of the monster that murdered his wife, had been conspicuously absent. Was it possible the incarnation known as F3 had picked up where his son left off? And was he preparing to release the virus at that very moment?

Or, worse, had F4 somehow survived? Mason clearly remembered the scarred man struggling to pry the chain from around his neck as it pulled him up into the darkness, but he'd never actually seen a body, as he'd been trapped in his debriefing while the remains were being collected, and any pictures of the monster's corpse that might have been taken were conspicuously absent from the crime-scene report.

And what, if anything, did either of them have to do with the chemical formula he'd found in the slaughterhouse?

It was time he demanded some answers from a man who wasn't likely to give them—at least not for free.

"Do me a favor, Gunnar," Mason said. "See if you can arrange a meeting with an old friend of ours. Emphasis on *old,* not on *friend.*"

"Are you sure that's the approach you want to take?"

"I have a hunch that if there's anyone who can help us figure out what's going on here, it's him."

6

DOWNTOWN DENVER

December 26

Mason glanced at the monitor of his laptop, which he'd set up on a table in the room he'd appropriated from Ramses. The clock read 11:13 A.M., and yet the screen remained blank.

"He should have logged in by now."

"It's all part of the negotiations," Gunnar said. "He wants to make us sweat a little first. Nothing tips the scales like desperation."

The man they hoped would be able to offer some insight into the continued elevation of FEMA's activation levels was already fifteen minutes late for the virtual meeting they'd arranged in an encrypted conference room, and that was on top of the six hours he'd made them wait for his initial reply to Gunnar's request for a sit-down, which he'd then scheduled for the following day, presumably to remind them who held all of the cards.

"Trust me, I'll get the answers out of him," Mason said. "One way or another."

He'd hoped they'd be able to conduct their business in person at the man's home, beneath which was a bunker that housed a veritable treasure trove of documents and artifacts available nowhere else in the world. He was certain that hidden within them, somewhere, were the identities of the Thirteen, which was undoubtedly why the man had insisted that their meeting be conducted online. He wasn't about to give up that information—assuming he even knew he had it—for nothing.

A chime announced the arrival of the man on the other end.

"Showtime," Ramses said. He'd run a cord from Mason's laptop to a separate monitor on the other side of the room so that he, Alejandra, and Gunnar could watch from the couch. "Let's see if this guy's really got that hair-trigger-personality thing going on, like you seem to think."

Mason checked his image in the box in the upper right corner of the screen to confirm that the wall behind him didn't betray any secrets that the other man didn't already know. He wanted the pictures of the crime scenes to serve as a visual reminder of their shared history, both for what they'd accomplished and what they'd lost, in the hope of forging an emotional connection.

He approved the man's request and the screen went black for several seconds before an elderly man with a full head of white hair and a beard like Santa Claus appeared. He wore flannel pajamas buttoned all the way up to his neck and a fuzzy blue bathrobe. The smile on his ruddy face was genuine and without so much as a hint of the true nature of the man himself.

"Young James Mason!" the old man said. He'd positioned a dry-erase board behind him to provide a seamless white backdrop. "I am pleasantly surprised to see you again so soon."

Ramses looked at Mason over the top of the monitor and raised his eyebrows in disbelief.

"I trust you enjoyed your holiday season," the old man said. His eyes clouded and his smile became a frown. "In so much as someone in your position can. I understand better than most how you must feel, especially under the circumstances. Fortunately, I can still see my beloved Dolores in the eyes of my children and grandchildren, despite their being scattered to the four winds. I am not so technologically adept that I am overly proficient with such things as Skype and FaceTime, but they allowed me to share each and every one of those eight magical nights with them."

His face abruptly brightened and his smile returned.

"Thanks for agreeing to meet with me, Johan," Mason said. "I only wish we'd been able to do so in person—"

"So you could scour my archives for the information you didn't know to look for when you were here last?" The old man smirked and playfully wagged his finger at the camera. "One does not reach such an advanced age without learning a few things in the process."

Johan Mahler was the ultimate dichotomy, a perfect schizophrenic who was not only aware of his human and inhuman sides but embraced both with everything he had. This half was not only impossible not to like but made it hard to believe that the other half actually existed. He and Mason had been introduced by Gunnar, who'd used his considerable skills at even greater monetary gain to follow the paper trails of men he believed Johan had targeted for their financial interests or professional vulnerabilities. Instead, his services had been utilized to track down some of the most elusive Nazi war criminals who'd escaped justice at Nuremberg so that Johan's pet assassin—a man who called himself Seraph—could execute them in cold blood. Photographs of their lifeless faces now hung beside the old black-and-white pictures of their younger selves during the war. Those keepsakes adorned the walls of Johan's trophy room, hidden in the secure bunker underneath the Mahler mansion, which had been built by his grandfather, whose entire extended family had been eradicated during the Holocaust. His son, Johan's father, had joined forces with the Nakam Group to make sure that not even the lowliest Nazi Anwärter or Bewerber escaped their wrath.

In Johan's eyes, they'd deserved to die for the crimes they had committed against his people, his heritage, his family. Mason, in turn, had used him to find and subsequently kill those who were responsible for the death of his wife. He'd never forget the expression on Johan's face when he explained how much the two of them were alike. Nor would Mason forget how he'd felt when he realized the old man was right.

"I don't know what Gunnar told you, but I need—"

"Oh, I know exactly what you need, James. In fact, I am rather surprised it took you so long."

As if on cue, a man wearing a gray sweater vest and a cranberry button-down shirt materialized at Johan's side. He had pale skin, bushy eyebrows, and thick, dark hair, and while he appeared to be the old man's caretaker/butler, Mason knew he was much more than that. Asher Ben-Menachem had been a battalion commander in the Golani Brigade of the Israeli Defense Forces, through his service to which he had first come into contact with Ramses in the Middle East, although Mason didn't know any of the details and wasn't entirely sure he wanted to, given everything else he knew about the man, who now placed a stack of photographs on the table in front of Johan and took his leave.

"You are concerned that you didn't completely eliminate the threat, that some unknown reservoir of the virus or, heaven forbid, the Hoyl himself has survived," Johan said.

"Something to that effect," Mason replied.

"I do not have all of the answers you seek, but perhaps I can at least offer peace of mind."

He lifted the first photograph from the top of the stack and held it up to his webcam. Pictures could be doctored in any number of ways, from something as simple as changing the color of the eyes to more dramatic alterations that could reshape the structure of the face and render the subject unrecognizable. At the same time, however, there were some things that simply couldn't be Photoshopped. Chief among them was the spark of animation, the intangible quality of life. There was no artist or computer program on the planet that could effectively give life or take it. Anyone who'd ever seen photos of a murder scene recognized this universal truth, which was why the picture erased any doubts Mason might have had.

"This is one of my most treasured possessions, and I have you to thank for it," Johan said. "Do you question its authenticity?"

Mason was 100 percent certain that this was the man he'd last seen being hauled up into the rafters by the chain wrapped around his neck. Someone had wiped the soot from his face, but it had been a rushed job, and a gray paste remained along his hairline. The quality of the lighting made his skin look waxy and his scars more pronounced. His blond eyebrows and hair were patchy and grew in wiry tufts. His nose and mouth were skeletal where the bacterium he'd meant to use to accelerate the decomposition of those killed by his virus had eaten through his flesh. The deep lacerations he'd inflicted upon his own neck were raw and puckered. But it was his eyes—those awful blue eyes—that proved that the Hoyl was utterly and unmistakably dead.

"No," Mason said.

Johan lowered the picture and set it aside.

"I will spare you asking your next question and give you the only answer I can," he said. The expression on his face was one of sympathy. "We have not detected the presence of his replacement, although we remain vigilant. When another Hoyl emerges, as we have no doubt he will, we will make certain he joins the rest of his lineage in the grave."

The remainder of the stack contained pictures of each of the previous generations of Hoyls. Johan held them up to the camera, one after the other, to illustrate his point. Their faces were dissimilar enough that when viewed in sequence, the differences were apparent, although much less so than the obvious similarities. They all had the same blond hair and blue eyes and shared the same bloodline, one that could only be traced as far as the surname Fischer, the fourth most common in Germany. The first two photos—F1 and F2, respectively—were in black and white and showed only the faces of the dead men, their lifeless eyes staring fixedly at the camera. Powder burns surrounded the coins on their foreheads. The third was in faded color and featured F3 slogging through a mangrove swamp with men in white isolation suits, but unlike his predecessors, he was still very much alive. There was still at least one more Hoyl out there, one who specialized in hemorrhagic fevers and likely didn't take kindly to Mason's having killed his son.

"How can we be certain he didn't just pick up where his son left off?" Mason asked.

"Every Hoyl has a unique signature. Believe me when I say that you would know if F3 were here. He is anything but subtle."

Whether Mason liked it or not, their destinies were forever entwined, but wherever the third incarnation of the Hoyl was now, he couldn't have been responsible for the elevated activation levels of the emergency operations centers, which had been raised long before he could have found out about his son's death. Plus, the risk of exposure was too great; if there was one thing the Hoyl knew how to do, it was to strike when least expected and vanish again as though he'd never been there at all.

Mason recalled what Kane had said before he'd been forced to shoot him.

You think ours was the only game in town?

Between the discovery of the chemical formula for Novichok A-234 and the distinct MO exhibited by the sadistic death traps in the knocking pen and the gas chamber, he was starting to believe that a second would-be mass murderer had been inside the slaughterhouse, preparing a backup plan in case the flu virus failed, one reliant upon the most lethal nerve gas ever imagined. If his instincts were right, by killing F4, he'd eliminated the only witness who knew his identity.

He could almost hear the Hoyl laughing at him from beyond the grave.

"Did any of the Fischer incarnations have known accomplices?" he asked.

"Outside of associations of convenience, they were solitary creatures whose masters kept them on a short leash," Johan said.

"And you know who these masters are, don't you?"

"They have had many through the years."

"As many as thirteen?"

"Very good, James. Perhaps there is hope for you yet."

"What do you know about the Thirteen?"

"More than you are capable of understanding as of yet, I'm afraid."

"You'd be surprised what I'm capable of understanding."

"And you would be more surprised by what you are not," Johan said.

Here was where Mason needed to tread carefully. He needed to find out what Johan knew about the initial activation of the emergency operations centers, but he had very little in the way of collateral and couldn't risk giving it up too quickly.

"Are you familiar with FEMA's system of emergency operations centers?" he asked.

Johan stiffened ever so slightly.

"I assume you are referring to the current level-two activation status," he said. "You suspect there is a reason for its current state of elevation, considering you thought you had eliminated the threat posed by the virus."

Mason didn't reply.

"Neither the elevation of FEMA's activation levels nor the timing of its decision to raise them strikes me as unusual, given the nature of the Hoyl's plot," Johan said. "In fact, I am somewhat perplexed as to why it did not raise the activation status to level one, especially here, which leads me to believe they have no reason to suspect the viral threat has not been contained."

"If that's the case, then why not lower the activation to level three?" Mason asked.

"That is a question for which I have no answer, at least not a direct one."

"What's that supposed to mean?"

"I fear the truth lies in the fact that the activation level was raised in several states six weeks prior to its ultimate elevation in the remainder."

"Which ones?" Mason asked.

"California, Texas, Florida, New York, and Washington, D.C."

"Is there any significance beyond the fact that they contain the highest population centers and standard terrorist targets?"

"That I do not know. Not for sure anyway."

Mason was quite confident he did, but that information would come at a price, one he was more than prepared to pay. The time had come to put all of his cards on the table.

"Do any of the Thirteen have an affinity for chemical weapons?"

Johan looked him dead in the eyes. Gone was the affable grandfather with the endearing affectations. In his place sat a man who might have looked like him, but who was completely unlike him in every way, as though the muscles he'd used to hold himself together had relaxed enough to let his inner beast claw its way out.

"There we go," Ramses said.

Mason glared at his old friend to shut him up and once more matched Johan's stare. He'd seen exactly what he'd expected during the transformation: a complete and utter lack of surprise.

"What do you know?" Johan asked. "Tell me, boy. Time is of the essence."

"While I was inside the slaughterhouse, I found a chemical formula written on a torn piece of paper."

"Why am I only now learning of this?"

"Because we can't prove that any amount of it was manufactured, and everything we've tested has come back negative for the presence of any of the precursor. . . ." His voice trailed off as everything came together in his head. "That's why FEMA raised its levels of readiness in the states with the highest-value targets and why you weren't surprised when I mentioned chemical weapons. The precursor chemicals were already in play."

Johan sighed and settled back into his chair. The fire faded from his eyes. When he spoke again, it was in a voice of resignation.

"Are you familiar with the Organization for the Prohibition of Chemical Weapons?"

"It's the international watchdog agency in charge of verifying compliance with the Chemical Weapons Convention," Mason said.

"On September thirtieth, the OPCW reported that a random audit of a Swiss chemical company revealed that every one of its shipments of hydrogen fluoride bound for Port Newark, New Jersey, over the past three years had arrived hundreds of pounds short, a negligible amount when dealing with thousands of metric tons, or millions of pounds. A few hundredths of a percent, in fact. Well within the standard deviation one would expect to observe between scales."

"What's the significance?"

"Hydrogen fluoride is a common compound used in the creation of hydrofluoric acid and the manufacture of fluorocarbons to be used as refrigerants. If you were to mix it with methylphosphonyl dichloride, however, you would create methylphosphonyl difluoride, which, when combined with isopropanol, produces sarin."

"And no one has any idea where thousands of pounds of it might have gone?"

"It's always possible the calibration of the scales was just far enough off to make it appear as though some seemingly insignificant amount of a substance transported in drums nearly as large as the industrial shipping containers that housed them was missing, when it actually wasn't."

"Hence the level-two activation level while the EOCs monitored the situation," Mason said.

"Which you have now confirmed, at least to some degree, is cause for more than mere concern," Johan said. His brow furrowed and his eyes turned momentarily inward. "I fear the enemy is much closer to implementing its plans than I suspected. I regret that I must take my leave if I am to reach out to my network and try to get to the bottom of this."

He reached toward his computer to terminate the connection, bumping it in the process. The camera swung wildly to the side, blurring past the old man and the whiteboard behind him before settling momentarily upon two other dry-erase boards that had been pushed together and covered with photographs and handwritten notes. They quickly vanished and Johan once more appeared, his features distorted by their proximity to the lens.

"Wait," Mason said. "You didn't answer my question. Tell me who we're up against so I can end this once and for all."

Johan paused, his face pale, his expression unreadable.

"You are up against the clock, James, and you are already out of time," he said. A rustling sound and the screen darkened. His disembodied voice emerged from the speaker a heartbeat before he exited the virtual conference room. "We all are."

7

"There's nothing out there about the missing hydrogen fluoride beyond a few brief notations saying pretty much what we already know," Gunnar said. He'd assumed Mason's place at the table, leaving him to watch over his old friend's shoulder as information scrolled past at dizzying speeds on the screen. "It's really not that uncommon an occurrence; it's the fact that it happened to the same supplier over such a long period of time and with such regularity that makes it raise a few eyebrows."

"More than a few, judging by FEMA's response," Mason said.

"That's the thing, Mace. Their reaction, even given the potential severity of the threat, is disproportional to the known facts. A level-three activation in the states immediately surrounding New Jersey, where the chemicals were diverted, appears to be the established protocol."

"They obviously know more than they're letting on," Ramses said from where he'd sprawled on the couch with his head on Alejandra's lap.

"Of course they do," she said. "We would be fools to think otherwise."

"I'm inclined to agree," Gunnar said. "Without additional intelligence, it comes across as a knee-jerk response to a situation that potentially doesn't even exist."

"Johan seemed to think it was real enough," Mason said.

"In case you didn't notice, that guy's got a serious case of Jekyll and Hyde," Ramses said.

"He is a sweet man," Alejandra said.

"Who has obvious trust issues." Ramses abruptly stood and walked a circuit of the room, studying the photographs of the crime scenes on the walls. "I mean, what's with the whole secrecy act? 'I fear the enemy is much closer to implementing its plans than I suspected.' Who says stuff like that? You'd think if he actually knew who was involved, he'd be happy enough to point us in the right direction and let us do our thing."

"I've been asking myself the same thing ever since I first met him,"

Mason said: "He obviously needs our help, but he's not prepared to tell us why. My gut tells me it's because there's something he doesn't want us to find out about him."

"I've worked with his kind many times before," Gunnar said. "He's trying to control the flow of information so that we see only what's in front of us. For my money, he's leading us toward some grand revelation, although at this point I hesitate to even speculate as to what it might be."

"That must be some serious shit he's keeping to himself if he's cool with telling people he hunts Nazis for sport," Ramses said. "Don't get me wrong. If I'd known they were in season, I would have applied for a tag—"

"He would have told us if he knew who was responsible for the chemical threat," Mason said. Johan had used them to help him ferret out and execute the Hoyl; he had no doubt the old man fully intended to do the same with whomever they were up against now. "Have any of the other precursor chemicals disappeared?"

"There are no reports of missing isopropanol, methylphophonyl dichloride, or dichloro(fluoro)nitromethane in anything resembling the kind of quantity one would require to convert that much hydrogen fluoride into Novichok A-234," Gunnar said. "That doesn't mean that smaller quantities couldn't have been legally obtained without setting off any alarm bells. As you well know, a couple gallons of the finished product would be more than enough to depopulate a city the size of Los Angeles."

"What about the company responsible for losing the chemical?"

"Ausland AG is a subsidiary of Royal Nautilus Petroleum, the sixth-largest corporation in the world. It specializes in the research and development of advanced materials and specialty chemicals, specifically the production of lightweight polymers and composites used in electronics, green technologies, and space travel. Its chemical-formulations wing primarily deals with soda ash and its derivatives and accounts for maybe thirty percent of its gross receipts, but it's growing at an astronomical rate thanks to its commitment to lessening the environmental impact of agricultural and industrial chemicals, including refrigerants."

"So what do your instincts tell you?"

Gunnar cocked his head and appeared momentarily contemplative. He had the uncanny ability of being able to intuit almost anything about a company with minimal information, and if he truly dug deep enough, there was no secret, no matter how well it was hidden, that he couldn't find.

"I sincerely doubt anyone at Ausland is involved. We're talking about a company with annual revenue in the tens of billions and facilities scattered throughout Europe. If someone on the inside wanted to divert any amount of a chemical, it would make more sense to do so at the source, where they'd have access to the raw materials prior to packaging and warehousing. And considering the volume of materials they produce and export, they're the perfect choice for someone at the destination looking to skim a little off the top. I'd be surprised if anyone would have ever noticed the missing hydrogen fluoride were it not for the OCPW's audit."

"So it must have gone missing directly from the shipping containers," Mason said. "While they were still on the boat."

"Anyone with access and opportunity—the ship's personnel, dockworkers, or even customs officials—could have transferred the chemicals to a separate container either prior to or upon reaching Port Newark and walked out with it right under the noses of the inspectors."

"Good luck tracking down the names of every one of those employees over the last three years."

"Exactly," Gunnar said.

Ramses brushed past Mason and leaned over Gunnar's other shoulder.

"Did you record that meeting?" he asked.

"Of course. What are you thinking?"

"Can you replay that section where the old guy bumped his computer?"

"Without breaking a sweat." Gunnar breezed through several windows, fast-forwarded through the digital file, and paused when he reached his target. "Voilà."

Mason leaned closer to the screen, a smile forming on his face.

"Well, what do you know?"

He immediately recognized the display from the rear chamber of

Johan's archives, where twenty dry-erase boards had been turned on end, arranged side by side and back-to-back, and covered with poorly focused photographs and handwritten notes. The central panel had been labeled MOST WANTED, and it had been on the one adjacent to it that the old man had posted everything he knew about the Hoyl. At the time, Mason had been so focused on the man who killed his wife that he hadn't paid close enough attention to the other boards, but it suddenly struck him that these subjects were quite possibly other mass murderers just waiting for the chance to do the apocalyptic bidding of the Thirteen. Perhaps one of them even specialized in nerve gasses like Novichok A-234 and had been at some unknown stage of its manufacture inside the slaughterhouse before it burned down.

The webcam had captured maybe half of each board and the junction where they'd been pushed together. Gunnar advanced through the individual frames until he found the clearest one and zoomed in as far as the resolution would allow. While it still demonstrated significant blurring at the edges, most of the words were legible and the pictures reasonably sharp.

On the board to the left were photographs of an unidentifiable blond woman captured at a distance in fields strewn with bodies. She wore black in every picture, while the armed men in her entourage changed camouflage fatigues to match surroundings ranging from tropical jungles to barren deserts. The words VALKYRIE, WORLD, RATLINES, and INTERNATIONAL were written above the number 4. To the right were pictures of a figure never revealed in more than partial silhouette, little more than a figment of the imagination within the shadows of fallen buildings and alleys near where medical personnel treated casualties on sidewalks and in the streets. Most of the words beneath them had been cut off, but he could still make out EPIDEMIC, PURIFICATION, NAKAMURA, and the numbers 731 and 5.

"What is 'Valkyrie'?" Alejandra asked. "I have not heard that word before."

"A valkyrie, or *valkyrja* in Old Norse, is one of a group of females, depicted either with wings or on flying horses, who determine who lives and who dies on the field of battle," Gunnar said. "They're described in the *Poetic Edda* from the thirteenth century as 'ladies of the War Lord, ready to ride,' who ultimately sort the dead and take the greatest warriors to Valhalla."

"We can only assume that's her code name," Mason said. "Either one she goes by professionally or one given to her by Johan."

"The words *world* and *international* could literally apply to any location, organization, or event, which essentially obviates their use. Unless they're part of a specific name or title, of course, but there's no way of knowing for sure without being able to see the words preceding or following them."

"What about 'ratlines'?" Ramses asked.

"It's likely in reference to the system of escape routes used to smuggle Nazi war criminals, enormous amounts of stolen wealth, advanced weaponry, and, many believe, even Hitler himself out of Germany and into South America after World War Two. Unless this woman is in her seventies or eighties, though, she couldn't possibly have had anything to do with them. I would imagine it was one of the historical trails Johan followed to find her."

"The Germans were behind the creation of just about every early chemical weapon, from mustard gas to sarin," Mason said. "It's not unreasonable to think that the men who were evacuated along those ratlines continued to develop them in Argentina. They could very well have figured out the Novichok formula on their own."

"What about the number?" Alejandra asked.

"Four must indicate either her position in Johan's most wanted or the member of the Thirteen with whom she's affiliated," Gunnar said. "It's the number attached to the second individual I find most intriguing, though. The only real possibility beyond an area code in western Tennessee is that it corresponds with Unit 731, the covert biological and chemical research and development unit of the Imperial Japanese Army during the Second World War. It was responsible for experimentation on POWs that would have made even Mengele blush."

"What kind of experimentation?" Alejandra asked.

The conversation had suddenly taken a very personal turn for her. While she'd survived the Hoyl's testing, albeit permanently disfigured, her younger sister had not.

"Injection of diseases disguised as vaccinations; exposure to fleas infected with the plague; deliberate infliction of frostbite and syphilis; forced pregnancy; food and water deprivation; and death by electrocution, pressure chamber, gas, anthrax, cholera, typhoid, and—Jesus— vivisection."

"What is that?"

"Dissection of a living specimen," Mason said.

"Unit 731 was responsible for the deaths of more than three thousand men, women, and children at its facility in the Pingfang District of China alone," Gunnar said.

"What about 'epidemic' and 'purification'?" Ramses asked.

"It was officially known as the Epidemic Prevention and Water Purification Department of the Kwantung Army, but I can't find any association with 'Nakamura,' which is the seventh most common surname in Japan. There's plenty of information about its first chief medical officer, Lieutenant General Shirō Ishii; the microbiologist who succeeded him, Lieutenant Masaji Kitano; and Yoshio Shinozuka, who was conscripted at sixteen years of age to perform autopsies and vivisections and ultimately testified against the Japanese government, which has yet to officially acknowledge the unit's existence."

"I can see why these guys would appeal to the Thirteen," Mason said, "but surely everyone associated with them is dead by now."

"Not this guy," Ramses said, and tapped the screen where the indistinct figure barely stood apart from the dark mouth of an alley framed by mountains of rubble. "He's still out there somewhere."

"So is this woman in black," Alejandra said.

"And either one of them could be armed with knowledge of biological and chemical warfare gained from some of the most atrocious experimentation ever conducted," Gunnar said.

"Chemical experimentation that could have been continuing inside the slaughterhouse where the Hoyl was testing his decomposition agent," Mason said. "They had all of the right equipment, not to mention the formula for Novichok A-234."

He stared at the pictures of the woman in black and the silhouette lurking in the shadows. His unconscious mind picked up on details his conscious mind had failed to recognize. He'd been so focused on the subjects and the bodies strewn all around them that he hadn't immediately noticed that the woman's armed escort and the medical professionals attempting to save the silhouette's victims were wearing gas masks.

"Johan doesn't do anything by accident," he said. "I think he deliberately bumped his laptop. He wanted us to see those boards."

"Why?" Ramses asked.

"Because he thinks one of these two is involved."

PART II

The real menace of our Republic is the invisible government, which like a giant octopus sprawls its slimy legs over our cities, states and nation.

—John Francis Hylan,
ninety-sixth mayor of New York City (1922)

8

December 27

Mason was now convinced there'd been a second operative working inside the slaughterhouse, one potentially responsible for producing mass
quantities of Novichok in case the plot to release the flu virus failed. If
either the blond woman with the Nazi roots or the shadowed figure associated with Unit 731 were involved, then he had to consider the possibility that what they were dealing with was no mere backup plan; it
was a tactical escalation. A disease could be blamed on Mother Nature,
but there was nothing natural or accidental about a chemical weapon
attack. It was an open declaration of war against their entire species, a
war that would be over before the first shot was even fired, unless he
figured out a way to stop it, and the only place he could think to start
was at what he considered ground zero.

"I can't shake the feeling that someone was actively manufacturing
chemical weapons in this place," Mason said.

"Despite the lack of physical evidence?" Locker said.

"I know, right?" Mason offered a half smile for the forensic specialist's benefit. "I just keep thinking about those stainless-steel vats, the
mattress I remember seeing in the room next to them, and how good
these guys are at covering their tracks. Throw in the level-two EOC

activation and potentially hundreds of pounds of missing hydrogen fluoride, and physical evidence is just about the only thing we don't have."

He followed Locker through the field of rubble that had once been Steerman's slaughterhouse, the building at the end of the underground tunnel that connected it to the former AgrAmerica complex, CS4. The forensics specialist hadn't been surprised to learn about the missing chemicals but, considering he'd found no trace of them, didn't seem overly concerned.

"We're already taking every conceivable precaution," Locker said. "I have my team retest the soil after every vertical inch we clear. There's no way I'd let my people work out here in anything less than Level B hazmat suits if there was the slightest chance of exposure to anything stronger than chlorine bleach, let alone a nerve gas."

It had been within the walls of this awful place that Mason had found dead immigrants hanging from meat hooks, left to rot. Men and women who'd succumbed to the Hoyl's virus, unwilling participants in his testing of what the Centers for Disease Control and Prevention had confirmed to be a strain of highly pathogenic avian influenza engineered from the original Spanish flu, HPAI H1N1. The bacterium that piggybacked on its viral envelope—a species genetically similar to one oil companies dumped into the ocean to consume the crude spilled from tankers—had been designed to accelerate the process of decomposition to a matter of weeks, dissolving the remains of the infected to a consistency that could be hosed down industrial drains.

Locker guided him along a narrow cordoned walkway running between sections of the ruined building that had been gridded off and painstakingly excavated a single millimeter at a time.

"In addition to my team, we have more than fifty archaeologists of various specialties from the Museum of Nature and Science working out here on a voluntary basis," Locker said. "We've collected a significant number of meat hooks and pieces of the overhead tracks they were once attached to, but we haven't been able to find anything remotely identifiable of the people who'd been suspended from them."

They passed a woman crouching over one of the floor drains. She reached inside with a pair of tweezers as long as chopsticks, extricated a small bone, and set it on a collection tray. The man in the adjacent grid wore a welder's mask and used an acetylene torch to break up a mass of metal and calcified matter that had been fused to the concrete by the intense heat of the blaze.

"You're only now getting down to the killing floor?" Mason said.

"No one's ever had to investigate a crime scene of this nature before. Instead of inadvertently discovering we were dealing with the site of a mass murder after removing tons of debris, we entered into the investigation with that knowledge, meaning that every speck of dust potentially contains evidence. Throw in the confirmed presence of a lethal virus, an unclassified decomposition accelerant, and a potential chemical threat, and we've been forced to proceed with such extreme caution that we've had to move most of the larger debris by hand in an attempt to preserve what little is left of the victims. We're talking unidentifiable bone fragments and handfuls of teeth, most of them at least partially consumed by a fire chemically fueled to such high temperatures that the foundation itself buckled. We can't even conclusively determine how many people died here, let alone begin the process of identifying them."

Mason nodded his understanding. Even with complete skeletons, they likely still wouldn't be able to ID the victims. The Hoyl had specifically chosen them for his twisted experimentation for that very reason. They were undocumented and hailed from countries where most couldn't afford proper medical or dental care, and certainly not the kind of X-rays they'd need for comparison. Most of the countries in question didn't even collect DNA for missing-person cases.

The larger evidence was stored inside a chain-link enclosure that had been erected in one of the crowd pens where cattle had once grazed while awaiting their turn in the knocking pen. The vats he'd seen on the second floor were near the back. The stainless steel was scored black with carbon, scratched to hell, and deformed by the weight of the collapsed roof. The handwheels had broken off, the digital displays had melted, and the surviving pressure valves had been collected in a bucket.

"We found twenty of these containment vessels in quadrant four," Locker said. "They're modified fermenter units, the kind used by microbreweries, capable of holding a little under eight hundred liters."

"That's not as bad as I thought," Mason said.

"Each. We're talking about two hundred gallons apiece, or four thousand gallons between them. If someone had access to Novichok A-234 in that kind of quantity and dispersed it strategically enough, he could easily wipe out the entire population of the Earth several times over. But, like I told you before, we didn't detect any chemical agents on the inner surfaces or functional components. That's not to say there never were any, only that trace amounts would have burned off."

"So you can't tell what they might have been used to produce," Mason said.

"Or if they were ever used to produce anything at all. All I can tell you with any confidence is that they hadn't been filled at the time of the explosion, or they wouldn't have flattened like that. Some residual amount of their contents would have been spared as a result of the internal pressurization."

"I guess that's something."

"That's not to say they didn't intend to use them to produce chemical weapons or hadn't used them to do so in the past."

"Just when I was starting to feel better, you had to go and ruin it."

Locker's transceiver crackled from the holster on his hip. He excused himself, answered the call, and lowered his voice so as not to be overheard.

Mason walked around the cage, surveying the collection inside. He recognized the crumpled remains of the mini refrigerator he'd seen in the room with the mattress and the table saws that had been mounted to the counters in the packing room. What he didn't see, though, were any containers that could be used for the storage of toxic chemicals. Granted, the larger plastic variety would have melted, but the corrosion-resistant kind necessary for the precursor chemicals would have survived the blaze. Maybe they'd actually caught a break and derailed the plot before it was set into motion.

Locker tugged on the sleeve of his jacket.

"You'd better come with me," he said. "We found something behind the false wall."

Mason knew exactly which wall he was talking about. He remembered seeing it at the end of the underground tunnel when he'd first arrived at the slaughterhouse weeks ago. It was maybe a little too close to the door leading into the building and a slightly different shade of gray than the surrounding concrete. Nothing incredibly overt, just enough to have given him pause. It was about time the forensics team finally reached it.

Locker struck off into the ruins, his stride so long that Mason practically had to jog to keep pace. They navigated the wending path through the rubble, skirted the surviving framework of the structure, and headed straight for the concrete pad that marked where a massive commercial garage had once stood. The loading dock was now little more than an uneven slope of gravel and fractured concrete. The iron staircase that had once reached the elevated office had melted into a hellish snarl. Not so long ago, Mason had stood in this precise spot with liquid fire raining all around him, seconds before the entire building had collapsed.

A portable bank of metal-halide lights shone down into a square shaft in the ground. The iron hatch that had saved him from the fire stood wide open. He hopped down and descended the stairs to the terminus of the twenty-two-mile tunnel, where he'd first encountered the tram that serviced the hidden line.

The men waiting at the bottom turned to face him with matching expressions of anticipation and excitement. He recognized forensics specialists Dave Andrews and Josh Wilkinson from various crime scenes he'd worked. They stood beside a tripod that supported a device reminiscent of an old-time camera, only with a digital readout and an LED display. A series of cords connected it to a laptop computer on a folding table beside a red first-aid kit. Another bank of lights had been positioned to shine at the southernmost wall.

"This marvel of technology here is what we call a through-wall radar," Locker said, and gestured toward the camera. "It utilizes continuous-wave, ultra-wideband random-noise waveforms to see through walls. Sound waves of such low frequency that they can't be detected from the other side."

"What does it show?" Mason asked.

"Nothing."

"But you said there was something back there."

"Right. And that something is nothing."

Talking to Locker when he was in full-on forensics mode was often a maddening experience. He seemed to start at random points in a conversation, like a star in the night sky, and expect everyone around him to envision the same constellation he did.

"You're telling me you can see through that wall and there's nothing there," Mason said.

"We are speaking the same language, aren't we?"

The others chuckled. Mason shot them a glare that caused them to disperse.

"This radar generates sound waves and fires them through the wall. When they encounter something on the other side, they bounce back. This detector receives those returning sound waves, converts them into a digital signal, and sends it to this laptop, which runs a program that filters the incoming data, interprets it, and forms a three-dimensional representation of what's on the other side. As you can see, right now it's showing us approximately eighteen inches of nothing."

"So why are we still talking about it when we could be tearing down that wall?"

"Because it's not entirely empty."

Mason squeezed his temples in an effort to stave off a burgeoning headache.

"Look at the monitor." Locker turned the laptop so he could see it. Mason could somewhat discern the representation of depth behind the wall. Red pinpricks materialized within that space, only to vanish again, like fireflies floating in the foot-and-a-half space between the false wall and the true end of the tunnel. "You have to understand that the concrete wall attenuates ninety-nine percent of the sound waves on their way through, and another ninety-nine percent on the return trip, leaving a fraction of a percent of the original sound waves to form an image. Not nearly enough to create a comprehensive, detailed model of anything on the other side, which is why this unit features continuous-wave radar architecture that emits a ceaseless barrage of sound waves. It can easily distinguish a hollow space from open air or packed earth, but it requires a large number of data points to identify specific objects in between. It's like trying to draw a picture using just dots from the tip of a sharpened pencil, with someone erasing them as quickly as they appear. There's no way of plotting these data points in three dimensions unless—"

"You collect enough of them over an extended period of time," Mason said.

He looked at the smile on Locker's face, then at the screen again.

"You're saying these little flickering dots prove there's something behind the wall," he said.

"Let me see if I can figure out how to use the time-lag feature."

Mason stepped back and gave Locker room to work. He clicked through a series of prompts that caused more and more dots to appear on the monitor. It was like witnessing the birth of a galaxy, as thousands of stars coalesced into cloudlike masses that slowly defined two unmistakable shapes.

"Jesus," Mason whispered.

He again looked at Locker, who was no longer smiling.

9

Locker's mobile crime lab was an ambulance that had been painted black, gutted, and retrofitted to his precise specifications. While it might have been a Playskool version of his main lab, it featured a digital command center on one side and a scientific suite on the other. Two RV-style seats were bolted to the floor in the middle of the aisle. He and Mason each commandeered one and watched the twin LCD flat-screen monitors mounted to the wall. Six digital audio receivers, attuned to as many frequencies, were fitted into slots below them and above the corresponding two-way communication devices. Locker wore a wireless headset that allowed him to switch between the frequencies, connecting him to all of the various members of his on-site team with the tap of a button.

"Can you get me any more light?" he asked. "I want a clear look at everything back there. We don't want any surprises."

The image on the right monitor subtly brightened as the camera passed through the six-millimeter-wide hole they'd drilled into the base of the wall and emerged into darkness marred by motes of dust. The articulating video borescope's depth of field was limited and the spherical shape of the lens caused a walleyed distortion that took some getting used to, but the resolution was phenomenal and it was able to capture still images even while it was transmitting in real time.

A camera mounted to the lighting array behind and above Andrews transmitted to the left monitor. It offered a decent view over the advanced-level evidence specialist's shoulder as he hand-fed the snake camera through the hole, using the six-inch LCD monitor attached to it to control its movements. Wilkinson flirted in and out of the right side of the picture, where he monitored the thermal-imaging camera and the spatial relationship between Andrews's probe and the objects on the other side. Both of the evidence-collection specialists wore white TECP—totally encapsulating chemical protective—suits and CBRN—chemical, biological, radiological, and nuclear—hoods with face shields and respirators, both for their protection and to prevent the transfer of so much as a single fiber or strand of DNA that might contaminate the evidence.

Three other teams were positioned at strategic locations around the site. The first was in the van parked beside the lab and served as operational support, while the second and third manned blockades at either end of the only road into or out of the property.

"Advance the probe three inches higher and turn the camera slowly from zero to ninety degrees," Locker said.

The borescope moved in somewhat disorienting lurches. The view rotated toward the center of the enclosed space. A blurry line of light cut diagonally across the screen before resolving into what looked like a thin wire.

"Spiderweb," Locker said. "Anything on thermal imaging?"

"Might as well be packed earth back there, for all I can see," Wilkinson said. "The infrared sensors haven't detected a single radiant heat source to suggest anything actively drawing power on the other side. Of course, it's also a million degrees down here with all of these lights, so I question their sensitivity."

The probe resumed its advance and a dark shape appeared on the right monitor. It was purplish black and shriveled like a prune.

"Continue upward. And turn maybe ten degrees counterclock-wise."

Mason leaned closer to Locker and spoke into his microphone.

"Can you widen the field of view?"

The prune shape drew contrast as the camera neared. It was more black than purple and featured a whorl pattern he recognized even before the crescent of the toenail appeared, which confirmed that the vague shapes they'd seen on the through-wall camera were indeed the bodies of two distinct individuals, suspended above the ground, with their arms over their heads.

"Lord have mercy," Andrews said.

"Can you move the camera farther away from the body so we can get more anatomy in the frame?" Locker asked. "That's it. Keep going. Just try not to touch anything."

"Easier said than done."

The majority of the foot came into view. The skin was desiccated and clung to the bony framework like plastic wrap. It took all of about a second to figure out why.

Spiderwebs stretched away from it in every direction. Long, taut strands, white with dust, sparkled in the light. There were no readily apparent patterns, just seemingly random crisscrossing webs that radiated outward from a dense funnel near the ankle, from which long, spindly legs slowly emerged. One at a time. Front appendages held high. A tiny head preceded a disproportionately large body that tapered to a point at the rear end.

Mason's flesh crawled.

"*Latrodectus hesperus*," Locker said. "The western black widow."

It dropped from the funnel, dangled in front of the lens, and spun to showcase the trademark red hourglass on its abdomen.

"Jesus," Andrews said. He scooted away from the wall on the left screen. The image on the right screen swung wildly. "Did you see that thing?"

The camera struck the victim's foot and went momentarily out of focus. The widow dropped from its web. Andrews gasped and swatted at his isolation suit.

"Get it together in there," Locker said. "Their fangs are barely long enough to penetrate the epidermis. They can not—I repeat, *can not*—bite you through your suits."

"Is that true?" Mason asked.

Locker covered the microphone.

"I guess we'll find out."

Andrews returned to his post, however hesitantly, and again crouched with his back to the camera. The borescope continued its ascent considerably faster than before. Not haphazardly so, but it was obvious that neither of the men wanted to be down there any longer than absolutely necessary.

Mason didn't blame them. He was aboveground and a hundred feet away, and still it felt like he had spiders all over him.

The image on the screen rose up the length of the shin, extending to the knee. The patella tented the skin, which was so tight, it appeared mummified. The camera passed the thigh, the groin, the belly. Thick webs parted before it, momentarily blinding the lens. More spiders scurried away. Smaller. Brown, with white-striped abdomens. Juveniles. They dropped out of sight, crawled into fortresslike webs, and squirmed into lesions in the parchment flesh.

Only occasionally was the second victim visible as an indistinct shape through the webbing, hanging to the right of the first.

The camera continued its jerky ascent. Past the chest and shoulders. The victim's arms were stretched straight up to the ceiling, pinning his head in place. The tendons of his neck stood out like cords beside the bulge of his trachea. There was nothing left of his lips. Something moved through the gap between his parted teeth. His nose had collapsed and there were webs in his nostrils. His eyelids were sunken into the sockets. What little was left of his hair looked like steel wool.

"Stop right there," Locker said. "Turn forty-five degrees to the right. Toward the rear wall."

"What did you see?" Mason asked, but the words had barely passed his lips when he saw it, too. "A video camera."

"Directed right at the victim's face."

"Why would anyone want to watch these guys get bitten to death by spiders?"

"The widows didn't kill these men," Locker said. "They're solitary creatures by nature. My guess is either several egg sacs were already inside when the victims were entombed or this is the result of several hatches, although based on the fact that this species ordinarily lays its egg sacs in the summer and these bodies appear closer to six months old than eighteen, I'm leaning toward the former. This level of insect activity is fairly unprecedented, though. Spiders don't generally consume human remains, so there's no way to estimate how much they accelerated the rate of desiccation."

"Can you tell what did kill them?" Mason asked.

"Any speculation at this point would be premature. I won't even consider waging a guess until after we get the bodies out of there and— Hold on. Stop. Right there. Back up a hair. Angle the probe about fifteen degrees higher."

The camera followed the skeletal arms upward toward the shackled wrists. The chain between the cuffs had been run through an eye ring screwed into the ceiling.

"Higher still," Locker said. "And turn maybe ten degrees to the left."

The man's hands came into focus. They'd curled in upon themselves like the feet of a dead bird.

Locker turned from the monitor with an expression of triumph on his face. Mason leaned past him to get a better look. He could clearly see the right hand and, above it, a section of the concrete ceiling smeared with dried blood. The index finger was blurred by proximity to the lens, but the bone protruding from the lacerated fingertip and ruined fingernail was unmistakable.

"He left us a message," Locker said.

The victim had scratched the ceiling until his finger bled and painted a series of eleven numbers, practically right on top of one another.

16207524874.

"Yeah," Mason said. "But what does it mean?"

10

"It's too long to be a phone number or a Social Security number," Mason said.

"Maybe a bank account," Locker said. "A wireless routing number. An IP address. A code of some kind. It could mean absolutely anything. Or it could mean nothing. We're talking about a man hung up by his wrists and sealed behind a wall with another man, who might not have been alive at the time. He had to understand on a primal level that he was about to die. For all we know, he could have just been writing random numbers to keep from giving in to panic, which would have caused him to deplete his finite amount of oxygen even faster."

"You don't believe that any more than I do."

"We have to consider every possibility. If we only look for what we expect to see, invariably we'll find it."

The Hoyl had employed a specific MO at each of the sites Mason had used to track him. He'd recruited test subjects desperate to cross the border, injected them with a cocktail of viruses and bacteria, and then hung them from hooks so he could study them as they decomposed. When he moved to a different location, he incinerated every trace that he'd been there, leaving behind so little physical evidence that no one would ever know the horrors that had transpired there. And while his victims had endured unimaginable suffering, he hadn't exposed them to an unnecessary element of sadism. As vile as his actions had been, they'd been clinical in their execution.

This crime scene didn't fit his mold.

These men had been cuffed and forced to watch helplessly as they were entombed behind a solid foot of concrete. An unconscionable amount of evil had been invested in their torture, much like the death traps he was now certain had been rigged by someone other than the Hoyl, a second monster, someone who either had no fear that his work would be discovered or simply didn't care, but what were the odds of two unique mass murderers using the same base of operations? And what did the numbers mean?

They needed to get behind that wall.

The other victim drifted in and out of focus at the edge of the camera's range. Another man. Same physical condition. No immediately identifiable characteristics.

The probe advanced toward him—

"Wait." Locker leaned forward so quickly that he had to grab his headset to keep it from falling off. "Back up. Back up. Retract two inches and turn ten—no . . . fifteen degrees. There. Right there." He sat back again. "Well, what do you know?"

A white box protruded from the rear wall. It had a black half sphere on its face. A lens of some kind.

"Can you get a little closer to it?" Mason asked.

"Move in," Locker said. "Carefully."

The borescope lurched closer and closer to the black dome. The thin cords extending from the housing were nearly concealed by spiderwebs. The one on the left was connected to the camera facing the first victim. Mason could only assume the one on the right similarly led to the camera focused on the second.

"It's a motion detector," he said.

A third cord went straight up. The camera traced its course to the ceiling, where it bent sharply to the right and disappeared beneath a mass of webbing. Extrapolating its path revealed a silver casing that would have been indistinguishable from the webs had the light not reflected from it. An enormous widow scurried away from the camera, throwing its nightmarish shadow across the narrow side wall.

"And that's the power source," Locker said. "Movement triggers the motion detector, which causes the cameras to start recording. The victims must have been unconscious when they were walled in there."

"But even if that were the case, they would have remained unconscious for only so long. Why go to the effort of installing a motion detector when the cameras could have just been set to record for the entire duration? Can you track the signal to see where they were transmitting the feed?"

"Cameras like that broadcast on a predetermined frequency that's sent out in all directions at once. Any receiver within its range could intercept the signal."

"How far are we talking?"

"I'd have to evaluate the camera to know for sure. I can't imagine it would be more than a mile, although a signal repeater could add another mile, mile and a half."

Mason grabbed the transceiver corresponding to the frequency for operational support, pressed the button, and spoke into it.

"I need to know every physical structure within a three-mile radius," he said.

"Copy."

He released the button and turned to Locker.

"It was probably just transmitting to someone watching inside the slaughterhouse, but we need to make sure we're not missing something out there."

"We're definitely missing something in here," Locker said.

Mason knew exactly what he meant. A crucial detail was staring him right in the face, and yet, for the life of him, he couldn't see it. He imagined waking up and finding himself entombed in darkness, his arms starting to go numb from diminished blood flow and shackled above his head. He could almost taste the stale air, growing warmer and thinner with every inhalation. His first instinct was to panic, to pull against his restraints, to kick at the walls, triggering the motion detector within a matter of seconds.

That reaction didn't fit with what he saw on the screen, though.

He thought about the condition of the remains. The skin on the wrists was intact. The same was true of the knees. In their situation, he would have practically ripped off his own hands trying to pry them from the cuffs and banged his knees bloody against the wall. Unless they'd been tranquilized, the physical evidence didn't add up.

"Andrews," Locker said. "Can you see if there are any more cords coming off of that box?"

"There could be a hundred, for all I can tell. That mass of webs is so thick, you'd need a flamethrower to cut through it."

The man who'd painted the numbers in his own blood would have known without a doubt that he was never getting out of there alive. He would have reached a point where he was laboring to breathe, and still he'd only moved a single finger. Why? A cervical injury could have caused near-complete paralysis, but that didn't mesh with the need to install a motion—

That was the key.

"They knew it was there," Mason said. "The motion detector. They held perfectly still, even knowing they were about to die. One of them gambled on moving a single finger. That's all he dared. One digit, high and hopefully outside the range of the sensors. He scraped his fingertip against the concrete with enough force to split the skin and peel back the nail. The message was so important, he risked triggering the motion detector, which has to be connected to something that scared him a hell of a lot more than any camera."

"I don't like this," Locker said.

"Get your men out of there."

"Retract the cable and seal the hole," he said into the microphone.

"With pleasure," Andrews said. "I can't wait to take off this infernal suit. It feels like there're spiders crawling all over me."

Mason watched the silver box fade back into the darkness. The dead man's hand materialized from the edge of the screen, followed by his mummified arm, the distorted profile of his face.

On the left screen, Wilkinson crouched behind Andrews with what looked like a caulk gun, waiting for him to reel in the camera.

"Slow it down," Locker said. "Give me a nice steady pace."

There was something in his voice that hadn't been there a moment ago. Mason was just about to ask Locker what he'd figured out, when it suddenly hit him.

"They left this for us to find," he said. "If we'd demo'd the wall instead of going in with a borescope, we'd have triggered the motion detector ourselves."

"Exactly," Locker said. "We need to take a step back and evaluate everything we know. Like you said, that motion detector has to be connected to something else, and we'd damn well better make sure we know what before we set it off."

The camera retreated in halting increments.

Slowly.

Mason thought about all of the widows crawling around in there, about the dead man and his ruined finger. The motion detector looked like the kind people mounted above their garages to turn on the porch light when someone approached, definitely not the most sensitive variety.

A black shape emerged from a web in the victim's armpit and dropped straight down toward the camera. Its red hourglass came into sharp focus, then blurred as it repeatedly struck at the lens.

"Jesus!" Andrews said.

The camera raced downward and to the side. The spider continued to strike at the lens. The probe grazed the dead man's flank, and the widow skittered off into a tear in the skin along the curve of the lower ribs.

"Careful in there," Locker said. "Try to maintain a steady pace."

"There are four buildings within the prescribed radius," a voice said from the transceiver. "And we've already been over each of them with a fine-tooth comb."

Mason pressed the button and spoke into the transceiver without taking his eyes from the monitors.

"Nothing out of the ordinary?"

"Everything's either abandoned or condemned. These guys picked the perfect place. We couldn't find anyone to question inside of ten miles."

"Check them again."

"Copy that."

The borescope retreated maybe an inch before abruptly stopping.

"It's snagged on something," Andrews said.

"Extricate it as gently as you can," Locker instructed.

Mason watched Andrews on the left monitor. The specialist's back hunched as he pulled on the articulating cord. The view on the right remained unchanged for several seconds, then jerked quickly downward. Rebounded from the knobby knee. Whipped sideways and hit the other leg.

"Everything okay down there?" Locker asked.

"That's about enough excitement for one day," Andrews said.

A faint hissing sound emanated from the monitor. Or maybe from one of the transceivers underneath it.

The image on the right screen went momentarily out of focus. When the aperture rectified, there were spiders everywhere. Scurrying through the webs. Streaking past the camera.

Andrews resumed retracting the borescope and everything became a blur. Mason caught a glimpse of blackened skin. Ankle. Foot. Toes. Webs. And then the floor, which was positively covered with dead spiders. The screen turned black as Andrews pulled the camera through the wall.

"Close her up," he said.

Wilkinson pumped the sealant into the hole while Andrews coiled the remaining length of the borescope. When he looked back at the camera, his entire face was beaded with sweat behind his face shield.

"And all without letting a single one of those bastards out of there," he said.

Mason felt a sinking sensation in his stomach.

Andrews pulled off his hood and wiped his forehead on his upper arm. His hair was positively drenched with sweat, which rolled down his cheeks like tears.

"How do you want to handle this from here, chief?" Andrews looked directly into the camera, as though he could see Locker. "We can have a demo crew out here in under an hour—"

"Put your helmet back on," Locker said in little more than a whisper.

Mason glanced at him in time to see the color drain from his face. He turned back to the monitor, where Andrews dabbed his eyes with the back of his wrist. His upper lip glistened. Twin vertical lines. Mucus, not sweat.

"Say again, chief?"

"Put your helmet back on!"

The hissing sound.

The falling widows.

The carpet of dead spiders.

Mason finally realized why the dead men inside the wall had been so scared to move. They'd known the kind of agonizing death that awaited them if they activated the motion detector, but the trap hadn't just been set for them.

It had been set for those who would inevitably find their bodies.

Andrews looked straight into the camera. His brown eyes widened a heartbeat before his pupils constricted to pinpricks. The corner of his mouth pulled sharply back toward his ear. The tendons in his neck tightened. He gagged and tugged at the collar of his isolation suit. Fell to the ground. Arched his back. Bared his teeth.

"Jesus!" Wilkinson shouted. "He's seizing!"

He stood over his convulsing partner, paralyzed by indecision.

"Listen to me very carefully," Locker said. "There's a first-aid tackle box on the table. Inside you'll find the Mark One Kit. It's in a black pouch with two syringes inside." He switched to the third team's channel. "Standby with decontamination. And get a hazmat team out here."

"What's going on—?" a voice responded, but Locker cut it off when he switched back to Wilkinson.

"You know what to do from here. Inject the smaller of the two—the atropine—directly into his lateral thigh muscle. Right through his suit. Don't jab it. Just push the needle all the way in and hold it there for ten seconds. Follow with the pralidoxime."

On the left screen, Wilkinson ran to the table, threw open the first-aid kit, and spilled the contents onto the table. Rummaged through them until he found what he was looking for. Held it up to the camera.

"Hurry," Locker said.

Wilkinson fell on top of Andrews. Struggled to pin him down. Stabbed the autoinjector into his thigh.

Mason closed his eyes as everything came together in his head. The Novichok had been removed before they even knew this place existed. That's why they hadn't found any traces of precursor chemicals in the rubble. Had everything gone as planned, no one would have known that the crushed vats had been used for the creation of the deadly nerve gas and the only people who could have figured it out would have been killed when they broke down the concrete wall, effectively crippling the investigation before it even started.

They'd finally caught a break, such as it was.

At this very moment, an unknown quantity of the deadliest nerve agent known to man was in play.

And they needed to find it.

11

Mason stood at a safe distance and watched the Hazardous Materials Safety and Response Team, a veritable army of specialists in blue full-body CBRN suits, erect decontamination corridors upwind from the lone entrance to the tunnel. They couldn't evacuate the men trapped underground until they cleared their route to the medevac chopper waiting to take them to Buckley Air Force Base for emergency medical intervention. And no one would be able to get down there to investigate until after the tunnel was decontaminated, which could very well take days.

The grumble of tires on gravel announced the arrival of the FBI's mobile command center, which was essentially an armored Winnebago stuffed with a miniaturized version NORAD. It pulled up to the cordon and parked next to Locker's mobile crime lab.

"It's about time," Mason said.

He jogged over to it, threw open the door, and almost collided with another agent. The woman was nearly a foot shorter than he was and wore her long black hair in a ponytail, which was pulled through the back of her FBI ball cap. She stepped back, squared herself, and proffered her hand.

"Special Agent Mason?" she said. "I'm Special Agent Jessica—"

"Now's not the time."

He slipped past her, headed for the back of the vehicle, and burst into the office without knocking. Gabriel Christensen, special agent in charge of the Denver Division, was seated at the lone workstation.

"You can't let the DHS take over this investigation," Mason said. "I'm the one who originally identified these guys and tracked them all the way from Mexico. If you want to pick up their trail again, you're going to need my help."

"Somebody certainly has a high opinion of himself," Chris said. The acoustics of the small office lent his voice a hollow quality.

"Do you want to catch these guys or not?"

The Bureau was still ostensibly in charge of the investigation into the trafficking organization responsible for murdering countless undocumented immigrants and smuggling the deadly virus across the border, but the release of a chemical weapon of mass destruction, no matter how small the quantity, changed the dynamics. It was imperative they establish themselves in the formal pecking order before they found themselves sidelined, and the only way to do so with as little time as they had at their disposal was by forming a task force.

"What world do you live in where I don't?" Chris said. The events of the last month had taken their toll on him. His wrinkles were more pronounced, his hair was thinner, and his suit hung from his frame, but his eyes were still as sharp as ever. He studied Mason as though probing his defenses for weaknesses. "You're not the only one with a personal stake in this investigation, you know."

His department had been infiltrated by agents whose allegiance had been to an organization beyond his understanding, a powerful entity that pulled their strings from shadows so deep, Mason had yet to fathom their depths. Chris wasn't stupid, though. He recognized that Mason knew more than he was letting on, and, while he understood his reasons for doing so, there were limits to his patience.

"All I'm saying is that once Homeland throws up the screen of national security, we're both out of the loop," Mason said.

Calling for a hazmat team to rescue Andrews and Wilkinson and decontaminate the tunnel meant alerting FEMA's emergency operations center, and thus the Department of Homeland Security, which had had state troopers diverting traffic at every conceivable access point within minutes and an incident management team on-site in under twenty. A press release had crossed the wire before the thirty-minute mark, detailing a ruptured pipeline and accidental gas leak, which had caused the closure of several rural routes but posed no danger to the general public.

"They need our resources," Chris said. "Hell, they need all the resources they can get. But if they intend to keep a lid on this thing, they need discretion even more."

Mason smirked when he realized where Chris was going with that line of thought.

"You're going to blackmail the DHS?"

"They can't afford mass panic. And they sure as hell don't want whoever has that nerve agent catching wind that we're on his trail and accelerating whatever timetable he's working on. Besides, I think it's only fair we maintain a seat at the table, don't you?"

"I want in. I'm already up to my neck in this one."

"I can't make any guarantees. You were suspended barely a month ago. If I were you, I'd count my lucky stars I still had my badge. If Trapp hadn't conveniently died—"

"Then your division would still be compromised," Mason said. "You don't have anyone else you know you can trust."

"What makes you think I trust you?"

"For God's sake, Chris."

"Trust is a two-way street, Mason. We both know the official account of what happened up north is horseshit."

"Now you're blackmailing me?"

"I'm incentivizing your cooperation." Chris leaned back in his chair, smiled, and laced his fingers behind his head. "It's called 'creative management.' Picked it up at an in-service training session a couple years back."

"Just get me on that task force."

The expression of amusement on Chris's face vanished, as though it had never been there at all. He leaned across his narrow desk, hit the speaker button, and spoke toward the phone. His voice echoed from the command center on the other side of the door.

"Connect me with Deputy Secretary Marchment."

Mason had worked with Rand Marchment before, so he knew just how quickly the former DEA administrator, now the number-two man in the entire Department of Homeland Security, would move on the situation. He'd been in charge of the Bradley Strike Force, whose investigation into drug trafficking had led them to the Hoyl and the deadly virus he was smuggling through the desert via infected immigrants. The last time Mason saw him, Marchment had been sitting in the chair beside his hospital bed in Arizona, describing how his partner and the majority of his team had been killed in the ambush that had nearly claimed his life, as well. Only in D.C. did such a colossal failure warrant a promotion, and to a position one rung shy of a cabinet-level post at that.

"So we're good?" Mason said.

"You need to recognize when you've overstayed your welcome."

Mason had taken less subtle hints.

"Thanks, Chris."

He rose from the chair and headed for the door. Chris spoke to his back.

"Those answers had better be forthcoming, Mason. I've given you enough rope to hang us both."

"You won't regret it."

"I already do."

A voice erupted from the speaker on the phone.

"I have Deputy Secretary Marchment on line two."

"Get out there and find me that Novichok," Chris said.

He hit the button to kill the speaker, snatched the handset from the cradle, and spun his chair in the opposite direction.

Mason blew through the office door into the command center and practically slammed into the same agent again. She cocked her head and stared up at him from beneath the brim of her cap. Her blue eyes were deceptive, the kind that made her appear to be an open book while simultaneously concealing her thoughts.

"Look," she said. "We got off on the wrong foot. I'm Special Agent Jessica Layne and I'm—"

"Later," he said.

He brushed past her and strode down the aisle toward the front of the vehicle. There were three workstations, each of which featured a touch-screen monitor, short-range and satellite communications, and audio- and video-surveillance capabilities. Locker was already seated at one of them, the computer networked with his digital forensics system and a handful of transceivers lined up in front of him to connect him with his team in the field. Layne assumed the middle workstation beside him and glared up at Mason. The agent next to her had shoulder-length blond hair with purple streaks and wore her badge on a lanyard around her neck. Special Agent Gardner, Criminal Justice Information Services. They all swiveled in their chairs to face him.

"We don't know how much nerve gas was produced here, but we have to assume that each and every one of the vats recovered from the debris was filled to capacity," Mason said. "That's a total volume of more than four thousand gallons of what we believe to be Novichok A-234 in liquid form. And we don't have the slightest idea where it is now."

"Anyone could have filled a flask or a bottle and carried some amount of it out of here in a pocket," Gardner said. "For all we know, there could be hundreds of people like that out there, and we'll never be able to find them."

"Any kid with a chemistry set and Internet access can make a couple liters of most nerve agents in his garage. That's the kind of threat we face every single day. This is the major leagues. Novichok agents are fourth-generation chemical weapons so deadly and so complicated to manufacture that until today experts didn't believe it was possible for nonstate actors to produce them. No one would take that kind of risk just to splash a little from a flask. We have to look at the big picture and focus on locating large quantities capable of doing significant damage."

"So where do we start?"

12

"We're looking at an advanced chemical weapon synthesized from sarin and a chemical called dichloro(fluoro)nitromethane," Locker said. "Under normal conditions, sarin is a binary compound; its primary precursor chemicals remain separated until they're combined at the time of release, which prevents its rapid degradation and eliminates the risk of nontargeted exposure. You can't just store it on a shelf without killing everyone within range. The dichloro(fluoro)nitromethane solves that problem by stabilizing the reaction between the precursor chemicals, effectively allowing the Novichok to persist in the environment long after sarin would have completely dissipated. Fortunately, every batch of sarin has a specific signature, like a fingerprint, defined by chemical impurities that pass, unchanged, from the precursor chemicals, which we can use to trace those precursors back to their suppliers and ascertain a list of buyers. I've made arrangements with Homeland's incident response team to acquire a sample to run through the GC-MS to generate an impurity profile we can compare against our database of commercial chemical samples."

"We do the same thing to trace heroin and meth through distribution channels and back to their origin," Gardner said. "It can take days to get any actionable intel from manufacturers, and even longer to follow the trail."

"We're lucky in this case that there are so few suppliers, each of whose products have distinct impurities caused by the fossil fuels used as manufacturing feedstock and the hydrocarbons present in the air during processing, and we all know how persuasive the DHS can be when it comes to compelling answers from even the most unwilling subjects," Locker responded.

"I have no doubt they'll be able to find the source, but we can't afford to sit around waiting for them to do so," Mason said. "That Novichok didn't walk out of here on its own. They had to have moved it somehow, and they couldn't have done so in just any containers."

"Precisely," Locker said. He brought up an image of an industrial unit that looked like a cross between a propane tank and a torpedo. "While Novichok A-234 might be a whole lot more stable than its German predecessor, that doesn't mean its transport isn't without risk. Its main component is still sarin, which decomposes tin, aluminum, and cadmium-plated steel. Any decrease in pH will cause it to hydrolyze and form hydrofluoric acid. Exposure to heat can lead to combustion and vaporization, killing everyone for miles. They would have used ASME-rated cylinder tanks like this one—seven-foot-long barrels that hold roughly a hundred gallons apiece. They're readily available and used to move any number of hazardous chemicals, which makes tracking the purchase of an unknown quantity impossible but limits the means by which up to forty of them could be transported out of here."

"They would have needed a fleet of trucks to accommodate that much weight," Layne said.

"The way I see it," Mason said, "we're dealing with a minimum of two twenty-foot shipping containers loaded onto flatbed heavy haulers.

They'd blend in with highway traffic and could be stored invisibly on any industrial lot."

"So we're never finding them."

"At some point in time, they were driven onto this property and then driven back off again, which means that somewhere there's a record of it."

"We don't have any satellite imagery for nearly two years predating our arrival," Gardner said.

"True, but there are only two ways out of here. Can you bring up an aerial map?"

She pulled up the image on her monitor and leaned back so they could all see.

"This is where we are right now." Mason tapped the touch screen and the image zoomed in on a ten-mile square. "As you can see, the only access to this place is by County Road Thirty-seven, which originates at CR Eighteen to the south and ends at CR Twenty-six to the north. Regardless of which one you take, the only way out of this area is by getting on Highway Eighty-five either right here or . . . here."

"Those are just ordinary off-ramps," Layne said. "They don't have traffic lights with cameras we can access."

"But there are weather cams for road conditions."

The special agent smiled.

"I'm on it," Gardner said. "I have access to the Department of Transportation's archives, but it would save me a lot of time if I had a theoretical window."

Mason recalled how the second floor of the slaughterhouse appeared to have been abandoned in a rush, and not too long before he arrived.

"Try thirty to forty-five days ago and work your way backward from there."

"I'll check to see if any shipping containers or vehicles have been reported missing," Layne said.

"Good idea," Mason replied. "And I want aerial photographs of everything within a hundred-mile radius. Those shipping containers are the size of railroad cars. Any number of them should be easy to spot."

"My guys can scan the satellite footage of the entire eastern plains in a matter of minutes," Locker said. He grabbed one of the transceivers and started giving orders.

Mason felt the pressure of lost time bearing down on him. Those tanks could have traveled anywhere in the world by now. If they didn't find that convoy and at least pick up its trail soon—

"I've got them," Gardner said.

He leaned over her shoulder and studied the image on her screen. The resolution wasn't nearly as sharp as that of a traffic cam, but he could clearly see two heavy haulers descending an off-ramp from the vantage point of what he assumed to be a light pole. Both trucks were flatbeds with anonymous corrugated shipping containers on the back, the kind bulk carriers shipped to every port around the world. They were old and rusted and looked just like every other he'd seen.

"When was this?" he asked.

"November sixth. Fifty-one days ago."

Mason closed his eyes. He knew the date well. It was the same day the Thirteen had murdered his wife. While the Hoyl was burning Angie alive, a team had been hurriedly extricating the Novichok, due to the window of vulnerability she'd exposed.

"This picture was taken on the northbound ramp onto Highway Eighty-five at nine-forty-three A.M.," Gardner said. She switched to a different image. "Here they are arriving two days earlier, November fourth. Ten-fifty-eight P.M. The off-ramp from Eighty-five, six miles to the south."

He opened his eyes and studied the picture, which showed two flatbed trucks in the bottom right corner of the screen as they turned east onto County Road 18. The angle was different, but he was certain they were the same vehicles.

"I'll search the surrounding highway cams," Locker said. "They had to have originated somewhere. We should be able to pick them up again and follow them back—There. Ten-thirty-six P.M. Merging onto northbound Eighty-five from Highway Fifty-two east."

"Keep going," Layne said.

"There are only a handful of cameras between there and the Kansas border, all of them on I-Seventy-six, but I'll check them anyway."

"What do we know about these trucks?" Mason asked.

"Give me a second," Layne said. She imported the picture into the database and waited for the system to produce a match. "Sterling flat-beds. Model LT9500. Year: 2006. Twenty-four-foot bed." She closed the window with the hauler's specs and opened the database for stolen vehicles. "No matching models have been reported missing."

"Can you clean up these pictures?" Mason asked. "See if we can get a better look at the trucks themselves?"

"Give me just a second," Gardner said.

A series of filters passed over the image, one after another.

"What does that say?" Layne asked. "On the side of the container."

Gardner zoomed in on the blurry letters.

"Triton," she said.

"It's a global lessor of marine shipping containers," Locker added.

"So there should be a record of who leased them," Mason said.

"Not necessarily. Their business model is for their product to main-tain the youngest age profile of all containers in service. Something that old would have been retired and sold wholesale years ago."

"License plates?"

"I don't have the angle," Gardner said. "I can't get a clear shot of either end. These cameras were designed to capture the road conditions, not the cars themselves."

"Zoom in on the side of that truck," Mason said. "The one turning right. What's that on the passenger door?"

Gardner did as he asked. There was a logo beneath the window with words stenciled above it and to either side. They were old and faded and half-concealed by mud spattered from the tires. She again worked her magic with the filters and the logo resolved as well as it was going to, but the lettering remained out of focus and pixilated.

"Is that an ampersand?" Mason asked.

"There are two local hauling companies whose registered names use an ampersand," Locker said. "Errol and Sons Junk Removal and Front Range Transportation and Hauling."

Mason leaned closer to the screen. If he looked closely enough, he could see the jagged line of a stylized mountain range cutting through the symbol and, above it, arched lettering he could almost imagine reading Front Range.

"What do we know about the second one?"

"Front Range? It's incorporated as an LLC doing business at 19640 East County Road Forty-five."

"Where is that?"

"North of Wray," Gardner said. "Near the Kansas border."

"That fits with the trucks coming in from the east," Mason said.

"The business is registered to a man named Peter Cavanaugh," Locker said. "Seventy-two years old. No kids. Divorced twice. One wife lives in Reno, the other in Cheyenne. He inherited both the land and the business from his father upon his death in 1994. It looks like he was a one-man operation, hiring himself out locally through Craigslist and subcontracting for larger trucking operations moving agricultural supplies throughout Colorado, Kansas, and Wyoming."

"Can you track the GPS beacons in his trucks?"

"That model predates the routine installation of global-positioning beacons," Layne said. "I can try tracking them by their VIN numbers, but we would have already found them if he'd reported them missing."

"Then either they aren't stolen," Mason said, "or Cavanaugh isn't around to report them."

"What do we know about him?" Layne asked.

"There hasn't been any activity in either his personal account or his business account for more than two months," Locker said.

"Credit cards?" Mason asked.

"Maxed out a year ago."

"He could be working under the table."

"A distinct possibility, given his field, but it's nearly impossible to drop off the grid like this."

"What about phone records?"

"He doesn't have a landline and the last outgoing call from his cell phone of record was sixty-two days ago."

"GPS location of his phone?"

"Nothing," Locker said. "Either he removed the SIM card or the battery's dead."

"Last known location?"

"His home address."

"Bring up satellite imagery of that property," Mason said.

Gardner switched programs and zeroed in on the eastern plains near the town of Wray. Several zooms later, Mason was staring at a small farmhouse with a large outbuilding, a barn, and a grain silo. There was nothing around it but endless fields and scattered groves of trees. The nearest house was at least a dozen miles away.

"When was this picture taken?" Mason asked.

Gardner closed the image and opened the archives, which listed the sequential photographs by date.

"November twelfth," she said.

"Bring up the previous image. May seventeenth."

She clicked it and the photograph appeared. It looked identical to the one from six months later, only with the notable addition of the trucks parked in front of the outbuilding. Both had rusted shipping containers loaded onto their beds.

"Send everything you have to my phone," Mason said. "And contact the Wray PD and county sheriff's department. I want that property locked down right now. No one gets in or out of there until I arrive. And have them dispatch a K-9 unit. We're going to need help covering that much ground in a short amount of time."

He rushed down the aisle, opened the office door, and leaned inside.

"We ID'd the trucks they used to transport the Novichok out of here," he said. "They're registered to a guy named Cavanaugh. I'm on my way to his place right now."

Chris looked up from his computer monitor and covered the mouthpiece of the phone.

"Take Layne with you."

Mason glanced over his shoulder at the diminutive agent, who was already putting on her windbreaker and heading toward him, and then back at Chris.

"Why would I do that?" he asked.

"Because she's your new partner."

13

Mason turned north from the highway and had to ride down into a ditch to get around the police cruiser parked lengthwise across the dirt road, which cut straight through the endless grasslands toward a swatch of barren cottonwoods, barely visible against the gloaming. If Mason was right, their destination was just on the other side of them.

He'd made the 140-mile drive in under an hour and a half, during which time the brain trust back at the command center had been able to discover little they didn't already know. Cavanaugh had been honorably discharged from the army in the early eighties and earned his Class A driver's license shortly thereafter. He'd driven for various interstate-trucking companies until his father's passing, after which he'd seemingly settled into his old man's life. Not a single arrest or traffic ticket. Nothing to suggest he'd so much as crossed paths with the men Mason was hunting.

Gunnar's search had proven considerably more fruitful, but the opportunity to view the results had yet to present itself. Mason had tasked his old friend with finding out everything he possibly could about his new partner, Special Agent Jessica Layne. He wished he'd been given a chance to thoroughly vet her prior to her assignment, but he had to believe Chris had left no stone unturned, considering his department had been compromised by Mason's last two partners, who'd served interests other than their country's. Not to mention the fact that they'd tried to kill him on multiple occasions. He needed to forearm himself with every iota of information he could find, and not just to protect himself. If she were similarly corrupted, then maybe he could use her to lead him to the Thirteen.

Layne's assignment had been to coordinate the search of the property on the eastern plains with local law enforcement, but between calls, she'd been reasonably forthcoming with her answers to the few personal questions he'd asked. She'd graduated in the top 25 percent of her class at Colorado State and the top 10 percent at Quantico. She had a degree in psychology and advanced certifications in various subspecialties. Her prior posting had been in Virginia, where she said her duties had been largely administrative, but since her family lived up north, in Fort Collins, she'd jumped at the chance to return home and get out into the field. If she knew anything about the situation she was stepping into, she did a good job of hiding it.

Mason watched her from the corner of his eye. His new partner rode with her feet on the passenger seat, her knees drawn to her chest, and the grip of a Glock 27 protruding from the holster on her hip. She looked to be somewhere in her mid- to late twenties and couldn't have been more than five six in heels, although he doubted she owned any, but she carried herself in a manner that made her seem much larger.

He turned right and watched the cottonwoods, willows, and birch trees until they revealed a narrow driveway wending through the maze of trunks. The pool Crown Victoria splashed through water that looked a whole lot shallower than it turned out to be and nearly bottomed out on the other side. The driveway was grooved from the tires of heavy machinery and rutted by runoff from the fields. Branches raked against the siding with a sound like nails on a chalkboard.

The trees fell away and the headlights spread out across what at one time must have been the front yard. Grass had given way to thigh-high weeds. The frame of a swing set stood beside the rusted twin Ts of a clothesline. The charcoal gray Tahoe of the Colorado State Patrol's K-9 Unit had pulled in on the other side of them. A Wray PD cruiser had parked beside it, its high beams spotlighting the front porch, where two uniformed officers stood beneath the overhang, looking more than a little uncomfortable in their nitrile gloves and full-face air-purifying respirator masks, which they probably never thought they'd have to remove from their riot-control kits. This was undoubtedly the first time they'd been instructed to use such stringent precautions, but Layne had managed to convince them that it was standard federal operating procedure when working a potential crime scene where they were likely to encounter bodily fluids or a dead body.

The old farmhouse's whitewash had faded to gray and the windows were opaque with dust and cobwebs. Most of the shingles were gone and the overhang leaned in the opposite direction of the porch below it. A three-story grain silo that would probably stand the test of time lorded over it. The outbuilding to the right was far newer than everything else. It was a prefabricated unit that looked just about large enough to house two massive flatbed trucks.

A flock of crows wheeled in the distance, where seamless fields of feral crops, dead sunflowers, and wild grasses stretched off into the night.

Mason parked next to the cruiser and pulled his own respirator mask over his face. He stretched the gloves onto his hands as he climbed out. Layne donned her protective gear and met him in front of the hood. They waited for the officers to descend from the porch before flashing their badges.

"Tell me you haven't touched anything," Mason said.

"You kidding me?" the taller of the two officers said. He wore a regulation Stetson and cowboy boots, and conveyed the air of a man accustomed to reaping praise for doing very little. "You guys tell us we have to wear these plague masks and then think we're going to rush right down here and start touching stuff?"

"What Officer Dodge means to say is that we did exactly as we were instructed," the other officer said. He was shorter and stockier and undoubtedly came from stock that had earned its keep on the land. His badge read SENIOR OFFICER A. HILL, WRAY 3. "Our instructions were very specific. Control all access to the property. Touch nothing. Do nothing. Wait on-scene until agents arrive to debrief us. Not a whole lot of space to read between those lines."

"I'm not entirely sure I heard an answer in there," Layne said.

Mason smirked. He had no idea what life events had led her to join the FBI, but she certainly hadn't been recruited for her congeniality.

"No, ma'am," Hill said. "We did not touch anything."

"We made sure both egresses were covered before banging on the door," Dodge said.

"Did you check to see if they were locked?"

"That would have required touching."

Layne glared at him.

"No, ma'am," Hill said. "We couldn't hear anyone inside, so we looked through the few windows that aren't boarded over. Doesn't appear as though anyone's been here in a while."

"What makes you say that?" Mason asked.

"Everything's covered with dust," Dodge said.

"He's old and single," Layne said. "I doubt he spends much time with a feather duster."

"Pete's trucks tear up the roads out here," Hill said, "as you can tell from his driveway. The county generally has to grade that road you drove in on every other month, mostly because of him, but they haven't had the tractor out here since September and it's still in decent condition."

"Has anyone heard from him since then?" Mason asked.

"Like most of the people who live out on these rural routes, Pete keeps to himself."

"So you wouldn't notice if he'd gone missing," Layne said.

"We don't patrol out here," Dodge said. "We've had units in this area maybe a dozen times in the last month, but we don't go knocking on doors unless we have a good reason to do so."

"No one's reported anything out of the ordinary?" Mason asked. "Domestic disturbances? Gunshots?"

"You can't drive through here during prairie-chicken season without hearing gunshots."

"Have you encountered any vehicles you don't recognize in town?" Layne asked. "Anyone hanging around that you haven't seen before?"

"That's the kind of thing we'd definitely notice," Hill said. "New faces stand out in a town this small. And if anyone had any cause to suspect something was going on out here, we'd have heard about it."

Crunching noises from off to the left.

Mason turned on his mini Maglite and shone it toward the source. A state trooper approached through the tall weeds from the same general direction as the crows, his masked face nearly concealed beneath his Smokey Bear–style hat. A flashlight swung at his side. He wore a dark blue uniform with cargo pants, and his name was stenciled on his breast pocket: *G. Henderson, K-9 Unit*. A Belgian Malinois in a tan harness trotted at his side. It looked like a cross between a German shepherd and a jackal, with dark eyes, a lolling tongue, and blood on its muzzle.

"You guys FBI?" he asked.

"Was it the windbreakers that gave it away?" Layne said.

Mason held up his badge.

"Special Agents Mason and Layne. Denver Division."

"There's something you need to see," Henderson said, and headed back in the direction from which he'd come.

Mason and Layne followed him into the field. An old tractor emerged from the overgrowth beside the path; its rusted hood stood open, revealing its gutted engine. The plow it had once towed behind it had been claimed by tumbleweeds.

"Whatever it is we're dealing with, it's not contagious to canines, is it?" he asked.

The dog looked back at them with a huge grin on his bloody snout before falling back into stride with his handler. Mason felt guilty that he hadn't even considered the potential threat a chemical agent posed to the dog.

"What'd you find?" Layne asked.

"I can't take the credit. Atlas here found it."

"Found what?"

"I don't think I can adequately put it into words, ma'am. You really need to see it for yourself."

The cornstalks ahead were taller than all of them and looked like they'd been dead for several seasons. They were brown and crisp and rattled in the cold breeze that blew in from the northeast. Crows circled in the dark sky overhead, cawing and squawking. They perched on top of the stalks and jostled for space.

"Where's a good scarecrow when you need one?" Mason asked.

Henderson cast him a look he couldn't interpret.

Their combined lights barely illuminated the adjacent rows of corn, which cast shifting shadows that appeared to move with a life of their own. A narrow strip of broken stalks led deeper into the field. The dog bounded ahead and nearly vanished into them.

"I wasn't out here but fifteen minutes when I heard your car on the road," Henderson said. "We'd barely made a circuit of the house itself when Atlas picked up a scent and led me straight into this field."

Mason glanced up at the sky, where the black birds blended into the darkness. Clouds were creeping in from the east, swallowing the stars as they went. A breeze rattled the dead crops and raised the hackles on the back of his neck.

The fallen stalks tangled around his ankles and grasped for his feet. Pressed in from all sides. Clawed his face, grabbed at his arms. He couldn't see more than five feet ahead of him and the sky was all but lost overhead. The only thing he could tell with any kind of certainty was that Atlas hadn't cut this path. The signs of wear predated the most recent storm.

Mason knew they were getting close when he heard the buzz of flies.

His hand unconsciously sought the butt of his Glock in the holster beneath his left arm.

The dog barked from somewhere ahead of them. A murder of crows erupted from the stalks. Screaming. Beating one another with their wings. Shedding feathers like leaves.

Another step and they emerged into a small circular clearing.

A dark form reared up in front of them.

Mason drew his pistol.

Sighted.

Froze.

"This guy had probably better look for a new line of work," Layne said as she shoved past him. "He really sucks as a scarecrow."

14

Mason's first impression was that the man had been crucified. Someone had used thick, frayed rope to tie him to a wooden cross by his ankles, waist, shoulders, and wrists. His unsecured head hung forward, chin to chest. His red-and-black flannel shirt and denim overalls showed signs of both wear and extended exposure to the elements. A broad-brimmed straw hat concealed most of his facial features. What little Mason could see was crawling with flies and had been picked clean to the bone, presumably by the crows, which he was beginning to think had developed a serious superiority complex after feasting on human flesh. He shooed away one that had the audacity to land on the dead man's arm right in front of him.

"I do believe we found Peter Cavanaugh," Layne said. "How long do you think he's been out here like this?"

"I'm not sure," Mason said. "It's hard to tell with this much scavenger activity."

"Your gut?"

"A couple months, maybe more. Definitely within our theoretical time frame."

"Whoever did this didn't just kill him so he wouldn't report his trucks missing," she said. "This seems personal to me."

"I agree. The victim's been put on display. Posed. Whoever did this wanted him to be found. Wanted us to appreciate his work."

"For something meant to be found, the killer did an awfully good job of hiding it."

She had a point. Were it not for a blurry logo captured by a roadside camera and the work of a highly trained canine unit, who knew how long it might have been before anyone found Cavanaugh out here in the corn.

Atlas barked from somewhere off to the right. Henderson disappeared into the stalks after him.

"This feels somehow separate from the reason we originally came out here," Layne said.

"They could have gotten trucks from just about anywhere," Mason said. "Why drive more than a hundred miles to the middle of nowhere?"

"So they wouldn't get caught?"

"Then why leave this display at all?"

"There's another one over here," Henderson said from about fifteen feet diagonally to the northwest. He waved his flashlight so they could see him through the corn.

Mason raised his arm in front of his face and pushed through the stalks.

The second victim was displayed in the same fashion as the first. He was taller and thinner than the last and his flannel was blue instead of red, but otherwise every conceivable effort had been invested in posing him in an identical manner. He'd also been out here longer, if the relative disinterest of the flies and the crows was any indication. His bones were bleached by the elements and—

Mason eased closer and scrutinized the bones in the victim's hand and wrist. It took several seconds to identify the reason something had bothered him about their appearance. It was the outer layer of the bones. The cortices. They all showed subtle signs of remodeling. Plus, the saddle at the base of the thumb was worn, as were the small joints in the fingers.

He stepped back, tilted his head so he could see up underneath the hat, and studied the man's teeth. They were coffee-stained and the sockets had receded from the roots, making them appear longer than they actually were. While he certainly wasn't a forensic odontologist, he had enough experience to recognize that this man wasn't the typical victim of a serial killer.

This guy was old.

Mason went back to the first body, using a broken stalk to slide back the victim's sleeve. The bones were in much better shape than those of the second, but there was still clear evidence of arthritis. The teeth were long and discolored, too.

He stood on his toes and turned in a full circle. The only thing he could see above the corn was a whole lot of dark sky and the very top of the grain silo.

"There's a third one over here," Layne called.

Mason didn't reply. He'd latched onto a thought and wanted to see where it took him, starting with heading out of the field and back toward the farmhouse.

Despite historical precedent to the contrary, it was entirely possible that a serial killer would target old men. Maybe he chose victims that reminded him of his father or grandfather. Killers thrived on the hunt, though, and there were few victims less challenging than the elderly. Whoever did this had spent considerable time posing his victims and yet hadn't raised the curtain for the world to see. Was it possible the display was designed solely for this monster's personal enjoyment?

He was pretty sure he heard Layne call out the discovery of a fourth victim from somewhere behind him as he fought through the cornstalks, heading toward the silo. It was maybe thirty feel tall and composed of smooth ceramic tiles. The top was flat. Maybe by design. More likely the domed roof had blown off.

Rusted rungs led up the eastern side, nearest the house. He climbed slowly. The wind grew stronger as he ascended. He could hear the voices of the Wray police officers around the front of the house, but not well enough to make out their words.

He paused to take in the view when he reached the top. The path from the house drew a crooked line through the field to the first victim, around which the corn appeared to have been cleared just enough to see the body from this distance. Another path led to the north-northwest, and the second victim. Then west-northwest to the third. The fourth was to the southwest. Crows shrieked and burst from the corn farther to the south, where Layne followed the overgrown path toward the fifth. The pattern was clearly evident. The victims were arranged in a circle, or would have been if there had been two more of them, one between the third and fourth and another between the fourth and fifth. He scrutinized the middle for some sort of centerpiece but saw little more than a riot of shaking stalks he attributed to the dog.

A thin ledge encircled the inner rim of the silo, granting access to another ladder. He followed its descent with his flashlight beam, all the way down to the bottom, where, set into the ground amid the grain dust and trash and weeds, there was a metal hatch.

Mason climbed down the rungs, knelt over a hatch that reminded him of a coal chute, and inspected it with his flashlight. It was designed to open by using a lever outside the silo, but he was able to slide it on the metal runners without much difficulty, revealing an underground tunnel framed by wooden cribbing.

The killer could very well be hiding down there in the darkness. Mere feet away.

He drew his Glock, aligned the barrel with his flashlight beam, and aimed down into the earth. He saw aged timber and smooth, packed earth. The passage was obviously old, and yet there were no cobwebs.

He opened his mouth to quiet his breathing and listened for any sound to betray the presence of someone below him.

Silence.

"Screw it," he whispered, and risked a peek. He'd already recoiled by the time his brain sorted through what his eyes had seen. The tunnel extended beyond the range of his light, but there'd been no one and nothing in between.

He dropped through the hole and landed in a squat. The air sparkled with motes of dust and smelled faintly of mold and age. The dirt roof was maybe three feet high. Just tall enough to allow him to move in a crouch, his pistol raised in front of him. Every footstep sounded like a block of sandpaper striking wood.

The tunnel was roughly twenty-five feet long and terminated against a nearly petrified wooden door with an old iron latch that was surprisingly free of rust.

Mason leaned closer and pressed his ear against it.

Listened.

No sound from the other side.

He pushed the door open a crack.

Ducked back.

Waited for the thunder of gunfire, which, fortunately, never came.

He took a deep breath and shouldered open the door. Crawled out from behind it, low and fast.

Swept his light and pistol from one side of the room to the other.

Took in everything as fast as he could.

He was in a cellar of some kind. Belowground. No windows. Bare earthen floor. Timber planks overhead. Fieldstone and mortar walls. Inset slanted cellar doors to the left, black with coal dust. Wooden stairs straight ahead. Single bulb with a pull cord above them. Rusted metal shelves with jars full of nails and screws and washers. Preserves. Canning wax and glass jars. Dented cans of paint and kerosene. Bags of potting soil in the corner. Fertilizer. Seeds. So old that the bags had disintegrated and the contents spilled out. Weathered boxes and crates.

It was a tornado shelter. When the owner saw a funnel cloud, he just pulled the plug on the silo and gravity sucked the grain down into the tunnel so that he didn't lose his entire store. Solid planning. There were enough supplies to hunker down in here for an extended period of time. Or at least there had been decades ago, when everything was last stocked.

The door leading into the house was set flush with the ceiling. He'd be poking his head up from the floor like a gopher from its hole. The moment he raised the hatch, he'd be completely vulnerable.

He climbed the wooden stairs, careful to minimize the creaking of the ancient planks. Cocked his head toward the floorboards. Listened. Nothing.

Mason slowed his heartbeat, steadied his nerves, and went up fast. He shoved the door upward. Hurdled the final few stairs. Jumped out of the floor in the middle of the main room. The door struck the floor behind him with a resounding crash.

He pivoted in a circle, inspecting everything around him down the barrel of his pistol.

Bare plank floor. Faded paths of wear. Behind him: a potbellied stove, disconnected from the ductwork. Low ceiling. Cobwebs from the corners to the light fixture overhead. To his left: a rear window, broken and boarded from the outside. No curtains on the bent rod. Straight ahead: a wall where framed pictures had once hung, a threadbare couch against it. To his right: the kitchen, through which he could see the living room. The front door, twenty feet away.

He advanced in a shooter's stance. Dust on the counters. The dishes in the sink had been there for so long that the flies wanted nothing to do with them.

The living room showed more recent signs of habitation. A pillow and a blanket on the couch. A glass of water on the end table. But it was the front wall that immediately caught his attention. It was covered with photographs. Newspaper clippings. Computer printouts. All of men he didn't recognize. Their eyes scratched out in every single one. New pictures. Old pictures. Young men in clothes that appeared to date all the way back to the fifties. Old men from the here and now. Most featured men in military uniforms. As individuals. In groups. The same faces through the years.

A shadow passed across the seam of light around the boarded front window. The officers outside. One of them must have heard movement from inside the house. They had no idea he'd entered through the grain silo.

Mason glanced at the front door. The dead bolt was in the horizontal position. Unlocked. There was duct tape across the door strike. On the inside. Silver. Flush. Recently applied. Wires trailing from it to a corroded tractor battery. The handle of a paint can connected the terminals. A small square of cardboard prevented it from touching the positive side and completing the circuit. Beneath the arch was a glass jar with amber fluid at the bottom and a pile of white powder separated from it by another piece of cardboard. Beside it, a second jar. Full of nails.

The knob turned as if in slow motion.

"Don't!" Mason shouted.

A spark snapped from the battery.

He turned and dove into the kitchen.

A sound like a shotgun blast behind him.

Clattering noises like hail.

A high-pitched hum inside his head.

Smoke rolled over him.

White powder shivered from the plaster walls.

Flames crackled.

Only then did he feel the pain.

15

A town with a population smaller than most shopping malls on a Saturday afternoon was accustomed to small-town problems. Everyone knew everyone else. More important, everyone knew everyone else's mother. There was undoubtedly no one in town who would have ever imagined a day would come when a full two-fifths of Wray's police force would be shredded by an improvised explosive device merely by opening the front door of a house they all knew as "the old Cavanaugh place."

Senior Officer Anthony Hill and Officer Drake Dodge hadn't suffered. At least that's what the medical examiner said. Their families would, however. Of that, there was no doubt. The entire town would, for that matter. Any loss of life in such a small community was like the amputation of a finger. It might not consume every waking thought, but there would always be reminders of what was missing.

The explosion had been both violent and contained. The nails had done the real damage. Sharp one-inch roofing nails expelled outward at a speed of ten thousand feet per second squared. From a distance of roughly two feet. The ME's office had needed shovels to collect the officers' remains. Mason had been lucky. The kitchen wall had intercepted or altered the course of most of the nails. Those that passed through barely had enough momentum to embed themselves halfway into his right buttocks, thigh, and calf. Eleven in total. He'd thought the paramedic was joking when he produced a pair of pliers, but it pulled them right out. The wounds still hurt, though. As did the opposite cheek, where he'd been given a tetanus booster. He shifted his weight uncomfortably as he surveyed the damage to the inside of the house.

"Believe it or not, that was an ingenious weapon," Layne said from behind him.

He turned around to face her.

"That's not very comforting."

"It's not supposed to be. Building a bomb like that takes serious training and skill, especially to be able to improvise it from the items on hand. You can't just pluck little pieces of ammonium nitrate out of fertilizer. Producing it involves a complex chemical reaction. Never mind combining it with the right amount of fuel oil at the right time. This is one very smart individual."

"Definitely the kind of person you'd hire to produce a large quantity of Novichok."

"Then how do you read the five victims out there who look like they've been crucified?" Layne asked. "We can't possibly be dealing with another crime scene shared by two distinct mass murderers."

"I don't want to speculate until the ME determines cause of death, but I'm inclined to agree. This feels disturbingly intimate. It's like he chose this place specifically so he could take his time with his victims. So he wouldn't miss a moment of their suffering."

"That's why I was looking for you," she said. "There's something you need to see."

They passed the wall that had saved his life on their way out of the living room. It looked like it had taken a shotgun blast, as did the ceiling in the main room. There was little left of the front wall. The majority of the plaster was gone and the wooden support posts were scorched. The photographs lay in tatters amid the chunks of debris on the floor. Mason managed to get a decent shot of the only reasonably intact one on his cell phone.

The main entrance had been widened by a good five feet. They'd found the doorknob across the yard, embedded in the trunk of a tree. He tried not to look at the brownish red spatters on the porch or think about the sound the little booties he wore over his shoes made when they peeled from the sticky surface.

The entire yard was awash in the glow of portable lighting arrays. Shards of glass sparkled from the ground. The trees seemed to glow with the alternating red and blue glare from the cruiser blocking the driveway. The ambulance was still parked next to the Wray PD Caprice Classic and Mason's pool Crown Victoria, both of which were dented to hell, pocked with chunks of biological matter, and filled with glass from the shattered windshields. They were going to have to find another way home.

Layne led him past the cars and around the side of the house, toward where the cornfield glowed in the distance. The barking of tracking dogs echoed from the surrounding darkness.

The temperature had fallen precipitously. Mason's breath trailed him over his shoulder. The frosted weeds crunched underfoot.

He'd assumed she was taking him out into the field, where the dead men were posed like scarecrows, right up until she veered from the path in the opposite direction after passing the tractor. The gap where the battery had been was readily apparent. They skirted a mountain of hay that looked like it had once been baled and found a ponderosa pine that grew forked from the ground, as though its trunk had split when it was little more than a sapling. One half stood reasonably straight; the other bent sideways before eventually righting itself.

"He sat right here," Layne said. "That's where the dogs picked up his scent."

"The killer?"

"He sat right there, fifty feet from his victims, and listened to them die. Maybe even talked to them while they did."

"Were they able to track him?" Mason asked.

"He'd obviously been in this place for a while. His scent's every-where. They're following it in any number of directions." She turned away from him. "But that's not why I brought you out here."

Mason followed her stare to the upright portion of the tree, beside the killer's surveillance position. The bark had been removed and four symbols carved directly into the pulp. The dribbles of sap were crusted on the outside but appeared to still be soft in the middle.

久延毘古

"It's Japanese," she said. "It translates to 'Kuebiko,' which is the name of the Shinto god of knowledge and agriculture. He's traditionally depicted as an all-knowing, all-seeing scarecrow."

"I get the allusion to the way the men in the field are posed, but we figured that out on our own in all of about two seconds. Invoking the name of an obscure god to draw attention to the obvious doesn't mesh with everything we know about this guy. There has to be more to it than that."

"My thoughts exactly. So I googled scarecrows in general and Kue-biko specifically." Layne woke her cell phone and read from the screen. "'By definition, a scarecrow is a decoy designed to resemble a human being. It's placed in a field to discourage birds from consuming recently planted seeds or crops throughout the growing cycle. Large-scale and corporate farms use more modern means, like automatic noise guns and aluminum PET film ribbons to minimize crop predation. There are as many names for them as there are myths for their creation. Tattie-bogle, murmet, mommet, flay-crow, mog, shay, rook-scarer, and Feathertop. The earliest known historical account, however, comes from *Kojiki*, the oldest surviving book in Japan.'"

"There we go."

"'He's known as Kuebiko or, euphemistically, Yamada no Shodo, which translates to "someone left soaking wet from standing guard over mountain rice fields." He's incapable of walking, yet possesses a broad knowledge of all things.'"

"The knowledge thing seems to fit, especially if we're dealing with a man with a highly developed ego."

"Interesting you should mention ego. In Jungian terms, the scarecrow is the shadow, the inverse archetype of the ego."

"The darkness of our own creation."

"Kind of gives you goose bumps when you say it like that," she said.

"I'd imagine that's the whole point."

"A more metaphorical interpretation is of the scarecrow as a straw man, a distorted version of ourselves that is at once both foreign and familiar. One that's made of straw, essentially hollow inside. One that lacks some fundamental quality we ascribe to humanity."

"Like a conscience?"

"Like a conscience."

"So we're looking for a man who sees himself as an all-knowing shadow of a human being without a conscience."

"One who, like a scarecrow, is content to stand back and observe, a witness to the suffering of his victims instead of an active participant in it."

The way she said it made Mason's blood run cold.

It reminded him of the Hoyl, who must have spent countless hours studying his test subjects, from the moment symptoms manifested through the process of decomposition, although that was where the similarities ended. The Hoyl had been a clinician, detached from any emotional connection with his victims. He'd no more reveled in their pain than he had thrilled in their passing, unlike the man who'd brought his victims all the way out here so he could take his time with them and set up cameras to watch the men he'd entombed behind the wall at the end of the tunnel slowly suffocate.

This was a different kind of monster entirely, one capable of inflicting inhuman cruelty without remorse, one who possessed the skill sets required to design the traps that had nearly killed Alejandra and decimated his SWAT team during the hunt for the Hoyl.

One who could very well have access to thousands of gallons of the most lethal nerve gas ever developed and no compunction about using it.

16

Kuebiko's entire life had been an execution by *lingchi*—the death of a thousand cuts—and with the final figurative slice, the last drops of humanity trickled to the concrete floor and drained through the rusted grate. All that remained now was the physical vessel, a vaguely human form stuffed with pain and misery, a husk animated by hatred and rage. The time had come to revisit that suffering upon the men who had taken such pleasure in inflicting it.

"All . . . will . . . know . . . the . . . truth."

And with those words, Kuebiko became no more, leaving behind the Scarecrow, an all-knowing, all-seeing creature no longer constrained by the frailty of the flesh or the threat of damnation. Those were the failings of man and it was no longer one of their kind. It embraced its role in the coming nightmare, for, being dead already, it no longer felt fear. At long last, it would shine a light into the shadows and reveal not just the monsters but those who chose not to see their atrocities, making them complicit in the horrors perpetrated upon innocent men, women, and even children. They would pay for what they'd done—the whole godforsaken world would pay—starting with the men responsible for the interminable agony and culminating with the man who was ultimately to blame, even if he was too blind to see the role he'd played.

"Blind . . ."

The Scarecrow pressed its skeletal fingertip over the stoma in its throat and issued a harsh, rasping laugh. The sound echoed throughout the cold, insensate chamber, where it sat in complete darkness, by itself and yet not alone, breathing the dusty air and listening to the hum of machinery and the soft, dysrhythmic breathing of another from the live feed on its cell phone. In a matter of days, even that would be gone, but there would be no one left to bear witness to the silence.

For the first time, it noticed the alarm beacon at the top of the screen. Someone had triggered the early warning system that it had built into the improvised explosive device attached to the front door of the farmhouse. The hunt would soon commence in earnest, but there was no hope of stopping the course of events that had already been set in motion.

Millions of people would die, just not where anyone expected, especially the man who'd commissioned the Scarecrow's services, the same man who'd unknowingly created it in the first place.

A hiss erupted from the hole in its throat, a roar to which it couldn't even give voice. It crawled over the earthen mounds, struggled to its feet, and stormed out of the main room. Its wheezing exhalations trailed it down the hallway and into the room it had created with a single purpose in mind. The old man locked in the cage in the corner attempted to cry out at the sound of the approaching footsteps, but the duct tape turned the noise into a muffled grunt. His wrists and feet were bound together, forcing him into a fetal position, making it impossible for him to move in the slightest. He struggled to breathe through the mucus burbling from his nose. His eyes widened, but it was so dark that the old man couldn't have seen his hand in front of his face, let alone the silhouette standing before it.

The Scarecrow could, though. It could see everything.

"Do . . . you . . . remember . . . me?"

A desperate flurry of grunts to the negative. The old man tried to speak, but there would be no talking his way out of what was to come.

The Scarecrow reached up, grabbed one of the handcrafted objects hanging from the ceiling—starlike designs made from wooden tongue depressors bound together with yarn to form what almost looked like little men, or perhaps stick-figure dolls—and thrust it through the cage, into the old man's hand.

"How . . . about . . . now?"

The old man turned it over and over until recognition dawned.

He screamed into the duct tape and thrashed against his restraints.

The Scarecrow savored the exquisite sounds of his suffering.

PART III

If destruction be our lot, we must ourselves be its author and finisher.

—Abraham Lincoln,
Lyceum Address (1838)

17

Considering their pool car was covered with evidence and not going anywhere for the foreseeable future, a deputy from the Yuma County Sheriff's Department had been assigned to drive Mason and Layne back to the FBI building on East Thirty-sixth Avenue. Mason had taken the backseat, so he had room to shift uncomfortably on his rear end as the painkillers slowly wore off. Layne had fallen asleep in the passenger seat pretty much right away, her arms tucked into her jacket and her forehead resting against the window, which finally gave him the opportunity to review the results of Gunnar's research into his new partner's background.

The email consisted of a short note—*She looks clean, at least on paper*—and three attached files: a summary of findings, a basic financial audit, and her federal personnel file. Mason started with her finances. She hadn't received any large influxes of cash and didn't appear overly vulnerable to being bought. She had a solid four figures in her savings account, a decent start on a 401(k) plan, and rented a reasonably priced condo in an affordable neighborhood. Minimal credit-card and student-loan debt. Responsible, if not entirely frugal, spending patterns.

He moved on to Gunnar's summary of her personal history, a bullet-pointed list that told a reasonably comprehensive story. Born in Topeka and moved to Colorado at age four. Athlete in high school. Held down the same job through college. Applied to the FBI months before graduation. Her father was a Lutheran minister, her mother a teacher. Her younger sister had been killed at fourteen by a drunk driver, the son of a city councilman, who was later acquitted of manslaughter and sentenced to community service and a temporary suspension of his license. It was likely this injustice that had driven Layne and her older sister, an assistant district attorney, into law enforcement.

Her personnel file described an agent who was tenacious and driven, and yet one whose ambition didn't drip from every page. Details of her previous assignment were sparse to nonexistent, which essentially meshed with an administrative role. She had a TS/SCI security clearance, meaning she'd been vetted as thoroughly as humanly possible by the FBI and subjected to additional polygraph testing in order for her to be able to access sensitive compartmented information. Her performance reviews were simultaneously exemplary and marred by caveats. Maybe not caveats so much as backhanded compliments. One in particular seemed to sum up all of them. Her most recent supervisor had written: "She's bullheaded and deterministic, which will serve her well in the field." The way Mason read it, she required a certain measure of autonomy and didn't necessarily play well with others. In a nutshell, she didn't like being told what to do.

While everything he'd read painted a picture of a dedicated agent on the rise, he couldn't afford to blindly trust her. Not yet anyway. The field was a poor proving ground, though, so he was going to have to keep an eye on her. Underestimating her could be the last mistake he ever made.

Mason's phone vibrated to alert him to an incoming text as the cruiser pulled around behind division headquarters. He glanced at the message. Chris had worked his magic and gotten him on the task force, which was set to convene at 8:00 A.M. Layne's phone chimed about ten seconds later, rousing her from her slumber, to inform her of the same.

The deputy let them out at the rear security gate. They thanked him for the ride and headed toward the nearly empty parking structure. Before they split up at their respective vehicles, Mason made Layne promise to go home and squeeze in an hour or so of sleep, knowing full well she had no more intention of doing so than he did.

He needed time to think.

Something about the nature of the trap at the farmhouse was eating at him. Like Layne had said, while primitive, the design of the bomb had been perfect. The moment anyone opened that door, that person would be killed instantly. There was no doubt about it. The explosion itself would have more than done the job, but the container full of nails added an unnecessary element of brutality. There'd been more than enough fertilizer and fuel oil down in the cellar to increase the size of the bomb exponentially, enough to convert the entire acreage into a smoldering crater. Instead, the unknown subject—UNSUB—had built a device that was relatively intimate in proportion, yet one that would cause the most egregious physical damage to the intruders.

The IED—like the chemical dispersal unit that had killed the men behind the wall, the death trap in the knocking pen, and the methane bomb that ripped through the SWAT team during the manhunt for the Hoyl—had been designed for the victims to trigger it themselves. Surely there was some sort of underlying psychological motivation there, perhaps a means by which the killer could distance himself from the act of killing, and yet there was an undeniable element of cruelty at odds with that assessment. He'd wanted the men behind the wall to know they were going to die in the worst-possible manner, unless they opted for a slow asphyxiation. For Alejandra to experience the agony of her neck snapping a heartbeat before the captive bolt punched through her forehead. For the SWAT team to smell the gas, feel air rushing past them, fueling the fireball that would consume them. For the officers at the farmhouse to hear the sound of the tape peeling and the click of the paint can's handle striking the battery terminal, to see the spark, then the flash of light that propelled the nails through them. He wanted his victims to understand with their final thoughts that there was no escaping what was about to happen.

Finding the Novichok was their priority, though.

They'd have all the time in the world to examine the UNSUB's twisted signature and speculate about his motivations once the greater threat was eliminated. Right now, they had to believe that he knew they were coming for him and was undoubtedly already accelerating his timetable. They needed to find him in a hurry and it was going to take all of the task force's resources to do it.

But first he needed to shower, change into a pair of pants that didn't have holes in the ass, and pack a travel bag in case things started to move in a hurry.

Mason wasn't used to driving to his new house and certainly didn't think of it as home. It was simply the place where he slept and showered. And while he didn't know if his wife had ever even seen the building in which he now resided, he felt her absence within its walls. Every now and then he swung by his old house and parked across the street, but it didn't feel like home, either. Not anymore. Now it belonged to a couple who wore business suits and carried briefcases. All he really knew about them was that they were young and they smiled a lot, which made him feel good. He'd smiled a lot in that house, too.

That life was over now. His wife's murder was a fresh wound that tore open every single day. Everyone who'd contributed to the events leading to her death was dead. Everyone except for the entity that had set those events into motion, an entity he would track to the ends of the Earth if he had to. Hunting it down was the only thing that mattered. Everyone needed a reason to live. In that sense, he was lucky.

He had thirteen.

His new place was in an industrial corridor close enough to downtown that he could hear the omnipresent racket of construction, but far enough off the beaten path that few cars even inadvertently turned down his street. Fifty years ago, it must have been a hotbed of activity. Maybe even fifteen. At one time or another, the building had been a tire shop, a construction company, a used-car lot, and a showcase for aspiring graffiti artists. He'd bought it on a whim and had regretted it immediately, and yet somehow he warmed to it a little more every day.

The renovations were moving at a snail's pace, though. He would have thought that a crew being paid by the job and not by the hour would approach its work with a sense of urgency, but it was undoubtedly better to have the job done right than fast. For what he was paying them, he *really* hoped they were doing it right.

He'd replaced the windows with glass of the bulletproof variety and added a set of doors with the kind of lock that couldn't be picked with a battering ram. He'd chosen to leave the appearance largely untouched, although he'd applied what he liked to think of as a renewal of anonymity by mounting broken shutters and coiling razor wire through the top of the chain-link fence. His only real extravagance was a set of remote-control openers for the front gate and the garage doors.

The inside was another story. Having the whole thing gutted and stripped down to the bare framework had taken only a few days, but he was beginning to think the actual construction might take another twenty years. It was his own fault, he knew. He'd commissioned several challenging alterations of the structure itself, namely a panic room off the main living area, a storage room reminiscent of a bank vault, staircases behind walls, and an underground tunnel that let out by the river behind the property.

Considering the kind of power against which he'd aligned himself, he needed his house to be able to withstand a full-on assault. And it wasn't like money was an issue. He figured Angie would have approved of him using her inheritance to track down and destroy the cabal that had used and then discarded her entire family. It was probably the only thing he'd ever done of which her old man would have approved.

His own father, however, was a different story.

The gate was open and the crews were gathered around their trucks, which looked like they'd been worked on more recently than his house. They were parked on what he only loosely considered his yard and the men were either sitting or lounging with thermoses and smokes. Chatting and laughing. Music blaring. Surely at some point they'd want to head inside and do some actual work, if only to break up the monotony of doing nothing.

Mason wasn't in the mood this morning. He was tired and preoccupied and would have enjoyed a confrontation, which was a good-enough reason to avoid one. The foreman nodded to him as he drove through the gate and pulled into the middle of the three garages. He hadn't even opened the driver's side door when the reflection of a black Town Car flashed across his rearview mirror.

He closed his eyes and fought the urge to repeatedly pound his forehead against the steering wheel.

As if this day couldn't possibly get any worse.

18

J. R. Mason was a second-term United States senator. He was tenacious and driven, not to mention largely absent from Mason's life after his mother died and he was shipped off to a prestigious prep school, from which he'd been occasionally checked out for major holidays and photo ops. Or at least that was how it had felt at the time. Lately, though, it seemed as though their relationship was in a state of transition. Especially since Angie's death. His father had been there to help him through the worst time of his life and make the arrangements he'd been unable to handle on his own. Maybe his reasons for doing so were self-serving, but that was just his way.

His reward for helping Mason wash his hands of the AgrAmerica disaster was being stuck with the bulk of the shares at a time when unloading them was impossible. To his credit, he never once complained. He simply thrust out his chin, took his lumps from the media, and challenged himself to right the ship. Of course, that meant hiring a fleet of MBAs and PR guys and lawyers who could actually do the job, not necessarily rolling up his sleeves and doing it himself, as the papers made it sound.

Although he loved his father, Mason wasn't happy to see him. Drama followed him wherever he went like special interest groups at budget appropriations time. All he wanted to do was grab a quick shower, pack a bag, and get to the task force meeting, which, unfortunately, was probably the whole reason the senator was here.

"I like what you've done with the place," he said. "When are you going to tear the rest of it down?"

"Funny." That joke was really getting old. "Shouldn't you be in Washington, voting yourself a pay raise?"

"We did that weeks ago, before the session adjourned. Have you already forgotten how these things work?"

"I know. Christmas with the Constituency. I'm just grateful you didn't buy us matching sweaters this year."

"I only did that once, and yet you find a way to bring it up every chance you get. You were a child, for crying out loud."

"I was sixteen, Dad. That's the kind of thing that scars a kid for life."

"It doesn't hurt to show a little Christmas spirit, you know." As if on cue, his driver entered with a small decorated tree. He looked around, shuddered, and set it down in the middle of the main room. "Ah, yes. Thank you, Rodney."

The driver tipped his cap and took his leave.

Mason couldn't help but smile as he stared at the tree. It was maybe three feet tall, plastic, and more blue than green. It looked like the kind of display a downtown bookstore might put in its window, but it was a grand gesture of the type he rarely attributed to his father.

"What?" he said. "Worried it'll scare off the rats?"

"Christmas was three days ago, Dad."

"I've stopped by multiple times during the past few days, as you'd know if you ever checked your voice mail." The senator winked. "Unless you're deliberately trying to avoid the man responsible for giving you the gift of life—"

"It's perfect. Thank you."

His father clapped him on the back and strolled deeper into the skeletal structure.

"I try not to tell people how to do their jobs—Lord knows how little I enjoy being told how to do mine every waking second of the day—but I believe more would get accomplished if your foreman were somehow able to coax his workers *inside* the house."

"Look, Dad. I appreciate your stopping by, but—"

"Oh, I know. You have a busy day ahead and I did show up unannounced. I just wanted to check how things were going with the investigation up north. I realize you're not obligated to share the details of an active investigation, but I've heard there's been a lot of activity out there recently. You know, at the end of a tunnel that leads directly into a building on my property. I think that entitles me to some answers, and I've encountered precious little cooperation through formal channels."

"It was a gas leak. Plain and simple. Someone ruptured a line."

"Strange they would need to activate a hazmat team for something so 'plain and simple.'"

"I'm sure you know more about that kind of thing than I do."

"You were there. At least that's what I heard from sources—none of whom was my own son, I might add—who thought I deserved to know, since it affected me on both the personal and professional fronts."

"Sorry my first thoughts weren't about how it would affect you, Dad. I'll try to be more considerate next time."

"Don't twist my words. That's not at all what I'm saying. My concern is that you're taking unnecessary risks now that Angela is no longer with us. I've already buried a wife and a daughter, James. I have no intention of burying my only son."

"I'm not opposed to cremation."

"I see I've caught you in a rare mood this morning. Perhaps we should find a more fitting occasion to catch up on current events. And invest in some new pants. Those have holes all up and down the back."

"I sat on a cactus."

"So I heard. You should really make an effort to be more careful. Like I said, don't think for a second that Angela will be happy to see you again so soon." He turned on his politician's smile and effectively switched personas. "Fifty dollars will buy you a coffeemaker and a space heater. The carrot always trumps the stick, son. This place will be finished in half the time."

He flipped up the collar of his overcoat and started for the door.

"Where are you staying?" Mason asked.

"The B Suite." The top floor of one of the buildings on the AgrAmerica lot had been designed to accommodate visiting investors and VIPs. Mason's father-in-law hadn't been known for doing anything half-assed. It was lavishly appointed and had stunning views of what had once been Paul Thornton's kingdom. "Swing by tonight if you're up that way. I'll treat you to a steak as thick as a dictionary. There are advantages to owning your own cattle, you know."

"As long as you're not the one cooking it."

"Perish the thought."

The senator offered a one-armed hug and headed for the door.

"Thanks for the tree, Dad. It really *spruces* the place up."

"Try not to sit on it."

His father stopped in the entryway and turned around. He looked at Mason, then past him, and nodded to himself as though confirming some deep inner thought.

"I'm going to be spending New Year's in the District this year," he said. "I'm heading back tomorrow afternoon. I'd like to formally invite you to come with me. There are some people I'd like you to meet."

"People?"

"Person, James." It struck Mason that his father was referring to a woman. "Don't make this any more uncomfortable than it already is."

The senator hailed his driver and ducked outside. A cloud of breath trailed him into the cold. Mason was just about to close the door, when his father abruptly turned around.

"I heard the, quote, unquote, 'gas' was actually a chemical warfare agent."

The words caught Mason by surprise. He was too slow with his reply. He opened his mouth, but by then it was too late. Anything he said would have been a lie and they both knew it.

"That's what I thought." The senator inclined his face to the sky and closed his right eye against the sun. He didn't look at Mason when he spoke. "Ask yourself a question, son. If you wanted to make something like that, who would you hire to do it?"

Mason stared blankly at him for a long moment. Sometimes he forgot that politicians had to have more than a megawatt smile and a firm handshake. Most were incredibly bright, whether or not the media decided to portray them as such.

His brain was already kicking into overdrive.

"Looks like it might snow after all," his father said, and then he was gone.

19

The Dodge-Hill Strike Force, named in honor of Drake Dodge and Anthony Hill, the Wray police officers killed in the explosion, was established as an offshoot of the Joint Terrorism Task Force, which was comprised of the combined assets of the ATF, DEA, FBI, ICE, and every other domestic agency responsible for counteracting foreign and domestic terrorism. Taking the investigation to the JTTF was a stroke of brilliance on Chris's part, not only because it prevented Homeland from supplanting them but also because it actually gave the FBI an element of control, since it was responsible for all funding, from the salaries of the agents on loan from the various agencies to vehicles and materiel support. It also meant that Chris could appoint a leader over whom he felt he could exert some amount of influence.

Assistant Special Agent in Charge Diana Algren's role was to liaise with department heads and field units, dole out assignments, collate evidence, and disseminate information for public consumption. While the media had yet to catch wind of either the release of the Novichok or the remains in the cornfield, it was only a matter of time before someone tipped them off to the sheer quantity of bodies piling up in the morgue.

From Mason's perspective, Algren's involvement didn't necessarily bode well for a speedy resolution. The cameras loved her, although not nearly as much as she loved them. She was as articulate as she was attractive, and fast-tracked for an SAC posting. Her chestnut hair was longer in front than in back and framed her face in such a way as to draw attention to her green eyes and perpetually pouting lips. The former were natural, the latter augmented, presumably by the same plastic surgeon who erased her crow's-feet and tightened the skin on her neck every so often. She wore a cream-colored blouse, a tapered suit jacket that emphasized more than the bulge of her sidearm, and a knee-length skirt that fit her like the upper half of a mermaid's tail.

She stood at the head of the polished rosewood table with a stack of black binders, which she slid to each of them in turn. The table was easily large enough to accommodate twenty people, so they spread out, but remained clustered by agency. The blinds were drawn and the recessed lighting had been dialed up, spotlighting photographs of Denver through the years, from black and white to color and all of the faded shades in between.

Algren's personal assistant wheeled around a cart with ice water and coffee before taking his leave. She commenced the moment he closed the door behind him.

"Considering the nature of the threat we're up against, we'll begin with a brief introduction and then get right down to business." She had a slight northeastern accent of the kind Mason attributed to a wealthy upbringing. Connecticut, maybe. "For those of you who don't know me, my name is Diana Algren. I'm one of the assistant special agents in charge of the Denver Division of the FBI. I've been appointed to head up this task force. My role will be to provide oversight for our investigative efforts, coordinate the responses of all agencies, and facilitate the flow of information—to wit, all communications will go through me directly."

She glanced at her notes.

"Also representing the Bureau are Special Agents James Mason and Jessica Layne, who were responsible for the initial discovery of the victims we're attributing to an UNSUB who has some sort of sick fascination with scarecrows." Mason nodded and Layne offered a half wave to those assembled. "Together, we bring to the table some of the brightest investigative minds in the world and a wealth of knowledge regarding the apprehension of serial murderers, a facet of this investigation we consider secondary to the manufacture and potential release of an unknown quantity of a Novichok agent theorized to be as much as four thousand gallons, although one we believe to be critical to the identification and apprehension of the principal parties involved."

One of the agents at the end of the table, sitting to Mason's left, whistled appreciatively. He obviously recognized the damage one could inflict with that volume of chemical weaponry.

"I would like to welcome Agents"—again, Algren looked at her notes—"Victoria Addison and Adrian Salazar from the Department of Homeland Security's Federal Protective Service. Their existing national framework of detection and response, including split-second activation of FEMA's national and state-level emergency operations centers, should the worst-case scenario arise, will surely prove beneficial."

Addison had thick arms and large hands and a scar that ran from the corner of her mouth to her ear, as if she'd been caught by a fishing hook and torn herself free. Her brown eyes issued a challenge she appeared more than capable of backing up. Salazar, who had smooth tan skin and a broad chest, made eye contact with each of them. He looked out of his element in the conference room, but Mason could easily see him swinging a baton and cracking skulls in the field with a smile on his face.

Algren turned to the newest arrivals, who'd entered after she'd already started and assumed the seats at the foot of the table so as not to interrupt. Mason glanced at them for the first time.

"The contingent from the Bureau of Alcohol, Tobacco, Firearms and Explosives is comprised of Special Agents—"

"Becker?" Mason said.

Special Agent Travis Becker looked up from beneath the brim of the ATF baseball cap that concealed his face. He was one of the few survivors of the Bradley Strike Force, which had stumbled onto the Hoyl's trail in the Arizona desert a year ago. Had he not been outside the range of the explosion that destroyed the stone quarry, there would have been no one left to drag Mason from the burning rubble.

"Glad to see you're still among the living, Mason," he said. "I wouldn't have wagered my last dime on it."

"I'm encouraged to see that several of you already know—" Algren started to say.

"Special Agent Marilu Johnson," Becker's partner said. She had dark skin and eyes, wore her hair in cornrows, and made no effort to hide her impatience. "What do you say we wrap up the formalities so we can get down to work?"

"Agreed," Algren said. "Our Bomb Recovery and Analysis Team is already on-site and eagerly anticipating any insight you might be able to provide into the signature of the IED." Johnson nodded, suitably placated for the moment. "Field support will be provided by the Weld and Yuma County Sheriff's Departments; the Denver, Fort Lupton, and

Wray police; and the Rocky Mountain Regional Forensics Laboratory. And again, I must reiterate, all communications are to go through me." She speared each of them with her gaze to drive home the importance of her request. "Now, if we're all on the same page, I would like to direct your attention to the second page in your binders."

Mason opened his and leaned back in his chair. Algren was definitely on top of things. She'd already gathered pictures of the farm and the victims and assembled a significant amount of lab data.

"For those of you who don't know, the name Novichok—which means 'newcomer' in Russian—collectively refers to a group of fourth-generation chemical weapons developed by the Soviet Union under the guise of Project Foliant and known officially by their A-series designations. We believe that as many as five of these agents—A-230, 233, 234, 242, and 262—have been adapted for military use. Our intelligence, what little we have, is limited at best and owed to a whistle-blower named Vil Mirzayanov, who went public in 1992, on the eve of Russia's signing of the Chemical Weapons Convention. While their scientists claim these chemical weapons are the deadliest ever made, they've never been tested on human beings. At least not officially. The British government believes that A-234—the same agent we're dealing with here—was used in the attempted assassination of Sergei and Yulia Skripal in 2018.

"It's essentially an evolved version of sarin, the most lethal of the four G-series agents developed in Germany prior to World War Two. While we have no data regarding exposure to A-234 specifically, the lethal dose of sarin in humans is a tenth of a milligram per kilogram subcutaneously, one milliliter in direct contact with the skin, or thirty-five milligrams per cubic meter of air. The most severe symptoms include bronchorrhea and bronchospasm—the combination of which leads to the victim drowning from the fluid in his lungs—and a host of more common signs you'll be able to recognize by the mnemonic SLUDGE—salivation, lacrimation, urination, defecation, gastrointestinal distress, and emesis."

"That's some very specific data," Layne said. "I thought the Nazis never used it."

"They didn't. Had they, the war might have had a different outcome."

"So how did we get this information?"

"The sarin attacks in Iraq, Japan, and, most recently, Syria corroborated data extrapolated by our own military," Algren said. "The army conducted its own experimentation with sarin in the fifties, but that's neither here nor there."

"The Chemical Corps had its own production facilities back then," Addison said. "The stockpiles are long gone, but surely some of the men responsible for creating them are still around. Salazar and I can reach out to the National Personnel Records Center and requisition their files. Maybe they can help identify the uniformed men in the photographs we collected from the farmhouse, too."

"I trust Homeland can expedite the process," Algren said. "Now, if you'll all turn to page five, the first picture is an aerial view of the Cavanaugh property at 19640 East County Road Forty-five. The location where each victim was found is marked with an X. Of particular note is their relationship to and distance from one another. While they form a ringlike pattern, it's premature to conclude that a circle was the intended design, when it's apparent we interrupted the UNSUB before he completed it.

"The following pages show each of the five victims from various angles. We've only been able to identify one of them so far: the owner of the property, Peter Cavanaugh, marked as number two on your diagram. I want you to pay special attention to the detail images, especially those on pages twenty-three, twenty-eight, and thirty-two."

The first picture displayed a man's leg from roughly mid-thigh down. The soft tissues were black and eroded where the rope had been used to bind it to the post. The discoloration extended all the way from the knee through the swollen foot.

The second image was similar, although the subject displayed much more advanced stages of decomposition. An arrow marker had been placed beside the leg to indicate a diagonal fracture line through the tibia, the edges of which were visibly coarse.

The third featured a forearm proximal to the wrist. The rotting skin on the radial side exhibited significant damage from avian activity. The ulnar side, which had been bound inferiorly, was distended with the purplish swelling of settled blood, or hypostasis.

Mason immediately recognized the significance.

"He kept them alive for several days after tying them up there."

"Precisely," Algren said.

"Has the ME determined COD yet?"

"We anticipated having a preliminary report of findings prior to this briefing, but we're assured it's forthcoming."

"You said there were pictures of all five victims," Johnson said. "I assume that doesn't include the officers killed in the explosion."

"Correct. Their deaths are to be considered superfluous to our investigation and the stated mission of this strike force. While the murders are a tragedy—one I fully expect you to use as motivation to catch this monster—these two officers, specifically, were not the UNSUB's intended targets. It could just as easily have been Mason and Layne who opened the door."

Mason hadn't actually thought about it like that until she said it out loud. He was grateful not to have received more than eleven nails in his leg and butt, no matter how badly the wounds still hurt. Everything was moving so fast that he hadn't paused to contemplate how much differently things could have gone had he entered through the front door instead of the silo.

"The explosion was designed to serve the same purpose as the trap he laid for us in the tunnel below the slaughterhouse," he said. "The dispersal of the chemical weapon and the IED connected to the door were both designed to eliminate the lead officers and set back, if not outright derail, the investigation from the start."

"Which means he's familiar with law-enforcement procedure," Layne said, "but not intimately so. For my money, his background is in a field tangential to ours."

"A solid observation," Algren said. "I'll submit it to Behavioral with our profile request."

The last page featured a close-up photograph of the Japanese *kanji* characters the killer had carved into the pine trunk. Mason couldn't shake the feeling that they were more than a calling card; the killer was sending a specific message, but what did it mean and who was the intended recipient? Anyone even remotely familiar with law-enforcement procedures would know they wouldn't allow the message to be released to the media, and there were too many variables involved with the discovery of a crime scene and the establishment of jurisdiction to guarantee the presence of a specific agency. The message had to be for someone other than the responding officers, although presumably someone who would receive the message through them, a theory that meshed with Layne's assessment.

There was a knock at the door. Algren's PA entered without waiting for a reply, strode across the room, and whispered into her ear. Her expression remained unchanged.

"Thank you, Roger." She rose and smoothed her jacket and skirt. "You'll have to excuse me."

Her assistant held open the door to the anteroom for her. A man stepped into view from the right and proffered what looked like a photograph printed on plain paper. She took it from him and furrowed her brow.

The door closed and concealed her from view.

"What do you think that's all about?" Layne asked.

Mason could only shake his head. Something was happening. He could feel it.

Algren opened the door and returned to the head of the table.

"We found the trucks we believe were used to transport the Novichok from the slaughterhouse."

"Where?" Mason asked.

"New Jersey."

20

Rocky Mountain Metropolitan Airport

The agent assigned to drive Mason and Layne to the small commercial field delivered them right to the door of a Cessna 560 Citation, the pilot of which waited just long enough for them to close the door behind them before ramping up the engines and starting to roll. They navigated the narrow aisle, dropped their bags on two of the rear-facing seats, and sat across the small tables from them. By the time they fastened their seat belts, the plane had already left the ground and commenced its steep ascent. They spent maybe twenty minutes reviewing the case file before agreeing that they'd better take advantage of the opportunity to sleep while they could.

Layne kicked off her shoes, drew her feet up onto the seat, and leaned her head against the closed shade. By the time Mason zipped his binder into his travel bag, she was already snoring softly.

The small plane was one of the older models in the FBI's fleet, as attested to by the gray vinyl upholstery and the frayed edges of the seat belts, but it had been upgraded to incorporate Wi-Fi and surveillance equipment that probably saw a lot more use than anyone cared to admit. He logged in to his federal email account to make sure there was nothing urgent he needed to deal with before sacrificing the next three hours to what he anticipated to be the slumber of the dead. The only message was from Algren, who'd sent him a link to the secure cloud she'd set up for the task force to share files and a brief note saying she'd arranged for them to meet with a representative of the New Jersey State Police at the lot in Port Norris, where the missing trucks had been impounded.

Mason set his federal phone on the table and was just about to close his eyes, when he felt a vibration against his left hip.

He glanced across the aisle at Layne to confirm she was still sleeping before removing his stealth phone from its holster and allowing it to scan his thumbprint and face. The screen awakened and revealed a message from Gunnar.

CAN YOU TALK?

Again, he checked to make sure his new partner was asleep before texting back.

NO, BUT I CAN LISTEN.

Mason plugged a wireless bud into his ear, leaned against the window, and tilted the screen so that only he could see it. He answered the call the moment his phone started to vibrate in his hand. Gunnar materialized a heartbeat later, with Ramses' kitchen behind him.

"I take it you're on the job?" he said.

Mason tipped the phone just far enough for his old friend to see the porthole window of the private plane.

"Then I'll make this quick," Gunnar said. "When it comes to the two possible suspects from Johan's top twenty—the woman in black and the man in the shadows—I'm afraid we're way behind. Like seventy-five years, the end of World War Two. While I'm still nowhere close to being able to identify them, it's important that you understand the historical perspective, because, if I'm right, we're dealing with some really bad individuals and it's imperative that you don't underestimate them."

Mason nodded for him to proceed.

"In many ways, the backgrounds of the two subjects are a lot alike, at least in so far as what we believe to be the trail that led Johan to them, although I have yet to pick up the scent of either, which ought to tell you everything you need to know about how closely guarded their identities are. Maybe not in the sense of state's secrets, but, rather, the effort invested in covering their historical tracks. You see, in order to smuggle anyone even peripherally related to the Nazis out of Germany under the noses of the occupying Allied forces, new identities needed to be created out of thin air, obliterating anything resembling an actual paper trail."

Gunnar disappeared and a series of documents appeared in his place. They were yellowed and faded and worn around the edges. Each contained both typed and handwritten material and dates ranging from the late forties to the early fifties. They were written in French, Italian, German, and languages Mason didn't immediately recognize. And each had been stamped with an unmistakable red logo, long since faded to pink, a plus sign encircled by words readily identifiable in any language: International Committee of the Red Cross.

"There were two primary ratlines," Gunnar said. "One ran from Germany to Spain, and then to Argentina; the other from Germany to Rome to Genoa, then to various destinations from Mexico to Chile, and everywhere in between. The majority of these emigrations were arranged by the, quote, unquote, 'humanitarian efforts' of the Catholic Church, quite possibly even under the direction of the Holy See. You have to remember that Mussolini's Italy was part of Hitler's Axis, so it should come as no surprise that the Vatican would be sensitive to the plight of Roman allies seeking to avoid the trials at Nuremberg, which were viewed as essentially rubber-stamp death-penalty hearings. A network of priests and bishops arranged for false identification papers to be issued by the Vatican Refugee Organization, which could then be used to obtain displaced persons passports from the Red Cross, providing the documentation these people needed to obtain legitimate visas, effectively killing off their true identities and starting over again with completely untraceable new names."

Mason opened a dialogue box and texted a question.

WHAT ABOUT THE WOMAN?

"I'm still trying to pick up her trail," Gunnar said. "She obviously had to have been born sometime after that, which implies that Johan found her by tracing her lineage, and I think I have a pretty good idea of where she might have been at some point. Remember, these weren't your standard rank-and-file Nazis. We're talking about people like Klaus Barbie, the Butcher of Lyon; Adolf Eichmann, architect of the Holocaust; Franz Stangl, commandant of the Treblinka extermination camp; Josef Mengele, the Angel of Death at Auschwitz; and Paul Shäfer, a medic in the Wehrmacht who worked his way into central Chile and started a closed community rooted in Nazi ideology and a kind of revivalist Christianity. He called this place Colonia Dignidad—Dignity Colony—and within its walls, he and his devotees continued their vile experimentation on political prisoners supplied by Chilean dictator Augusto Pinochet and his secret police. While there's little actual evidence of the horrors perpetrated by this community over the next forty years, it wouldn't be a stretch to assume they continued working with both biological and chemical weaponry."

A CULT? Mason typed.

"Exactly. And not just there but in Japan, too. Bear with me."

He brought up a black-and-white image of maybe a hundred men, lined up in five rows for a group picture. They were all of Asian descent and wore military uniforms with peaked caps. It was so old and faded that it was hard to distinguish one man's face from that of the next, but there was no mistaking the caption scratched into the emulsification: Epidemic Prevention & Water Purification Department. The pictures that followed all featured men wearing white smocks and surgical caps, uniforms and gas masks, rubber hoods and goggles.

"It was the Red Army that ultimately pushed down into China and annihilated the Japanese army," Gunnar said. "When Unit 731 found out that the Soviets were coming, they immediately began destroying evidence and got the hell out of there while they still could. After all, Chinese POWs weren't the only ones they subjected to their experimentation. Considering no one knew exactly who they were, they blended in with the retreating forces and reintegrated themselves into society. A society that four decades later gave rise to a cult called Aum Shinrikyo, led by a nearly blind pseudoprophet named Shoko Asahara, who assembled an all-star team of disaffected professionals and set about creating his own version of the apocalypse."

A different series of photographs scrolled past, only these were in color and far more recent. Mason recognized the glaring similarities to the pictures he'd seen in Johan's archives, the ones of the silhouette watching from the shadows as medical professionals treated the injured right there on the streets.

"These guys launched two separate sarin attacks," Gunnar said. "Including the 1995 attack on the Tokyo subway."

FOCUS ON THIS LINE OF INQUIRY, Mason typed. WE FOUND A SERIES OF JAPANESE CHARACTERS AT ONE OF THE CRIME SCENES THAT SPELLED KUEBIKO. SHINTO GOD OF KNOWLEDGE.

"I haven't encountered him through the course of my research, but I'll see what I can find."

RELATIONSHIP TO THE THIRTEEN?

"So far, everything I've found points to entities established on the fringes, isolated groups steeped in secrecy and bereft of affiliations, individuals whose very existence is closely guarded."

LIKE THE HOYL.

"You don't have to remind me what we're up against," Gunnar said. "Trust me, I'll ferret this guy out, but it's going to take time."

I'M AFRAID THAT'S ONE THING WE SIMPLY DON'T HAVE.

"I'll get back to you," Gunnar said, and terminated the call.

Mason put his phone to sleep and returned it to its holster. He cast a sideways glance at Layne, who was still in the exact same position, but he couldn't shake the feeling that she'd hurriedly closed her eyes right as he'd turned to look.

21

Algren had arranged for a Crown Victoria to be waiting for Mason and Layne at the airport in Wilmington, Delaware. It had taken just over an hour for them to drive to the New Jersey State Police impound lot in Port Norris, where a trooper named Barrie, who wore a blue flat cap, a light blue uniform shirt, and navy slacks with yellow stripes down the sides, had been waiting for them at the gate. He led them past the guard shack and into a dirt lot filled with beat-up vehicles from every era.

"The cars out here on the main lot are your standard impounds," Barrie said. "Maybe a dozen belong to lowlifes in county lockup or the pen up in Bridgeton. We keep all the cool stuff in the warehouse. You know, high-ticket seizures and vehicles used in the commission of crimes. I figured those trucks of yours were probably used for hauling drugs, so I had them moved straight in there myself."

He led them down a row of SUVs toward a massive aluminum warehouse with closed-circuit cameras mounted on the roof.

"What makes you think those trucks were carrying drugs?" Layne asked.

"If there's one thing I know, it's cars. Those Sterling flatbeds are worth good money. Even older models like these will still easily bring in fifty grand apiece. There aren't many people willing to just abandon a hundred grand out there in the Barrens besides drug runners."

Barrie used the key chain clipped to his utility belt to unlock the door and gestured for them to precede him into the darkness. The over-head lights came on with a resounding thud and cast a flickering pale glare over the vast space. Half was lined with shelves overflowing with a seemingly random assortment of parts, while the other half was like a garage from *MTV Cribs*. There were sports and luxury cars, seized vehicles of all kinds. Layne traced the contours of a Rolls-Royce with her fingertips as she passed.

"Sound reasoning," Mason said.

The trooper swelled with the compliment.

"And the dead guy, of course. Definitely fits the MO of the major cartels."

Both Mason and Layne stopped in their tracks. Barrie was five paces ahead before he noticed they'd fallen behind and glanced back.

"They're just over here," he said.

"What dead guy?" Mason asked.

"You mean you didn't know?"

"Enlighten us," Layne said.

"We found him inside that truck right there," Barrie said as he led them out from behind the racks. The flatbeds they'd traveled all this way to find were in the back left corner. At least what was left of them. "You ever see someone after they're cremated? That's what it was like. Nothing but ashes and chunks of bone on the floorboards."

The trucks were totally black, from bumper to fender. The paint had been burned to the bare metal and all that remained of the seats in the cab was the wire framework. The windows were gone and glass had fused to the remnants of the dashboard. The tires had melted to the bare rims.

"Were you able to identify him?" Mason asked.

"There wasn't enough of him to ID. Or at least that's what I heard. Had the Forest Fire Service not responded as quickly as they did, there wouldn't have been anything left of him at all."

"Was the fire response unusually fast?"

"I wouldn't say so. At least not by our standards anyway. They have one of those Helitack units ready to go at all times. Had that fire out before it even burned through five acres. The handcrew found the trucks and called the sheriff's department. They pawned it off on us when they saw what was left of the driver."

"How long ago was this?" Layne asked.

Mason was happy to let her take the lead. She'd slept nearly the entire time they were on the plane, while he'd struggled to find a comfortable position in a seat designed for a person half his size, and undoubtedly one whose rear end wasn't riddled with puncture wounds.

"November twenty-eighth. So that's what? A month ago today?"

"How long had they been out there?"

"There's no way of knowing. Had it not been for the fire, we might never have found them."

"Why's that?"

"I don't know if you've ever been out to the Pine Barrens, but that area's like Jersey's version of the Everglades. The forest is so dense that those trucks could well have been lost out there for fifty years before anyone ever found them."

"Awfully fortunate that fire happened when it did," Mason said.

"You'd be surprised how many fires we have out there. More than fourteen hundred a year. That's the whole reason we have a dedicated fire-response unit ready and waiting."

"So you didn't suspect arson?"

"Should we have?"

Layne climbed up onto the warped runner of the truck and leaned through the window, into the cab.

"No VIN?" she said.

"No license plates or U.S. DOT numbers, either," Barrie said. "Everything was either removed or burned off in the fire."

"So there was no way of tracking down the owner."

"We kind of figured that's who the dead guy was. No one reported any missing trucks matching the description of these two. You guys are the first to even ask about them."

"Why go to the trouble of burning them when you've already stripped all identifying markings?" Layne asked. She'd been thinking out loud, but Barrie answered.

"Those trucks could have been out there for more than a decade before the fire. I mean, they're like fifteen years old. If someone didn't want them to be found, the easiest thing to do would have been to leave them where they were and let the forest grow over them."

"What about shipping containers?" Mason asked.

"You mean those big bulk numbers?" Barrie said. "We didn't find anything like that. There was no sign of what they might have been hauling."

Something wasn't right. Mason could feel it, but he couldn't pin down what. His instincts were crying out for him to recognize something that was staring him right in the face.

"Did you test for traces of chemical accelerants?" he asked.

"Each of those gas tanks holds eighty gallons," Barrie said. "Those trucks were essentially giant bombs. Everything within a hundred-foot radius had to be drenched with a flaming layer of gasoline when they blew."

"What my partner's asking in the most roundabout way possible is where the fire started," Layne said.

"You'd have to check with the Forest Fire Service. The way we saw it, we had two abandoned vehicles, with no means of establishing ownership, and an unidentifiable body, with no evidence of a crime. You're lucky we even bothered to have what's left of these things brought here. Lord knows the state would have been happy to have them hauled to the junkyard, if only to wash its hands of them."

"What makes you say that?" Mason asked.

"My CO said the state didn't want to incur the expense, but once I explained my reasoning, he said he figured what they didn't know wouldn't hurt them."

"Who does he take his orders from?"

"Who doesn't he take orders from? Shoot, there are twenty-six deputies and commanders under the superintendent. Any one of them could have passed it down the chain of command."

"Is taking them to the junkyard standard operating procedure?" Layne asked.

"How many torched vehicles do you think we find?"

Layne met Mason's stare. Something obviously wasn't adding up for her, either.

"He's right," she said. "For all we know, these trucks could have been out there since 2006. We don't have any way of identifying them outside of the fact that the time line fits and they're the same model as the trucks missing from the Cavanaugh crime scene."

Mason nodded. That was precisely what was bothering him, although for entirely different reasons. Every conceivable effort had been invested in making sure these vehicles were impossible to ID— from killing the driver to stripping them of every registration and serial number and then burning them to the point that they were little more than skeletal black frames. The only way anyone would have known to look for them in the first place was if that person had discovered the bodies in the cornfield, in which case the investigation would have required that agents be dispatched for every potential match, even as far away as New Jersey. There was something here that the UNSUB didn't want them to find, but setting five acres ablaze seemed like the surest way to make sure the flatbeds were identified, when they might have otherwise remained hidden for years.

"He wanted us to find the trucks," Mason said.

"Why?" Layne asked. "What's the point when a month ago we weren't even looking for them and they'd been stripped of any identifying markings?"

"He didn't want us to find them until after we discovered his work in Wray. If he didn't strip the VIN, someone would have traced the trucks back to Cavanaugh. When the police couldn't get ahold of him, they would have gone to his house and likely either discovered what was in the cornfield or set off the IED on the door. Either way, his plans would have been interrupted."

"Then why'd he go back to Colorado at all?"

"That's a good question. It's like he finished one job and started another."

"One professional and the other personal?"

Mason walked around to the front of the trucks, which took up nearly a quarter of the warehouse all by themselves.

And then it hit him.

He turned to Barrie.

"I need a favor. Two of them, actually."

"From me?" Barrie said.

"I want to talk to the medical examiner about the remains. Can you call ahead and make arrangements for him to meet us in his office?"

"He's actually a she, but I'd be happy to."

"And I need you to see if you can find out who issued the order to dispose of these vehicles."

"That might take a little more doing. My CO already stuck his neck out for me on this one."

"Tell him he has my word it won't come back on him."

"I'll do what I can."

Layne took Mason by his arm and guided him out of earshot.

"What are you thinking?" she asked.

"The UNSUB displayed his victims in the cornfield. Incinerating the guy who theoretically drove the other truck reeks of pragmatism. It's not his style."

"Right. He wanted us to find his 'scarecrows.'"

"More than that, he wanted us to be able to identify them."

Layne recognized where he was leading her.

"But he didn't want us to be able to identify the dead man in the truck."

22

Pine Barrens | Cumberland County, New Jersey

Barrie had arranged for the Cumberland County ME, Dr. Mary Ann Quarrels, to meet them at the morgue in an hour. Considering her office wasn't far from where the flatbeds had initially been discovered, Mason figured it couldn't hurt to take a look at the scene for himself, so he requested a personal tour from the sheriff's department.

A black Chevy Tahoe with the county seal on the door was parked on the side of the highway at the prearranged location. The driver introduced himself as Deputy Karl Mills, offered a handshake meant to remind them of who was in charge, and led them off into the forest without any small talk.

The crimson glow of the setting sun filtered through the dense canopy of shortleaf pine and white cedar trees, creating slanted columns of light that only occasionally reached the detritus. Mason smelled the lingering scents of soot and ash long before the living trees gave way to the charcoaled carcasses of the dead. New growth was already rising from the rich black soil. They reached a decline so steep, they had to brace themselves against the tree trunks to keep from falling. An arrow-straight clearing about ten feet wide stood apart from the burned forest at the bottom. They were nearly on top of it before Mason recognized it for what it was.

"There are all kinds of abandoned railroad tracks running through the Barrens," Mills said. "They could have driven those trucks onto them just about anywhere. Hell, the nearest access point is about thirty miles north of here in Atlantic County. We aren't even a mile from the highway and we never would have known they were here if not for the fire."

"So you don't think this was a case of arson," Layne said.

"The handcrew would have said if something wasn't right. They deal with this kind of thing just about every day. In fact, it was one of their guys who said the fire didn't even start near the trucks."

"What made him think that?" Mason asked.

"Something about the porous nature of the soil and the properties of gas burning on top of a compact layer of soot. And the depth and angle of the char. He said he could read it like a book."

"So if your guys ruled out arson, how did the fire start?" Mason asked.

"It could've been any number of things," Mills said. "Kids playing with matches. Downed power lines. Debris burning. Hot brakes or exhaust particles from trains on the lines still in service. Most of the time, no one even knows. A full quarter of such cases end up filed as 'miscellaneous' or 'of indeterminate cause.'"

Mason and Layne fanned out and explored the clearing. The faint aroma of gasoline still radiated from the soot, which came away from the sandy soil on the tread of their shoes. Some animal or other moved covertly through the underbrush with the crackle of dead branches.

"We found what was left of them right here," Mills said. "It's impossible to tell now, but there were shards of metal and glass scattered as far as the eye could see. If you look over there, you can still see where the passenger door of the second vehicle went through that tree. We found it embedded in the hillside about thirty feet away."

"All of the evidence was gathered and moved to the New Jersey State Police's warehouse, correct?" Layne said.

"That's my understanding."

"And there were no identifying marking on either truck at the time."

"You mean like license plates and VIN numbers?" Mills said. "That was the first thing we looked for. Of course, we stopped looking once we found what was left of the driver. That made it the state's problem, not ours."

"What about bulk shipping containers?" Mason asked. "Any sign of what they were carrying?"

"The flatbeds themselves were just about the only parts of the trucks that withstood the explosion and there hadn't been anything on them at the time."

Layne looked Mason in the eyes.

"They could be anywhere by now."

Mason nodded. This was the perfect place to abandon the trucks. It was roughly equidistant from Washington, D.C., and New York City, with both Baltimore and Philadelphia a short drive away. There were 11.2 million people in those four metropolises alone, with millions more scattered in between, in cities like Atlantic City, Harrisburg, and Trenton. The shipping containers looked just like any others and could be sitting anonymously in any industrial lot or seaport within shouting distance of hundreds of thousands of people.

An attack on D.C. could wipe out the government and obliterate the chain of command, paralyzing the entire country and eliminating anything resembling a coherent emergency response. Any professional football team, from the Giants and Jets to the Ravens and Redskins, promised at least seventy thousand spectators at their games, whose deaths would be broadcast on live TV. There were 8.5 million people in New York City alone, all of them concentrated into an area that could easily be purged in a single afternoon with a handful of drones retrofitted with aerial-dispersion units. Not to mention the million people, most of them tourists, gearing up to cram into Times Square, while another billion watched the ball drop from their homes all around the globe. Four thousand gallons was more than enough to literally depopulate the entire eastern seaboard ten times over.

Mason removed his key chain from his pocket and turned on the mini Maglite. He alternately swept it across the ground and into the branches of the burned pines as he headed east from the tracks. If the firefighter was right about the fire starting elsewhere, then he needed to find the source. The responding officers might have believed the trucks had been abandoned out here for years, but he was convinced that wasn't the case, and yet there was something about the attempted incineration of the vehicles that didn't sit right with him.

"The UNSUB either doesn't think there's any way we can catch him or he doesn't fear the consequences," Layne said, as though reading his mind.

"He's playing with us," Mason said. "Taunting us. He's confident there's nothing we can do to stop him."

"Someone knows who he is. We find whoever that is and that person can lead us to him."

"So far, everyone who's come into direct contact with him is dead."

As soon as he said it, he realized that likely wasn't the case at all. In fact, he just might know someone who'd seen him and survived.

"What?" Layne asked.

"Nothing."

"You did this squinty thing and got all quiet. Something clicked for you, didn't it?"

A veritable wall of trees rose from the dead earth ahead of them. A shadow passed through the thicket and scampered behind the shrubs. They were nearly to the far side of the burn and hadn't seen any sign of where the fire might have started.

"Maybe."

"But you aren't going to tell me, are you?"

The carpet of pine needles and dead leaves had burned another twenty feet into the forest. The needles of the surviving pines were withered, their bark charred and dusted with white ash. Their blackened branches had frozen in the direction the wind had been blowing at the time and the leaves of the few surviving saplings curled toward the direction of the burn.

"The fire started somewhere around here," Mason said.

"Not going to answer my question?" Layne asked.

Scorched trunks stood around them like pillars supporting the rapidly darkening sky. Mason walked a winding path through them, shining his flashlight from the ground into the upper reaches. He had no idea what he was looking for, only that he'd know it when he found it.

It was Layne who did.

"Over here," she said.

Mason followed the sound of her voice. The aura of her flashlight limned what at one time must have been an exceptionally dense section of the forest. Several trees had fallen against one another and the adjacent rock formation, creating what almost looked like the frame of a tepee. Layne knelt inside of it, her back to him. He squeezed in beside her and followed her beam deeper into the darkness, toward where a handful of shards from a beer bottle reflected from the scorched earth at the base of the stone, its face scored black with carbon.

He recognized it immediately. Someone had ignited a Molotov cocktail and hurled it against the rock. But if even he could tell how the fire had started . . .

"Damn," Mason whispered.

He drew his Glock. Turned around. Found himself staring straight up the sight line of a pistol—And into the deputy's face.

"I really wish you hadn't found that," Mills said.

23

"Drop your weapons. Right there in the dirt. And keep your hands where I can see them."

Mason removed his finger from the trigger. Placed it along the length of the barrel. Held the pistol away from his body. He wanted the deputy focused on it, not on him.

"You can still walk away from this," Mason said.

He heard the crackle of detritus from off to his left. Maybe fifty feet away. Just beyond the edge of the forest. There was at least one other hostile out there. If the rock formation behind him was six o'clock, that placed the second man around eight.

"But I can't let you," Mills said. His voice was high and tight. Scared. He hadn't anticipated this situation and wasn't entirely prepared to deal with it. The fact that he hadn't shot them both in the back of the head meant he was waiting for someone else to do it for him.

"Now lay your weapons on the ground. Don't even think about trying anything stupid."

Another rustling sound from the thicket to Mason's right. Two-thirty, three o'clock.

He lowered his pistol to the ground and cautiously raised his hands to his sides.

"So you took a little cash to make some evidence go away," Layne said. She slowly turned her hips and shoulders so that she could see him. "I mean, who hasn't? Right? It's not like you killed anyone. We can work this out. It's not you we want anyway. Give us the guy who paid you and we all go home tonight. No one has to know."

The snap of a twig announced a fourth man. Behind Mills. Moving into position to get a clear shot around him.

They couldn't let him get there.

"You have no idea who you're dealing with," Mills said. He re-adjusted his grip on his pistol. Trying to work up the nerve. "These people? There's nothing they don't know. Nothing they won't do."

Mason glanced at Layne from the corner of his eye. Her left hand was flat on the ground, her right beneath her jacket. Her thighs were tensed underneath her. She licked her lips, slowly. Didn't blink once.

If she'd been compromised like his previous partners, then now was her chance to finish what they'd started. She could easily put a bullet in the back of his head before he could turn around. Or maybe she was simply biding her time, waiting to see if the deputy could find the nerve to do it for her.

"Think about it, Mills," Mason said. "You've already outlived your usefulness to them. You were dead the moment we came out here."

The truth of his words hit the deputy squarely in the face. His expression morphed from one of indecision to outright terror. Whoever they were, these people scared the living hell out of him.

Mills swallowed hard. Used both hands to steady his aim.

Three o'clock to Mason's right. Past Layne. No clear shot through the fallen trees.

Nine o'clock to his left. Again, no clear shot.

The deputy ahead of him. High noon.

A fourth man moving clockwise. He'd have a clear shot past Mills's left shoulder when he reached one o'clock.

The rock formation at his back, barring retreat.

Mason hoped he and Layne were on the same page, or this was going to be a painful team-building exercise, although the fact that she hadn't shot him herself was at least a step in the right direction.

"Just give us a name," she said.

"They know where I live. Where my parents live. My girlfriend. My little sister, for Christ's sake. I tell you anything and they're dead. All of them. Don't you see?"

The fourth man stepped out from behind a scorched tree and into the clearing behind the deputy.

It was now or never.

Mason lunged to his feet. Caught Mills by surprise. Got inside his arms. Grabbed him by the jacket. Lifted and shoved him sideways.

The bullet punched through the deputy's shoulder, screamed past Mason's ear, and ricocheted from the rock formation before he even heard the crack of gunfire. He dove for his Glock as the second bullet hit Mills squarely in the spine. Grabbed it and rolled to his left. Raised the barrel and fired toward the gunman, who was already on the move. Hit a tree trunk right behind him with an explosion of charcoal.

Layne was a blur in his peripheral vision. A flash of discharge and chunks of wood burst from the fallen trunk beside her head. She instinctively ducked, then started firing.

Mason popped up and dove headfirst into the burned debris. Crashed through sharp branches. Landed hard on his side. Rolled and used his momentum to propel himself to his feet. Right in front of a man wearing camouflage hunting gear. The man's eyes widened and he pressed his cheek to the stock of his rifle—

Mason shot him in the chest and was running again before the body even hit the ground.

There were at least two men still standing. Maybe more. And they undoubtedly knew these woods far better than either he or Layne did. He couldn't afford to let them vanish into the forest, at least not until he got some answers.

Mason sprinted around the scorched trees toward where he'd last seen the fourth man. Passed the trunk his bullet had struck.

Layne materialized to his right, running in the opposite direction of the third man, who was sprawled on the ground, his face buried in the soot. She had a bead on the fourth man and the angle to cut him off. He veered away from her and right into Mason's line of sight.

A single shot and the man grabbed his thigh. Tumbled to the ground with a shout. Pushed himself back up and tried to hobble. Fell again.

Mason followed him in a shooter's stance. He glanced from one side to the other and back again to make sure they weren't being led into another ambush.

"Drop your weapon!" Layne shouted.

The man crawled behind the trunk of a burned tree. Sat up and tucked his legs to his chest. Raised his weapon.

"It's over," Mason said.

The man peeked around the side of the trunk and Layne fired right past his face. He ducked back. His shoulders heaved with his heavy breathing. He knew there was no way out of this situation.

"You're right," he said. "It is."

He moved with the speed of purpose. Pressed the barrel of his pistol to his temple.

Mason aimed and prepared to shoot.

The other man beat him to it.

A flash of discharge from behind the tree. Spatters of fluid captured within its corona, as though frozen in time. Then darkness once more.

The report echoed through the desolate forest.

"Jesus," Layne said. "What the hell was that?"

The man's hand fell limply to his side, his blood sizzling on the barrel. He leaned slowly out from behind the tree and collapsed onto his side. The exiting bullet had blown out the entire side of his skull.

Mason sighted the forest down his Glock in case there were still any more of them out there.

"Welcome to my world," he said.

24

The lights from the state police cruisers stained the surrounding forest in alternating shades of red and blue, making the shadows lurking behind the trees appear to pulsate. The entire highway was shut down and every available officer in the county was either already here or well on his way. The forensic team's van was angled across the shoulder of the road, its headlights directed toward the forest, where the evidence response team documented the crime scene. The occasional flash of a photograph caused the distant trees to draw contrast from the night.

Mason sat in the back of the ambulance parked on the opposite side of the road, pressing an ice pack against the base of his skull and listening to his partner's phone call. Her side of the conversation anyway. She spoke quietly so as not to distract the paramedic stitching up the nasty gash on her forearm.

The DHS had yet to produce the list of the surviving members of the Chemical Corps with experience in either the production or decommission of chemical weapons that it had promised to Locker. The FPS contingent on the strike force—Addison and Salazar—had volunteered to follow up but had yet to make any headway. Now that they'd drawn out the enemy, though, there was no time to waste, so Layne had called an acquaintance at the Army Criminal Investigations Command in an effort to bypass formal channels and procure the personnel information they needed if they were going to figure out who had the kind of skill set required to produce the Novichok. It couldn't have been a very long list and the UNSUB's name had to be on it.

Mason watched a handful of criminalists in white jumpsuits comb through the sheriff department's Tahoe in search of answers they'd never find to questions they didn't know to ask. All they knew was that four of their colleagues were lying dead in the Barrens and they'd probably never understand why.

Deputy Karl Mills had been a decorated officer, an usher at church, and volunteer wildfire fighter in his spare time. Wes Phelps and Gino

Tomassi had been full-time firefighters with a combined twenty years of service to the New Jersey Forest Fire Service and not so much as a single misdemeanor between them. Only Tom Wahl, the man who'd decorated the forest with the contents of his skull, had anything remotely resembling a criminal record, which included little more than a single conviction for poaching and a pair of drunk and disorderly charges. All four of them had recently caught up on mortgages that had fallen several months behind.

Mason could only guess where the men had been approached about taking care of the flatbeds and the body inside, but they'd obviously received the carrot before they were shown the stick. Mexican cartels used similar tactics to guarantee the loyalty of their narcos, whose families were dragged into the streets and publicly executed if they skimmed so much as a peso, which was why officers had been dispatched to the homes of known family members of the decedents. Regardless of the locals' insistence to the contrary, Mason knew they weren't dealing with a drug-trafficking organization. The Thirteen were as patient as they were ruthless. The moment those four men failed to preserve their secret, the names of their loved ones had been written on a ledger somewhere, and would be checked off at some unknown time in the future.

"The army's going to send us a list of all personnel who either worked with the creation of or the subsequent decommission of their chemical weapons stockpiles," Layne said. "Apparently, it's a really long list that covers nearly eighty years."

"Did they give you a time frame?" Mason asked.

"Sometime tomorrow. The majority of the records are still on paper and housed at the National Archives in St. Louis, so someone's going to have to physically pull the files."

Mason nodded. He'd expected worse.

"What about Algren?" he asked. "What'd she have to say about all of this?"

Layne had reported the news of their ambush to the head of the strike force while Mason had cleared the area to make sure there weren't any other attackers.

"She's already reached out to the Bureau chiefs in Baltimore, New

York, Philadelphia, and D.C. to secure additional resources," Layne said.

"Did you ask her about the precursor chemicals?"

"Homeland's still working on it."

"There are only six domestic manufacturers."

"Right, which is why she's trying an end around with white-collar crimes to get their records through back channels."

"So she said a whole lot of nothing."

Layne smirked and pulled her sleeve down over the bandage on her forearm, baring her teeth when it grazed the wound.

"She scheduled a conference call for two hours from now. Hopefully, the other agents will be able to give us something useful."

Mason moved the compress from the base of his skull to his forehead. He was more angry than he was hurt, mainly at himself for the way everything had gone down. The men they'd killed weren't sadistic murderers. They'd simply been desperate and made a deal with the devil, then panicked when the FBI showed up, seemingly out of the blue. Had he and Layne not found the broken glass and recognized what it meant, those four men would still be alive, but they would have wasted even more time coming to the realization that the UNSUB's trail ended here. Their only actual leads were sitting in various morgues, awaiting identification and formal determination of cause of death, both of which were taking an absurd amount of time, especially considering that at any moment countless people could die in a manner he wouldn't have wished upon his worst enemy.

Layne's phone chimed to alert her to an incoming text message. She awakened the device and studied the screen.

"Algren says Behavioral's expecting our call."

"Didn't she already forward them everything we had on the UNSUB? Surely there's enough there to generate at least a preliminary profile."

"They apparently need help—and I quote—'qualifying a curious dichotomy of character.'"

Mason knew exactly what they meant. There was a duality to the UNSUB that defied classification, more than merely having personal and professional aspects of his personality. He simultaneously exhibited a desire to kill and an unwillingness to do so. He didn't murder his victims himself, so, technically, there was no blood on his hands. He'd given the men behind the wall the choice of either asphyxiating or triggering the release of the sarin. A case could be made that by doing so he'd demonstrated mercy, while at the same time subjecting them to an obscene level of cruelty. Had his only goal been to wipe out millions of people, they'd be dead already.

There was more to his plot than any of them could see. If he was anything like the Hoyl, then someone even more dangerous was pulling his strings. The Novichok A-234 was a means to an end for the master, but it was the suffering of his victims that fueled the UNSUB. They needed to be stopped before, like an eclipse, their motivations aligned and darkness descended.

"You okay handling this one?" Mason asked.

"Sure." She raised an eyebrow. "What are you going to do?"

"I have a few phone calls of my own to make, starting with the Yuma County ME. There's no reason we shouldn't have COD for the men in the cornfield by now."

Mason tossed her the car keys so she could have a little privacy to talk to Behavioral. Truth be told, he needed some space of his own. He knew exactly how Layne would feel about his utilizing help from outside their ranks, and he wasn't prepared to explain his rationale for doing so, at least not until he was certain he could trust her. Not killing him when she'd been presented with the perfect opportunity was a positive development in that regard, though.

He wandered away from the commotion and punched in the number for the Yuma County ME. The number rang several times before the call was routed to an automated service. He disconnected and tried again, but achieved the same result. They must have set incoming calls to the main line to forward automatically. He returned his phone to his pocket, drew the stealth model, and speed-dialed Gunnar, who answered on the second ring.

"What are you doing in New Jersey?"

That Gunnar could triangulate his location in a matter of seconds didn't surprise Mason. In fact, nothing his old friend did surprised him anymore.

"That's kind of why I'm calling," Mason said. "I was hoping you wouldn't mind reaching out to Johan on my behalf."

"Does this have anything to do with the sudden surge in energy futures trading?"

"That's your area," Mason said. "I'm trying to get some answers and encountering an unusual amount of resistance through routine channels."

"I take it this meeting will need to be virtual in nature."

"Time's of the essence."

"He'll want to know why."

"Let his curiosity get the better of him."

Gunnar was still chuckling when Mason ended the call. He was about to head back to the car, when he remembered the connection he'd made right before the ambush. He speed-dialed number three on his stealth phone. If he was right about the UNSUB and his MO, then there was a very real chance that Alejandra had seen him while he was rigging the knocking pen to kill her. Any detail she could remember about him, no matter how small, would be hugely beneficial right about now.

He glanced back at the Crown Vic, where Layne sat in the passenger seat with the door open and her legs hanging out the side. Her posture, specifically the way she hung her head, suggested her arm was bothering her considerably more than she let on. Had she been co-opted by the Thirteen, all she would have had to do was stand down and let the men take him.

Her voice carried to him from the distance. While he wasn't close enough to make out her words, the tension and frustration in her voice were unmistakable. She was either an incredibly gifted actress or maybe, just maybe, she was exactly who she claimed to be. He needed to figure out which was the case, and in a hurry, because he could positively feel the investigative momentum building. The time would soon come when he was going to have to trust her, and the consequences of being wrong would be catastrophic.

Alejandra picked up right before the call could go to voice mail. She sounded like he'd awakened her from a deep sleep.

"Hello, James," she said.

"Tell him this had better be important," Ramses said in the background.

"I wouldn't have even considered calling and dredging all of this up again if it weren't," Mason said. "There's something I need to know, and you're the only one who might be able to help me."

Alejandra was silent for so long that he feared the call might have been dropped.

"I will help you if I can," she said.

"Think back to that night at the slaughterhouse. I want you to try to remember everything you can, specifically about when you were taken prisoner outside the complex."

Her exhalations came faster, heavier, as she mentally returned to the woods near the slaughterhouse, where she'd been posted with a Thunderstorm bullpup assault rifle with an under-barrel grenade launcher, waiting for him to give the signal to blow the whole place to hell.

At that point, Mason had been out of contact with Gunnar and her for maybe five minutes, which he'd rationalized as their cellular signals being unable to penetrate the cinder-block walls. He hadn't been upstairs in the room with the massive stainless-steel vats for more than three minutes, tops. It was then that he'd recognized the nature of the trap he'd inadvertently sprung and sprinted back down the stairs to the killing floor, where he'd found her bound in the knocking pen. That amounted to roughly eight minutes for which he couldn't account. Eight minutes the Hoyl had used to abduct Gunnar and load him onto the tram in the underground tunnel. Eight minutes for an accomplice Mason now believed to be the UNSUB to rig Alejandra in a death trap designed to buy the two monsters time to escape.

"I did not hear him behind me," she said. "Not until it was too late. When I turned around, all I saw was a dark shape against the snow. It was blowing in my face. From behind him. He covered my mouth and nose with a cloth. It smelled of chemicals. Then everything went black."

"You lost consciousness."

"Yes, but not for very long. I do not think so anyway. I remember the snow. He dragged me through the snow by my arms."

"Did you see the man who took you? Do you remember anything about him?"

"I remember moonlight, and then darkness. Snow, then no snow. He took me inside."

"Was he still dragging you?"

"Yes. The floor was slick. Greasy. The smell . . . the feeling against my skin . . ."

"There was no light at all?"

"Not at first. Not until he turned on his flashlight."

"Did you see him then?"

She was quiet for a long moment before speaking.

"I saw his boots. Rubber soles. They squeaked on the floor. Black boots. Laces."

"Were they large? Small? What size do you think?"

"Average. I think. Perhaps slightly smaller." Mason imagined her closing her eyes while she relived the experience, an expression of torment on her face. "There was something else. The boots. They were taped where he tucked in his pants. I remember the tape. Black, like the boots. Like they tell you to do in Altar before you set out across the border and into the desert. To keep sand from getting inside."

"Or snow," Mason said. It sounded like the kind of thing a man would do if he were preparing to leave on foot rather than by way of an underground tram. "Anything else about him? Anything at all?"

"He led me to the pen. Dropped me on the ground. The metal was cold. Wet from his footsteps. I heard the screech of the chain. He held it in one hand, lifted my head by the hood of my sweatshirt with the other. Rested my neck on the . . . on the crush, then pulled my arms behind me. He placed the chain in my hands. Helped me close them around it. Squeezed them tight."

"He didn't say anything?"

"He did not have to."

"What about his hands?"

"They were cold. And the fingers. They moved like the legs of *la araña*. Of a spider. They were small but strong. Very strong."

"He had to walk around in front of you after that, didn't he?"

"He kept the light pointed in my eyes. I could not see his face. Only his *boceto,* his . . . *silueta*."

"His silhouette?"

"Yes. His hat, mostly. It was triangular. Like a cone, only flatter. The brim was very wide."

"The Hoyl wore those broad-brimmed hats, but that wasn't him, was it?" Mason said.

"Who else could it have . . . ?" Alejandra's voice trailed off as everything fell into place for her. "This man. He is the one we are hunting."

"Yeah," Mason said. He turned around and looked at Layne, who stared back at him from across the distance. She was undoubtedly wondering what was taking him so long. "And I need all the help I can get to find him before a whole lot of people die."

"You must promise me that you will make sure he can never do to anyone else what he did to me."

"With pleasure, but I need to find him first. Try to remember everything you possibly can. Anything you might have seen or heard. The sound of his voice. Any unique physical trait. Anything at all I can use to identify him."

Several seconds passed, during which he could hear only the harsh rhythm of her breathing. When she finally spoke, it was in a firm voice.

"Metal," she said. "He had metal on his face. After he taped the flashlight to the chair, he turned around and stared at me. Like he was judging his own work. I remember reflections from his face. From his eyes. Like stars. His eyes looked like stars."

25

It was a fifteen-mile drive to the Cumberland County ME's office in the town of Woodbine. Mason figured if he pushed it through the tight turns of the national forest, he could make it in under twenty minutes. Layne rode in the passenger seat, with her laptop open on her thighs, the photographs of the five victims in the cornfield and the two behind the wall arranged on her screen like some hellish version of *The Brady Bunch*.

"So we're dealing with seven victims that we currently attribute to our UNSUB," she said. "But what about the person who was incinerated in the truck? Where does he fit in?"

"You know as well as I do that the guys who attacked us tonight didn't kill him," Mason said.

"So you think he was already inside the vehicle when they set it on fire?"

"Stands to reason, and if they believed they were potentially looking at murder charges in addition to arson, that would justify their panic."

"Okay. So we have three subsets of victims."

"And three distinct MOs," Mason said. "The two men in the tunnel were presumably used as guinea pigs to test the efficacy of the Novichok, and the men in the cornfield were displayed in a manner that more closely fits the mold of a serial killer."

"We don't know how the man in the truck was killed, though."

"That's the point. We're not supposed to. There's something about either his identity or the manner of his death that would compromise their plans."

"'Their'?"

"We've already established that the UNSUB has no fear of getting caught, which means that someone else does. Someone threatened by the potential identification of the remains."

"Then what's the UNSUB's relationship to this second person?"

"I think you were right when you drew a distinction between the personal and professional nature of his crimes. Manufacturing the Novichok was professional. Testing it on the men in the tunnel and torturing the men in the field were personal."

"So where does the body in the truck fit in?"

"If we assume the second man in this scenario hired the UNSUB for his ability to manufacture a large quantity of Novichok and then the four men from tonight to clean up after him, then I'm betting the man in the truck is the link between the two."

"We need to figure out who he was."

"Or else this is where the trail ends."

Layne closed her computer, cradled it to her chest, and brought her feet up onto the seat. She rolled down the window and leaned her face into the breeze.

"You know what I don't understand?" she said. "Let's say we're right and one man hired another to mass-produce a chemical weapon.

That's a straight-up business transaction. Cash for Novichok. They could have built a lab anywhere, loaded the product onto any truck, and we would never have known. Why set up shop in a building where there's already other horrible stuff going on, and why kill five men on the same property where he stole the trucks? It's like he's leaving bread crumbs for us."

Mason thought about the chemical formula he'd found on the clipboard in the otherwise sanitized lab.

"He wants us to find him," he said.

"But we already know he's fully convinced that we can't."

"Then he's leading us toward something."

"His partner, the man who hired him?" Layne asked. "Why would he want to do that?"

"Because he has his own agenda."

"But is it separate from the dispersal of the Novichok? That's our priority. We don't have time to explore every tangent."

"There has to be a relationship between the first two subsets of victims and the UNSUB for him to have wanted them to suffer so badly before their deaths," Mason said. "And if my theory is right, the dead man from the truck somehow links him to his business partner, which means that the victims are the key to finding both of them."

"We need to ID them," Layne said.

The headlights diffused into the surrounding forest, which encroached from the sides of the road. They caught the occasional flash of eye shine from nocturnal animals in the deep shadows.

"Do me a favor," Mason said. He removed his cell phone from his pocket and handed it to her. "Scroll through my contacts until you find Locker's number, call him, and put him on speaker."

She did as he asked. Locker answered in an exhausted voice on the fourth ring.

"You're on speaker," Mason said. "Special Agent Layne is here with me. Tell us you have some good news."

"Wilkinson was released from the hospital today and they expect Andrews to be able to go home by the end of the week."

Mason had gotten so caught up in the hunt that he'd nearly forgotten about the men who'd been exposed to the Novichok in the tunnel.

"What happened to them isn't on you."

"Maybe not, but if we don't find this guy before he dips into his stockpile, the next time will be."

"We won't let that happen," Layne said.

"I like your optimism, but from everything I've heard, we're no closer to finding him now than we were yesterday."

"Who's your source?" Mason asked.

"Are you kidding? I've had Homeland crawling all over me since the moment they arrived."

"Even with their EOCs at heightened awareness, they had that hazmat team on-site awfully quickly, don't you think? It's almost like they were just sitting around waiting for something to happen."

"I have no doubt they know more about the situation than they're letting on. We only know as much as we do because they've allowed it to filter down to us."

"Are they starting to clamp down on the flow of information?"

"Not really. It's strange. It's almost like they're just hovering around the periphery, waiting for something to happen."

"You think they anticipate a mass-casualty event?"

"That's what I thought at first, but their level of involvement doesn't mesh with a theoretical threat level that high."

"Then what else could they be waiting for?" Layne asked.

"Good question. They've basically set up shop right here in my lab, and yet they're taking a hands-off approach. It's like their presence is meant to remind us of who's in charge, but they've yet to assume command. You know what that means, right?"

Unfortunately, Mason did.

The Department of Homeland Security was an autonomous agency whose directorship was a cabinet-level position, making it beholden neither to Congress nor the people of the United States. It fell under the auspices of the president of the United States himself, in effect creating his own private army. That wasn't to say that Homeland didn't have the best interests of the country at heart, only that it was under no obligation to divulge those interests. Or even justify the means by which it pursued them.

For Locker, that meant he had agents watching his every move, poring over his work, and using it to draw conclusions to which he wasn't privy, until such time as they either seized control or simply up and left. Their arrival had been too well timed and their actions strangely unpredictable. They merely maintained a presence inside the lab and on the Dodge-Hill Strike Force, waiting for the right moment to assert their authority.

Mason wasn't about to let that happen. He refused to be cut out of an investigation peripherally related to his wife's death, the aftermath of which had revealed a shadow entity powerful enough to influence global events and, he now suspected, utilize the DHS for its own ends. They'd stumbled upon a plot they'd never been meant to find and now the investigation was about to be usurped by an agency capable of making it disappear beneath the shroud of national security.

"It means we're running out of time," Mason said.

"Surely anyone purchasing isopropanol or methylphosphonyl dichloride in the kind of volume required to convert potentially thousands of pounds of hydrogen fluoride into a viable nerve agent should be pretty easy to find, don't you think?" Locker said.

"The Homeland contingent on the strike force is following that lead."

"That alone should tell you everything you need to know. Either they're grossly incompetent, which I highly doubt, or they already have a pretty good idea of where it originated."

"So why haven't they stepped in and taken over the investigation?" Layne asked.

There had to be an element Homeland still didn't know, something they were unable to find out on their own. That was why they hadn't thrown up the shield of the Patriot Act and sent them all packing. They needed Locker, or at least his resources, but what could he possibly have or be able to provide that they couldn't get on their own?

Mason slowed as he left the forest behind and entered the city limits. The traffic light at the main intersection flashed yellow, highlighting the darkened storefronts lining the sleepy thoroughfare. Another block and he turned into an asphalt lot beside a sign that read SOUTHERN REGION MEDICAL EXAMINER'S OFFICE. He parked right in front, beside a newer-model Escalade, which presumably meant the ME was already set up and waiting for them. They needed to pick her brain. There had to be a way to identify the cremated remains—

The final piece fell into place.

He suddenly understood exactly why the DHS was taking such a passive role. It needed something that only Locker was in a position to provide.

"You haven't ID'd the men behind the wall yet, have you?" Mason said.

"It's not as easy everyone seems to think. Such advanced stages of desiccation are notoriously challenging, even without factoring in the unprecedented level of insect activity. Those guys are practically mummified. We couldn't get a single useful fingerprint to save our souls and odontological molds and X-rays are only useful if we have access to the victims' dental records. I managed to sequence their DNA, but unless their families provided samples that were uploaded to the system when they went missing . . ." Locker's words trailed off. "They're waiting for me to identify the victims."

"Then I guess we'd better figure out who they were first," Layne said.

26

Mason hadn't spent a lot of time in medical examiners' offices, but this was definitely the smallest he'd been in. The pale light from the exposed halogen tubes made him instinctively squint. Everything was either gray or white, from the floor tiles to the countertops to the cabinets on the walls. One side of the room featured a work surface and an industrial sink, the other a lab station and a small desk with a computer. A portable X-ray machine stood in the corner beside a light box. A single stainless-steel table dominated the center of the room. Power tools were mounted to one end and what looked like a garbage disposal was attached to the drain.

The ME appeared to be in her early fifties. She was of solid build, and her hiking boots smelled of manure. Her face was florid and her dark hair was long and streaked with gray. She wore it in a thick braid that slithered down the back of her knee-length white lab coat, which hung open, revealing her buttoned cowboy top and jeans.

There was a single plastic container about the size of a dresser drawer on the autopsy table. Inside were ashes, soot, and bone chunks, collectively labeled JOHN DOE 02-0441. She wore a pair of examination gloves, which she used to extricate a bone fragment roughly three inches long.

"We could probably get a decent sample from this chunk of femur," she said. "If we pulverized it and spun it up, we might be able to isolate just enough DNA to generate at least a partial profile."

"None of the officers seemed to think there was enough left to do so," Layne said. She hovered equidistant from every surface, as though not wanting to touch anything.

"Those guys don't know what they're talking about."

"Then why haven't you done so?" Mason asked.

"For a truck driver who, for all we know, was sitting dead in that truck for a decade before the fire? If he was smuggling drugs for one of the cartels, like everyone seems to think, he's almost guaranteed to be an undocumented Mexican national anyway."

"We only need you to do the physical legwork," Layne said. "Sending the remains to another facility will cost us time we don't have. If you can generate a preliminary DNA profile, our lab can take it from there."

"This is a small county operation; we don't have the resources you do," the ME said. "Do you have any idea how much work you've already created for me? The state mandates that every victim of an officer-involved shooting be autopsied. That's nearly four hours apiece right there. Plus the days spent writing reports and collating lab results—"

"I totally understand," Mason said. "The FBI will reimburse you for your time and expertise."

"Identifying him is that important?"

"Lives are at stake," Layne said.

Dr. Quarrels looked from Mason to Layne and back again, as though in an attempt to discern the direness of the situation from their expressions. Mason hoped his conveyed the message that he'd be willing to force her to do it at gunpoint, if he had to.

"And you'll arrange for transfer of custody of the physical remains?" the ME said.

"How quickly can you have it done?"

"Four hours?"

"You have three."

The ME proffered her hand like a salesman closing a deal. Mason shook it and looked her directly in the eyes.

"You're on the clock, Doctor."

His phone vibrated in his pocket. He glanced at the number of the incoming call before answering.

"That was fast," he said.

"I found what we were looking for, and you're never going to believe it."

Locker had his full attention. Mason covered the phone and spoke to the ME, who was already rummaging through the cupboards.

"Is there someplace I can take this call?"

"My office is at the end of the hall. Pass the entrance to the lobby and you'll walk right into it."

The ME returned her attention to the cupboard and removed a centrifuge and what looked like a miniature copy machine labeled FREEZER/MILL.

"Give me a few seconds, okay?" Mason said into the phone.

He hurried out of the autopsy room and down the hall to the ME's office. Switched on the lights and waited for Layne to follow him inside before closing the door. Took the seat behind the desk. Propped the phone against a picture of Quarrels and her golden retriever.

"I'm going to put you on speaker, okay?" Mason said. "I want Layne to hear this, too."

He hit the button and Locker's voice erupted from the phone mid-sentence.

". . . already dead."

"Start over. I must have cut you off."

"I said I ID'd the victims behind the wall at the end of the tunnel, and they were already dead."

Layne took a seat in the vinyl chair on the other side of the desk and raised the question with her eyebrows.

"I don't follow," Mason said.

"The men behind the wall have been dead since November twenty-fourth, 2001."

"You and I both saw the bodies, Locker. There's no way they've been dead for two decades."

"That's the thing, Mason. The ME and I both independently worked time of death and came up with estimates within days of each other. Sometime between the end of June and the beginning of July. Six months ago."

"But you just said they'd been dead since November of '01," Layne said.

"Precisely."

"I'm going to need a translator."

"Start at the beginning, Locker," Mason said.

"Remember what we were talking about earlier? That started me thinking: Why would the identities of these men be so important to the DHS? I mean, there are potentially thousands of gallons of Novichok out there, but for some reason they're more concerned with what I'm doing? It doesn't make any sense until you boil it down to the most basic logic. These two men—for whatever reason—pose a threat to national security beyond their knowledge of or participation in plots against this country, both biological and chemical in nature. Homeland Security's primary mission is to secure our borders and counteract threats from abroad. To protect us from terrorists. From rogue countries and violent ideologues. From criminals trying to smuggle weapons into the country. And therein lies the inherent flaw in my initial approach. It's no wonder I hadn't been able to identify them. I'd been looking in the wrong place the entire time. All of our missing persons databases are essentially exclusive to American citizens."

Mason finally caught up with the conversation.

"So you tried INTERPOL," he said.

The global MPUB—Missing Persons and Unidentified Bodies—database was conceived as part of the FASTID Project, which was an attempt to do for the rest of the world what the Next Generation Identification System did for the United States by pooling the resources of all of the participating countries assembled under the banner of the European Commission.

"Exactly. And once I uploaded the DNA profiles, incomplete though they were, I hit the jackpot. Our victims matched samples submitted by family members with loved ones on El Al Flight 1086 from Bern to Tel Aviv. The plane crashed in the forest just a couple miles from the runway and went up in a ball of flames. The majority of the victims were dismembered and burned to such an extent that investigators couldn't even confirm that the number of dead matched the flight manifest, let alone positively identify more than a handful of the deceased. One hundred and eighteen ticketed passengers and the entire flight crew were legally declared dead, and yet seventy-three families held out hope and sent DNA samples to INTERPOL, among them the families of Nitzan Chenhav and Yossi Mosche, who reappeared two decades later, entombed with about a million spiders."

"How did two men who died halfway around the world end up walled beneath a building used for experimenting with biological and chemical weapons?" Mason asked.

"That's not even the most interesting part. Ask me what they did for a living?"

"Just tell us already."

"You're trying to spoil my moment of triumph, aren't you?"

"Locker."

"Chenhav was a microbiologist specializing in hematology and genetic disorders of the blood. He was one of the leading research scientists at Sourasky Medical Center in Tel Aviv and a pioneer of the development of both natural and synthetic anticoagulants. Mosche was a medical biochemist whose primary focus was neuromuscular regeneration. In addition to a professorship at Sackler School of Medicine, he served as a consultant to several major pharmaceutical conglomerates and—get this—the World Health Organization's Department of Bioterrorism Preparedness."

"Both were Israeli nationals?" Layne asked.

"You got it."

"And both were on the same flight from Switzerland to Israel."

"What are the odds, right?"

"What were they doing in Bern at the same time?" Mason asked.

"Definitely a question worth answering."

"Which one left the numeric message for us to find?"

"The biochemist. Mosche."

"You realize Homeland's about to descend upon you and shut you out of the case."

"They can try."

"Why are you in such a good mood?" Layne asked.

"Because we have an actual lead."

"That went up in flames two decades ago," Mason said.

"That's a problem for the investigative team," Locker said. "I did my part. The rest is up to you."

"Email me everything you have, okay?"

Mason terminated the call and stared out the window through the gap between the blinds while he organized his thoughts. Chenhav and Mosche obviously weren't random victims, nor could it possibly be mere coincidence that the bodies of a microbiologist and biochemist were discovered beneath a facility responsible for the production and testing of an engineered flu virus and a chemical weapon of mass destruction. Where had these men been since 2001 and what sequence of events had drawn them into the orbit of the Hoyl and the UNSUB, and, by extension, the Thirteen? What was the significance of the numbers the biochemist scrawled in his own blood?

And then there was Bern. The last person to mention the Swiss capital to Mason was his brother-in-law, Victor Thornton, who'd claimed in the days before his death to have recently been there to help establish an Eastern European presence for his newest venture, Global Allied Biotechnology and Pharmaceuticals. Mason didn't have the slightest idea what Victor might have done while he was there or what acquisitions he might have made to penetrate the biotech market, but it wouldn't be too terribly difficult to figure out. He knew someone who had all of the records he could ever hope to find.

"It's impossible to totally drop off the grid for any length of time," Layne said. "You can't go anywhere without being caught in a web of surveillance cameras."

Mason's phone vibrated to notify him that he'd received the file from Locker. He forwarded it to Layne, whose device chimed from inside her jacket.

"Call Algren," Mason said. "Tell her we need to move up our brief-ing. And see what you can do about summarizing Locker's report."

"My laptop's in the car."

He pulled the keys from his pocket and tossed them to her. She caught them and rushed toward the door. She grabbed the knob, paused, and glanced back at him.

"What are you going to do?"

"Try to get some background on Chenhav and Mosche before Homeland learns their identities and information becomes scarce."

Layne nodded and exited the office. The whirring sound of the cen-trifuge carried down the hall from the lab. The door slowly closed and once again there was silence.

Mason grabbed his phone, forwarded the information Locker had just sent him to both of the encrypted clouds, and called Gunnar on his stealth phone.

"I just sent you a link to a secure video chat room," Gunnar said. "Once you log in, the other party will be notified and receive an invita-tion to join you. Trust me when I say that our old friend's curiosity is suitably piqued."

"He's going to have to wait until I can break away," Mason said. "In the meantime, I need another favor. I just uploaded a file to the cloud. Find out everything you can about the subjects. And I mean right now. I have a feeling that whatever information exists is about to go away."

"I should warn you, Mace. There aren't many ways to make things vanish permanently and even fewer people capable of doing so. They're also the kind who'll be able to follow our footprints right back to us if they so much as catch a whiff of our scent anywhere it shouldn't be."

"Then you'd better do it fast, because they're going to be coming up behind you in a hurry."

27

The conference call commenced half an hour later, at 10:30 P.M. local time. It was 8:30 back home in Colorado, and exhaustion already showed on the faces of men and women who weren't about to get any sleep in the foreseeable future. The live display was divided into quadrants, with Algren featured in the upper left, the ATF team in the upper right, the DHS contingent in the lower left corner, and Layne in the bottom right. She sat at the medical examiner's desk, with her laptop in front of her and the wall of framed degrees and awards as a backdrop. Mason was sprawled on the couch running along the wall, his laptop open and primed to view his amassed information all at once.

"I want to keep this briefing concise and to the point," Algren said. "With as many seemingly disparate investigations as we're currently juggling, we need to do everything in our power to delineate and compartmentalize each. Let's start with the forensics report. Special Agent Layne?"

"I trust you've all had at least a few seconds to familiarize yourselves with case file number charlie sierra four one-two one-eight dash one-six," she said. There was a lag between the sound of her voice beside Mason and the movement of her lips on the screen. "The important part here is the identification of the victims recovered from behind the false wall at the slaughterhouse. DNA profiles were generated and compared against local, federal, and international missing persons databases. Ultimately, the samples matched those submitted by relatives of Israeli nationals Nitzan Chenhav and Yossi Mosche—a microbiologist and biochemist, respectively—who were purportedly killed on El Al Flight 1086 from Bern, Switzerland, to Tel Aviv, Israel, on November twenty-fourth, 2001."

"That opens up a whole new can of worms, doesn't it?" Becker said. The ATF agent sat directly in front of his laptop camera, a paper cup of steaming coffee to his right. Johnson sat on the edge of the bed, the painting on the wall behind her the kind of landscape that hung in every motel room in the world.

"The way I see it," Layne said, "we're dealing with four distinct lines of inquiry. First: What were both men doing in Bern at the same time? Second: How did these men survive a crash that killed everyone else on board? Third: Where have they been for the last twenty years? And fourth: What was the nature of their involvement with the flu virus and the Novichok agent being developed in the building above where they were entombed?"

"Of the four," Algren said, "the last question is of the greatest consequence."

"We'll run with that one," Addison said. She nodded to Salazar, who sat beside her at a wooden table. They'd exchanged their DHS uniforms for T-shirts with the Federal Protective Service logo. Stools were stacked upside down on a hotel bar behind them, the wall above it lined with shelves overflowing with bottles of liquor.

Layne cast Mason a sideways glance before speaking.

"Mason thinks he might be able to dig up some background on them."

"I don't want the two of you getting bogged down with tasks that can be handled remotely," Algren said. "You're on point out there. I need you unencumbered in the field, at least until I arrive."

"You're coming out here?"

"The attack on you and Special Agent Mason tonight represents an act of aggression against this strike force. I've already made arrangements for ASAC Hooper to take my place here while I transition into my new role. Agents Addison and Becker will be joining me; their partners will stay behind to ensure investigational continuity. Local intelligence operatives and tactical units will be provided by the Joint Terrorism Task Force under the direction of the Department of Homeland Security."

Again, Layne glanced back at Mason, who sat up and leaned into the frame behind her.

"Have you been able to figure out the route the trucks took to get here?" he asked.

"We acquired them outside of St. Louis on I-Seventy," Addison said. "And one final time on Highway Seventy-six between Morgan-town and Philadelphia."

"Did they still have their payload?"

"Affirmative."

"What about physical evidence inside the farmhouse?" Layne asked.

"We collected two distinct sets of fingerprints," Algren said. "One set belonged to Cavanaugh, as one would expect, but the other doesn't match any in the NGI. The UNSUB must have known his biometric data wasn't in the system."

"Do we have IDs or COD from the Yuma County ME yet?" Mason asked.

"It's a small office unprepared to deal with a case of this magnitude," Addison said.

"Then transfer the remains to Locker's lab."

"That's precisely what we intend to do once the ME finishes her examination."

"We don't have time to wait around for her," Layne said. "Have her send us what she has so far and we'll take it from there. At least we'd be able to establish a little forward momentum."

Layne's computer chimed to alert her to incoming mail. She abruptly stiffened and turned to face Mason, her eyes wide and a smile on her face.

"We just received the profile from Behavioral."

Mason glanced over her shoulder and saw the name of the sender. He recognized it immediately. Xavier Christensen. While his boss might have been a pro at separating his personal life from his professional, he apparently had no qualms about calling his son, a highly respected behavioral analyst, to expedite their profile.

"What does it say?" Algren asked.

"Give me a minute to read through it and I'll summarize," Layne said. "You should all be receiving a forwarded copy right about . . . now."

"We'll come back to you, then. Where do we stand with the precursor chemicals?"

"None of the registered suppliers reported any purchases out of the ordinary," Addison said, "let alone in the kind of quantity we're talking about, but we've subpoenaed their records to verify their claims."

"What about the signature of the IED?" Algren asked.

"There is no signature," Becker said. "We believe the UNSUB is just a very smart man who took advantage of the items he had on hand. Not a pro, but certainly not an amateur, either. With as much raw fuel as he had in that cellar, he could have easily launched that house into orbit."

"That was never his intention, though," Mason said. "The blast was localized to inflict maximum damage on whoever opened that door. He wanted us to be shocked by the carnage when we arrived."

Again, Mason was reminded of the cruelty of the trap in the knocking pen. Had he arrived any later, he would have found Alejandra with her spinal cord severed and a bolt halfway through her forehead.

"I agree, but we lack physical evidence to support that assertion," Algren said. "It's little more than a theory that presupposes we have the slightest idea of what's going on inside his head."

"Which brings us to our profile," Layne said. "Behavioral's reluctant to say he's of Japanese origin based solely on the characters carved into the tree. Traditionally, the Japanese have a much different relationship with their elderly than we do. More respectful. They revere their aging population as a source of wisdom and knowledge. They say it's possible the UNSUB could have developed a kind of animosity that caused him to seek out elderly victims, but such a specific emotional response likely wouldn't cross over to a different ethnicity. If he hated his elders, he would have sought out victims who most closely resembled them."

"Assuming he was of Japanese origin in the first place."

"Exactly."

"Were all of the victims Caucasian for sure?" Becker asked. "Anyone of Japanese descent would definitely blame white men of a certain age for the internment camps during World War Two. And, you know, the whole atomic bomb thing."

"As far as we know," Algren said, "but we can't say conclusively without the autopsy report."

"Which we should have had by now," Mason said.

"What else?" Algren asked.

"We've got your standard troubled childhood. Liked to torture animals. No overt elements of sexual aggression, although they're unable to completely rule out a sexual component without confirmation from the ME."

"We need to see if we can at least get preliminary findings."

"We're still out here in Wray," Becker said. "I'll follow up in person on my way to the airport."

"A couple other things stand out," Layne said. "They don't believe his overt demonstrations of cruelty are for our benefit alone. He draws immense personal satisfaction from hurting other people. It makes him feel powerful. And they all but confirmed what we were thinking. He displayed his victims in the cornfield because he fully intended to reveal his completed design when the time was right."

"Do they agree that the display is meant to convey a message?" Mason asked.

"It appears so, but they're unable to even speculate as to what that message is or who he hoped would receive it."

"What about the Japanese characters themselves?" Addison asked. "Kuebiko. What's their take on that?"

"The scarecrow motif speaks to him on a personal level. In the modern context, it's simply a human decoy meant to scare birds from a field, but it could also represent either a literal or metaphorical straw man. A being that looks alive from a distance but is actually dead inside. Or if we stick with the Japanese allusion, the scarecrow first appeared in *Kojiki,* the oldest surviving book in Japan. An all-knowing deity named Kuebiko assumed its form. Maybe he's trying to convey the message that he knows something other people would rather he not. Whatever the case, the scarecrow plays prominently into his message. He left the carving on the tree for us, the responding officers, but his victims were the message he meant to deliver to a specific faction privy to the confidential details of this investigation, one that already knows his true identity but he's certain won't divulge it. He has absolutely no fear of being caught."

"They're suggesting our investigation is compromised," Algren said.

"Not in so many words, but the implication is clear."

Algren's expression clouded and for the first time betrayed her age.

"What about the arrangement of the victims?" Mason asked.

"That's where the profile breaks from that of a traditional serial killer," Layne said. "The circular nature of the display and equal distance between bodies implies a finite number of victims. This isn't a man who intended to keep on killing until we eventually stopped him. They speculate he was going to kill three more people—two to complete the outer ring, and one, presumably the victim of the highest personal value, to be his centerpiece—and then he was going to sit back and watch the reaction from afar. In fact, they still believe he's going to do just that."

"So they're confident the victims were specifically targeted and not crimes of opportunity," Addison said.

"If you're willing to read between the lines a little."

"Which means that right now there are potentially three specific individuals who know that this man is coming for them," Mason said.

"What does any of this have to do with four thousand gallons of Novichok?" Becker asked.

"They believe he has a background not just in chemistry but in chemical engineering specifically. He's directly responsible for its manufacture, which he sees as his job. He doesn't care about where it's released or how many people die. It's the fulfillment of a contractual obligation. Like punching a clock. It's the other murders that matter to him on a personal level."

"So if we find these three men," Mason said, "we find the UNSUB."

"And the Novichok," Algren added.

"That's their theory," Layne said.

"Have we had any luck identifying the men from the photographs inside the farmhouse?" Mason asked.

"With their eyes scratched out, our techs hold out little hope, but they're still running the images through every available database and praying for a miracle," Algren said.

"I saw that wall before it exploded. Those pictures were like trophies to him. The men in that field? They were in those pictures. I'm sure of it. If we could identify them and subtract them from the picture, the remainder would hopefully give us at least one of our three intended victims."

"Again, the autopsies are the holdup," Layne said. She looked pointedly at Mason, who realized she finally understood what he'd been saying all along about Homeland. "We need to figure out who those men are."

28

Dr. Quarrels promised to call them the moment she had a serviceable DNA profile of the cremated remains ready to upload, at which time she'd turn over her work to Locker and wash her hands of it. She had a long night ahead of her and neither Mason nor Layne wanted to be there when the bodies of the men who'd tried to kill them arrived. There was nothing more for them to do in New Jersey, at least not until Barrie got back to them with the name of the superior officer who'd wanted to send the burned trucks to the junkyard, and it was only an hour's drive to Philadelphia, where Algren's plane wouldn't be arriving for another four hours. They debated renting a room where they could crash for a few hours, but they were too wired to sleep and figured they'd better eat while they had the chance.

They found a twenty-four-hour diner on the highway outside of Millville and took a booth in the front corner, which afforded them a view of both the interior and the street outside. The only other customers were sitting at the counter on the far side of the restaurant, facing the pass-through window and fountain drink dispenser, above which hung a television tuned to a muted cable news network. They wore flannel shirts, jeans, and ball caps, perched high on their heads in true trucker style, and ate with their faces in their meals, totally oblivious to the banging and clanging coming from the kitchen.

The waitress was petite and attractive, with short, dark hair and the legs of a runner. She introduced herself as Erica and took their orders on a paper guest check. Mason ordered the chicken fried steak, while Layne opted for a burger and fries. They asked the waitress to leave the carafe of coffee to minimize interruptions. She seemed more than happy to oblige and disappeared through the swinging door into the kitchen.

"We're wasting our time here," Layne said. She rolled her head on her shoulders to work out the kinks in her neck. "We should be out there trying to track him down."

"I'm open to suggestions."

"Like you said, someone at least peripherally involved with this investigation knows him. We should hunt that person down and get the information out of him."

Mason agreed with her, but the intended recipient of the UNSUB's message undoubtedly wielded the kind of power that insulated him from the scrutiny of his subordinates. Whoever it was had to be rattled, though. There was no doubt he'd reveal himself in time, assuming catastrophe didn't strike first.

"Trust me on this one, Layne. The UNSUB knows this guy is pissing himself and fully intends to draw out his suffering—"

Mason's cell phone vibrated inside his jacket pocket. He recognized the Arizona area code but not the number itself.

"Mason," he answered.

"It's Becker. I got the answers we needed."

"ID and COD?"

Layne raised her eyebrows.

"COD," Becker said.

"Did they just release it?"

"The ME knew this afternoon."

"Then why the hell didn't she tell us?"

"She did."

"Then who dropped the ball?"

"It's not that simple."

Mason suddenly understood exactly what had happened.

"Homeland," he said.

"I couldn't get within a quarter mile of her office, even this late at night. I could see at least half a dozen black sedans and SUVs in the parking lot, though. Government vehicles might be subtle on their own but not when they travel in packs."

"So how'd you find out?"

"The officer redirecting traffic was a Yuma County Sheriff's deputy named Mack. He went to high school with the medical examiner, who passed along some information I'm pretty sure the DHS wouldn't have approved of."

"Why would she tell him?"

"One of the police officers killed in the explosion was her husband's cousin. Small towns and all that. She didn't want his death to get swept under the rug, and it was starting to look like that was going to happen, so she gave a copy of her handwritten notes to Mack, who gave them to me."

Mason mimed for Layne to grab him a writing utensil and pulled a napkin from the dispenser. She hopped up from the table, plucked a pen from the hostess stand, and tossed it to him.

"So what's the verdict?" he asked.

Layne leaned across the table in an effort to hear Becker's side of the conversation. Mason wasn't about to put the call on speaker. They probably shouldn't even have been discussing it on an open line. He glanced up at the truckers, who appeared to be in the process of finishing their meals. Neither appeared to have the slightest interest in anything that wasn't on their plates.

"Suicide," Becker said.

"What?"

"You heard right," Becker said. "Suicide."

"How does a man climb up onto a wooden cross, secure all of his limbs, and set about killing himself?" Mason asked.

Layne looked at him like he'd lost his mind.

"That was pretty much my reaction, too. Believe me. You need to take a step back and look at it purely from the ME's perspective. Her job is to tell us how the victims died—plain and simple—using inarguable scientific facts. And in this case, the facts are conclusive that these five men killed themselves."

"Walk me through it."

Layne switched to Mason's side of the table and scooted right up against him. She practically leaned her head on his shoulder in an effort to better hear Becker's voice.

"We already knew the victims were tied up there for some length of time while they were still alive. Best estimates suggest somewhere between seventy-two and ninety-six hours, but that's entirely speculative. What isn't is that each of the men was given a small glass ampoule about the size and shape of a Tylenol capsule. By given, I mean placed into their mouths. Inside that ampoule was a solution of saxitoxin, the neurotoxin produced by the puffer fish. It's about a thousand times more toxic than sarin if ingested and promises a quick but extraordinarily painful death."

"He gave them the ampoules intact?"

"The ME pulled glass shards from between their teeth and under their gums."

"The victims held them in their mouths for three to four days?"

"I'd wager a kidney that the UNSUB told his victims what it contained before putting it in their mouths. He gave them a means to end their suffering. To kill themselves when they couldn't take it anymore."

"What suffering?"

"Here's where I need to consult her notes. Bear with me, okay?"

Mason scribbled on the napkin to make sure the pen worked and prepared to write down everything Becker said.

"The ME found trace amounts of a powdery yellow residue inside their sinuses and airways," Becker said. "She thought it was pollen at first, but considering the season, she had it sent to the lab with the blood and tissue samples for toxicology screening while she performed the physical evaluations. No defensive wounds on the hands or forearms. No outward expressions of trauma. The only broken bones occurred either during the process of being tied to the posts or shortly thereafter. The worst of the external soft tissue injuries were, and I quote, 'localized necrosis of the eyelids and acute corneal injury.'"

"What exactly does that mean?"

"It'll all make sense when I'm finished," Becker said. "Their insides apparently looked like they'd been through a blender. The oral and pharyngeal tissues were swollen nearly to the point of closure. There were massive accumulations of fluid in their lungs. The mucosal linings of their bowels had dissolved and their livers were the size of footballs."

"Jesus," Layne whispered.

"The blood work showed elevated red and white blood cell counts and unusually high levels of a liver enzyme called *carboxylesterase*, which is responsible for—and again, I'm going to read straight from the report—'the selective hydrolysis of the C-4 acetyl group of known toxins.'"

The waitress arrived with their food and set the plates in front of them. Mason thanked her and watched her until she returned to the counter, where she distractedly wiped it with a damp towel while perusing a magazine. One of the truckers rose from his stool and headed for the restroom. The other leaned onto his elbow and glanced up at the TV screen.

"That's when the toxicology results came back," Becker said. "The problem was the DHS came with them."

"What did they show?" Mason asked.

"A mycotoxin of the trichothecene group, similar to the kind manufactured for use as a weapon in Cambodia and Vietnam."

"Yellow rain?"

"Not exactly. This is a specific mycotoxin known as nivalenol. It's produced by a fungus called *Fusarium nivale*, a naturally occurring species prevalent in rural areas of—you guessed it—Japan."

Everything suddenly made sense. These men had been incapacitated, bound to the crosses, and then hit directly in the face with a controlled burst of nivalenol when they awakened. They'd inhaled it, ingested it, and taken it in through their eyes. And then their killer had placed an ampoule of saxitoxin in their mouths and given them the means of ending their pain when it became too great.

Their eyelids would have blistered and popped, making them impossible to close. The sensitive linings of their mouths, noses, and throats would have eroded, producing the constant flow of blood that accumulated in their lungs. The abdominal symptoms would have followed shortly thereafter. Along with the pain. Agony so excruciating that their cries must have carried for miles, if only anyone had been around to hear them.

They'd held out for as long as they could, hoping their bodies would miraculously withstand the assault. They'd screamed through the night while the toxin ate through the linings of their intestines, gasped for air as their lungs filled with fluid, and fought hunger and dehydration and the blazing sun, against which they couldn't even close their eyes.

"They understood how the nivalenol worked," Mason said. "They knew that they could be saved if someone found them in time."

That was why they'd endured more pain than any human should have to bear, suffered through symptoms they had the means of making go away. They hadn't survived for three full days because they feared death, but, rather, because they were intimately familiar with the mechanisms by which both toxins killed. Only when they reached the point of no return, when even rescue and immediate treatment offered no chance of recovery, did they bite down on the ampoules they'd held in their mouths through the unimaginable pain. Only then did they relinquish hope and utilize the only means at hand to end their misery.

Mason scribbled four words on the napkin and underlined them multiple times.

"Who else knows all of this?" he asked.

"Outside of the ME, the DHS, and however many people Mack told, only us," Becker said. "Johnson agreed that we should bypass reporting this to Algren, at least until I can do so in person, and see if we can figure out where this thing is going. I can't imagine Homeland isn't every bit as eager as we are to get the Novichok off the streets, but they're slow-walking, if not actively shunting, the flow of information critical to a federal investigation, and I want to know why."

"You're not the only one," Mason said. "Let me know the moment you find out anything, okay?"

"You do the same," Becker said. "And keep your eyes open, Mason. Something's really wrong here. I can feel it."

29

Mason ended the call and stared at the words he'd written on the napkin. His conclusion made total sense. Someone who didn't understand how the nivalenol worked would have ended his suffering long before the third day. Instead, all five of the victims had waited at least seventy-two hours before biting the ampoules. It was always possible the UNSUB had painstakingly explained the escalation of symptoms, but there was no reason for men who were about to die to take him at his word. Not unless they had a specific background. Not unless they were—

"Chemical engineers like him?" Layne said, reading what he'd written on the napkin.

"He knew his victims through the course of his work," Mason said.

"They must have done something a whole lot worse than getting him fired for him to kill them in such a brutal way."

The waitress abandoned her magazine and returned to the kitchen. Mason could see her through the porthole window, leaning against the wall and texting on her phone.

"But where did he work with them?" he asked.

"I think we're on the right track looking into a military background."

"Then his victims should have already been ID'd."

"Who's to say they haven't been?"

Mason set down his mug harder than he'd intended. The waitress glanced up from the kitchen. Their eyes met through the porthole window. He waved an apology and she returned her attention to her phone.

"If any chemical engineers have been reported missing over the past six months," Layne said, "there ought to be record of it somewhere. Especially if they have working knowledge of WMDs. We can then cross-reference it against the personnel list from the army."

"There's still something we're overlooking here, though," Mason said. "This guy is like an evil MacGyver. He can make a bomb out of the junk on hand, a suicide pill using bad sushi, and a biological torture device from mushrooms. It's not just about inflicting maximum damage for this guy; it's about putting his victims in a position where they literally hold their lives in their own hands."

"But Chenhav and Mosche were different. They were an extension of his professional persona."

"Were they?" Mason asked. "Maybe there's some amount of overlap between the two."

The trucker emerged from the restroom. He returned to his stool and glanced up at the TV, where a reporter stood framed against the backdrop of a forest stained red and blue by the light bars of police cruisers.

"The one who left the message on the ceiling," Layne said. "He was a scientist, too, wasn't he?"

"Right. So what are numbers to a scientist?"

"They could mean anything."

"Of course, but why use a code to deliver a message unless you only want a certain faction to be able to decipher it, especially when the message itself is more important than the potential for a few additional minutes of life?"

"There's no evidence to suggest that either of them was involved with the military, the flu experimentation, or the production of the Novichok. For all we know, these two guys were nothing more than successful scientists at the top of their respective fields. What kind of people would they expect to find their bodies and recognize the code, let alone be able to crack it?"

"Someone who would understand the implications of what had happened to them."

"You think it's a warning?"

The larger trucker elbowed his companion, who looked up at the screen. The ticker on the screen read POLICE CLOSE NYC CENTRAL PARK.

"Mosche worked with WHO's bioterrorism readiness program," Mason said. "If someone wanted to negatively impact the international state of preparedness in anticipation of releasing a deadly virus, eliminating one of the men responsible makes a lot of sense."

"As far as the world knows, he's been dead for two decades. Surely every single military and medical response protocol has been updated multiple times since then."

"But he's definitely the kind of guy you'd want if you were trying to anticipate and counteract those protocols."

"They can't be closely held secrets if they expect to be able to coordinate emergency responses with agencies on both the federal and local levels."

"We're missing something obvious," Mason said. "Mosche had to know his remains would be found by someone who recognized the slaughterhouse for what it truly was. He left the message for someone who would have known to look behind the false wall. Someone familiar with the layout of both the building and the tunnel."

"You think Chenhav and Mosche were complicit in what went on there?"

"It makes sense."

"Then why kill them?"

"Probably caught them by surprise, too," Mason replied.

"So they left a warning for other people like them," Layne said. "One that whoever found it would recognize the moment he saw it."

"We've already ruled out phone and Social Security numbers, bank accounts and wireless transfer confirmations."

"It's not an IP address and the corresponding geographical location is in the middle of the ocean."

"We're thinking too broadly. How would one scientist use numbers to communicate a specific message to another scientist?"

"He was a microbiologist, right?"

"Chenhav was the microbiologist. Mosche was the biochem . . ."

Mason's words trailed off as he caught the tail of a thought that had eluded him until now.

"What?" Layne asked.

"Son of a bitch."

Mason set his phone on the table in front of him, grabbed a fresh napkin, and scribbled down the numbers Mosche had written in his own blood on the ceiling of his tomb.

1 6 2 0 7 5 2 4 8 7 4.

"Talk to me, Mason. What are you thinking?"

His mind was moving too quickly to formulate a reply. He opened a browser and entered a search at the prompt. Brought up the resultant image. Zoomed in. Positioned his phone right above the napkin so he could clearly see both the numbers and the screen.

"The periodic table?" Layne said.

Mason tuned out everything around him and set to work.

One: hydrogen. Six: carbon. Two: helium. Zero? No zero.

"Damn."

Hydrogen was H. Carbon, C. Helium, He.

H-C-He?

His phone vibrated. He swiped away the incoming call. He needed to be able to see what he was doing.

One and six could be sixteen. Sixteen was sulfur. Two and zero? Twenty. Twenty was calcium.

Sulfur was S. Calcium, Ca.

S-Ca.

The rest tumbled into place from there.

Seven and five was seventy-five. Seventy-five was rhenium.

Two and four was twenty-four. Twenty-four was chromium.

Eight and seven. Eighty-seven was francium. No. Separate the eight from the seven. Eight was oxygen.

Seven and four. Seventy-four was tungsten.

"Sulfur, calcium, rhenium, chromium, oxygen, and tungsten," he said.

"An organic metal of some kind?" Layne asked.

"No."

Mason wrote the abbreviations for the elements on the napkin beneath the corresponding numbers.

16 20 75 24 8 74.
S   Ca Re Cr O W.

"It's more than just a metaphor to him," Layne said. "Like the killings themselves, it has personal significance. He not only thinks of himself as a scarecrow—"

"He is the Scarecrow."

Layne's cell phone chimed. She removed it from her pocket and checked the caller ID.

"Algren," she said, and answered on the second ring. "This is Layne."

Mason checked his phone log. His missed call had come from the strike force leader, too.

"What?" Layne said. She lowered the phone from her mouth. "Check your email, Mason. Hurry."

Mason opened his mailbox and tapped the incoming message from Algren. It contained a picture that took several seconds to open. At first, he couldn't tell what it was. Everything was either dark or grainy. There were trees everywhere, and between them, what almost looked like—

He glanced up at the TV and then back at the picture. Pulled out his wallet and tossed two twenties on the table. Grabbed his coat.

"Finish the call in the car," he said, and headed for the door.

The behavioral analysts had been right. The UNSUB wasn't done. He'd left another dead man bound to a cross.

Right in the middle of Central Park.

30

ELSEWHERE

The Scarecrow felt neither elation nor sorrow. In fact, it felt nothing at all, a regrettable consequence of the abandonment of its humanity. Even the death of one of its primary tormentors failed to trigger an emotional response, not even a hint of satisfaction. It had merely watched from a distance as the man suffered through the sheer agony for as long as he could bear before ending his own life. The duration of his misery had seemed to pass in the blink of an eye, little more than a morbid reality show playing in the background of a fever dream.

In a sense, the being that had once inhabited this form had already preceded this body into the grave, casting aside this empty shell to implement a plan quarried from the mind of a terrified child, forged by an advanced education, honed to a razor's edge during the subsequent years in hiding, and now ready to be plunged into the heart of a world that had used it and thrown it away, a diseased slab of meat rotting from the inside out, a final insult mirrored by the slow death of its opposite half—its better half—the half that had been the only thing tethering it to its former life. It cared nothing for the man who thought himself its master or the internal war waging within his organization. Let the Thirteen destroy one another and the entire world with them. They were responsible for all that was wrong with this damned species, the living embodiment of the greed that had led to the deliberate infliction of such horrific pain upon a group of powerless children in a cold, sterile room. One lineage in particular: Quintus. The memory of the agony that family had inflicted had been purged from its blood, the sins of the father washed away, and thus the bloodline itself needed to come to an end. And the last man bearing it was so caught up in his attempted coup that he didn't even realize that he'd invited the fox into the henhouse, and it was about to slaughter everything inside.

A frigid breeze howled across the roofline.

The Scarecrow again pressed its eye to the telescope and watched the shadowed forms moving through the trees in the red and blue glare of police lights, scurrying like roaches around a crumb, unaware that the entire place was about to be fumigated. If only they could see it, silhouetted against the roofline, and recognize their communal fate, but they'd never seen it in life, so why should the moments before death be any different?

The long process of transformation, the release of all of the sadness and rage, the stripping away of its humanity, like so many layers of skin, had stranded it in a form of purgatory, neither alive nor dead, a figment of its own imagination, a ghost haunting its own life, such as it was. Even when it had shared its work and living space—while brewing its ultimate creation and inserting that infernal oil-consuming bacterium into the viral envelope of that wretched disease—the others had gone out of their way to avoid it, as though its physical deformities were a contagion, rather than the result of the cruelty of savages just like them. Only the man with the blue eyes, the man for whom its other half had designed the respirator following his unfortunate accident, had been different. In the Hoyl, the Scarecrow had found not just a kindred spirit but a mentor and, in many ways, the closest thing it'd had to a friend in as long as it could remember. They'd shared many commonalities, from their disfigurements and the prosthetics that caused others to look away in disgust to their desire to lash out at a world that had done everything in its power to break them.

The screech of tires drew the Scarecrow's eye to the Seventy-ninth Street Transverse, where a black Crown Victoria skidded to a halt at the police barricade. Agents in federal windbreakers disgorged from the front doors. The man who'd been driving the vehicle turned and surveyed his surroundings.

Here was one more thing they had in common: the man looking back at it from the distance.

This was the same man who'd walked right past the Scarecrow in the darkness on the killing floor of the slaughterhouse, the man for whom it had rigged one of its most ingenious traps, the man who'd murdered the Hoyl. It smiled at the realization that this man would die with all of the others, despite the assurances it had made to its true master, who wanted to end the Quintus bloodline nearly as badly as it did.

Soon, the investigators would figure out the nature of the tableau in the park and orchestrate a siege on its staging ground, but by then it would be long gone and there would be nothing they could do to stop it.

The Scarecrow tucked the telescope under its arm and retreated into the shadows.

Let them come.

They'll find hell waiting.

PART IV

For you see, the world is governed by very different personages
from what is imagined by those who are not behind the scenes.

—Benjamin Disraeli,
Coningsby (1844)

31

December 29

"Who found him?" Mason asked.

Special Agent Nick Barbieri had been waiting at the police cordon off of West Drive when they arrived. He had dark eyes, a hawkish nose, and permanent five o'clock shadow. The back of his windbreaker was stenciled with *FBI* in large letters, and beneath them, in smaller print, *Joint Terrorism Task Force.* He wore an olive green Kevlar vest underneath it, his sidearm in a tactical holster strapped to his thigh, and talked over his shoulder as he led them deeper into the park.

"The report was called in anonymously through the main JTTF tip line," he said.

"Counterterrorism?"

"Domestic section."

"Why'd they call you?"

"That was the first question we asked ourselves when we got here."

"Did you trace the call?" Layne asked.

"To the number assigned to a disposable cell phone purchased at a Duane Reade in Chelsea."

"Voiceprint analysis?"

"Computerized."

"He wanted us to find the body," Mason said.

"More like he got tired of waiting for us to do so."

Barbieri guided them away from the main path and uphill into a dense thicket of sycamore, oak, and black cherry trees, their bare branches sparkling with frost. The ground was carpeted with dead leaves that crunched underfoot. They were in the very center of Central Park, at the heart of one of the most populous cities in the world, and yet it almost felt like they were out in the country, as they couldn't see a single skyscraper.

"What's this?" Layne asked. "Some sort of nature conservatory?"

"It's called the Ramble. Thirty-eight acres of some of the densest forest you'll find on the eastern seaboard. You could easily get lost if you ditched the trail."

"How is it possible no one saw anything?" Mason asked.

"There are people everywhere out here in the summer," Barbieri said. "Not so much in the winter, especially not at night. And definitely not where we're going."

An aura of light radiated from behind the trees in the distance. The hill grew steeper, the damp leaves slicker. Jagged crests of Manhattan schist rose from the slope, dictating a wending course through the maze of tree trunks. A stream trickled somewhere nearby.

"Who all knows about the discovery?" Layne asked.

"Just my team," Barbieri said. "And now you."

"How much does the media know?"

"We told them we're conducting a joint red team exercise with the DHS. Their Office of Counter Terrorism's Public Safety Unit does that kind of thing all the time to audit our infrastructure and response times. Generally not in Central Park, though."

"They won't see through it?"

Barbieri looked back at her and winked.

"They report what we tell them."

The lights grew brighter. They heard voices and saw shadows moving through the trees. Two officers wearing navy fatigues and Kevlar vests with the words *Police DHS* stenciled across the front materialized from the glare of portable lights positioned in a half circle around them.

A handful of forensic techs from the FBI's Evidence Response Team crashed through the forested area in their white jumpsuits, sweeping their flashlights across the mat of dead leaves and marking potential evidence with numbered placards. Two stood together in the middle of a small clearing barely wide enough for the horizontal bar of the cross. They turned at the sound of crunching leaves and shone their handheld spotlights into the faces of the newcomers.

Mason shielded his eyes with one hand and flipped open his badge jacket with the other. The light lingered as a bright red stain in his vision even after the techs returned to their work. He stepped between them and stared up at the cross. The base had been wedged into a deep crevice in a massive rock formation. Scraggly evergreen shrubs grew from cracks in the stone and obscured the bare feet of the victim. He could tell by the texture of the skin near the heels and the thickness and color of the toenails that the victim had been elderly, like the others.

"Tell us what you see," Layne said.

The taller of the two evidence response specialists glanced back at them. Mason caught a glimpse of brown eyes and a caramel complexion through her face shield. Dark bangs spilling out from underneath her hard hat. She spoke with a heavy Puerto Rican accent.

"We believe he'd been dead for between six and eight hours when we arrived, placing his time of death somewhere between fourteen and sixteen hundred hours."

"The middle of the afternoon in Central Park? You're sure?"

"His skin was still slightly warmer than the ambient air and he was in fixed rigor," the other said. He was shorter and stockier, with a broad jaw and thick-rimmed glasses. "At the same time, however, there was significant hypostasis in his ankles and feet. That generally doesn't develop until livor mortis."

He shone his beam onto the victim's feet below the rope that bound them to the post. They were purple and swollen and shot through with black veins.

"Which means he was bound up there long enough for the blood to settle into his feet before he was killed," Mason said.

"Our best guess is somewhere between sixteen and twenty-four hours."

"Between ten P.M. and dawn, yesterday."

"And no one saw him?" Layne asked. "No one heard him calling for help?"

"There's a good reason for that."

The female investigator shone her light up toward the victim. Mason caught a blur of blue jeans, a flannel shirt, and a down vest before the beam settled on the dead man's face. His purplish tongue was engorged and protruded from his mouth. There was a black, necrotic laceration right down the middle. The corners of his lips pulled downward. His entire face was swollen and his eyes bulged beneath his heavy lids. The muscles in his cheeks sagged, as though a massive stroke had affected both sides.

"What the hell happened to him?"

"We haven't even had a chance to document the site yet," the female officer said. "When someone calls the terrorism hotline with a report of a suspicious-looking man wearing a vest, this isn't what you expect to find."

"We had to clear the area first," the stocky officer said. "Make sure there was no immediate chemical, explosive, or radiological threat before we could even get close."

"And you're certain there isn't?" Layne said.

"Nothing registered on the calorimetric array or the dosimeter."

"You would have been able to detect it if a chemical weapon had been employed on the victim, right?" Mason said.

"I can tell you right now, just by looking at him, that some sort of chemical was used on the poor bastard. The way both sides of his face droop like that? And the protrusion of his eyes? Those are acute physiological responses associated with toxins like BTX."

"Botulism?"

"That would be a safe guess based on the bilateral flaccid paralysis and certainly explain why no one could hear him, what with not being able to speak and all."

Mason turned on his own mini Maglite and used it to inspect the victim. His best guess was that the man was somewhere between sixty-five and eighty, although the facial deformities made it impossible to narrow that range. The overalls were ill fitting, dirty, and worn through at the knees. The bib, buckles, and flannel shirt were concealed beneath a down vest with feathers blooming from countless tears. He caught a glimpse of what almost looked like a fat quill, and then it was gone. It took several seconds for him to find it again.

"What's that right there?" he asked.

The female investigator stepped forward, climbed up onto the rock, and sifted through the feathers until she isolated a thin tube about half the width of a drinking straw. She carefully pulled on it until it slithered all the way out, revealing that it connected to . . . nothing. She patted down the vest. Stuck her fingers inside. Pulled on the fabric and shone her light into the stuffing.

"There has to be something . . ." Her words trailed off when she brought the tube close to the plastic shield over her face. She held it higher and studied the bottom, as though trying to look at the stars through it. "There's a bulb on the end. And some sort of fluid inside."

"What is it?" Layne asked.

"There's only one way to know for sure." She carried the tube to her evidence-collection kit and removed a small jar. "We have a GC-MS in the mobile lab. It shouldn't take more than half an hour to figure out what we're dealing with."

"But you're sure it's not a chemical warfare agent," Layne said.

"Trust me. If it were, you'd be dead by now."

"There's a cheery thought."

The evidence response specialist tipped the open end of the straw over the jar. A small amount of clear fluid drained out, barely enough to cover the bottom of the container. She upended it and gave it a gentle shake. A phlegmlike gob swelled from the opening and dropped into the water. It unraveled on the bottom into what looked like a pale worm with horizontal striations.

"Is that a tapeworm?" Layne asked.

"I could be wrong, but it looks an awful lot like the tentacle of a jellyfish," the female investigator said.

Mason shone his light up at the dead man's face—at his swollen tongue protruding from between his lips and the black erosion that resembled a split in a burned hot dog.

An ulcerous wound that had been inflicted by a venomous tentacle.

32

Mason watched the men from the medical examiner's office carry the body bag downhill through the trees, toward the path. Flashlight beams slashed through the underbrush as the forensics team fanned out into the woods, scouring the damp leaves and trampled weeds for evidence.

"This guy didn't just walk into the park dragging an unconscious man behind him," he said. "Someone would have seen him, regardless of how late at night."

"How many entrances to the park are there?" Layne asked.

"You can get in just about anywhere along the six-mile perimeter," Barbieri said.

"Security cameras?"

"Thirty-some inside the park itself and traffic cams at all of the surrounding intersections."

"Are there any blind spots?" Mason asked. "If you knew where the cameras were, could you transport an unconscious body into the park without being recorded?"

"Probably. There's a ton of forested areas. Especially along Central Park West. But this park even has its own police precinct. We're talking mounted and foot patrols, day and night."

"The victim could have lived nearby. Or maybe he took a walk along the same path every night. Our guy could have stalked him. Learned his routine. Picked this spot for the abduction and dragged him away from the path."

"There are no signs of a struggle anywhere around here," Barbieri said

"A guy with a background in chemistry wouldn't have much difficulty getting his hands on some chloroform. Or even making his own with some acetone and bleach."

"Regardless," Layne said, "he had to have entered the park at some point in time, either with the victim or by himself. If it was captured on film, we need to find it."

Mason climbed up onto the rock formation and knelt at the base of the cross. It was made from four-by-four fence posts. The first was wedged into a crevice, the bottom of which was filled with concrete. It had been formed with a square metal bracket large enough to insert the post, and so long ago that it had already collected a season's worth of dead leaves and pine needles. The second post had been bolted horizontally to the top of the first and stabilized with L-shaped brackets. The wood was scarred where the cords binding the victim had worried into the grain. At the wrists and shoulders. Around the chest, waist, and ankles.

"Accessing those cameras won't be a problem," Barbieri said. "Picking him out of the forty-some thousand people who enter this park on any given day without a physical description will be, though."

"What about the victim?" Layne said. "If we can isolate him and establish a pattern—"

"There's a reason he was subjected to an agent that would distort his features," Mason said. "Unless he walked in here looking like that, facial-recognition software is useless. If we knew his name, we could get a picture from his driver's license or social media accounts."

"It's just a matter of time," Barbieri said.

"Not the way things have been going for us lately," Layne replied.

Mason stood and pressed his back to the cross. Shone his light into the surrounding treetops.

"He had to have gotten these posts up here somehow," he said. "Carrying them into the park would have attracted attention. Check and see if there are any active construction sites within the boundaries of the park. If there are materials of any value out here, they're within range of a security camera."

"On it," Barbieri said. He turned and started barking orders into his two-way before he was even out of the clearing.

There was a tiny gap between the interwoven branches of the canopy where Mason could see a sliver of the concrete path downhill. It wasn't a clear view by any stretch of the imagination. He wouldn't have been able to describe anyone walking past, but he'd know someone was there. Within shouting range, if only he could raise his voice.

"The Scarecrow wanted his victim to cling to hope for as long possible," Mason said. "He wanted him to see the people walking past on the path. If any one of them had turned and looked into the forested area at just the right moment, they would have seen this guy looking back at them. He couldn't move and he couldn't talk, but he was conscious of everything going on around him. And inside him. Like the others, he knew he was dying."

"He recognized the point of no return."

"Exactly. He understood how the toxin worked and mentally checked off the symptoms. Botulism makes total sense. His vision would have become blurry and his speech slurred. His muscles would have grown weaker and weaker, until he couldn't control them at all. He wouldn't have been able to swallow. The mere act of breathing would have grown increasingly difficult, until he realized that if he didn't use the last of his strength to inhale from the straw, the suffering would be more than he could bear."

"So he took a big slurp of jellyfish stingers?"

"A means to end his suffering."

"What was he, allergic?" Layne asked. "I got stung as a kid. It hurts like you wouldn't believe, but it's not the kind of thing that's going to kill you."

"Catch," Mason said, and tossed her his phone.

While the ERT had been removing the body from the cross, he had, in addition to learning about the physiology of botulism, initiated a quick Internet search using the key words *jellyfish, venom,* and *Japan.* The results had been exactly what he expected. *Chironex yamaguchii.* Commonly known as *habu-kurage.* A species of box jellyfish found in the coastal waters surrounding Japan, and one of the most venomous life-forms on the planet, capable of causing respiratory failure and cardiac arrest within a matter of minutes.

Layne nearly dropped his phone when it vibrated in her hand. She held up the screen and read the caller ID.

"Southern Region Medical Examiner's Office."

"It's about time," Mason said. He was about to take the call, when he realized there was a commonality among the other crime scenes, a detail he had yet to find, but one that had to be around here somewhere. "Go ahead and answer it. Have Dr. Quarrels send the DNA profile to Locker. And give him a heads-up to let him know it's coming. Make sure he knows to drop everything and call us the moment he has a positive ID. I need to follow this line of thought and see where it leads me."

He grabbed one of the portable lights, which were about a hundred times brighter than his flashlight, shone it into the trees, and turned slowly in a circle as he visually scoured the branches from the lower canopy to the upper, searching the shadows for what he knew had to be there.

"It has to be around here somewhere."

"What does?" Layne asked. She returned his phone and craned her neck to follow the progress of the spotlight through the limbs of the densely needled cedars and skeletal sycamore and oak trees.

"The camera. The Scarecrow took a huge risk setting up right in the middle of Central Park. There's no way he could have walked away without seeing the payoff. He rigged the video surveillance behind the false wall at the end of the tunnel and sat either on that tree trunk behind the farmhouse or on top of the silo, watching those men suffer for days on end. He wouldn't have missed a single second of this guy's agony for anything in the world."

"This could just be a distraction to keep us occupied while he enacts whatever plan he has for the Novichok."

"True, but he also could have stood in this very spot, dispersed it with a remote-controlled drone he bought at any store, and wiped out the entire city."

"But by doing so, he'd risk dying with everyone else."

"I'm not convinced that's not his ultimate goal. The profile suggests he's selected a finite number of victims. Maybe he's no longer able to complete his design, but he can still make sure everyone on his list dies before he checks out."

"A mass murderer's bucket list?"

"That would be the logical culmination of both his personal and professional lives." Mason thought he saw something. He stopped turning and focused the light at the highest point among the trees. "Wait."

"What?"

"Grab Barbieri."

Mason gathered his bearings. The victim had been positioned facing to the west. He was currently shining the beam about ten degrees south of that bearing. It wouldn't have provided a perfect view of the man as he died, but it would have been more than good enough.

"What'd you find?" Barbieri asked.

"Climb up here. Next to me."

Mason scooted a few inches to his left, just far enough to make room for the other agent. Layne climbed higher on the formation, behind the cross.

"What's that over there?" Mason asked.

Barbieri leaned right up against him and aligned his line of sight with the beam.

"All I see are trees."

"Past them."

"I can't—"

"Keep looking at that same spot," Mason said. "Right between where those branches fork."

He switched off the light. The night sky limned the boughs with an almost ethereal glow. Beyond the canopy, at the very edge of sight, was the top corner of a skyscraper.

"Which building is that?" he asked.

Barbieri stood on his toes. Leaned from one side to the other to get a better look.

"Mayfair Towers," he said. "It's an apartment complex on Seventy-second. Half a block from Central Park West."

"We need to get inside that apartment," Mason said. "Assemble a tactical team. And do so quickly. If he's watching us, he knows we're coming."

33

"It's the penthouse apartment." Barbieri spoke into the microphone inside his tactical gas mask as they jogged up the stairwell of the thirty-six-story tower. His voice was loud in Mason's earpiece. "The owner's listed as Aegis Asset Management, a wholly owned subsidiary of Royal Nautilus Petroleum."

"The oil company?" Layne said. She was still trying to Velcro the straps of her Kevlar vest over her chest, a feat made even more difficult by the full-body CBRN outfit underneath it. The black GORE CHEMPAK tactical suits made them look like Imperial TIE fighter pilots from *Star Wars,* but they were Class 3–rated for protection from chemical, biological, and radiological threats. "Why would an oil company need an apartment?"

"Diversification? Executive compensation package? Half of these luxury apartments are owned by corporations or foreign nationals. One like this goes for upward of four million dollars."

Mason's heavy breathing echoed inside his mask. The visor narrowed his peripheral vision to an uncomfortable extent, making him feel like he was playing a first-person-shooter video game.

"Who's the registered occupant?" he asked.

"Charles Raymond. Managing director of Research and Development."

They rounded one bend after another, hot on the heels of the other tactical officers. The team was divided into four units, each consisting of four highly trained FBI SWAT officers. One ascended the south stairwell, the other the north. The third had already secured the main level, and the fourth was currently on a helicopter, preparing to rappel onto the roof of the building. From there, they could reach the private terrace surrounding the penthouse apartment, cover the back door, and prevent the Scarecrow from jumping down to one of the balconies of the units underneath it.

"What do we know about this guy Raymond?"

"Next to nothing at this point. Seventy-three years old. Divorced. Two adult children. Doctorate in mechanical engineering from Stanford. No criminal record."

"Military experience?"

"None that I'm aware of."

Layne glanced back at Mason as she hit the landing and launched herself up the next flight. The door to the thirty-fifth floor flashed past behind her. They'd been counting on the victim in the park being the owner of the suite and having a military background. Maybe the apartment had simply been the only one that offered the Scarecrow the view he needed and the body of Charles Raymond was waiting inside, although it couldn't be coincidence that this was now the second time they'd heard the name Royal Nautilus in conjunction with this case.

Two agents took up position at the top of the staircase, one on either side of the door. They examined the seams for trip wires while a third slid an articulating camera underneath the door and surveilled the hallway on a handheld monitor. There was a single elevator to the left, its surface a golden metal polished to reflect the light of the overhead fixture like the midday sun. The walls were hardwood-paneled, the floor marble. There was nothing between them and the opposite stairwell.

"South stairwell clear," the third man whispered through the earpiece.

"North stairwell clear," an unfamiliar voice whispered. "We go on my mark."

There was only one residential penthouse on the top floor. It was roughly 2,400 square feet and surrounded on two sides by a private L-shaped balcony. They'd enter into a blind foyer, with the entire suite to their right, at the end of a short corridor that terminated in a trident-shaped fork. To the left were the bedroom and bath. Straight ahead, the great room. To the right, the study and, beyond it, the narrow kitchen.

"Go."

An officer opened the door—slowly, carefully—and the others fell into formation, one behind the other. They converged on the apartment at the exact same time as the second team from the far stairwell. One of the men removed from his bag a compact through-wall radar unit that looked like a massive iPad with vertical handles. He ran it along the plaster to make sure there was no one lying in wait on the other side and then stepped back to make room for another officer, who used a crowbar to remove the trim around the door, revealing a half-inch gap metered by wooden spacers, between which they could see that the dead bolt wasn't engaged. There was no sign of trip wires or remote sensors, either.

The rubber sweep at the bottom of the door left just enough room for the tech specialist to feed the articulating camera underneath. He held up the monitor so they could all see while he turned the camera to look at the back side of the door. There was nothing connected to either the knob or the dead bolt, and the chain wasn't hooked. He turned the camera to view the corridor. To the left, a coat closet. Door closed. No apparent trip wires. To the right, a hallway with open thresholds on both sides and the aura of moonlight from the great room.

"Give me infrared," the voice in Mason's ear whispered.

The color on the screen turned a pale shade of green but didn't reveal any laser beams rigged across the hallway.

"You know your assignments," the team leader whispered. "Keep your eyes open and don't touch a goddamn thing. No heroes today. Are we clear?"

Mason raised his pistol and stepped into position to follow the men into the apartment. He sensed Layne at his right hip, felt the nerves radiating from her. Cleared his mind and concentrated on regulating his breathing. Time slowed to a crawl. He became acutely aware of everything around him.

He heard the order in his left ear as though from a great distance. The world around him sped up with the opening of the front door. He funneled through the doorway and into the narrow corridor.

The men in front of him moved like specters through the darkness, the fabric of their suits shimmering in the moonlight flooding through the wall of glass overlooking the park. Some veered left, others right. Mason led the remainder past the outer forks and into the great room. All of the furniture had been shoved to the sides, leaving the area rug in the middle of the room bare. The drapes had been torn down and cast aside. The entire rear wall was composed of windows that granted a spectacular view of the city skyline through the railing along the terrace. The silhouettes of their external penetration team darted past on their way to the lone outside egress, around the corner to the right, near the kitchen.

A telescope had been mounted on a tripod right against the glass and angled down toward the park. It was two and a half feet long, with a barrel easily eight inches wide. While Mason knew little about such things, he figured it must have had some impressive magnification. More than enough to get a good close-up of the man staked to the cross in the distant park.

Voices erupted from the earpiece.

"Bedroom clear."

"Study clear."

"Kitchen clear."

"Terrace clear."

"Something's not right," Mason said. The Scarecrow had outthought them every step of the way. Every move he'd made had been carefully planned and executed. He'd led them here for a reason, and based on everything Mason knew about him, that reason was to simultaneously flaunt his brilliance and attempt to derail their investigation. He'd led them here to kill them all. "He wouldn't have left without arming whatever trap he'd set for us."

"I agree," Layne said. "We're missing something."

Mason tried to put himself inside the Scarecrow's head. He would have anticipated the tactical units coming in from both the front door and the terrace. To inflict maximum damage, he would have wanted them all in the same place at the same time. He liked the killings to be intimate in proportion, yet devastating in their ferocity.

Mason ducked out of the living room and slipped past the other men into the bedroom. Again, the rear wall was composed entirely of windows, through which the pale glow of moonlight passed. There were no photographs on the nightstand, nothing of an even remotely personal nature. The bed was perfectly made and the walk-in closet stood open. Shirts on one side, suit jackets on the other.

"Maybe we got here faster than he anticipated and didn't give him enough time to set a trap," Layne said. She followed Mason across the hallway and into the study. The furniture was leather, the lighting recessed. A bookcase adorned with tomes that appeared to have been chosen for aesthetic value dominated one wall; another was nearly concealed behind a monolithic flat-screen TV. A vase of withering flowers and a marble statue of a reclining nude sat on the glass coffee table. "Surely we would have seen it by now if he had."

The kitchen was on the other side of the bookcase. The countertops were bare and the stainless-steel appliances sparkling clean. Mason resisted the urge to check the drawers and cabinets and passed the terrace door, which the fourth team had left open, admitting the night air and the constant din of traffic.

"The false wall in the tunnel looked different from the others," Mason said. "He'd known we'd eventually recognize it, but he'd expected us to just knock it down, which would have triggered the motion detector and released enough Novichok to kill us all. He'd rigged the IED to the door at the farmhouse for the same reason. Whether or not we found the bodies in the cornfield, he knew that if we'd tracked him that far, when no one answered the front door, we'd try to open it, and—*boom*—no more investigators."

"So what's obvious here?" Layne asked. "What stands apart from everything else?"

The answer hit him squarely in the face.

He turned to his left, toward the great room. The majority of the agents were gathered in there, near where the telescope sat on its tripod. All by itself.

Barbieri stepped away from the others. Leaned closer to the eyepiece, pressed his mask against it.

Mason heard the click from across the room.

"What the hell?" Barbieri said. He brought his eye away from the lens. "I can't even see—"

"Down!" Mason shouted, and tackled Layne through the open door leading onto the terrace.

The explosion tore through the room and everyone in it. A fist of fire hit Mason from behind and hurled him across the tiled balcony. Glass exploded outward like buckshot. He lost his grip on Layne, then visual on her as the churning smoke overtook them.

His back struck the railing.

Layne collided with him a split second later.

The railing tore from its moorings with a metallic screech.

Mason felt it give, then lean outward over the nothingness.

He wrapped his arms around Layne. Tried to roll away from the railing as it toppled backward over the roofline and plummeted toward the street. He heard it crash onto something behind and below them.

Flames raced across the terrace.

A wave of superheated air buffeted them over the edge.

And into the open air.

34

A sinking sensation in the pit of his stomach.

Weightlessness.

Wind whistling past his ears.

A solid mass of fire raced out over the rooftop and across the sky overhead.

Mason caught a glimpse of the building across the street from the corner of his eye, its windows rushing upward.

The bricks to the other side of him were a blur.

He pulled Layne tightly against him. If he could absorb the brunt of the fall, then maybe she might survive—

Impact.

Parallel bars bit into the muscles of his back. Bent. What little breath he'd managed to inhale on the way down burst past his lips.

He toppled forward and lost his grip on Layne. Tumbled down the fallen railing, bounced from the balcony, and slammed into the thick glass door of the apartment below Raymond's.

Came to rest.

Mason pushed himself to his hands and knees. Struggled to recapture his breath. Felt the pressure in his chest break and air flood into his lungs.

"Layne!"

She lay facedown on the concrete, her gas mask broken, her eyes closed. Her entire face was black with soot and glistened with blood. She groaned and tried to rise. Failed. Bared her teeth in determination and tried again. Managed to roll onto her right hip.

Mason knelt beside her and helped prop her up against the wall beside the door leading into the apartment. They'd landed on its balcony, which was maybe fifteen feet long but only five feet deep. The railing that had fallen from the roof was bent nearly in half and folded over the side.

A car alarm blared from the street far below them. Sirens erupted in the distance.

"Are you all right?" he asked.

Layne thrust out her hand in response. He grabbed it and helped her to her feet. She staggered to the edge of the balcony and leaned out over West Seventy-second Street, thirty-five stories below. Stepped back and closed her eyes. Breathed out a long, slow sigh of relief.

Smoke still gushed from the roofline above them, but there was no sign of flames.

Mason grabbed the doorknob, which turned easily in his hand and opened into the great room. There was no furniture. The floor was hardwood and the walls were bare. He was about to conclude that it was empty when he detected a flickering light from the corner of his eye.

"We have to get back up there!" Layne said.

"Go," Mason said. "I'll be right behind you."

She limped past him, hit the hallway, and rushed for the front door.

Mason followed the source of the light around the corner and into the bedroom. Blackout curtains covered the windows. The closet doors stood open, revealing deep shadows. There was no furniture. Only a telescope that lay shattered in the corner, a TV mounted to the wall, and a mat made of woven straw underneath it. The power was on and the screen was divided into quadrants. The bottom two were uniformly black, while the upper two were gray and marred by a wavering glow. He recognized what he was seeing as smoke when a man's silhouette passed through it, clearing a passage, through which he caught a momentary glimpse of a bed and a nightstand. The quadrant beside it

looked nearly identical, only the wall underneath the camera was actively burning. He deciphered the outline of the reclining nude on the
coffee table.

The television was just bright enough to illuminate the photographs covering every inch of the wall surrounding it. They all featured
the same man in various poses, never once looking at the camera. On
the street. In the park. Getting into a Town Car. Through the window of
a restaurant. His eyes were scratched out in every one of them.

"Jesus," Mason whispered. And then it hit him. "The Scarecrow
was right underneath our feet."

He sprinted out of the room, down the hallway, through the front
door, and into the main hallway. The recessed ceiling fixtures snapped
off and the dim red emergency lights came on. The fire alarm blared.

The door across the hall opened and a terrified woman peeked out.

"Did you see anyone come out of this apartment?" he shouted.

"No one's been there in a month. What's going on?"

He pressed the button for the elevator a dozen times, but it didn't
light up. It must have shut down automatically when the emergency
systems kicked on.

"Where's the nearest emergency exit?"

She pointed past him down the hallway. He turned and raced
toward the closed door at the end. Burst through it into the stairwell.
Grabbed the railing. Jumped down to the landing. Careened from the
wall. Propelled himself down to the next floor.

Mason pressed the button on the side of his mask to open the main
communication channel.

"Cover every exit from the building," he said. "He's heading down
one of the stairwells right now. Make sure he doesn't get out!"

The only response was a faint hum of static from his earpiece.

He cleared the stairs two at a time. Used the railings to swing
around the landings. One floor after another. The bottom was so far
down, he couldn't even see it.

The door to the thirty-second floor opened and he barely avoided
slamming into the man entering the stairwell. Gray hair. Pajamas. Slip-
pers and a robe. A woman behind him, silk nightie, eyes wide.

He blew past them and tried his comlink again.

"Can anybody hear me?"

The explosion must have damaged his transceiver. He couldn't even hear his own voice through the speaker.

Walls blurred past. People emerged from the doorways leading to the floors, all wearing hurriedly assembled outfits and matching expressions of confusion and terror.

"Coming through," Mason said, and wove between them.

One landing after another. He hurdled the railing and jumped across the gap to get past an elderly couple. Dodged a woman carrying a fluffy dog with a pink bow. Thundered all the way to the bottom. Shouldered open the door and emerged into an enclosed courtyard backing onto Seventy-third Street. There was debris everywhere. Police cruisers screeched to the curb, painting the growing crowd in swirling shades of red and blue.

Mason fought his way through it and sprinted toward a black Yukon with government plates, which skidded to the curb and bounced up onto the sidewalk. An agent wearing an FBI windbreaker and ball cap was halfway out the door before he even killed the engine. He brought a portable transceiver to his lips and cocked his head up toward the smoke roiling into the night sky.

"Seal off the building!" Mason shouted.

An ambulance screamed down the street toward them. A fire truck converged from the opposite direction, going the wrong way down the one-way street.

The agent turned toward him, reached for his weapon, and nearly drew it before recognizing a fellow agent beneath the soot.

"What the hell happened up there?"

Mason snatched the transceiver from his grasp and pressed the button.

"This is Special Agent James Mason. Badge number victor-tango-alpha-zero-one-one-two-nine-six-three-two-three. I need the Mayfair Towers sealed off right now. No one leaves the premises."

"There are over four hundred apartments in that building," the dispatcher said. "We can't contain every single occupant."

"We already have officers in place directing evacuees to the nearest shelters," the agent said.

"Then round them up. None of them gets out of here until I say so."

"We have to move everyone to a safe distance until we know the structural integrity of the complex hasn't been compromised."

Policemen were already breaking up the crowd in the courtyard and leading them out onto the street, where even more people congregated on the sidewalks. Some walked, others ran, but most stayed where they were and aimed their cell phones at the top of the tower. An officer in a yellow reflective vest guided a group of people out from the courtyard on the far side of the building, presumably from the opposite stairwell.

Mason watched helplessly as they dispersed.

An NYPD helicopter thundered across the sky and hovered above the penthouse, its spotlight sweeping the roofline.

Firefighters and paramedics raced past. Pushed through the throngs disgorging from the stairwell.

A news crew took up position across the street and started filming.

The residents around Mason were little more than silhouettes dissipating into the shadows. For all he knew, the Scarecrow was long gone. Then again, he could have been standing mere feet away and Mason wouldn't have recognized him.

He tore off his mask and spiked it on the ground in frustration.

"Get me the footage from every camera that records so much as a single floor of this building," he said, and thrust the transceiver into the agent's chest. "One of them must have captured him."

35

Mason and Layne worked their way through what was left of the penthouse apartment while emergency response team agents in white jumpsuits took photographs and collected evidence. The windows were all gone, the support posts between them charred and smoldering. Mounds of rubble filled the great room. The furniture had burned to the charcoaled framework and bare springs. Mistlike spatters of blood decorated the walls. Metal fragments from the rigged telescope were embedded in what was left of the scorched ceiling.

The other rooms had survived relatively unscathed, along with the agents who'd been inside them when the bomb went off. The eight men within the blast radius, however, had been killed instantly. The tube of the telescope had served to funnel the blast, blowing straight through the men and the upper half of the wall behind them. The agents in the study and the kitchen had been peppered with shrapnel but were going to recover, thanks to Layne and the officers from the bedroom, who'd dragged them out into the hallway.

The IED had been shaped to inflict the most visceral damage possible to those within a relatively narrow blast radius. Had it been designed to explode outward in all directions, Mason and Layne would have been killed with the others, rather than hurled over the edge of the thirty-sixth-floor terrace, five hundred feet above the ground.

The lead ERT agent caught up with them and led them out onto the balcony. Despite the police lights flashing from the street below them, the remainder of the city remained dark and oblivious.

"We found traces of ammonium nitrate, ethyl alcohol, nitromethane, and powdered aluminum," the woman said. She was short and pale, which made her freckles stand out like beacons. "In the hands of a skilled chemist or a munitions expert, those are the ingredients one would use to make homemade C-4."

"Where can you buy those supplies?" Layne asked. "Maybe someone working there will be able to remember him and give us a physical description."

"The ammonium nitrate can be prilled from most common fertilizers. You can get the alcohol from an auto-parts store and the rest from any college chemistry lab."

"What about the detonator?" Mason asked.

"We haven't found any traces of it, but the way you described how it worked, he could have easily made it himself from a doorbell, some nichrome wire, and a lithium-ion battery."

"So that's a dead end," Layne said.

"Not necessarily. He didn't make the explosive here and we found no traces of the chemicals in the apartment below us. Homemade C-4 doesn't have the same shelf life as weapons-grade plastic explosives. It's the kind of thing you want to use pretty much right after making it, which means his base of operations can't be too far from here. Definitely in the city."

"Who owns the apartment downstairs?" Mason asked.

"A company called Maledict Management Services."

"Never heard of it."

"I thought you might have, since its corporate headquarters is in Colorado and the IRS is currently investigating it for fraud."

Mason connected the dots. During the hunt for the Hoyl, he'd stumbled upon a criminal enterprise that incorporated hundreds of fictitious companies, created verifiable histories for them, and set them up on shelves to age like bottles of wine.

Maledict must have been one of them.

"It's a shelf company," Mason said. "Does it own any other properties?"

"Not anywhere around here."

"The woman across the hall said she hadn't seen anyone in the apartment downstairs in a month."

"Your guys are conducting the interviews. All I can say is, the evidence doesn't support that observation."

"Someone must have seen him, then."

"You'd think so, wouldn't you?"

"Let us know if you find anything else," Mason said. "Anything at all."

She nodded and walked back into what was left of the great room.

"That wasn't very helpful," Layne said.

"Maybe not, but it supports our theory that the Scarecrow has some amount of military experience. Get ahold of your contact at army CIC and see what you can do about expediting the personnel list of everyone who was involved with the production and decommission of its chemical arsenal. And while you're at it, find out if they have anything on the guy who lived here. Charles Raymond. The Scarecrow targeted him specifically and stalked him for what looks like months, judging by the pictures."

Despite the victim's facial deformities, identification had been a piece of cake, thanks to a birthmark on Raymond's temple that appeared in just about every picture ever taken of him.

"Why kill him here when he could be made to suffer for days on end in the middle of nowhere, like the others?" Layne asked. "The Scarecrow was lucky to get a single day in a place like this. Even with as well as he chose the location."

"We must have discovered the victims in the cornfield too soon and forced him to enact a fallback plan he already had in place," Mason said.

"What makes you say that?"

"He poured the concrete for that post bracket at least a year ago, and think how long it must have taken to secure the apartment underneath the victim's."

"He has to have been planning this for years."

"Maybe even longer," Mason said. "I can't shake the feeling that this all goes back to the army. We need that personnel list."

"I'll follow up with my contact," Layne said. "And one of us had better update Algren, too."

"You handle the calls and I'll set up a meeting with the woman who lived across the hall from the Scarecrow. She must have gotten a good look at him at some point and ought to be able to provide a physical description, if nothing else. Maybe your guy will come through and she'll be able to ID him from the personnel files."

"It's worth a shot."

"I should also grab a couple of rooms," he said. "There's a hotel a block over, on Seventy-first. We're going to have to sleep sometime, and we could probably use a base of operations for the time being."

"I'll call you if I find out anything," Layne said.

Mason nodded and headed back through the ruined penthouse suite. While he wanted nothing more than to scrub off the soot under a hot shower, it would have to wait. What he needed most right now was some time on his own. Until he was completely convinced that Layne hadn't been compromised, like his two previous partners, there were certain aspects of the investigation he needed to keep to himself— namely, his sources. With Homeland actively attempting to prevent the release of the autopsies of the victims in the cornfield and dragging its feet on providing the names of the men who'd served in the chemical corps, he was going to have to find a way to work around them, especially if he wanted to figure out why they were obstructing the investigation.

There was only one man he knew who might be able to help him find out the truth and, fortunately, he was already expecting Mason's call.

36

On his way to the hotel, Mason arranged an interview with the woman from the apartment across the hall from the one the Scarecrow had used to surveil Charles Raymond. He'd already logged into the secure virtual conference room by the time he reached his room on the tenth floor, alerting Johan to his arrival. If Gunnar had piqued the old man's curiosity about the nature of the call as well as he thought he had, then Mason wouldn't have to wait very long. In fact, he'd barely set down his laptop on the small table when the screen brightened and Johan appeared on the monitor, wearing a fuzzy blue bathrobe over linen pajamas. His eyes were bloodshot from lack of sleep. The corner of his mouth twitched, betraying his impatience.

Mason wished they were having this conversation in person. There was so much he wanted to know and even more he didn't yet know to ask, but right now, there was specific information he needed from this man and he didn't have the time or patience to jump through hoops to get it.

"Hello again, my young friend," Johan said. "I must confess I am somewhat perplexed as to why you insisted upon meeting again so soon, and under such auspicious circumstances. To what do I owe this rather unexpected pleasure?"

"I need answers and I've encountered an extreme amount of resistance trying to get them," Mason said.

"I am flattered that you think I might be of assistance and, of course, I will help you in any way that I can."

"What do you know about Novichok agents?"

Johan raised his brows, as though mildly surprised.

"I am only peripherally aware of the attempts of the Soviet Union to improve upon the foundation laid by German scientists."

"This version in particular—A-234—is an upgrade of sarin that makes it not only chemically stable but persistent in both liquid and gaseous forms."

"Are you certain we are dealing with one based upon sarin and not one of the other G-series agents? Think carefully. The answer is of great consequence. We do not wish to find ourselves following the wrong trail."

Mason thought of the whiteboards in Johan's archives that had displayed the pictures of the woman in black and the shadowed figure. The answer to this very question likely determined which one of them was waiting at the end of that trail. The former led to Colonia Dignidad in Chile via a network of ratlines, the latter to the dissolution of Unit 731 and the eventual formation of a cult that had launched a chemical attack on the Japanese parliament, a cult he was beginning to believe had given rise to a man who thought of himself as the Scarecrow. A man who'd never been photographed as more than a silhouette among the shadows, spawned from the residua of an organization without conscience or compassion, a vile entity responsible for the horrific medical experimentation resulting in the deaths of thousands of prisoners of war. A man who now had access to enough Novichok A-234 to extinguish all life on the planet and the willingness to use it.

"There's no doubt in my mind," he said.

"Have you seen it with your own eyes?"

Mason didn't reply.

"Then we must proceed with alacrity," Johan said. "I fear we might already be too late."

"What do you know?"

Johan sighed and settled back into his seat.

"I told you about my great-uncle Wilhelm, who worked as a chemist for IG Farben, the German industrial conglomerate that developed the Zyklon gas used to kill millions of my people in the concentration camps. He was part of a team that developed a pesticide that demonstrated applications above and beyond the mere extermination of insects, as he ultimately learned for himself. It was shipped off to the German Army Weapons Office, along with the other chemicals that were rushed into mass production and would come to be known as the G-series agents—tabun, sarin, soman, and cyclosarin—stockpiles of which were estimated to have reached as much as ten tons."

"If Hitler had weapons that deadly at his disposal, why didn't he use them?" Mason asked.

"Not for lack of want, I assure you. Some speculate it was because of the indiscriminate manner by which they kill, but considering his willingness to send his own troops to the slaughter, I refute any theories of conscience. I believe he had a plan, but he simply ran out of time. His development department was on the verge of perfecting the V-2 rocket, which was rumored to be able to reach even our distant shores. Had the tides of war not turned when they did, he would have wiped out his opposition from afar and paved the way for the conquest of Asia and the Americas."

"So the war ended and there were ten tons of chemical weapons just sitting around, waiting for someone to take them?"

"You would think so, would you not? And yet there is no record to indicate what happened to those stores, one way or the other. It is rumored the Soviets took them. As you must know, by the end of the war, ours was an uneasy alliance at best. The fate of those weapons, however, is of no consequence in the grand design. Now that everyone had the recipe, the former Allies could simply go back home and begin manufacturing it for themselves. Which is precisely what we did. After all, the most effective weapon is the one everyone has. The fear of reprisals—mutually assured destruction—obviates its use. Hence, the need to tinker with the formula to improve upon the design."

Mason recalled the question his father had posed: *If you wanted to make something like that, who would you hire to do it?* That was the question at the very heart of the investigation, the answer to which the DHS seemed desperate to prevent them from learning, the reason why it had attempted to conceal the results of the autopsies of the victims in the cornfield, why it had so desperately needed Locker to identify the dead men from behind the wall, and why it had yet to provide the list of military personnel with working knowledge of the production of chemical weapons.

It feared that the Scarecrow was one of its own.

"Who was responsible for its manufacture? Where does someone find the kind of men willing to produce Nazi-designed weapons of mass destruction?"

Johan blinked several times and for a moment appeared genuinely confused.

"You mean you do not know?"

Mason did his best to maintain a neutral expression.

"The same Nazis who were making it over there," Johan said. "The very same ones who devoted their lives to exterminating every Jew on the planet. We brought them back to America with us. You must understand that our country did not enter the First World War as the global force it is today. We celebrated our victory in that war by roaring through the twenties and colonizing within our borders. Europe, on the other hand, was faced with the daunting task of rebuilding. Cities lay in ruin. Entire populations were displaced. All around these people were signs of death and destruction. It wasn't enough to defeat a momentarily re-united Germany; it needed to be ground beneath their collective heel."

"All while millions were dying from the Spanish flu," Mason said. "Just so the companies holding the patent for the cure could make billions."

"And billions more could be stolen from Germany, or at least that's how its citizens perceived it. While their fathers and brothers were still rotting in the fields and trenches, the victors began systematically dismantling their country. They were stripped of their colonies and saddled with prohibitive sanctions. Their perceived oppressors, aided by 'evil' Jewish bankers, imposed crippling financial reparations. When they were unable to pay, what little they owned was taken from them."

Mason glanced at his watch. He was already running late. Layne was going to have to interview the woman from the apartment across the hall from the Scarecrow's without him.

"An entire generation was raised in poverty and steeped in resentment," Johan said. "It was only natural that it had a twenty-year head start on the rest of us when it came to preparing for what it considered a war to reunify the Germanic peoples, a Second World War we easily could have—and probably should have—lost. We could not allow ourselves to be caught off guard again, especially with the Communist tide rising over Eastern Europe. So we set about building an arsenal the likes of which the world had never known."

It was strange that Johan could talk about the prewar Germans in an almost sympathetic manner, even while actively hunting Nazi war criminals and anyone who might have aided them along the way. Mason supposed it was all a matter of choices, and theirs had placed them on a collision course with an assassin with a .22, a camera, and a sack of worthless coins.

"Two decades is an eternity in an arms race," Johan said. "We had tanks and planes, but that was nothing compared to intercontinental rockets and weapons of mass destruction. We could not smuggle them out of Germany under the noses of the Soviets, so instead, we collected the scientists and engineers who designed and built them. We struck a deal with the devil under the guise of Operation Paperclip and seemingly overnight went from lagging behind to leading the race toward Armageddon."

"What does this have to do with what's happening now?" Mason asked.

"Everything," Johan said. He grew increasingly animated as he talked. "We offered amnesty to murderers responsible for the deaths of millions from the safety of their offices and labs and executed their minions at Nuremberg. We brought them to America and they picked right up where they'd left off. In exchange for citizenship, they gave us the fields of nuclear chemistry and atomic physics. We granted them safe passage to and from both Germany and Argentina, and they reciprocated with uranium enrichment and NASA. They gave us the advanced technology of their air force, and we delivered it into the hands of Lockheed and Martin Marietta. We welcomed the enemy into our midst and built our entire scientific and military infrastructure around them!"

Mason was familiar with Operation Paperclip. There'd been plenty of recognizable public figures among its organizers—like James Forrestal, the first secretary of defense, and Sheldon Boscage, grandfather of a future president—and even more among the recruits. Walter Dornberger, a major general in the Luftwaffe, had developed guided and air-to-surface missiles for the U.S. Air Force. Wernher von Braun, a major in the SS, who'd helped design the V-2 rocket, had used his expertise to help land the first men on the moon. Reinhard Gehlen, a Wehrmacht lieutenant general, and his network of spies had been integrated into the CIA to keep tabs on the Soviets.

"The marriage of Paperclip and the armed forces birthed the facilities at Fort Detrick—home of the U.S. Army Medical Research Institute of Infectious Diseases and the National Interagency Confederation for Biological Research—from which sprung specialized installations all across the country, including one of the largest chemical weapons manufacturing sites in the world, within miles of downtown Denver."

"I've lived in Colorado my entire life," Mason said. "I'd know if that were the case."

"You've been to the airport, haven't you?"

"Of course."

"All of that land from Commerce City to DIA was once the Rocky Mountain Arsenal, a secured base responsible for the production and warehousing of the majority of the country's chemical arsenal. Around the turn of the century, it was designated a Superfund site by the Environmental Protection Agency, which remediated it and transformed it into a wildlife refuge—at least the parts that aren't still hazardous—but it was only one of many, most of which are still in use today, in one capacity or another."

"So for the better half of the last century, if you were in the market for someone with ready access to or working knowledge of the manufacture of chemical weapons of mass destruction, you could have found him within shouting distance of the Capitol Building."

"Among other places, but you obviously see my point. It would not be difficult to find someone with practical experience making sarin if you had connections within the military-industrial complex."

"Then if I were looking for someone to help mass-produce a large volume of sarin to serve as a precursor to A-234, then odds are that someone served at one of these installations."

"If you were in the market for a professional anyway," Johan said. "Now, young James, I have told you everything I know. I beseech you do the same."

Mason nodded and carefully composed his words.

"During my pursuit of the Hoyl, I encountered a room inside the slaughterhouse filled with metal vats like the kind microbreweries use. Huge stainless-steel models. Maybe twenty of them, each capable of holding roughly two hundred gallons. Any one of them—maybe even all of them—could have been filled with Novichok."

Johan closed his eyes, took a deep breath, and blew it out slowly. Mason could almost see the gears turning as the old man worked the mental calculations.

"Thank you, James. I was aware of the vats recovered from the rubble, but I knew nothing of their intended function. What about the victims you discovered inside the tunnel?"

"They'd been dead for roughly twenty years," Mason said.

"I find that hard to believe, considering the history of the building."

"The date can be easily corroborated."

"You have an actual date?"

"November twenty-fourth, 2001."

Johan furrowed his brow and glanced to his left, an instinctive re-action to searching through the part of the brain associated with the recall of specific information.

"You recognize that date, don't you?" Mason said.

"I have given you what you need, James. And you, in return, have given me much to contemplate. I regret that I must retire in order to do so. The hour is late and my mind is not as sharp as it once was."

Johan's eyes grew distant, as though he'd already terminated the call before physically reaching for his computer to do so.

Mason stared at the blank screen while he sorted through what he'd learned.

They desperately needed those military personnel files.

There was no doubt in his mind that the identity of the Scarecrow was hidden somewhere within them.

37

Layne was waiting underneath the aluminum awning outside the main lobby of the Mayfair Towers when he arrived.

"What the hell took you so long?" she asked. "I had to interview the lady from across the hall without you."

"It took longer than I'd anticipated to get the rooms," Mason said. "What did she have to say?"

Layne cocked her head and stared at him for several seconds, as though deciding whether or not his story held water.

"She thought his first name was Ichiro, although she only ever called him Mr. Nakamura on the rare occasions she encountered him in the building."

"Nakamura?" he said. He felt the ground shift beneath his feet. He'd seen that name before. On the screen grab of the whiteboard in Johan's basement. The shadowed figure connected to Unit 731. "Are you sure?"

"Yeah. Why?"

"It's nothing. Keep going."

"Apparently, he only lived in that apartment a few months out of the year, a week or so at a time. She said he was very respectful and always wore a suit with an overcoat, a fedora, and dark glasses. Not sunglasses, but tinted glasses, as though he were sensitive to even indoor lighting."

"Could she give you a physical description?"

Layne removed her notebook from her jacket pocket and flipped through the pages until she found the right one.

"Asian-American. Late forties to early fifties. Somewhere around five five or five six in height. No facial hair, scars, or tattoos. Thin frame. She didn't think he could have weighed more than one twenty and described his manner as being almost effeminate."

"Not the mold one would cast for a military man."

"That's why I wasn't overly surprised when she failed to identify him from the photographic lineup I put together from the personnel files for the Chemical Corps."

"Your army contact came through?"

"Do you not check your messages? Yeah, he came through. Unfortunately, the list only goes back to the mid-eighties, but Locker's team was able to weed out the deceased and put together a list of the scientists who'd worked directly with sarin, those of Asian origin, and a subset of both. The older files have to be physically pulled from the National Archives in St. Louis, so that'll take time."

"Which we don't have."

"I also talked to Algren," Layne said. "Her plane just touched down at JFK. A car's supposed to pick her up on the tarmac and take her to the New York Field Office. She wants us to get there as soon as we can."

"Did you tell her what happened here?"

"Seems like she knows more about it than we do, but she did say she was glad we were all right."

"No, really."

"She said we should have been more careful. We could have used whatever evidence might have been inside the apartment."

"That sounds more like her."

Mason's stealth phone vibrated against his hip. He knew exactly who was calling, if not why it had taken him so long.

"Why don't you check in with forensics one last time while I go get the car," he said. Layne nodded and headed back into the apartment building. He waited until she was out of sight before answering. "I found Nakamura."

"Does he have anything to do with the men in white suits crawling all over the scorched roof of the building behind you?" Gunnar asked.

Mason looked up into the sky, where the first hint of dawn stained the clouds a pale shade of pink, and toward the distant satellite his old friend had obviously hacked into.

"He knew we were coming and had an IED waiting for us," he said.

"I'll take another crack at the name. Maybe I'll have better luck approaching the search from a different angle. What've you got?"

"The apartment he was living in is registered to a company called

Maledict Management Services and the woman across the hall thought his first name was Ichiro."

"I'm on it."

"You saw the pictures on Johan's whiteboard," Mason said. "We need to take this guy off the board before it's too late."

"You're certain he's the Scarecrow."

"Without a doubt, but I'm no closer to catching him than I was before," Mason said. "Tell me you had better luck with the dead guys from the tunnel."

"You weren't kidding when you said information was going to disappear," Gunnar said. "Even with my not inconsiderable skill set, I was only able to find seven occurrences. That's all. And they're probably gone by now, too."

Mason found a relatively private spot behind the tree-lined retaining wall of the adjacent apartment complex, away from the commotion.

"I'll take what I can get," he said.

"You don't have much choice in the matter," Gunnar said. "My program didn't have time to run through the whole protocol. Fortunately, I initiated it to search both faces together before searching for each individually. I figured that would get us the most useful information the fastest. And it's a good thing, too. With as quickly as Homeland moved, we might not have gotten them at all."

"Are you certain it was the DHS?"

"This was professional work, Mace. We're talking military-grade hackers or cyberwarfare experts."

"So what did you find?"

"The first picture is from June seventh, 1989. The Fourth Annual Global Symposium of the Society of Clinical Microbiologists and Virologists in Stockholm. Our guys stand apart from the crowd. Chenhav has a disproportionately large head and Mosche has eyebrows so big and bushy, he probably only wears glasses to keep them out of his eyes."

"What are they doing?"

"What every other human being on the planet does at a professional convention," Gunnar said. "They appear to be networking and getting hammered."

"Keep going."

"November 1991. A group photo taken at a conference of the Israel Medical Association. All you can see are their faces. There's another picture from the same event. Mosche is front and center, with a woman identified as Dr. Lirit Har-Even, vice president of the IMA. Chenhav's in the background. There's really not much to work with in either of these."

"There has to be something useful or it wouldn't have been worth the trouble to erase them."

"Here's an interesting one. August 1994. The Twentieth Assembly of the Society for Lasting International Peace in Copenhagen." He paused. "Didn't your grandfather found SLIP?"

"Great-grandfather. More important, why would a microbiologist and a biochemist be there? What are they doing in the picture?"

"Just standing there. Five men smiling for the camera. I'll read you the caption. 'Leading the charge for the global transition to a new energy-based economy and socialized health-care model: Dr. Nitzan Chenhav, World Medical Association; Andreas Mikkelson, managing director of Royal Nautilus Petroleum; Dr. Yossi Mosche, secretary of the International Supplement and Pharmaceutical Standardization Organization; Stephen Whitner, CEO Ford Motor Company; and Lyle Amendola, U.S. congressman from Pennsylvania.'"

"That's the second time I've heard the name Royal Nautilus tonight alone."

"In what capacity?"

"One of its subsidiaries is listed as the owner of a penthouse apartment of significant interest at the moment."

"What's the name?" Gunnar asked.

"Aegis Asset Management."

"Give me a second." Headlights approached from the distance. Mason leaned against the gray brick facade and settled into the shadows. "Aegis lists more than two thousand properties among its assets, fifty of them in New York City alone. Looks like your standard corporate real estate management firm, the kind of operation massive international companies set up in every country to handle their physical holdings, as their total assets are too large and diverse for a single entity."

"Nothing out of the ordinary?"

"At least not superficially. Of course, it was another of Nautilus's subsidiaries that lost potentially thousands of pounds of hydrogen fluoride, so I'll definitely have to dig deeper."

"What about the SLIP conference?" Mason asked. "You know how that kind of thing works. What do you read into the picture as it pertains to the two Israelis?"

"The photo reeks of a PR photo op for Royal Nautilus and Ford," Gunnar said. "You know, to show they're committed to the idea of renewable energy, despite the crushing financial impact it will have on both of them. If there's something else, I don't see it."

A pair of unmarked black Tahoes pulled up and parked against the curb opposite the Mayfair, but no one got out.

"What's the next instance?" Mason asked.

"New York City. May 1995. Economic Strategy Conference of the U.S.-Israel Science and Technology Alliance. I'm familiar with these guys. Their goal is to improve Israel's economic stake in the global market by making long-term arrangements with a bunch of American-based multinational corporations to locate and maintain research and development facilities in Tel Aviv. I don't think there's anything nefarious about this one, either. All I have here is our two scientists in the background of someone else's photo. Uncredited."

"Two more, right?"

"The United Nations Summit on Sustainable Population Growth. Bonn, Germany, 1999. Mosche shaking hands with some UN official wearing a fancy medal. Chenhav standing behind him, like he's waiting in line. The caption's in German. 'Top Israeli scientists receive award from Mr. Lothar Schubert, under-secretary-general for the General Assembly, for their commitment to stable population design.' That's a literal translation. I assume they mean 'population models.'"

"If they were looking for ways to curb population growth, nerve gas would be a good way to get it done in a hurry."

"I'm pretty confident the UN doesn't sanction the indiscriminate extermination of millions of people."

"There has to be something there, though. It's right in the wheelhouse of both the Hoyl and the Scarecrow. What's the last one?"

"May eighth, 2000. Saint-Tropez, French Riviera. The World

Congress on Chemical, Biological, Radiological, and Nuclear Threat and Terrorism."

"Finally." Mason couldn't get a good look through the tinted windows at the men in the SUVs, but he had a pretty good idea who they were. "What's in the picture?"

"A couple of pale white guys on a beach in polo shirts and khakis. Both wearing sunglasses. Chenhav has a really big hat. Very formal for the weather. Behind them is a row of hotels. I recognize the Château de la Messardière. Our guys are just sitting at a table, looking serious. That's all."

"There has to be something else."

"You're welcome to look for yourself."

"Don't send them to me directly," Mason said. "It looks like I'm going to be working under a whole lot more supervision."

The doors of the Tahoes opened in unison and agents climbed out of both front seats. They wore navy fatigues and bulletproof vests. Mason recognized the two DHS agents he'd seen near Raymond's body in Central Park as they passed underneath the awning and headed into the lobby of the Mayfair.

"Do me a favor," he said. "See what you can find about Nautilus and a guy named Charles Raymond. And make it quick. I have a feeling things are about to get a whole lot more interesting."

38

The Jacob K. Javits Federal Building was a forty-one-story skyscraper with vertical window slits that had been deliberately misaligned to create a zigzagging pattern reminiscent of woven fabric. Situated in the Civic Center of Lower Manhattan, it housed a veritable who's who of government agencies and a dedicated immigration court. Mason parked in the substructure and he and Layne rode the elevator up to the lobby, where an administrative specialist wearing a gray skirt suit waited for them, the expression on her face one of inconvenience. She guided them through the security gauntlet and to an elevator that took them to the twenty-third floor, home of the New York City Field Office of the FBI.

A handful of agents moved about the hallways, but not nearly as many as Mason would have expected, given that thousands of gallons of Novichok were potentially out there in the city at this very moment. Their escort led them to a conference room, wished them luck, and took her leave. Mason knew something was wrong the moment he opened the door. He took in the room at a glance. A long hardwood table. Video conference call units. At least a dozen faux leather chairs on wheels. No water or coffee on the service cart. A solitary man stood at the window with his back to them, watching the sun rise over the East River. He turned at the sound of their approach.

"Becker?" Mason said.

"What's going on?" Layne asked.

"I was hoping you might be able to tell me," the ATF agent said. "The agent who picked me up at the airport brought me straight here."

"Where's Addison?" Mason asked.

"The DHS agent?" Becker said. "She wasn't on my flight."

Mason felt a sinking sensation in the pit of his stomach.

"Son of a bitch," Layne said.

The door opened and Algren strode into the room. Her makeup was freshly applied and there wasn't a single crease in her skirt suit. The hint of lace from her bra showed through her blouse. She'd obviously taken the time to change since landing, which was the kind of thing one did when preparing to meet with somebody important, not a group of exhausted field agents who hadn't slept for more than a few hours during the past few days.

Addison entered behind her and leaned against the front wall. The pale industrial light made the scar on her cheek look like a worm trying to squirm from the corner of her mouth into her ear.

"Everyone please take a seat," Algren said.

Mason watched her from the corner of his eye as he rounded the table, drew back a chair, and sat down. She deliberately looked anywhere other than in his direction. Layne chose the chair opposite his and met his stare. She knew the score.

Becker slouched into the chair at the foot of the table and cocked his head in such a way that the shadow from the brim of his ball cap concealed his eyes.

"As you are well aware," Algren said, "this is a fluid situation. It's imperative that we're able to adapt to changing circumstances in real time. The explosion at the Mayfair Towers marks a dramatic escalation beyond the limited experience and response capabilities of this strike force. Had there been so much as a single gallon of a chemical WMD inside that apartment, the force of the blast would have dispersed it over an area several blocks in diameter and thousands of people would have been killed in a matter of seconds."

"That wasn't our fault," Layne said.

"Be that as it may—"

The door opened behind Algren, who stepped aside to make room for the newcomer at the head of the table. An aura of authority radiated from him. His silver hair was slicked back from his long forehead, which drew the focus to his dark eyes. He wore an expensive watch with an oversize face and a tailored Brooks Brothers suit. Mason recognized him immediately.

"Deputy Secretary Marchment," Mason said. "You've certainly moved up in the world since I saw you last."

"The Department of Homeland Security was so impressed by the success of our strike force in Arizona that they made me an offer I would have been a fool to decline."

"Our team was wiped out."

"Were it not for our timely intervention and the sacrifices of heroic agents like yourself, Lord only knows how many people we might have lost to that virus."

"Congratulations. You got yourself a seat at the big table."

"I'll choose to take that at face value, Special Agent Mason." He paused before addressing them as a group. "I'll do my best to wrap this up quickly. For the sake of formality, my name is Rand Marchment and I'm deputy secretary of the United States Department of Homeland Security, in which role I supervise operations of critical importance to the safety of our nation and liaise directly with the secretary of the DHS and the president of the United States, both of whom would like me to personally express their gratitude. It is men and women like you, leading the charge on the front lines, who make it possible for us to keep our citizenry safe. We thank you for your hard work and sacrifice."

"Wait," Layne said. "Are you sidelining us?"

Mason had sensed that something along those lines was about to transpire the moment the DHS agents had pulled up in their SUVs outside the Mayfair Towers.

"I've requested that you remain on standby for operational support," Algren said.

"What about you?" Layne asked.

"My position will be integrated into the existing infrastructure of the counterterrorism network."

"So we get screwed and you get a promotion?"

"We need our most experienced and capable agents on point," Marchment said. "So as of this moment, the Counterterrorism Section of the National Security Unit, under the stewardship of the Department of Homeland Security, has assumed jurisdiction over this case, effectively disbanding this strike force. We ask that you turn over any and all pertinent materials and data, desist from further investigation, and sever all current lines of inquiry."

Mason turned his stare upon Marchment.

"Is it the Novichok that's the greatest threat to national security?" he asked. "Or is it the Scarecrow himself?"

The deputy secretary's eyes widened ever so slightly at the mention of the Scarecrow.

"I am no longer at liberty to discuss the details of this case with you, Special Agent Mason. And considering the nature and severity of the threat, each of you will be required to sign a confidentiality agreement and you will be expected to uphold the status of your station by denying any knowledge of this investigation or disclosing any information even peripherally related to it, under penalty of law."

"So what are we supposed to do now?" Becker asked.

"That's no longer within my purview, Agent Becker," Marchment said. "Agent Addison will lead you down the hall to secure offices, where a team of specialists will conduct your debriefings. You are dismissed."

He turned without another word and headed out the door, leaving

Algren scrambling to catch up with him. The moment it closed behind them, Layne slammed her fist on the table.

Addison assumed the head of the table and offered a smile that looked as uncomfortable on her face as it made the rest of them feel.

"Now, if you'll come with me . . ."

"Screw this," Layne said.

Addison opened the door for them and stepped to the side. Mason exited the conference room and glanced down the hallway to his right, where several DHS agents were already waiting for them with digital clipboards held to their chests.

Hopefully, this would be a relatively quick and painless process, because he really needed to get back to work.

A chiming sound behind him announced the arrival of the elevator.

He turned around in time to see Marchment enter the elevator. The deputy secretary looked up and their eyes met across the distance.

Mason held his stare until the doors closed between them.

Something clicked inside him, like a puzzle piece snapping into place.

He suddenly understood why the DHS had been hovering over the investigation from the start, why the hazmat team had been so quick to arrive at the slaughterhouse, why the FPS contingent on their strike force had interceded to prevent the release of the autopsy reports of the men in the cornfield and the personnel list from the army, and why the number-two man in the entire Homeland Security apparatus had been on-site, in the middle of the night, mere hours after the discovery of the victim in Central Park. He should have recognized it the moment he noticed that Algren had taken the time to change her clothes and freshen her makeup. Marchment must have contacted her sometime between their last briefing and her arrival, made her an offer she couldn't refuse, and used her ambition to effectively usurp the investigation and hide it behind the veil of national security.

One piece after another tumbled into place.

Marchment had been placed in charge of the Bradley Strike Force to make sure the investigation into the Hoyl focused on the drugs being smuggled through the open desert and not on the virus. He'd brought in Spencer Kane so he had a man he trusted on the inside, one who would keep him informed, shape the course of the investigation, and lead them all to their deaths if they got too close to the truth. And when it was all over, after the Hoyl had escaped with the virus and the strike force had been eradicated, he'd flown to Arizona to personally control the flow of information. He'd sat mere feet from Mason's hospital bed and shared the details of the deaths of his colleagues without so much as hinting that he'd been the one who betrayed them.

Now here he was again, directing his agency to make sure no one got too close to the Scarecrow, using the might of his position to enact the genocidal plans of the same men who'd tried to cull the global population with their flu virus, men with enough power and political currency to arrange for his appointment to one of the highest positions within the national security apparatus and use him to derail the investigation into their plot to release a chemical weapon of mass destruction. And through him, they now controlled a quarter of a million highly trained law-enforcement officers, a veritable army already assembled in every state of the union and along every physical border.

He could see it all so clearly now.

Rand Marchment was an agent of the Thirteen.

39

ELSEWHERE

The Scarecrow watched the jagged lines streak across the monitor, the peaks growing farther apart even as they diminished in amplitude. A high-pitched alarm erupted from it, but the Scarecrow pressed the button to silence it, leaving the warning light flashing impotently. The equipment was no longer strictly necessary, as there was no mistaking the direness of the situation. The blankets hardly rose with each labored inhalation, and the unmistakable stench of death was a physical entity stalking the room, like the grim reaper himself.

"Just . . . a . . . little . . . longer," the Scarecrow whispered.

It drew a cold hand from beneath the covers and kissed it with lips that had not known human contact in as long as it could remember.

It was surprised to feel the warmth of a single tear trickling down its cheek, and not simply for the lack of emotions it felt.

The Scarecrow carefully tucked the hand back underneath the sheet and ran its fingertips along the contours of a face it knew nearly as well as its own, or at least once had, before the life had dissolved beneath the skin, transforming the features into a skeletal mockery of the formerly radiant being. It tried not to think about how the eyes had begun to sink into the skull or that the mouth no longer appeared capable of closing. All that remained now was inevitability, the inevitability of victory and loss, vindication and vengeance, triumph and tragedy.

Death.

"The . . . bogeyman . . . has . . . come," it rasped. "His . . . master . . . cannot . . . be . . . far . . . behind."

Whether real or imagined, the Scarecrow sensed the hint of a smile tug at the corners of those waxen lips and rose from the bedside. There was still much work to be done and it was imperative that everything stayed on schedule, especially if it intended to separate the monster it had always thought of as the bogeyman from his security contingent. His role in the final act was the most important of all, for it was through his suffering that the Scarecrow would enact the final phase of the plan it had devised with its true master, a plan that would see the deaths of millions and expose all of those responsible for a lifetime of pain and misery.

It passed several rooms enclosed by walls made of rice paper before entering one filled with the bluish glow emanating from the aquarium housing the jellyfish, which floated inside like gobs of mucus. Unseen creatures scurried inside their tanks, snakes slithered across the detritus lining their cages, and insects tapped against the sides of their enclosures. It knelt before one in particular and tapped the glass, eliciting a frenetic buzzing sound.

"Your . . . time . . . has . . . come."

The final countdown would soon commence.

Three would become two, who would know the fear it had once felt and experience pain beyond anything they had ever known, before only one remained. One who, with his final breaths, would understand exactly what he had done, that he would die with countless others, no better or worse, and that the name he cared so much about would be worth less than nothing, his legacy defined by his atrocities.

And when the timer hit zero, everyone would finally see the Scarecrow—truly see it for the first time—and recognize the role they had played in the massacre.

40

Mason awoke with a start. Something had roused him from a dead slumber. It took him a moment to identify his surroundings. The clock on the dresser read 5:16 P.M. in glowing red numbers. A faint aura of light filtered through the drawn curtains, defining the radiator below them and the nearby table and chair, upon which rested his overnight bag. He heard car horns in the distance and the din of life on the street below. A dull ache spread throughout his body, radiating from the puncture wounds he'd received from the IED on the eastern plains of Colorado, the knot at the base of his skull he'd incurred while being hunted through the Pine Barrens in New Jersey, and the bruises covering his back and shoulders from being hurled off the top of a thirty-six-story building in New York City.

By the time he and Layne had finished their debriefings, the adrenaline that had sustained them since leaving Colorado had worked its way through their systems and exhaustion had set in with a vengeance. He remembered finding her asleep in a chair in the hallway of the federal building, driving them both back to the hotel through brutal midday traffic, and riding the elevator together to their rooms on the tenth floor, where they'd agreed that a few hours of sleep would do them both some good. They needed to remain as sharp as possible, both mentally and physically, in case Algren called in operational support. Of course, Mason knew that Layne had no more intention of sitting around and waiting for that to happen than he did, but if there was one lesson he'd learned from experience, it was that he should rest when he had the opportunity to do so, because there was no telling when he might get another chance, especially if things were about to start moving as quickly as he anticipated.

He was debating sneaking in a few more minutes of shuteye when he heard something outside his door, a sound that triggered his internal alarm system: the subtle creak of footsteps in the hallway.

Suddenly wide-awake, he slid out of bed in just his boxers, grabbed his Glock from the nightstand, and ran across the room. Pressed his back against the wall beside the door. Slowed his breathing and listened. No squeaking of wheels from a housekeeper's cart or the hinges from the door of a nearby room.

Something bumped against the other side of the wall.

There was definitely someone out there, someone who had no business being there.

More creaking.

A shadow passed across the faint line of light passing underneath the door.

Mason gripped the handle in his left hand. A quick twist and a tug and the door would be open. Whoever was on the other side wouldn't be expecting it. He'd come around the door low, using it to shield his body, and—

An electronic beep from the other side, followed by the click of the disengaging lock.

The door opened inward.

A rectangle of light spread across the floor and onto the rumpled bed. Two overlapping shadows nearly eclipsed it. Movement through the crack near the hinges.

They were coming in.

The moment they cleared the door, Mason shouldered it closed and stepped behind the second man. Grabbed him by the back of his jacket. Ducked behind his shoulder. Jammed the barrel of the pistol into the base of his skull.

"Jesus," the second man gasped.

The first stood silhouetted against the rear wall. He turned around. There was something in his right hand, something Mason couldn't immediately identify.

"I don't care if you shoot him," the man said, "but for the love of God, put on some damn clothes."

Mason jerked the second man backward so he could reach the light switch with his elbow. The recessed bulbs filled the room with a hard yellow glare. Ramses stood at the foot of the bed with a paper cup of coffee in his hand.

"Why the hell didn't you just knock?" Mason asked. "I could have killed you both."

Gunnar raised his arms just high enough that Mason could see that he held a cup in either hand. The coffee had splashed out of the small holes and covered both the lids and the backs of his hands.

Mason lowered his weapon, released Gunnar's jacket, and smoothed the fabric.

His old friend turned around and offered the cup in his left hand.

"You didn't reply to any of our messages," Ramses said. "What were we supposed to do?"

"Only you would go straight to breaking and entering," Mason said.

He set down his coffee on the table, dumped out the contents of his bag, and put on a clean T-shirt and jeans.

"What can I say? I'm a man of action."

"Let's just hope those actions don't get you killed," Mason said. He sat on the edge of the bed to put on his boots and sipped the hot coffee. "Why are you even here?"

"You said things were about to get interesting," Gunnar said. "We didn't want to miss any of the fun."

Mason smirked.

"I wouldn't dream of starting it without you," he said. "Have you found anything on Nakamura?"

"These things take time. Especially when someone's gone to great lengths to scrub the Internet of any mention of him. Trust me, though . . . if there's anything out there, I'll find it."

Ramses paced the room, an expression of revulsion on his face. He opened the curtains to expose the view of the building next door, the bricks of which were so close, he could have reached out and touched them, had he been able to open the window.

"The FBI must really hate you to put you up in a place like this," he said. "I don't even want to sit down, for fear my ass will come away sticky."

"Where's Alejandra?" Mason asked.

"Are you seriously asking why someone in the country illegally and without any form of identification didn't travel with us through an airport to the city with the most police officers while it's on heightened terrorism alert?"

"It couldn't have worked out better," Gunnar said. "Less than twenty minutes after we left, our anonymous friend circumvented my firewall again, which you'd already know if you'd bothered to check your messages."

"What'd he say?"

"He was fishing for what we knew about what happened here in the city."

Mason furrowed his brow as comprehension dawned.

"This guy's on the inside," he said. "As far as anyone outside the investigation knows, Central Park was closed for a red team training exercise and the explosion at the Mayfair Towers was accidental and unrelated."

"My thoughts exactly," Gunnar said. "He has to be wired into the national counterterrorism network to know as much as he does about FEMA's emergency activation levels and the JTTF's response to last night's events."

"So what did Alejandra tell him?"

"That we didn't know anything about it," Ramses said, "which is more or less true."

"He suggested we look into the supposedly coincidental explosion," Gunnar said, "which brings us to Charles Raymond, who, at the time of his death, was the managing director of Research and Development for Royal Nautilus Petroleum, the sixth most powerful position in the corporate hierarchy. He was hired straight out of grad school and worked in the exploration sector for a short period of time before being transferred to R and D, where he remained for the duration of his career. While his role on the executive council was likely more ceremonial than managerial, he wasn't so far removed from his department that he didn't still have his fingerprints on most of their active projects, including the development of liquid natural gas as a transport fuel, carbon-neutral production facilities, and green construction materials."

"Sounds more like an environmentalist than an oil company executive," Ramses said.

Mason finished his coffee, tossed the cup into the miniature wastebasket, and took a seat at the table.

"What about military service?" he asked.

"As a student, he received a draft deferment," Gunnar said.

"Anything related to chemical manufacturing or engineering? He had to understand what the Scarecrow had done to him and recognize the symptoms."

"In one way or another, everything he did was related to chemical engineering. He signed on at a time when oil was the only game in town and had to continually pioneer new technologies to keep up with the demands of an ever-changing world."

"What about Royal Nautilus itself?"

"It's the largest energy exploration company in the world, with annual revenue in the hundreds of billions and operations in nearly every country," Gunnar said. "Between oil and liquid natural gas, it produces nearly four million barrels of oil equivalent every day. As far as corporations go, it's somewhat sprawling and unwieldy, with countless subsidiaries and joint ventures in just about every industry even peripherally related to the energy sector, specifically those that fit into its four business groupings: the upstream search for and recovery of crude oil; the downstream refining and shipping of by-products; the integration of new energies and low-carbon opportunities; and the research and development of new products and technologies, which also encompasses chemicals and biologicals."

"Biologicals?" Mason said. "You mean like the kind of bacteria they use to clean up oil spills and the Hoyl integrated into his flu virus as a decomposition agent?"

"I was thinking more along the lines of vaccines and therapeutic agents, although that's a distinct possibility, and also part of the challenge of evaluating a company of this nature. There isn't a single industry it hasn't at least dipped a toe in. . . ." Gunnar furrowed his brow and looked Mason dead in the eyes. "That's not the kind of answer you're looking for, though, is it? You want to know if anyone associated with Nautilus wields the kind of power that could place him among the Thirteen."

Mason hadn't realized it until he heard the words spoken aloud, but that was precisely what he was asking. Someone at the top of the hierarchy of such a massive and profitable corporation would undoubtedly have access to the kind of wealth and connections that would make him a viable suspect.

"Well?" Ramses said.

"The problem with a company this large and diverse is that its power structure is divided and spread out across the entirety of its financial interests. Executive councils, management groups, and numerous boards of directors all functioning under the same umbrella. It's like the federal government in that sense. There are so many checks and balances that no one person is ever in complete control, and the majority of the time the left hand has no idea what the right is doing. The closest thing it has to what one might consider a presidential-type leader is Slate Langbroek, the chairman of the executive board, which in his case is more of a figurehead role, since he doesn't possess any true operational influence. He's the guy the executive council keeps in the public eye so it can get the real work done behind closed boardroom doors."

"People like Charles Raymond."

"Exactly."

"So how does someone with so much influence and prestige end up murdered in the same manner as the victims from the cornfield? He and Peter Cavanaugh were on the complete opposite ends of the socioeconomic spectrum. What do a self-employed truck driver and a corporate executive have in common?"

"The Scarecrow," Ramses said.

Mason grabbed his cell phone and flipped through his saved images until he found the snapshot of the photograph he'd found inside the farmhouse after the explosion. It had obviously been taken on a military installation and featured a group of twelve uniformed men, all of whose eyes had been scratched out. Raymond and his birthmark weren't among them, but it stood to reason that whatever he'd done to incur the wrath of the Scarecrow was likely related to these men.

"Can you try running this picture through your program?" Mason asked. He slid his phone across the table to Gunnar. "I'm confident one of these guys is Cavanaugh, but our forensics team hasn't had any luck conclusively identifying him, let alone any of the others. This is where everything started, and the key to figuring out the Scarecrow's ultimate goal."

"I don't know, Mace. My program works by generating a faceprint that maps the relative location of facial features to one another, half of which involve the eyes specifically. Their color. Their width and shape. The distance between them and the breadth of the nose. The space between the outer corners and the sides of the face. The thickness of the eyebrows. The configuration of the eyelids. The rest of the face is far more susceptible to the ravages of age, too. A picture this old? These men have to be in their seventies by now. At least. I'd be surprised if even their closest friends at the time would recognize them anymore."

"Will you at least try?"

"Of course. I just want you to understand that you're asking for a miracle."

He headed for the door.

"Where are you going?" Mason asked.

"Do you see me carrying my laptop?" Gunnar asked.

"No."

"Then I'd probably better go get it, don't you think?"

Ramses laughed.

Mason glared at him. First of all, it wasn't that funny. Second, he didn't want to have to explain the presence of his unexpected guests to Layne, who was asleep just down the hall, if they woke her up.

"Come on," Ramses said. "How often does Gunnar say anything remotely humorous? Try taking that stick out of your ass for a few minutes and see how it feels."

"There could be as much as four thousand gallons of a lethal Soviet nerve agent right outside that door at this very moment. If someone so much as tossed a water balloon filled with it from the roof, you and

I, and every single person within a half-mile radius, would be killed in just about the most horrific way imaginable."

Ramses leaned his head to the side, causing his neck to make an audible cracking sound. He worked his jaw behind his closed lips. When he returned his head to its natural position, his eyes were cold and flat.

"So what do you need from me?"

"Call Alejandra and have her send this Anomaly guy a message."

"What do you want her to say?"

"If he's on the inside, like we suspect, then he potentially has access to sensitive information, and right now we need to learn everything we possibly can about Rand Marchment, the deputy secretary of the Department of Homeland Security."

"Where does he fit in?"

"That's what we need to figure out, because if I'm right, not only will he lead us to the Scarecrow and the Novichok; he'll lead us to the Thirteen."

41

Gunnar's laptop hummed while his program ran the photograph Mason had recovered from the farmhouse in Wray through an exhaustive series of databases, comparing the few facial features it could accurately map against pictures that would essentially have to have been taken within a few years either way and from the exact same angle to conclusively identify the subject.

Mason hovered impatiently, only now realizing the futility of his request.

"Still nothing?" he asked.

Gunnar shook his head. Despite the mutilation of their eyes, it was hard to believe the program hadn't encountered a single photograph that was at least a partial match to any of them. Granted, their age placed their best years before the advent of the Internet, but their uniforms proved they'd been military at some point, which meant there had to be a record of them somewhere, and the fact that even Gunnar hadn't been able to find it was more than a little troubling.

"Are you reading this the same way I am?" Gunnar asked.

"We're looking for ghosts."

"Like I said, Mace, making people disappear is easier said than done in this day and age."

"There has to be a reason the Scarecrow left pictures like this one for us to find," Mason said.

Gunnar leaned back, inclined his chin, and looked momentarily contemplative.

"I have an idea," he said. "I'm not sure if it'll work, but it's worth a try."

"What are you thinking?"

Gunnar brought up the picture of the men standing in front of the government installation and zoomed in on the barracks.

"Look just above the roofline," he said. "See the crown of that red-and-white-checkered water tower to the left and what almost looks like the top level of a parking garage to the right? Over there. With the external walkways and the electrical works. It's possible that if I tweak the program so that it treats the physical structures like facial features, we might be able to use them to identify the location. We'd have to encounter another photograph taken from pretty much the same distance and angle or it won't generate even a partial match, but maybe if I'm able to broaden the tolerances, we just might get lucky."

"It's worth a try," Mason said. "It's not like you can get fewer than zero hits."

Gunnar set to work without another word. His fingers flew across the keyboard, opening and closing screens faster than Mason could visually keep up.

Ramses burst into the room from the outer hallway, his phone pressed to his ear.

"Allie sent the message like you wanted," he said. "She'd barely finished typing when Anomaly replied, but she doesn't know how to respond."

"What did he say?" Mason asked.

"That you're asking the wrong question."

Ramses put the call on speaker and handed his phone to Mason.

"Alejandra," he said. "What, exactly, did you ask him?"

"I wrote 'What do you know about Rand Marchment?'" she said.

It was a simple question that could have been interpreted in any number of ways, an open-ended query meant to draw out whatever information their anonymous source wanted to share. That Anomaly deflected implied not that he couldn't answer the question, but, rather, that they needed to rephrase it to get the answer they wanted. It suddenly struck Mason that Anomaly shared his suspicions about Marchment, the very ones he'd been contemplating since his debriefing last night. How had he been promoted into the right positions to manipulate the investigations into both the Hoyl and the Scarecrow? What was his relationship to the Thirteen, and to what lengths was he willing to go to carry out their plans?

"Type this," Mason said. "'What do you *not* know about Rand Marchment?'"

He heard the clicking sounds of Alejandra pecking at the keys nearly two thousand miles away.

"Let me see what I can find," Gunnar said. He opened a new window and set to work, lines of code blurring past. "I ought to at least be able to access his federal personnel file."

"Here is his response," Alejandra said. "'That is the right question.'"

"So what's the answer?" Mason asked.

Again, he heard her fingertips striking the keyboard.

"'How he came to power,'" she said. "What do you want me to—Never mind. He terminated the connection."

"That's not especially helpful," Mason said.

"This guy's just messing with us," Ramses said.

"Maybe he is," Gunnar said, "but there *are* several distinct gaps in Marchment's personnel file. The first corresponds to the late seventies and early eighties, when he went from a private in the army to a special agent in the DEA; the second, more than thirty years later, when he was promoted from chief of the regional office in Mexico City to assistant administrator of the Operational Support Division, the number-four man in the entire Drug Enforcement Administration."

"What did he do during those missing years?" Mason asked.

"To go from being an enlisted soldier in the army to a special agent in the DEA, he would have had to secure his discharge and then earn a college degree," Ramses said.

"That explains the first gap," Gunnar said. "What about the second?"

"The cartels are wired into everything in Mexico. The DEA can't afford for them to find out the names of its agents, both for their safety and the safety of their loved ones back home. It's a distinct possibility that those records were either never entered into a searchable database or deliberately deleted."

"So both of these gaps could be completely innocuous—"

"And our boy Anomaly is full of shit," Ramses said.

"Or it was during those missing years that he was co-opted by the Thirteen," Mason said. "We need to figure out exactly where he was and what he was doing."

"I'll look into his financials and see what I can find," Gunnar said. "It's hard to believe that a man so obviously ambitious could be bought with the promise of promotion alone. There's only so much power that can be amassed within the constraints of the system."

And yet here was a man who'd rocketed through the ranks into a position one step removed from a cabinet official, a man whose career trajectory could very well have followed that of Peter Cavanaugh and, quite possibly, that of the other men they'd found dead on his property. Based on their age and the pictures displayed inside the farmhouse, it was more than likely that the victims had served at the same time as Marchment. Maybe the deputy secretary's face was even among those with their eyes scratched out, which would explain his extreme reaction to the mere mention of the Scarecrow.

Mason had no doubt Marchment had been the intended recipient of the monster's message in the cornfield, the high-ranking official inside the investigation who knew exactly who he was and what he intended to do, but if Marchment had truly been corrupted by the Thirteen, then what did he have to fear from their pet monster? And why was he in the city if there were thousands of gallons of Novichok just waiting to be released? The answers they needed were hidden in the past, at a time when the most heinous war criminals were integrated into the military infrastructure and in a place where they labored to produce one of the most fearsome arsenals the world had ever known, weapons of mass destruction that had evolved into the threat hanging over their heads at this very moment, and there was only one place to look.

He turned to Ramses and held his stare.

"I need to know about the army."

His old friend's eyes narrowed. The expression on his face became one completely lacking in emotion. It felt as though the air had been sucked out of the room.

"Fuck you, Mason." He ground his teeth back and forth and glared at Mason without once blinking. "There are very few things that are off-limits to you. That's one of them."

"This isn't about you, Ramses. It doesn't have a damn thing to do with you at all."

"That part of my life exists at the bottom of a deep, dark hole. Nothing gets in or out. You hear me?"

"I need to know where you'd have to look to find someone who knew how to make chemical weapons."

"Go to YouTube and you'll find a dozen tutorials. It's not rocket science, man."

"I'm not talking about small quantities. The man who nearly killed Alejandra, the man with stars for eyes. He calls himself the Scarecrow and he's out there right now. Sitting on enough Novichok to wipe out this entire city a thousand times over. And we're running out of time to stop him."

Ramses was silent for a full minute. His eyes became distant. When he finally spoke, it was in a hollow voice.

"That kind of thing was way before my time. You probably know more about it than I do."

"Nearly all of the sarin was produced at facilities like the Rocky Mountain Arsenal in Colorado. Chances are the Scarecrow worked at one of them prior to their being decommissioned. I was hoping you'd be able to tell me something about them, or maybe what happened to the chemical engineers who designed those weapons."

"That's not the kind of thing they put in the recruitment brochure."

"What about the men who worked there? The people who actually mixed the chemicals and assembled the weapons?"

"You don't get it, do you?"

"Get what?"

"The army knows exactly who this guy is."

"If they did, they would have interceded by now."

"Rank and file, maybe, but not the bigwigs. This plays right into their hands."

"Under what circumstances does releasing a chemical weapon and killing millions of civilians benefit the military?"

"You're kidding, right? At this very moment, there are more than twenty thousand U.S. troops deployed on American soil in defiance of the Posse Comitatus Act and under the auspices of, quote, unquote, 'specialized training for urban conflict and general preparedness for civil unrest and CBRN attack.' Twenty thousand troops who can be dispatched at the drop of a hat and assembled in any city in the country within a matter of hours. We're not talking about the National Guard here, either. This is the First Brigade Combat Team of the Third Infantry, the same guys who spearheaded the coalition forces and took Baghdad during Operation Iraqi Freedom, some of the most highly trained men at our disposal. And right now, they're camped out at NORTHCOM, just waiting to step in and *assist* law enforcement and emergency management. Not just them, either. The Unified Command Plan puts nearly the entire mother-loving air force under USNORTHCOM's emergency command. You think it matters what we do? The powers that pull the strings? They release a ton of nerve gas and kill millions, they win. They turn the military loose in our streets in response and they win again. I don't know if you're paying attention, but this entire fucking game's already been rigged from start to finish."

"Do you really believe that?" Mason asked.

Ramses sighed and ran his fingers through his slick hair.

"Depends on when you ask. You stare at this stuff long enough and you start seeing patterns that aren't necessarily there."

"No one wants martial law," Gunnar said.

"If that's really what you think, then you aren't paying attention," Ramses said. "Getting power is one thing; keeping it is another. You can't rule the world without conquering it first."

"If you're suggesting the Thirteen have the ability to use the United States military as their own private security force, then we've already lost."

"Someone still has to try," Mason said.

Ramses looked him up and down, then nodded.

"The Scarecrow, you say? What's with these fucking nutjobs and the lame-ass names?"

"I don't know . . . Ramses."

He smiled.

"I don't have the answers you're looking for, but I think I know someone who just might."

42

If Mason's old friends were going to stick around New York for any length of time, they were going to need to find somewhere else to stay, which Ramses made abundantly clear every chance he got. The Plaza Hotel was just across Central Park, on Fifth Avenue, the walk to which would afford him the opportunity to discreetly observe what was going on inside the park and around the Mayfair Towers. He could probably also use some privacy to call the contact he believed would be able to illuminate some of the finer aspects of the art of chemical weapons manufacture. If Mason was right about the nature of their relationship, having a federal agent within earshot while doing so would likely cramp his style.

"You're going to seriously owe me for this one," Ramses said.

"Put it on my tab," Mason said.

"The whole point of extending a tab is so that it can one day be repaid. You know that, right?"

"What could I possibly do for you?" Ramses opened his mouth to reply, but Mason cut him off. "Don't answer that."

Ramses grabbed the doorknob and turned around.

"I'll call once I've made the arrangements. See what you can do about finding something a little nicer to wear. This guy's on the classier end of the scale."

He opened the door and nearly ran into Layne, who cradled two paper cups of coffee and a bag of what smelled like burgers to her chest. She'd just raised her fist to knock and held it awkwardly in the air as Ramses slipped past her. She followed him down the hallway with her eyes. When they returned to Mason, they were filled with fire.

"Who the hell is that?" she asked.

"Male prostitute," Ramses said as he stepped into the elevator. "Might want to take it easy on your boy here. He's going to be walking kind of funny for a while."

She raised her eyebrows but kept her gaze locked on Mason.

"He's not really a prostitute."

"I kind of figured as much." She transferred one of the cups to her free hand. "Are you going to invite me in, or is there something you need to tell me?"

Layne's eyes darted over his right shoulder, then back to his face. He could feel Gunnar standing behind him. She pursed her lips and pushed them outward with her tongue.

"Yeah," he said. "You should probably come in."

Mason stepped aside and Layne entered slowly. Her stare settled first upon the table, where Gunnar's laptop displayed the picture of the military men standing in front of the unknown installation, and then upon Gunnar, who offered an uncomfortable half smile.

"What the hell is going on here?" she asked.

"Is that for me?" Mason asked. He removed the cup from her hand, took a sip, and set it on the edge of the table. "Just what I needed."

She looked at her empty hand, then at Gunnar, before once more staring daggers at Mason.

"Layne, this is Gunnar Backstrom," Mason said. "Gunnar, Special Agent Jessica Layne."

Gunnar rose, shook her hand, and resumed his work without a word. He knew better than to risk striking a match near a powder keg.

"And the other one?"

"Ramses Donovan."

"The same Ramses Donovan who owns half of the marijuana dispensaries in Denver? In defiance of federal law, I might add."

"Is it too late to go back to him being a prostitute?"

"So let me get this straight." She set down the bag and remaining cup and got right in his face. "During the six hours I managed to sleep in the last two days, you brought two unauthorized civilians into an active investigation we're no longer working and shared classified information with them."

"They're old friends—"

"I don't care who they are. This falls on you."

"Look, Layne—"

"No, you look, Mason." Her eyes narrowed and her shoulders heaved. "I'm tired of you treating me like I'm stupid. Why don't you try telling me the truth for once? And I mean it, you try to feed me a load of crap and—God help me—I'll throw you out that goddamn window."

He studied her face and body language for any indication of deception. Her expression was one of genuine anger and betrayal. Her hand had found its way under her jacket, while his pistol was holstered on the nightstand. If she was compromised, like his past two partners, her only option was to kill both Gunnar and him.

Right here and now.

But if she didn't . . .

"There are elements of this investigation you aren't ready to understand," he said.

"Try me."

"You know about my partners before you, don't you?"

She waited several seconds before offering a subtle nod.

"What if I told you they'd been co-opted by forces outside of the Bureau?"

"I know about Special Agent Kane, but are you suggesting Special Agent Trapp didn't die in a car accident?"

Mason waited her out. This was a delicate matter. Convincing her of a cover-up at the highest levels was one thing; confessing to killing his last partner was another.

"Let's say, for the sake of argument, that I believe you," she said.

"That would mean hostile actors have not only infiltrated the FBI but compromised it."

"There are only a few of us who are aware of this, and we can only speculate as to the full extent to which we've been compromised."

"Does Chris know?"

"Most of it."

"So you're withholding evidence from your special agent in charge?"

"I'm not withholding anything. I can only tell him what I know, and unfortunately, that's not a whole lot."

"Do these guys know?"

Mason hesitated before answering.

"Yes."

"So two people with no law-enforcement affiliation—one of whom has a questionable relationship with organized crime—are privy to confidential details of an ongoing investigation that you haven't even shared with your direct supervisor. Or even your partner."

"It does sound bad when she says it like that," Gunnar said.

"You're not helping," Mason said.

"You want to know how this looks from where I'm standing?" She stepped closer and jabbed her finger into his chest with each point she made. "You claim your last two partners were dirty, but both of them are conveniently out of the picture. We found evidence of the attempted weaponization of the flu virus at the end of a tunnel originating in a building on property formerly belonging to your in-laws, yet none of them survived long enough to be questioned about their involvement. The IRS agent who stumbled upon the money trail that led to the discovery of the flu plot—one that also leads to the apartment the Scarecrow used to hunt the victim he staked in Central Park—is also unable to confirm your story—"

"Don't bring my wife into this."

"—because she's dead. They're all dead, Mason. Do you know the one thing they all had in common? You. And what did you gain from their deaths? Your partner couldn't attend the hearing that could have stripped you of your badge, your father now owns the multinational company tied to the development of the virus, and you inherited millions of dollars from your wife's estate. How much do you personally stand to make from all of this, huh?"

"You need to be careful here, Layne."

"Or what?" She stepped back, drew her weapon, and aimed it at his chest. "I'll die in a 'car accident,' too? You think the FBI's just going to keep sending you new partners? Don't you figure they already have to be taking a good long look at you?"

"Let them look. I have nothing to hide."

"You were there when we discovered the victims behind the false wall. You were there when we found the bodies in the cornfield. You were the one who entered the farmhouse through the silo when the front door was booby-trapped. You were there when the men who covered up the fire tried to kill us. You were the one who so conveniently discovered the apartment where the Scarecrow rigged the bomb that wiped out half of our team. You were the one who threw us over the edge of the roof and onto a balcony that just happened to be there."

"You should be really clear about what you're accusing me of doing."

"Either you're the luckiest man alive or maybe it wasn't your partners who were the dirty ones."

"Lucky?" Mason stepped forward until he felt the barrel of her gun against his sternum. "I've lost just about everyone and everything important to me. Kane and Trapp were more than my partners; they were my friends. And while I never had the greatest relationship with my in-laws, I didn't want them dead. At least not until the very end. And Angie . . ." He realized he was shouting and took a moment to compose himself. "My wife was my world. There's nothing I wouldn't give to bring her back. I don't care about the money. The only thing that matters is making sure the people responsible for her death are held accountable."

Layne's stare never wavered. She had to know he could easily disarm her at close range, which meant she had to be willing to pull the trigger if she sensed him so much as thinking about it. The fact that she hadn't done so yet meant that she was at least willing to hear him out.

"Then tell me," she said. "Tell me who's responsible for all of this. Who compromised your last two partners? Who conspired with your in-laws to create a flu pandemic? Who's to blame for everything that's happening now?"

Mason didn't respond.

"That's what I thought." Her eyes hardened. "What's to stop me from taking both of you in right now?"

"You want to find the Scarecrow and stop him from murdering millions of innocent people."

"Just because we're no longer part of the investigation doesn't mean no one's trying to catch him."

"You're smart, Layne. You've seen what's going on out there. Homeland's been obstructing the investigation from the very beginning and now they're the ones in charge. That's been their goal from the start."

"Then tell me why. Convince me."

"They sidelined Locker once he identified the bodies from behind the wall, they stepped in to prevent the ME from releasing the COD and IDs of the dead men in the cornfield, and now they cut us out after learning the identity of the man in Central Park. Think about the profile. The victims form a pattern, one that poses a threat to very important people involved in this investigation. The people for whom the message in the field was intended. The people who've been manipulating the strike force from its inception. The people who know exactly who the Scarecrow is. They need us out of the way so they can hunt him, but for reasons other than the fact that he possesses enough Novichok to wipe out every major city on the face of the Earth."

"It's personal for them, too," she said.

"Who was most threatened by our strike force? Who interceded every single time we started getting too close?"

"Homeland."

"And who do you think gave those orders?"

"Marchment," she whispered.

Layne lowered her weapon and allowed it to hang at her side.

"I don't know what his relationship to the Scarecrow is and I really don't care," Mason said. "They can have each other, as far as I'm concerned. I need to find the Novichok and make sure a lot of innocent people don't die, and I'm not about to let Homeland get in my way."

"Then you're going to need help."

Mason nodded.

"You're going to have to trust me, then," she said. "I have to know everything you know."

"I should warn you, though, there's an awful lot I don't know."

"And I should warn you that if you're lying to me about any of this, I'll take you in myself."

"I'd expect nothing less," Mason said, and proffered his hand.

Layne appraised him for several seconds before shaking it.

"Don't think for a second that my hesitation to shoot you means I won't do so if I have to."

"Perish the thought."

And if she turned out to be anything other than she claimed to be, he'd return the favor.

43

Ramses was waiting in the golden glow of the Fifty-eighth Street entrance to the Plaza Hotel when Mason pulled up behind the wheel of Gunnar's rented Cadillac Escalade. He rolled down the tinted window and gestured for his old friend to climb into the seat behind him, which he did, but only after leaning halfway through the window to see why he'd been relegated to the rear. He opened the door and slid in beside Gunnar, whose laptop sat open on his thighs while he simultaneously searched for a match to the unknown government installation in the background of the picture of the men with their eyes scratched out, researched Rand Marchment, Ichiro Nakamura, and Charles Raymond, and imported the list of personnel Layne had received from the army.

"They have the park sealed off behind portable barricades between Terrace Drive and the Seventy-ninth Street Transverse," Ramses said. He closed the door behind him and elbowed Gunnar to make more room. "There's no sign of the DHS, though. The whole operation is staffed by men wearing hard hats and reflective vests."

"Which agency?" Mason asked.

"State Department of Environmental Protection."

"That doesn't make sense," Layne said.

If Ramses was surprised she was there, he did a good job of hiding it, although not so well that Mason couldn't see him in the rearview mirror, carefully studying her from the corner of his eye.

"They didn't think so, either. They were told the penthouse explosion might have damaged some of the underground power lines, but the guy I talked to figured they must have been talking about the old water lines, because he didn't think any electrical cables had been run underneath the Ramble or so close to the lake."

"So what *did* he think?" Mason asked. He pulled away from the curb and entered the heavy evening traffic.

"That he was making twenty-eight bucks an hour to stand there doing nothing."

"That's not very helpful."

"He did say he heard that the explosion at the Mayfair was caused by a ruptured gas line, which apparently made some amount of sense to him. Something about these skyscrapers being built before the dawn of time."

"I guess that explains why the apartment complex isn't still locked down."

"And why the traffic's moving at all."

"They can't afford panic," Layne said. "If everyone tried to leave the island at once, it would be chaos."

"And Homeland's movements would be restricted," Mason said. "They'd never find the Scarecrow with eight million people all trying to get out of here at the same time."

"So they're using the unsuspecting population of one of the most crowded cities on the entire planet as bait to try to draw him out?" Gunnar said. "That's a big gamble."

"Why do you sound surprised?" Ramses said. "You think any of our lives are worth shit to these people?"

"I would have thought at least their own were."

"Where am I going?" Mason asked.

"Keep going straight," Ramses said. "You'll cross the Queensboro Bridge and turn right on Van Dam Street."

"I take it you were able to arrange a meeting?"

"Who do you think you're talking to here?"

"Why do I feel as though there's something you're not telling me?"

"Because there is."

"As long as we cleared that up," Mason said. "Where are we going?"

"Are you going to introduce me to your partner, or are we sticking with the whole male prostitute story?"

"You're changing the subject."

"Don't worry," Ramses said. "I'll let you know when we get there."

Layne turned around in her seat and thrust out her hand.

"Special Agent Jessica Layne, Federal Bureau of Investigation."

He smirked and shook her hand. If she'd been attempting to intimidate him, it obviously had the opposite effect on him.

"Ramses Donovan, entrepreneur." He released her hand and winked at Mason in the rearview mirror. "So I take it you're confident this one's not going to try to kill you?"

"I'm leaving that option open," Layne said.

Mason's cell phone vibrated in his pocket. He grabbed it and tossed it to Layne.

"Six oh nine area code," she said.

"Where's that?" he asked.

"New Jersey," Gunnar said without looking up from his laptop.

"Put it on speaker." The buzzing ceased and the car filled with the crackle of an open line. "Special Agent Mason."

"This is Officer Saul Barrie, calling from the NJSP impound lot here in Port Norris. Remember that thing you asked me to look into for you?"

"You found out who gave the order to dispose of the flatbeds?"

"I need your word that this won't come back to bite me or my CO in the butt."

"You understand I can't make any guarantees if this is actionable intel, but I'll do everything in my power to make sure no one ever knows the source."

"I knew this was a mistake."

"You're doing the right thing, Barrie. You realized from the start that something was wrong and trusted your gut when it told you to preserve the evidence. What's it telling you now?"

There was a long silence. Mason glanced at the screen from the corner of his eye to make sure the call hadn't been disconnected.

"Under ordinary circumstances, I wouldn't press the issue," Mason said. "I totally get your loyalty to your department and your commanding officer. I do. But those trucks were hauling something far worse than drugs, Barrie. A lot of people could die."

Still, the other end remained quiet. When Barrie finally replied, it was in a tone of resignation.

"Major Delvin Roybal. Commanding officer of the Special Operations Section."

"The New Jersey State Police have special ops?" Layne said.

"Not in the sense you're thinking. More like specialized operations."

"What does that mean?"

"The organization is divided into four branches: Administration, Investigations, Operations, and Homeland Security."

Mason glanced at Layne.

"Let me guess, we're dealing with Homeland Security."

"Right, but the branch is further broken down into sections: Emergency Management and Special Operations. So Major Roybal's on the third tier of the pyramid, with the commanding officers of five bureaus directly underneath him: Aviation, Deployment Services, Marine Services, Technical Response, and my bureau, Transportation Safety."

While the mention of Homeland Security and special ops had initially piqued Mason's curiosity, the entire branch sounded like a standard bureaucratic entity that dealt more with customs and commerce than the actual process of physically securing the homeland.

"It doesn't seem unreasonable to think that someone in charge of transportation safety would be in a position of determining how best to handle the disposal of abandoned commercial vehicles," Mason said.

"True, but he's also in charge of the Technical Response Bureau, whose CO manages the Arson Unit, which was never called in to investigate." Mason felt the weight of Layne's stare upon him. She recognized it, too. It made no sense to bribe the firefighters without disabling the investigative body. "He's also in charge of the Hazardous Material Transportation Enforcement Unit. They have weigh stations set up on every highway entering the state and inspect every commercial vehicle that passes through. If you're right and they were hauling shipping containers, then the contents had to pass inspection somewhere along the line."

"Would there be a record of where the trucks entered the state and what they were carrying?" Layne asked.

"The data's entered manually."

Mason knew exactly what that meant. Someone willing to pass two bulk containers loaded with tanks of an unspecified liquid likely wasn't the kind of guy who'd enter the details into the log.

"Thanks, Barrie," he said. "You did the right thing."

"I hope to God you're right."

Layne terminated the call and set Mason's phone on the console.

"So we have a high-ranking official in charge of commercial-vehicle inspection and arson investigation making a unilateral decision to dispose of evidence potentially incriminating the owner in both trafficking and arson," she said.

"We need to find out more about this Major Roybal."

"Major Delvin Roybal," Gunnar said from the backseat. "Fifty-two years old. Twenty-nine years of service with the NJSP. His wife divorced him after twenty years, which means she hit the minimum threshold in New Jersey to receive alimony. Throw in two adult children, both of whom are enrolled at Rutgers, which isn't exactly cheap, and you have the recipe for financial disaster. Yet, somehow, the good major is not only keeping his head well above water; he just bought himself a new Harley, free and clear."

"Can you trace his income?" Mason asked.

"He draws a salary of roughly a hundred and fifty grand from the NJSP, which isn't chump change by any means, but— Here we go . . . a onetime payment of a quarter of a million dollars for his services as a consultant." Gunnar whistled appreciatively. "That's Clinton money and this guy isn't even in a position to influence policy."

"Who paid him?"

"A company called East Coast Transportation Services, which is a totally legitimate company based out of Newark. It manages a fleet of five thousand commercial vehicles that it leases to any number of corporations."

"What's its involvement?"

"They haven't filed their quarterly taxes, so the payment hasn't even been reported yet," Gunnar said. "I suppose they could have been trying to arrange for preferential treatment. Time is money in the trucking industry and bypassing weigh stations would be a competitive advantage, but they could have easily arranged accommodations through routine channels, and at a fraction of the cost. If I were to wager a guess, I'd say they made the payment on behalf of one of their clients, although they could have collected the funds through any number of aboveboard mechanisms without leaving a paper trail."

"Do any of its clients stand out?"

"Every major corporation is on the list. East Coast Transportation Services essentially provides subcontracted vehicles for companies with existing fleets when they need additional shipping help in a pinch."

Mason felt a tug at the back of his brain.

"What about Royal Nautilus Petroleum?"

"They're here, but so is every other oil company from Anadarko to Valero."

"Take your next left," Ramses said.

"You think the payment's legit?" Layne asked.

"The numbers are way out of line, but the payment itself is completely legitimate. At least on paper."

"Any payments to officials with similar positions in other states?" Mason asked.

"Not within the previous two quarters, and certainly not on the same scale."

"We should track down this Roybal and see if we can ruffle his feathers," Layne said.

"If he accepted a bribe of that magnitude to allow the trucks to pass inspection and then arranged for the destruction of the evidence," Mason said, "he was in the wind the moment he heard what happened to the men who tried to kill us."

"I'll handle that once we're done here," Ramses said. "I have a talent for finding people who don't want to be found."

"I'm not sure I like the sound of that," Layne said.

Ramses directed Mason into an industrial district filled with squat, single-story redbrick warehouses. Every available surface was covered with warring graffiti, all vying to be seen. They passed a salvage yard, a sweater mill, a lumberyard, and a wholesale furniture warehouse before turning down a side street defined by cramped apartment complexes on one side and abandoned commercial buildings on the other. Another left and they were on a dark, deserted street with a veritable twenty-foot wall formed by the bricked-over backs of the warehouses on the left and downtrodden shops with roll-up aluminum garages on the right. What wasn't already condemned looked like it should be.

"Up there on the right," Ramses said. "The one with the concrete blocks stacked on the roof."

Mason pulled up onto the curb in front of a building barely wide enough for a slender garage and a steel door, upon which the address had been spray-painted in uneven numbers.

"This isn't one of those places where they harvest your kidneys, is it?" Mason said.

"Would you just trust me for once?"

The adjacent building showed more recent signs of habitation, if only because someone had made the effort of boarding up the windows on the main level and erecting a chain-link fence around the Dumpster. What was left of the faded white letters painted directly onto the bricks above the third-floor windows hinted at a previous life as some sort of automotive-parts distributor.

Mason killed the engine and watched the still street. He sensed he was being watched the moment he climbed out of the Escalade. Whoever designed the building's security had done an amazing job. The cameras mounted to the roofline on the opposite side of the road were nearly invisible, while those on the garage and neighboring building were so well disguised, he wouldn't have seen them had he not been specifically looking for them.

"Leave me the keys," Gunnar said. "I'll stay in the car to make sure no one steals it."

"You just don't want to go in there," Mason said.

"There is that."

Mason tossed him the keys and caught up with Ramses, who stood in front of the steel door beside the garage and stared up into a camera designed to look like a broken light fixture.

"Remember when you asked if there was something I wasn't telling you?" he said. "Well, I hope you brought your checkbook."

"What's that supposed to mean?" Mason asked, but judging by the smile on his old friend's face, he suddenly wasn't sure he wanted to know.

44

The man who answered the door had to be seven feet tall and little more than skin and bones. He had long, stringy hair and a patchy beard to match. His black leather trench coat and camouflage bucket hat had seen better days. His movements were almost insectile, as though he possessed an abundance of joints found nowhere else in nature. He stepped aside and admitted them without a word.

Mason and Layne followed Ramses into a dark garage that reeked of motor oil and sawdust. A monitor displaying security footage from the street out front and the alley behind was mounted on the wall. It cast a dim glare onto the stained concrete and a lone rattrap in the corner.

The skeletal giant made strange, hollow breathing sounds as he led them through the doorway at the back of the garage and into a room stripped to the bare framework, through which they could see a toilet with a pull cord and a roll of toilet paper balanced on the lid. The carpet was worn to the mesh in a traffic pattern that led absolutely nowhere. The man abruptly stopped, turned to face them, and held out his hand, palm up.

"Your badges and guns," Ramses said.

The giant nodded as though in slow motion.

"You're kidding, right?" Layne said.

The giant sluggishly shook his head and revealed a jack-o'-lantern smile riddled with missing teeth. The gaps made it easy to see that he didn't have a tongue.

Mason handed over his badge and drew his Glock. He ejected the round from the chamber and the clip, flipped the pistol over, and passed it to the giant.

Layne glared at Mason as she reluctantly did the same.

The giant handed back their badges, but their weapons vanished into the deep hip pockets of his trench coat. He walked right up to the wall, knelt in a series of awkward motions, and pried up the edge of the carpet. His inhumanly long fingers moved like worms as he delicately rolled the carpet away from the wall until he revealed a square of cracked concrete that was a slightly different color than the rest of the foundation. There was a small hole at one end. He grabbed a crowbar from the sill of the boarded window, fitted the end into the hole, and levered the hatch open. A thin layer of concrete had been bonded to the wooden door to prevent it from producing a thumping sound if someone stepped on it, betraying the presence of the tunnel hidden underneath.

The intermingling scents of damp earth and mildew emanated from the dark hole. Mason could barely make out a series of rickety wooden stairs, which creaked and groaned as the giant descended. A faint light blossomed several seconds later.

"Do I want to know where he's going?" Mason asked.

"You mean where we're going," Ramses said.

"Down there."

"When has following a strange man into a dark cellar ever gotten anyone in trouble?"

"Let's just get this over with," Layne said, and climbed down the stairs.

"Does it bother you that she has a bigger pair than you do?" Ramses asked.

Mason ignored him and followed her. He had to duck his head under the packed earth and exposed cribbing to enter the tunnel connecting the shop to the three-story building next door. Layne didn't even need to lower her head to pass beneath the lone lightbulb or the conduits that powered it from the far end, where the giant ascended another staircase, the space above emitting a scent Mason would have recognized anywhere: gun oil.

The room that awaited them on the main floor was like none Mason had ever seen before. Everything was clean and clinical. Sterile.

The outer walls were reinforced and sealed with sheet metal. Racks filled the place from floor to ceiling. Halogen tubes lined the ceiling, providing enough illumination to display the contents of the recessed shelves, which were packed with what appeared to be every weapon ever manufactured.

"We shouldn't be here," Layne said.

Mason could only nod. While he'd been troubled by Ramses' personal arsenal on a professional level, he knew fellow agents with larger caches of weapons. Now that he was here, though . . . now that he'd seen . . . this . . . he worried that his old friend was in even deeper than he suspected.

There were assault rifles in all shapes and sizes and from every manufacturer under the sun. Full auto. Semiauto. Bolt action. Sniper. Handguns of all kinds. M2 .50-caliber machine guns. Shoulder rockets. Flamethrowers. Grenades. Incendiary and explosive devices. One-stop shopping for everyone, from your garden-variety psychos to wannabe dictators in the market for a quick coup.

"Pretty unbelievable, right?" Ramses said. "I told you to bring your checkbook."

Mason caught him by the elbow.

"What the hell have you gotten us into?"

"Relax, Mace. It's all military surplus. Nothing to get your sack in a twist over."

"Military surplus?"

"Maybe not ours, per se, but definitely someone's."

An elegant maple staircase with a plush crimson runner branched from the left side of the room. The giant grabbed the polished banister and ascended into a hallway that terminated in an anteroom decorated with framed black-and-white photographs of African trophy hunters from the twenties and upholstered furniture with clawed feet. It smelled of wood smoke, expensive cologne, and the barely detectable scents of formaldehyde and age.

"Tell me again how this guy is supposed to be able to help us," Layne said.

"He knows something about chemical weapons and the military."

"Good. As long as one of us is clear."

The giant approached the inset door in the opposite wall, from beneath which a flickering glow played across the hardwood floor. He gently rapped with his knuckles, turned once more to face them, and gestured for them to take a seat.

"What's this guy's name?" Mason asked.

"Ryan O'Leary," Ramses said. "But everyone calls him 'Rhino.'"

"I'm not calling a grown man Rhino," Layne said.

"Just a moment." The voice from the other side of the door was soft but firm, the kind that people tended to heed the first time. The inner locks disengaged with a series of heavy thuds and the door swung inward. Classical music flooded out on a wash of firelight, silhouetting the man standing before them against the roaring blaze in the hearth some distance behind him. "Thank you, Mr. Church."

The giant nodded and presented the visitors with an awkward bow and a flourish of his arm.

Ryan O'Leary was barely taller than Layne, but his shoulders spanned the width of the doorway and tested the fabric of his silk evening jacket. His neck was like that of a bull, thick and corded, and seemingly a swallow away from popping off the top button of his shirt and sending his bow tie spinning at them. He wore his white mane bushy, a mustache that spanned his lip and swept up his sun-leathered cheeks to his ears, and a pair of magnifying lenses resembling goggles, which he'd flipped up against his forehead so he could see them.

"Rhino," Ramses said, and proffered his hand.

"Put that thing away before you hurt someone with it," O'Leary said. He engulfed Ramses in a one-armed hug around the waist. "I haven't seen you in the flesh since Torkham. Did Donovan here ever tell you about what happened there?"

Mason could only shake his head.

"They don't want to hear about that," Ramses said, but O'Leary plowed on regardless.

"There we were, streaking through the Spīn Ghar Mountains above Khyber Pass in a Black Hawk, skimming mere feet above the ground, attempting a daring rescue of a special ops unit that had been ambushed across the Afghani border in Pakistan, where the army couldn't go without causing an international incident. Or at least where it wasn't supposed to go."

"You're a mercenary?" Layne asked.

"I've been many things in my time," O'Leary said, winking. "So we swoop down toward their last known location and follow this dry creek bed into a slot canyon positively littered with bodies. We're talking twenty-some hostiles, all of them wearing their baggy tan *shalwar kameez* and *shemagh* scarves, their beards flapping in the rotor wash. And this guy here. Somehow he'd escaped the cave where his team was slaughtered, only to end up surrounded. I don't know how he did it, but he must have been like an animal, killing every single one of those men with any weapon he could find until all he had left were rocks, his bare hands, and his teeth. We found him covered with blood, both arms broken, bleeding from at least a dozen—"

"Now's not the time," Ramses said in a tone that brooked no argument. Mason looked at his old friend, whose eyes had taken on a faraway cast. He knew something horrible had happened in the army, but he'd never imagined it could have been something so awful. No wonder Ramses had never told him what happened. "This is Special Agent James Mason and his partner, Special Agent Jessica Layne."

Mason and Layne flashed their badges for the sake of formality.

"Put those things away," O'Leary said. "I'm not the least bit intimidated by the implied threat of such totems. I told Donovan I'd help you and, if it's within my power, I fully intend to do just that. I would hope that should the need arise, you'd be willing to do the same for me."

He smiled and thrust out his hand, his liver-spotted skin betraying the advancing age he worked so hard to conceal.

Mason caught the expression of disapproval on his partner's face, but they didn't have any other options and they were running out of time. He sealed the deal with a firm shake.

O'Leary stepped aside and gestured for them to enter a cavernous chamber that appeared to occupy the entirety of the second floor. The inner doorways had been widened to open up what at one time must have been numerous separate apartments but now functioned like so many museum exhibits. The walls were adorned with dead animals,

be it their entire bodies, select portions, or just their heads, all painstakingly stuffed, posed, and displayed in rooms devoted to their sites
of origin. One featured North American animals ranging from elk and
deer to mountain goats and bighorn sheep, their marble eyes appearing
to track the procession walking below them. A Kodiak bear stood on its
hind legs in the center of the room, its paws raised, claws unfurled, head
touching the ceiling. It loomed over a mountain lion with its jaws open
and its haunches flexed as though preparing to lunge.

"*Ursus arctos middendorffi* and *Puma concolor*," O'Leary said. "The
former mauled a woman on the oil sands of Alberta and took nearly four
full days to track. The latter killed and partially devoured a man in his
home, but didn't put up nearly the fight I had hoped it would."

"Seriously?" Layne said.

O'Leary smiled patiently at her, as though she were a child, and
guided them through the South American room, which showcased jag-
uars and caimans, tapirs and vultures, and even an enormous snake
nearly as thick as the trunk of the dead tree upon which it was posed.

"*Eunectes murinus*. The green anaconda. This one removed a
sleeping child from his bed and led me on a three-day hunt through
the Amazon basin. You can still see the stitching where I removed the
remains from its digestive tract."

Mason caught a glimpse of the Asian display through the doorway
to his right, where a Bengal tiger appeared ready to pounce from its
hind legs and a cobra struck from the wall behind it, on their way into
the African room. Gorillas and apes, crocodiles and pythons, and even
the heads of a rhinoceros and a hippopotamus stared down from their
mounts, all of them seemingly focused upon the lion frozen mid-roar in
the center of the room.

"Both the *Panthera leo* before you and its Indian cousin *Panthera
tigris tigris* in the exhibit we just passed developed a taste for human
flesh and killed fifteen men between them," O'Leary said. "I wish I
could have better captured the sheer ferocity they displayed in their
final moments."

He ran his fingertips along the lion's flank on the way into his inner sanctum, a workroom housing tables covered with taxidermy tools.
The head of a baboon was clamped in an enormous vise on the central

table, its teeth bared and its hollow sockets staring accusingly at them. Flames nearly overflowed from the hearth behind it and cast a strange wavering glare over the entire room.

"I didn't see the smoke from the street," Mason said.

"It's vented on the back side of the building, above the industrial laundry."

O'Leary assumed his position before the primate's skull, tilted it to better see into its left eye socket, and lowered his magnifying lenses. He clipped a cigar and clenched it between his teeth. A flick of his Zippo and he puffed until the cherry glowed bright red. He commenced working as though they weren't even there.

"Aren't these things flammable?" Layne asked. She waved vaguely toward the trophies in various stages of completion on the surrounding tables, the racks of preservative chemicals, and the bags of stuffing material.

"I've got news for you, Special Agent." O'Leary smiled and revealed bright white teeth seemingly too large for his mouth. His black eyes, magnified by the lenses, glowed like charcoal on the brink of igniting. "Everything burns."

45

"I was eighteen years old when I joined the army," O'Leary said. He spoke with the same tone of longing and nostalgia old people generally used when talking about meeting their spouses or bringing their first child home from the hospital. "That would have made it '64. They enlisted me in the Chemical Corps and shipped me off to Vietnam before my signature was even dry. As it turned out, I liked it so much, I stayed until they physically forced me onto a plane in '73."

Up close, the signs of age were more readily apparent. The creases in his cheeks and at the corners of his eyes became furrows in the shadows cast by the fire. The joints of his remarkably dexterous hands appeared arthritic.

"What did you do in the Chemical Corps?" Mason asked.

"What didn't I do?" He tweezed stray lashes from the baboon's eyelid, set them delicately onto a small collection tray, and consulted a basketful of glass eyes of all different sizes, appraising one after another until he found the exact one he wanted. "I sprayed Agent Orange, launched mortar rounds, and shot every weapon at my disposal, but there was nothing I enjoyed more than watching the Vietcong and that infernal jungle of theirs burn."

"Napalm," Ramses said.

O'Leary winked at him and blew a mushroom cloud of smoke up toward the ceiling.

"It wasn't about the killing, though. There was just something awesome about watching that shell disappear through the treetops. There's a moment when time stands still, right before the world turns to flames, a single second where everything goes quiet and if you listen closely, you can hear the whoosh of the fire god drawing his first breath of life."

He set his cigar in the ashtray so he could use both hands to shoehorn the eyeball into the socket. The golden iris reflected the firelight.

"Maybe we haven't been especially clear about why we're here," Mason said. "Ramses thought you might be able to help us figure out whom one would hire to produce mass quantities of nerve agents and where we might find him."

"I'm trying to do just that, but you must understand the historical context," O'Leary said, clenching his cigar between his molars. Smoke drifted from his nostrils as he spoke. "Guys like me? We're only useful in wartime. We came home to hippies and protests. You think any of them wanted to reintegrate us into their new society of free love and flower power? We were bona fide killers and no one had any use for our particular skill sets. Not even the army. The brass knew the coming war would be a cold one. We were in a race to see who could destroy the world the most times over, which meant the Chemical Corps had a new mission, and on a much grander scale, so they sent us to Buckley Air Force Base in Colorado."

"And put you to work at the Rocky Mountain Arsenal."

"That's right. I did my job like a good soldier, but I never cared for the kind of chemical weapons they had us making, invisible gasses that killed indiscriminately and without mercy. Without honor. And I saw them in action, too. Mostly on rabbits, and more times than I care to recall. Ugly things to watch. I even saw a man get exposed once. Poor bastard knew he was going to die and there was nothing he could do to stop it. That's when I said enough's enough and got the hell out of there. I bounced around Central and South America for a while after that, selling my services to the highest bidder until there were no more revolutions to fight, and then hooked up with a defense contractor that paid in cash, asked very little in return, and helped finance a comfortable retirement."

"Dealing weapons?" Layne said.

"I provide hardware for connoisseurs and collectors, men like myself, who have what one might consider nontraditional needs. Not these gangbangers and street thugs. None of my products have been used in the commission of a crime, and every single one of them still has its serial number."

"So why the tunnel?"

"To make sure it stays that way. You want to see my weapons in action? Deploy the military in the streets and my clients will come out of the woodwork. The people who buy my wares are the kind who hope to God never to have to use them."

"And people like Ramses serve as the middleman," Mason said. "How much money does my good friend here bring in for you?"

"Enough to negotiate a deal to help federal agents I wouldn't otherwise have been inclined to invite into my home," O'Leary said.

Mason had to remind himself that Ramses was merely a broker who connected sinners with their vices and not an active participant in their damnation. Besides, the conversation had strayed and needed to be brought back in line.

"The men who made the nerve gasses?" he prompted.

"We're talking about scientists who dreamed up ways of killing people in the worst-possible ways. From far away, where they wouldn't get any blood on their hands. And you never saw them anywhere near the North Plants, where we manufactured sarin in those enormous vats. The only guys I really got to know out there were the ones working inside the hazard suits, moving drums from one bunker to another."

"Could any of those guys make it?"

"What do you think we were getting paid to do? You have to

understand the difference between making it and *creating* it. We essentially worked an assembly line. Spin this wheel. Monitor that gauge. Log the volume and flow rates. Switch drums. It was almost like making beer. Everyone had a role in producing it, but none of us ever really had the whole recipe."

"What about the scientists in charge of creating it? How many of them do you think there were?"

"We didn't spend a whole lot of time with the brain trust. You have to remember that this was the army and there was a chain of command. A grunt like me didn't rub elbows with officers."

"Do you remember if any of them were of Asian origin?"

"You mean like the Vietcong? There wouldn't have been any of them back then, not with so many of us fresh from fighting in Vietnam and having lost so many friends."

"What about the scientists themselves?" Mason asked. "Do you remember any of their names?"

"Some days, I don't even remember my own." He smiled wistfully and readjusted the baboon's head in the vise so he could view the opposite socket. "Time and age take a steep toll, I'm afraid, no matter how hard you rage against it. It's one of nature's most backhanded gifts: We forget much of the past so we don't have to see how little the present resembles it or recognize that there's no role for us in the future. It's been so long since I even thought about those days that not a single name springs to mind, but I might be able to recall something about them if you can refresh my memory."

Mason removed his phone from his pocket and passed it to O'Leary.

"How about faces? Do you recognize any of these guys?"

The older man held the smartphone sideways and at arm's length. The inverted image reflected from his magnifying lenses.

"Kind of difficult to place them with their eyes scratched out." He flipped up his lenses. "When did you say this was taken?"

"We're not sure," Layne said. "What do you think?"

"Maybe '68? Or '70, at the very latest."

"Do you recognize where it was taken?" Mason asked.

"Could be any base anywhere around the world. All of them looked the same back then."

"How about the men themselves?"

"You can hardly see any part of their faces, the way they've been disfigured."

"We really need you to try," Layne said. "Identifying these men is of critical importance to our investigation. Believe me when I say we wouldn't be here otherwise."

O'Leary blew one final gust of smoke up into the cloud trapped against the ceiling and stared at her for several seconds, as though truly seeing her for the first time.

"There's a chemical weapon in play and you don't have any idea where it is, do you?" he said.

"You're partly right," Mason said.

"Which part?" O'Leary stubbed out his cigar and seemed to inflate with an unspoken challenge. "The part about a chemical weapon being in play or the part where you don't know where the hell it is?"

Mason's patience had already worn thin and he wasn't in the mood to justify his situation to an arms dealer who had no more qualms about killing than the man they were hunting.

"Just look at the picture again," he said. "Tell us what we need to know and we'll be on our way."

"It's like that, is it?"

Ramses stepped between them and locked eyes with O'Leary.

"You know me, Rhino. I wouldn't have brought these guys here if we had any other option. This is an active situation and we need your help to end it."

"Does this have anything to do with what's going on in Central Park?"

Ramses stared Rhino down for several seconds before the older man slowly nodded, lowered his lenses, and looked at the picture again.

"You need to understand that it's been half a century. None of these guys look even slightly fam—Hold up. Him there." He tapped the screen. "That guy right there."

Mason walked around behind him and looked over his shoulder. He was pointing at one of the taller men, standing third from the right. The man had broad shoulders and an elongated head with a buzz cut. He had big front teeth and showed his gums when he smiled. Mason pinched the man's face between his fingers and drew them apart to magnify the image.

"Yeah," O'Leary said. "I remember him. Second Lieutenant Vance Edwards. Guys used to call him 'Mr. Ed' because of those big old teeth. That's the only reason I recognize him. He didn't go anywhere without that guy who looked like a pug. Denver, maybe. No, Danvers. And Milton Bradley, like the board-game maker. I don't know if that was his name or just what they called him, though. And bear in mind, '68 was before I met any of them. They might not have known each other way back then, but they were thicker than thieves by '73. If I were a betting man, I'd say at least one of those scratched-out faces belongs to them."

O'Leary handed Mason's phone back to him. He tried to push it back to encourage the old man to take another look, but it was clear he had nothing more to offer.

"Thank you for your time, Mr. O'Leary," Layne said.

"Come back anytime you want, Special Agent."

Mason scribbled his number on a piece of scratch paper and dropped it on the counter beside the one-eyed baboon's head.

"In case you think of anything else."

"Can I interest you in an AK-12 or -74 while you're here?"

"You do realize we're federal agents, right?" Layne said.

"That doesn't mean the government won't take away your guns with the rest of ours."

Mason could still hear him laughing all the way through the anteroom and into the hallway, where Ramses caught up with him and spun him around.

"What the hell were you thinking back there? This is my world out here. Not yours. It's my name, my reputation on the line."

Mason nodded his understanding. He knew his old friend had gone out on a limb trying to help him, but something about O'Leary had rubbed him the wrong way, something more than being surrounded by the carcasses of his conquests.

"Show some respect, Mace," Ramses said, and started down the stairs. "This is the underworld, and now you're in it."

46

Mason drove on autopilot, allowing Ramses to guide him out of the industrial district while his mind ran through what they'd learned. O'Leary had been able to provide a positive ID for one of the men in the picture, and possibly enough information about the man's entourage to track them down, too, but he hadn't been able to shine any light on the Scarecrow himself. If he were truly in his late forties or early fifties, he wouldn't have been in the army at the same time as those men anyway. In fact, he might not even have been born yet, which meant he encountered those men after O'Leary took his leave, and presumably sometime during the era when the country was ramping down its production of chemical weapons and starting to actively dispose of them. So if he'd been a chemical engineer for Uncle Sam, his face should have been among those from the personnel files Layne had received, unless he'd deliberately altered it, which brought Mason to what Alejandra had said about his eyes.

The stars intrigued Mason. His first thought was that Alejandra had seen the reflection from the face shield of a gas mask, but it should have cast a single reflection, not two, which made him think of what the woman from across the hall had said about Nakamura wearing tinted glasses, presumably due to sensitivity to light, but lenses like that were made with scratchproof and antiglare coatings. While he couldn't entirely exclude the use of eyeglasses, or even magnifying lenses like O'Leary had been wearing, what else could possibly look like metal reflecting from a man's eyes?

Perhaps the Scarecrow wasn't specifically of Japanese descent after all. It was always possible that something about the culture spoke to him. The *kanji* characters were one thing, but the mycotoxin from the *Fusarium nivale* mushroom, the saxitoxin derived from the puffer fish, and the venomous tentacles of the *habu-kurage* hadn't been chosen at random. They were integral to the message he was trying to deliver. Either he viewed that culture as part of his identity or he'd taken on his identity in response to a cultural wrong. There probably weren't many

MICHAEL LAURENCE

Japanese citizens who hadn't at least considered the notion of avenging the deaths of the two hundred thousand people killed in Hiroshima and Nagasaki, but these men, specifically, were the Scarecrow's targets, not their flag. Releasing a chemical weapon in a major city center would definitely qualify as a proportional, if belated, response, although that would be considered a personal motive, whereas the Scarecrow had been treating every aspect of the production and transport of the Novichok as a professional obligation.

And everywhere Mason turned, he found himself looking back in time at the Rocky Mountain Arsenal and finding the Department of Homeland Security hurriedly setting up roadblocks all around it. The men in the pictures were the key. While that was where their association began, it wasn't until some unknown number of years later that they crossed paths with the man who would become the Scarecrow.

They dropped Ramses off at a car-rental place near the Transit Authority and went around the corner to wait for him at a trendy café that was mercifully still serving coffee. They'd be able to cover twice as much ground with a second SUV, and suddenly Mason felt like heading south, away from the city. Lost in the accumulation of bodies were the two Israeli scientists, who now stood apart from the rest of the victims specifically for their lack of direct involvement with the U.S. military, and yet identifying them had been of great consequence to the DHS. He needed to figure out why, and it all started with Bern, their last known location before their staged deaths.

Layne ordered at the counter while Mason and Gunnar sat outside on the dark street. A bitterly cold breeze assailed them from the east. Tiny snowflakes accumulated on the umbrella above their table and tapped against the front window, through which he could barely see Layne in the line of the crowded, dimly lit coffeehouse. Photocopied handbills advertising concerts and protests were posted in the window beside a professional poster promising a sneak peek at the future of renewable green energy in Times Square.

"You were right," Gunnar said. "Peter Cavanaugh is on this personnel list your partner got from the army."

"Can you access his Official Military Personnel File?"

Layne backed out the front door with four mugs balanced on a wooden tray. She set them on the table and squeezed behind Mason to get to the chair next to him.

"His OMPF is long gone," Gunnar said.

"Homeland probably made it disappear the moment we figured out who owned the trucks," Mason said. "What do we have on him?"

"All I see here is his name on a list, which at least confirms what you already knew, I guess."

"We need to know where he was stationed and when he was there," Mason said.

"What about his health records?" Layne asked. "There should be a list of dates and treatment facilities we could use to establish a time line of his postings."

"The military routinely filed the health records as part of the personnel files until '92," Gunnar said.

"What about his ex-wives?"

"Excellent idea. Assuming they were seen on the government's dime, we ought to be able to figure out if he was ever stationed at the RMA."

Mason's phone vibrated in his jacket pocket. He grabbed it and checked the caller ID. The main line out of the Rocky Mountain Regional Forensic Laboratory. He made sure they were alone on the freezing street before putting the call on speaker so the others could hear.

"Mason."

"SEAL," Locker said.

"What?"

"It's an acronym for sea, air, and land."

Mason rubbed his temples with his thumb and middle finger.

"Start at the beginning, okay?"

"Your guy's in the navy," Locker said. "Or at least he was anyway. I ran the DNA sample I received from the Cumberland County ME through the Combined DNA Index System and got a hit pretty much right away, only it was for a six-year-old child in San Diego."

"They incinerated a kid?"

Gunnar and Layne both stopped drinking and looked directly at Mason.

"You're not listening. You know how CODIS includes pretty much every DNA sample ever uploaded, right? Well, in this case, a sample from a newborn was submitted as part of a paternity suit. This sample matched one belonging to an enlisted seaman, only when I attempted to access the corresponding data, there was nothing there. I mean gone. Poof. Totally missing. Someone with a serious clearance level had to physically go into the database and remove it. But since the kid's sample was there, I was able to jump through a few hoops and get a peek at his birth certificate. That's why it took so long to call you. I mean, jeez, you'd think I was trying to get a peek at the First Lady's gynecological records—"

"Locker."

"Major Ashley Marshall Saddler. Male. Thirty-four years old. Or at least he was. He was part of the SEAL team stationed in Damascus during the 2013 sarin attack, and I only know that much because it's part of the *Congressional Record.* His trail ends in 2017, when he re-signed his commission."

"Where's he been since then?"

"Sounds like a question worth answering."

"Does Homeland know about this?"

"I don't think so. The whole team packed up and left yesterday afternoon. My cheeks are starting to hurt from smiling so much."

"Where did they go?"

"Let's see. Where did they leave that note? It's got to be around here somewhere."

"Funny. Did they take everything with them?"

"Are you looking for something in particular?"

"The bodies of the Scarecrow's victims."

"Are you kidding me? They never even arrived."

"Do you still have the pictures you guys took of them?"

"Of course. Even if they cleaned out my system on their way out the door, I utilize off-site backup to routinely save all data every hour. With as much evidence as we deal with here for open investigations and pending trials, we'd have to be the world's biggest idiots to keep it all under one roof with a big old bull's-eye on it."

"Can you send them to me? Just the faces, okay?"

"What good can they possibly do you at this point? I heard you got the rug ripped out from under you, too."

"We're technically on standby for operational support."

"Sounds like a paid vacation to me," Locker said. "But you're not letting this one go, are you?"

"Are you?"

Locker chuckled and hung up.

Gunnar jumped in the moment he was certain the call had ended.

"Major Ashley Saddler entered the private sector as a security consultant for a company called Kenward, whose stated mission is to 'provide professional and efficient turnkey support services for commercial enterprises and developing governments.' It specializes in risk management solutions and security services for government agencies and commercial industries from construction and mining to oil and gas."

"It's a private defense contractor," Layne said.

"With a focus on the energy sector . . ."

Gunnar's words trailed off and his eyes became distant.

"You said something earlier about a surge in energy futures trading," Mason said.

"That can't be a coincidence, but how did a private contractor end up as ashes inside a truck used to haul chemical weapons?"

Mason's phone vibrated to alert him to the arrival of an email. Five of them, actually. Each labeled by victim number. He opened them and flipped through the attached pictures. Five men in varying stages of decomposition, photographed from several different angles. With and without their hats. Their flesh ravaged by birds, their eyes pecked out. Even had they still been there, they wouldn't have done him any good, considering those of the men in the picture against which he compared them had been scratched out. Only one man stood apart, thanks to a prominent gold incisor tooth.

This was a long shot and he knew it. Even if the Scarecrow's goal had been to hunt down eight of the twelve men in the picture and deliver his message to the remainder, the odds of the one man Mason hoped to find among the dead were at best less than fifty-fifty, but, for once, luck was on his side.

The man he was looking for was victim number two.

Mason had stood right in front of him and never known. The desiccated remains of the dead man's musculature and tissues distorted the shape of his face and his skull to such a degree that he hardly looked human. Fortunately, all Mason needed was the teeth.

"What are you smiling about?" Layne asked.

He tilted the screen so she could see it, then passed the phone across the table to Gunnar.

"Hello, Mr. Ed," she said.

"Second Lieutenant Vance Edwards," Gunnar said. "In the flesh. Or what's left of it anyway."

They might have closed the book on his story, but perhaps men named Danvers and Milton Bradley were still out there somewhere. And there was one place where they knew all three men had been stationed at the same time, the same place where all of the various threads of the investigation appeared to converge.

The Rocky Mountain Arsenal.

47

Elsewhere

The Scarecrow waited until it was certain the man was fully incapacitated before reaching through the bars of his cage and checking his pulse and respiration rate, just to be sure. It unlocked the cage, grabbed the man by his collar, and pulled him out onto the floor. His wrists bled from where he'd attempted to use one of the tongue depressors to sever his bindings, reminding the Scarecrow of how it had once done the same thing, although for entirely different, and equally futile, reasons. In response, they had taken away all of the tongue depressors and the scarecrows it had made from them. The very same man who had demonstrated how to make them had gathered them all in a bag and taken them away, the same man now lying unconscious at its feet.

A hissing sound erupted from its throat and it kicked the man. Over and over. Until blood trickled from his ear.

"No . . ." the Scarecrow said aloud. "Not . . . yet."

For as much as it wanted the man to suffer, it had been planning his death for so long that it needed everything to be perfect, the precise way it had envisioned his denouement for nearly half a century, during which time it had tried to create a normal life for itself, only to see it derailed by the painful and degenerative conditions that not only consumed it from the inside but also caused the physical deformations responsible for the expressions of revulsion on the faces of those it passed on the street, forcing isolation upon it, trapping it within its own mind, where it rehearsed its ultimate transformation and the misery it would inflict upon its tormentors through the lonely days and sleepless nights, at least until it had found a group of like-minded individuals, a family, for as long as that had lasted.

Now, with its other half dying and its family destroyed, all it had left was the vengeance it had been plotting since the first time the men in their white lab coats entered its room, since the first time it breathed from the mask, electrifying the passageways of its nerves, like so many lightning bolts striking beneath its skin, triggering the muscular contractions and the nausea that would cripple it for days at a time. It had spent years meticulously stalking those responsible, tracking their movements, cataloging every aspect of their lives, not merely waiting for the perfect opportunity but creating it. Carefully inching closer and closer to the man whose family had been behind everything, working its way into his sphere of influence until such time as it was able to plant the seed of its revenge with his most trusted adviser, who, in the end, had proved that trust to be misplaced. His time would come soon, only on the grandest stage possible, one from which everyone in the world would see him fall, taking his godforsaken name with him.

It had received a far better offer for the services it had rendered anyway, one that would serve as the perfect posthumous insult, a proposal relayed to it by the Hoyl, a faithful believer in the mission of his true master, whose goals aligned perfectly with those of the Scarecrow. A master who wanted Quintus to realize with his final thoughts that he had never had any control over the coup he believed he had started, that he'd been outmaneuvered from the very beginning by another, the mastermind whose machinations had set the coming war into motion, who'd used the Hoyl to orchestrate the downfall of Secundus and now employed the Scarecrow to destroy Quintus. It cared nothing for the internal politics of the Thirteen. The only thing that mattered was knowing that it would live long enough to kill Quintus, and die knowing that it was taking millions of people with it, achieving a dream first envisioned in the mind of a terrified child, a dream its family had failed to achieve a quarter of a century ago.

The Scarecrow dragged the man down the hallway, through the dirt, and into the cold room, its breath pluming from its lips. It released the man's arms and let them fall to the floor. The back of his head rebounded from the concrete hard enough to make his teeth click. It rolled him over a mound of broken flooring and packed earth to the edge of the hole. With a smile, it nudged him over the edge, descended the ladder behind him, and stepped down, planting one foot to either side of his head. It watched the man's chest rise and fall and blood flow from a laceration on his cheek for several minutes before scooting him onto the travois and strapping him down.

A faint tapping sound emanated from its backpack, which caused its smile to grow even wider.

The Scarecrow donned its harness, hooked the straps to the contraption, and struck off into the darkness.

PART V

An invisible empire has been set up above the forms of democracy.

—Woodrow Wilson,
The New Freedom (1912)

48

"I found it," Gunnar said.

Mason set aside his laptop, crossed the aisle, and sat on the opposite side of the table from his old friend. He'd ridden in private jets before, but Gunnar's Cessna Citation XLS was unlike any he'd ever seen. It was only fifty-two feet long but had been customized to more closely resemble an apartment than an aircraft. The seats were bluish gray and upholstered with leather as soft as butter, the woodwork maple and polished to a reflective shine. The fore cabin featured a functional kitchen, and the aft cabin had been turned into a bedroom.

The flight from Republic Airport in East Farmingdale, New York, to Washington, D.C., was an hour and ten minutes, about half an hour less than it would take Ramses and Layne to drive from Brooklyn to the New Jersey State Police Headquarters in West Trenton. She'd insisted upon going with him to track down Maj. Delvin Roybal to make sure everything was handled the proper way, which was fine with Mason, because his was a task that needed to be conducted in person.

Gunnar spun around his laptop. The aerial photograph on the screen was in faded color and taken at such an angle as to suggest it had been snapped from a plane shortly after takeoff. A gray sky filled with clouds. The jagged blue line of the Rockies on the distant horizon. Brown prairie in between. A red-and-white-checkered water tower

stood on tall striped legs maybe a hundred yards west of a row of buildings, including a warehouse with a radio tower, an industrial plant
crowned with smokestacks, and a six-story building that looked like
a parking garage, with exterior walkways and electrical works on the
roof. And in front of them, at the point where the main road entered
from the south, a plain white L-shaped building with a flat roof. If one
were to gather a dozen uniformed men in front of it, a picture could
be taken in such a way as to show the crown of the water tower above
the roofline to the upper left and the massive structure to the right.

The caption had been scratched directly into the picture itself,
scraping away the emulsion.

It read simply: RMA. North Plants. 1967.

"What are the odds, right?" Gunnar said.

Mason nodded. He grabbed his laptop, searched the Internet until
he found detailed imagery of the Rocky Mountain Arsenal on a site
devoted to Superfund's various remediation projects, and set it up next
to Gunnar's so he could view both screens at the same time. The RMA
had been built on a grid composed of twenty-five equal squares, each a
mile to a side. The majority of the plants were clustered on the six in the
center. The South Plants were separated from the North Plants by an
open-air chemical evaporation basin and a series of disposal trenches.
Apart from the occasional dirt road, the remainder of the site had been
left undeveloped. There were dozens of outlying lakes to the east, most
of which had been earmarked for sediment remediation, and a network
of chemical sewers to the north and west more reminiscent of the roots of
a tree than the standard right angles of military construction.

Gunnar leaned closer so he could see.

"What are we looking for?" he asked.

"I'm not sure, but something happened here that no one wants us
to know about."

Mason opened the file containing aerial photographs from the site
survey during the early eighties, shots taken by a camera attached to the
underside of an airplane, detailing each of the grids, one by one. Dirt
roads stood apart from flatlands composed of yellow and brown weeds
and grasses. Tree-lined streams and gullies. Natural lakes ringed with

cattails and asphalt-lined evaporative basins shaped like diamonds. Both the North and South Plants were the size of small towns.

He tracked down the legend to see what had once been housed there. The North Plants, as O'Leary had described, featured buildings for chemical production, weapons assembly, and warehousing. The South Plants, on the other hand, formed a veritable city unto itself in the middle of the sprawling Rocky Mountain Arsenal complex, one that hadn't belonged to the army at all, but, rather, to a private corporation, simultaneously allowing it to share the same facilities as a military regiment amassing the largest chemical arsenal the world had ever known and shielding it from regulatory oversight.

Mason had to read the name twice to make sure his eyes weren't deceiving him.

Royal Nautilus Petroleum.

His head swirled with the implications. He thought about the chemical subsidiary from which the hydrogen fluoride had been diverted, the decomposition bacterium reminiscent of the kind oil companies used to consume spills, Charles Raymond with his bulging eyes and split tongue, and the picture Gunnar had found of Mosche and Chenhav—the two dead Israeli scientists—with Andreas Mikkelson, managing director of the very same company that had occupied the South Plants of the Rocky Mountain Arsenal while the twelve men with their eyes scratched out had been stationed there.

"Holy shit," Gunnar said.

Mason's phone vibrated. He recognized Layne's number and answered on speaker.

"I was just about to call you," he said.

"My contact from the army finally got back to me about the guy we found in Central Park," she said. "Turns out Charles Raymond was never actually in the military, but he was registered as a civilian contractor from 1968 to 1992, which makes his records just recent enough to have been uploaded to the modern system. And you'll never guess where he was assigned."

"The Rocky Mountain Arsenal."

"You really know how to take all the fun out of this, don't you?"

"We only just learned that Royal Nautilus Petroleum owned a large portion of the South Plants."

"Which presumably puts Raymond in the same place at the same time as the rest of the Scarecrow's victims."

"Did your guy know the nature of the arrangement between the army and Royal Nautilus?" Mason asked.

"No, but he was able to confirm that Raymond's credentials listed him as Research and Development," Layne said.

"The presence of an R and D contingent suggests a relationship beyond the simple manufacture of precursor chemicals."

"Precisely," Gunnar said. He toggled between windows as he read from the trove of information he'd amassed in a matter of minutes. "Nautilus Chemical Company, a division of Royal Nautilus Petroleum, purchased on-site operations in 1952 and used them for the manufacture of herbicides and pesticides. Among the chemicals it produced were dichlor—an integral component of sarin—and aldrin, dieldrin, and malathion, all of which have since been banned. They discharged millions of gallons of liquid waste into natural depressions in the ground and buried solid waste in unlined holes. Accidental spills in the range of hundreds of thousands of gallons precipitated a plan to inject chemical waste into a twelve-thousand-foot-deep well, which caused earthquakes throughout the Denver area. They discontinued on-site operations in 1982."

"Raymond was long gone by then," Layne said. "He was at a similar facility called the Edgewood Arsenal from 1972 to 1978."

"Where was that?" Mason asked.

"Where are you by now?"

"Probably somewhere over Maryland. Why?"

"Look down."

"You're kidding, right?"

"It's just outside of Baltimore, on Chesapeake Bay," she said. "It's now called the U.S. Army Edgewood Chemical Biological Center and is considered the principal research and development resource for nonmedical chemical and biological defense. We're talking gas masks, personal protective gear, detection devices, whatnot."

"So one manufactures the weapons, the other the defense against them." Mason paused and considered the implications. "That's why they needed an R and D team. They had to test their products."

"According to the Department of Defense," Gunnar said, "the U.S. Army Chemical Corps conducted classified medical experiments at the Edgewood Arsenal from 1955 to 1975 with the stated mission of testing protective clothing and pharmaceuticals and studying the impact of low-dose chemical warfare agents on military personnel. Roughly seven thousand soldiers were exposed to upward of two hundred different chemicals, among them anticholinesterase nerve agents like GB and VX, mustard gas, irritants and riot-control agents, and psychoactive drugs like LSD and PCP."

"You see why I don't want anything to do with these assholes?" Ramses said. "They were experimenting on their own people, for Christ's sake."

"Where did they get their test subjects?" Mason asked.

"They were solicited through the Medical Research Volunteer Program," Gunnar said. "Primarily from Baker Company."

"Later renamed Bravo Company, or Company B," Ramses said. "These were your standard enlisted infantrymen. Foot soldiers. Grist for the mill. Expendables."

"If the woman who lived across the hall from the apartment the Scarecrow maintained in Mayfair Towers was right about his age," Mason said, "he couldn't have been much more than a child during the time Raymond was participating in the experimentation."

"Which makes him unlikely to have been affected on a personal level," Layne said.

"Unless they experimented on his parents," Ramses said.

"We're getting ahead of ourselves here," Mason said. "We need to figure out if any of the other victims were at Edgewood. Can your contact get us a list of the men stationed there?"

"It's a work in progress," Layne said. "Hopefully, someone's pulling the records from the National Archives as we speak."

"What about the volunteers?"

"Long-term follow-up was practically nonexistent," Gunnar said. "By the early eighties, the National Academy of Sciences could only track down about sixty percent of them. There was a class action lawsuit filed in the early nineties, though. I could probably get a list of those who participated without much difficulty."

"Do it," Mason said. "What about our dead Israeli scientists? Chenhav and Mosche, the biochemist who left the message in blood. Can we connect either of them to the RMA or Edgewood?"

"At the time of the plane crash, both men were in their late thirties, which means they would have been teenagers during the time frame in question," Gunnar said. "I did find something interesting while looking into them, though. Another plane went down near the Russian border six weeks earlier, on October fourth. Siberia Airlines Flight 1812 was shot down by the Ukrainian Air Force en route from Tel Aviv to Novosibirsk, Russia. Everyone on board was killed, including thirty-eight Russians and forty Israelis, among them five microbiologists, three of whom worked in advanced medical research."

"What do you mean, 'shot down'?" Layne said.

"According to Ukrainian officials, it was inadvertently hit by an antiaircraft missile during testing. Supposedly, the main fuselage is on the bottom of the Black Sea at a depth of more than three thousand feet, too deep for divers to retrieve the black box, so no one can dispute their account."

"That's convenient."

"What were they all doing on the same plane?" Mason asked.

"There's no way of knowing for sure," Gunnar said. "What I can tell you, though, is that Novosibirsk is considered the scientific capital of Siberia. It boasts more than fifty research facilities and thirteen full universities in a city the size of metro Denver."

"That's seven dead Israeli scientists in a two-month span."

"Immediately following the terrorist attack on nine/eleven."

They were onto something of critical importance. Mason could positively feel it.

"What would five Israeli microbiologists do in the scientific capital of Siberia?" he asked.

"That's the million-dollar question, isn't it?" Gunnar said. "Let's look at it from a historical perspective. The Soviet Union dissolved in 1991 and left the country a shambles. The world's largest state-controlled economy suddenly had to transition to a market-oriented model, which nearly collapsed the central bank and caused double-digit inflation. They had to slash their Cold War military budget, eliminate their social-welfare systems, and run up the national debt just to remain afloat. Fortunately, they had a massive arsenal of weapons and trade partners willing to pay exorbitant prices, especially Iran."

"Which posed a credible threat to Israel's national security."

"Exactly, so if you were Israel, what would you do?"

"I'd make sure I not only possessed the same weaponry as my enemies but any possible advantage I could gain."

He was suddenly reminded of what Johan had said about America bringing the German scientists into the fold after the war to help ramp up its military for the seemingly inevitable conflict with the Soviet Union. Was it so hard to believe that with their geographical proximity, the Soviets had simply taken the technology itself?

"The Russian military became a clearinghouse," Mason said. "Proprietary assault rifles, machine guns, and pistols were popping up all over the world in the hands of people who shouldn't have had them. It wouldn't surprise me if they'd been willing to part with some of the nastier aspects of their arsenal, too. For the right price."

"You think the Israeli scientists were buying biological or chemical weapons?" Layne asked.

"I think they'd already bought whatever it was. You don't send microbiologists to negotiate a deal. You send them to train on technology or verify the authenticity of a sample. You send them because they're the only ones who know how to safely handle whatever they're bringing back."

"What do you think that was?"

"I don't know," Mason said. "But someone didn't want them taking it back with them."

"And the following month," Layne said, "two more scientists allegedly died on the return trip from Bern—which we now know not to be the case—only to magically reappear two decades later beneath a building used to manufacture biological and chemical weapons."

"If someone deliberately crashed their plane, they could have just as easily downed it on the way to Bern, instead of on the way back," Gunnar said. "They wanted Chenhav and Mosche to reach Switzerland before they made them disappear. More than a hundred people were killed so that no one would ever find out what they'd bought or what they intended to do with it."

"We need to know why they were there," Mason said.

He recognized the magnitude of the statement the moment it crossed his lips.

Bern was where the trails of both the Scarecrow and the Hoyl converged, mass murderers specializing in chemical and biological weapons, respectively. And if Mason was right, there was only one person who possessed that knowledge, whether he knew it or not: the new owner of AgrInitiative, formerly AgrAmerica, and almost Global Allied Biotechnology and Pharmaceuticals.

The Honorable J. R. Mason III.

His father.

49

WASHINGTON, D.C.

Mason arranged for a car to be waiting for them when they arrived at Ronald Reagan National Airport. He'd expected the service to send something fairly ordinary, but he'd apparently forgotten the kind of clout his name carried in the District, especially considering he shared it with his father. The Town Car had been idling on the tarmac, with the driver standing at attention beside the passenger door. If he was surprised to see the younger James Richmond Mason and not the senator, it didn't show on his expressionless face. He simply opened the rear door, ushered them inside, and assumed his seat behind the wheel.

His father's address was already programmed into the GPS. It was only five miles from the airport but promised to take twenty minutes, thanks to an accident on the George Washington Memorial Parkway and the standard Capitol Hill snafu. He hadn't visited his father in D.C. since right after his first election to the Senate, at which time he'd been staying in a mansion that essentially amounted to a frat house for elected officials, none of whom left their offices for longer than it took to sleep. Since then, however, his old man had acquired a town house about half a mile from the Capitol Building—using his own personal funds, despite the story the media had tried to sell at the time.

Gunnar opened his laptop on his thighs the moment he had his seat belt fastened and resumed his work. His fingers were a blur on the keyboard, and the images on the screen flashed past at lightning speed. Mason brought up the picture of the twelve men posed in front of the building at the Rocky Mountain Arsenal on his cell phone. The Scarecrow had already killed as many as half of them. Presumably time had contributed some amount of attrition, as well. If the profilers were right, two of the remaining men had been chosen to finish the design in the field, one of whom was to be the centerpiece. If he was right about Marchment's being one of them, the Scarecrow was going to have a hell of a time getting to him with a phalanx of DHS agents surrounding him at all times, but he'd undoubtedly taken that into consideration from the start and already had a plan in place, presumably one that would be enacted prior to releasing the Novichok. Or would he use its release to draw Marchment out into the open? Either way, both factored prominently into the endgame, which Mason could feel approaching with the inevitability of a thunderstorm building against the horizon.

He swiped away the picture, opened his email, and clicked on a new message from Locker, who'd attached several photographs of the man he'd identified from the ashes in the front seat of the flatbed. The first was from Maj. Ashley Saddler's personnel file and featured him standing in dress uniform in front of an American flag. He didn't look like an Ashley. In fact, he looked like the kind of guy who'd beat the hell out of anyone who called him by that name. His neck was thicker than his head and tested the strength of his collar. His ears were small and the lobes bowed outward. The muscles in his broad jaw bulged as a state of normalcy. His steel gray eyes were as flat as his buzz cut.

The remainder of the images had been taken in the field and showed a man who positively dwarfed his companions. He was the human equivalent of a tank leading a motorcade of Jeeps. His Colt M4A1 rifle looked tiny propped against his meaty shoulder and in the grasp of his massive hands. He wore camouflage fatigues and still stood apart from his surroundings like a bear from the forest.

"The odds of dying in a plane crash are one in five point four million," Gunnar said. "The odds of seven men in the same field and from the same country dying in the same manner over a span of two months are infinitesimal, so I broadened my search parameters and found a veritable run on scientists."

"What do you mean?"

"Seventy more of them died between 2001 and 2007."

"Is that statistically higher than any other profession?"

"I have no idea, but you have to hear the way some of them went out. A biomedical scientist found splattered on the sidewalk outside the parking garage of his office building. An expert on DNA sequencing slashed to death with a sword. An Australian scientist working on a vaccine to protect against biochemical weapons found dead in the air lock of his lab cooler. A renowned virologist found three hundred miles away from where he'd abandoned his car. A defected Russian bioweapons authority found dead after announcing his intention to exhume the bodies of ten victims of the 1918 Spanish flu in hopes of creating a vaccine. A microbiologist working on AIDS and liver cancer research found beaten to death outside his lab. Throw in your seven Israelis and that's thirteen dead scientists in the three months following nine/eleven alone, which verges on statistically impossible."

Mason closed his eyes and focused on his old friend's words. He felt as though he were on the brink of fitting two pieces of the puzzle into place, but the revelation eluded him.

"Listen to some of these other causes of death over the following six years," Gunnar said. "Bandit attack. Home invasion. Arsenic poisoning. Suicides. Stabbings. Plane crashes. Several hit and runs. Multiple counts of blunt trauma to the head. We aren't talking about minor players, either. The majority of these guys were leaders in their respective fields. A full third were developing vaccines for viruses with potential weapons applications. Another third were hematologists, doctors who specialize in the blood and blood-borne pathogens. Nuclear physicists. Biological warfare experts. The list goes on and on."

The timing couldn't be coincidental. The terrorist attack on September 11, 2001, had changed the world more than any single event in recent history, catalyzing the reaction that produced entire populations willing to exchange their freedom for safety, their privacy for security. People welcomed the NSA into their most intimate conversations, the government into their homes, and Big Brother into cameras on every street corner. All they asked in return was that they be able to go about their daily lives without the threat of fiery death raining down on them from the sky. They trusted the dawning police state not to abuse the power they'd bestowed upon it, powers custom-tailored to an entity like the Thirteen, which through strategic planning had planted operatives at the highest levels, wiring itself into every home in the Western world, entering without a warrant and monitoring every aspect of their lives, positioning itself to quell any potential resistance before it even started.

It made perfect sense that a syndicate that drew its power from fear would want to aggressively invest in other similar catastrophes all around the world to effectively complete the full transfer of authority, using biological or chemical attacks that would make the destruction of the twin towers at the World Trade Center pale by comparison. To pull off such an ambitious global coup, not only would it need to gather the scientists with the requisite skills to create those cataclysmic events; it needed to remove those who could derail their plans from the equation. And considering how quickly it had acted after the planes hit, there was no doubt that this had been the Thirteen's plan all along.

"Kind of has the feel of not only paving the way for bioterrorists but setting the fields involved with preparedness back in the process, doesn't it?" Mason said.

"A man with more than a decade's head start researching the Spanish flu could have certainly stood in the way of the Hoyl's plans," Gunnar said. "The same way an Australian scientist working on an inoculation against biochemical weapons of mass destruction might have been a big hindrance when it came to the release of large quantities of Novichok."

"Are you certain this is all viable intelligence?" Mason asked.

"I'm not pulling this off some conspiracy theorist's blog. We're talking about major sources. *The New York Times, Denver Post, Los Angeles Times, London—*"

"That's not what I mean. All I'm saying is that you can connect any pattern of dots if you try hard enough."

Gunnar smirked.

"You seem to have forgotten who you're dealing with."

The Town Car crossed Pennsylvania Avenue and Mason caught a glimpse of the Library of Congress in the distance. They passed Seward Square and entered a neighborhood marked by skeletal deciduous trees and nineteenth-century row houses that appeared to have been stretched vertically to compress as many units as possible into the allotted space. They had formal stoops and the kind of ornate cornices and woodworking details around the windows that Mason generally associated with museums.

"Here's what I don't get," Mason said. "If all of these scientists were killed and their bodies left to be found, why were Mosche and Chenhav kept around for so long before they were executed?"

The driver pulled up against the curb and parked in front of a two-story house with basement windows partially concealed behind an elaborate wrought-iron fence. The facade was greenish gray, the door a bright rose color, and the stairs black. A silhouette passed behind the drapes hanging in the oriel bay window of the parlor.

"They were obviously contributing in some way."

"And they couldn't possibly have done so for two decades without doing so of their own free will."

The driver opened his door and stepped out onto the street. The frigid breeze cut through the warm interior and chased dead leaves across the asphalt.

"This is the part I always find awkward," Gunnar said. He waited patiently for the driver to open his door before climbing out and stepping aside for Mason to do the same. He slipped the chauffeur a tip so discreetly that Mason nearly missed it. Sometimes it was hard to believe that this was the adult form of the kid who'd worn a hairnet and worked in the school cafeteria to send money back home to his grandparents. "Are you sure we shouldn't have called first?"

"What, and give him a chance to slip out before we got here?"

"To make sure he has access to the information we need."

"Trust me, he has it," Mason said. "He hired a cybersecurity firm to install servers and equip a remote-access terminal in his guest bedroom so he could network with his executives at AgrInitiative."

"You just didn't want to give him enough notice that he could have matching sweaters waiting when you arrived."

"You're just jealous."

"There are very few things that inspire jealousy in me," Gunnar said. "Your relationship with your father is not one of them."

"What do you say we get this over with, then."

50

Mason wasn't so self-involved that he imagined his father sitting by the phone, waiting for him to call, or peeking through the curtains every few minutes on the off chance he might drop by. They'd both known the chances of his actually accepting his father's invitation to join him for New Year's. As it turned out, he'd never once thought about what his father did when he wasn't physically present. Mason recognized that he was a United States senator and had a better idea than most of what that job entailed, but he hadn't really understood that the job was what he did and not who he was. When it came right down to it, Mason saw the job as his father the same way. It was what his old man did—sometimes better than others—not who he was. In fact, he knew absolutely nothing about who his father was when he wasn't wearing either hat. Surely he wasn't the first adult child to suddenly realize that his youth, while it had been everything to him, was just a phase in his father's life that had come and gone and that if he wanted to have an actual relationship with him now, it would be on different terms, ones that had yet to be clearly defined.

All of those thoughts ran through his head in the time it took for his father to open the front door and for him to barge right past him.

"Look, Dad. I—" His father held a glass of wine. The clatter of heels echoed from down the hallway. His cheeks were flushed, but not nearly to the same degree as his son's. "I . . . forgot you had company."

Mason knew that his father had seen other women after his mother died, but he'd never brought them home. Truthfully, he'd only brought Mason home for the rare holiday here or there, and he was the old man's flesh and blood, which surely meant that whoever she was, she was special to him in a way that however many others hadn't been.

"James, my boy. Do come in. And Gunnar, eh? I think the last time I saw you was, oh . . . long enough ago that you still had pimples. Not here to wrest my company from my grasp, are you? Then again, maybe that wouldn't be such a terrible thing after all."

He proffered his hand to Gunnar, who shook it with a crooked half smile on his face.

"Senator. It's kind of disorienting seeing you in person instead of on the news. I was starting to wonder if you didn't just play a character on TV."

"Touché."

He clapped Gunnar on the shoulder, gave Mason a fairly awkward hug, and guided them both into a hallway paneled with rough-hewn wood with a coat of lacquer so thick, it looked like wax.

"I still can't help but think of this as more of a hotel room than as a place that I own."

"We must stay in different hotels, Dad."

The living room was massive, and even then it hardly seemed to contain the white overstuffed suede furniture that looked like it had been made from giant marshmallows. There was a two-sided fireplace built into the wall straight ahead, through which he could see the dining room on the other side. To the right was an enormous saltwater aquarium filled with coral and fish of all sizes and colors. A small shark swished through a mountain of live rock before another shape passed across the glass from the opposite side of the tank. And with a click of heels, she emerged from the dining room, holding a crystal wineglass by the stem.

"Aren't you going to introduce me, J.R.?"

She was a stunning woman. Tall and slender. Tight charcoal skirt. Long legs. Snow-white skin. High heels. A silk blouse with a patterned scarf. Shoulder-length blond hair that partially concealed her right eye.

White-blue eyes. Almost clear, like those of a wolf. Full lips the color of the flesh around a cherry pit.

"It would be my pleasure," the senator said. He took her by the hand with an almost playful twinkle in his eye and led her to where Mason stood. "Boys, may I introduce Ariana Levine, who has graciously consented to ring in the New Year with me. Ariana, this is my son, James, and his childhood friend Gunnar Backstrom."

"I've heard so much about you." She transferred her glass to her left hand and extended her right in such a way that Mason wasn't entirely sure if he was supposed to kiss it, shake it, or admire her French tips. "The way your father talks about you, I imagined you to be seven feet tall and surrounded by a golden aura."

He'd initially thought she was way too young for his father, but up close the signs of age showed through. Or, more accurately, the signs where her age had been surgically erased showed through. Her skin was maybe a little too tight around her eyes, her forehead, and her jawline. Her neck was a slightly darker shade than her face, and the cleavage that bloomed from her blouse had that telltale look of skin stretched over time by the weight of her implants. Or maybe he was just looking as hard as he could to find her flaws.

"It's a pleasure to meet you," he said, shaking her hand. She radiated wealth and class in a way he generally only associated with his father at campaign time. "I've heard absolutely nothing about you."

He'd meant for it to sound a lot more flippant than it came out.

Her laughter was like the tinkle of wind chimes.

"Ms. Levine sits on the board of numerous corporations, trusts, and charitable organizations," Gunnar said. "She's responsible for the creation of the Foster Foundation, which funds research for Parkinson's disease. It was Parkinson's that claimed her husband, Milton Foster, who served as CEO of First Continental Bank throughout the latter half of the eighties and the nineties."

"Your reputation precedes you, Mr. Backstrom." She again offered her hand and he kissed it. Mason had never seen his old friend in his element before, nor had he imagined how effortlessly he could shift between worlds. "You've done fabulous work for several acquaintances of mine."

"It's an honor to meet you in person, Ms. Levine."

"We were just about to open another bottle, if you boys would care to join us," the senator said.

He whisked in and deftly took Ariana's hand from Gunnar's.

"Thanks for the offer, but we're actually just swinging by," Mason said. "I was really hoping you'd be able to help us answer a couple of quick questions, and then we'll get out of your hair."

"Just swinging by the capital?" His father raised an eyebrow. "I'd question if this was actually a social call if I didn't already know that your task force had been disbanded."

"I know my cue to leave," Ariana said. "I am pleased to have finally met you, James. And you as well, Gunnar. Perhaps our paths will cross again soon."

And with a swish of her hips, she rounded the wall and vanished into the dining room.

"Why, Senator, I had no idea—"

"Stow it, Gunnar." Mason's father turned to face him. "I was hoping to do that under different circumstances, but I'm way too old to hide a woman from my grown son."

"Does she make you happy?" Mason asked.

His father looked at him curiously for a moment.

"Yes," he finally said. "She makes me happy."

"Then that's all I need to know."

His smile when he clapped Mason on the back was genuine, the kind he used when there were no cameras around. He almost appeared relieved. It was strange. Mason couldn't remember a time when he felt as though his father had actually cared what he thought.

"So this is a business call?"

"And, unfortunately, we're pressed for time. I need to know why Victor was in Bern last year, and I really need you not to ask any questions."

"If this has anything to do with my company, then I have a right to know."

"Gunnar just needs a few minutes in your system. That's all."

"I hear rumors of chemical weapons and counterterrorism exercises in Central Park and now my son, the federal agent, shows up un-announced at my door. How worried should I be?"

"Everything's under control."

The senator looked him squarely in the eyes for several seconds be-fore reluctantly nodding. They might not have ever had the closest rela-tionship, but his father had always been able to tell when he was lying.

51

The guest bedroom faced the rear of the row house and looked out upon the slate-tiled courtyard; or rather, it would have had the windows not been blacked out with tinted film and covered with drapes heavy enough to make the rod bow. While the senator's computer setup was the kind hackers used in movies, with half a dozen monitors and glow-ing components stacked to either side and bolted to the walls, it was all for show. Mason knew his father had simply paid for whatever top-of-the-line package the cybersecurity firm recommended for powerful people who didn't know any better. He undoubtedly just used it for videoconferencing and accessing AgrInitiative's system, which was ac-complished by clicking an icon on his home page. The user name and password autofilled, eliciting a groan from Gunnar, who sat in the high-backed leather chair at the keyboard like the captain of a spacecraft.

Mason rolled a second chair across the small room and took a seat beside him. He couldn't help but think of his wife as Gunnar typed commands, breezed through directories, and scrolled through data for-merly belonging to the Thornton empire. His father waited until they were networked to the corporate mainframe before adjourning to the living room, from which they heard the occasional clinking of glasses and snapping of knots in the fire.

"Whoever's managing your dad's affairs has already made signifi-cant strides in distancing AgrInitiative from the mess AgrAmerica made of its holdings, not to mention its reputation," Gunnar said. "Its portfo-lio's been purged of anything that could possibly be perceived as tainted and most of its less wieldy subsidiaries have been sold, closed, or are in the process of being dismantled. We're talking wholesale slaughter, corporate-style."

"I take it that's a good thing," Mason said. "Or are you trying to tell me you might not be able to find the information we need?"

"You have to understand that the finances of a company of this size essentially have a life of their own. They're in a constant state of fluctuation and at any given time provide little more than a snapshot of the larger picture, like a photograph taken through the window of a moving car. Liquid assets, by definition, are fluid. Cash flow can be manipulated, the value of investments varies from one day to the next, physical assets are depreciated on seemingly arbitrary schedules, and mergers and acquisitions are never simple transactions. They're often complex arrangements that involve combinations of stocks and cash and subsidiaries and board seats and trade secrets and intellectual properties and any number of intangibles whose worth is dictated not by the market but by their value to the buyer."

"That doesn't answer my question."

"But it does explain how Victor was able to weasel his way into the biotechnology game. Your brother-in-law couldn't simply cut a check for millions of dollars to buy an existing business without tipping off the competition to his aspirations, so he acquired one piecemeal."

"You found it."

"Was there ever any doubt?"

"So what do we know?"

Gunnar populated all six of the monitors with information and glanced from one to the next as he spoke.

"We're dealing with a Swiss company by the name of Aebischer Pharma AG. Certainly not a juggernaut in the world of pharmaceuticals like Novartis or Roche, although it does have an interesting history. It launched in 1996 with the stated mission of producing cutting-edge medical-grade pharmaceuticals using a unique fusion of man-made and natural sources, but it was woefully unprepared for the continual assault of environmental interests, which forced it to develop synthetic versions of the naturally occurring components. Not only was that contrary to its own stated mission; it ended up being significantly more expensive, so by 1999, it was actually worth less than its physical assets. Fortunately, its facilities were state of the art, its location outside of Bern was ideal, and the Swiss were notorious for their lack of governmental regulation, which made it the perfect European outpost for an American pharmaceutical research group that received its start-up capital from the Richter Foundation."

"The charitable entity of the very same dead man who conspired with my wife's great-grandfather to develop a deadly strain of influenza on a hog farm," Mason said. "We should have known his name would pop up at some point."

"It gets better. That company was called Advanced Medical Defense Solutions and the group that launched it was composed of medical research scientists who all served in the U.S. Army Chemical Corps and passed through Fort Detrick at some point. While technically a limited partnership under the Aebischer name, the deal was a whole lot more complicated than that. The original Aebischer ownership group retained a thirty-two-percent share, which it subsequently sold to chemical giant Bayer. For its initial investment in AMDS, the Richter Foundation was rewarded with a full third of Aebischer, which it converted into private shares and sold to several different international corporations, which then sold those shares to even more international corporations. By the time all was said and done, the ownership of the company was like a jigsaw puzzle that could only be assembled by picking up the pieces, one by one, and fitting them back together, which was how Victor, over the span of a decade, patiently accumulated controlling interest in a firm headed by former Defense Department scientists who, in addition to manufacturing a solid and reputable line of generic antibiotics, vaccines, and prescription drugs, expanded into the arena of agricultural insecticides and fungicides."

"Definitely the kind of place where guys like Chenhav and Mosche, a microbiologist and a biochemist with ties to the World Health Organization, the United Nations, and the World Medical Association, might be sent in the aftermath of nine/eleven," Mason said.

"Especially considering that in the wake of the merger, Aebischer became the exclusive production facility for Bayer's proprietary drug ciprofloxacin, a second-generation fluoroquinolone antibiotic used to

treat inflammatory conditions of the urinary, gastrointestinal, and respiratory tracts. Not to mention anthrax. In fact, once the CDC and
WHO recommended that it be prescribed prophylactically to everyone
who might potentially come into contact with respiratory anthrax, it
sold its existing stockpile—one point two billion pills—directly to the
U.S. Department of Defense on the day after Senate Majority Leader
Tom Daschle received a letter filled with spores. At a profit of close to
three billion dollars."

Mason suddenly understood exactly why his brother-in-law had
acquired Aebischer.

"Let me guess," he said. "They also just happened to be sitting on
an inoculation against the swine flu."

"Aebischer has an entire R and D department devoted to the production of vaccines and prophylactic treatments with defense applications, so if it didn't already have one, it was definitely the kind of place
that would be able to produce one."

With Victor controlling both the release of the Hoyl's virus and access to the cure, he could have staged a pharmaceutical revolution that
very well could have made him as powerful as any of the Thirteen, which
was quite possibly why they'd had him killed. Or maybe he'd never been
in control of his own hostile takeover of his family's agricultural empire
and the Thirteen had been manipulating him from the very start.

"What kind of damage could Aebischer do to my father if anyone
found out about its potential involvement?" Mason asked.

"None that I can see," Gunnar said. "At least not on paper. I don't
have access to sensitive projects, and the lack of governmental oversight
means no one outside of the company really knows what they're developing beyond what's been publicly reported. For all we know, whatever
plans Victor had for it never reached the execution phase. Then again,
if he were truly looking for a legitimate foothold in the Eastern European pharmaceuticals market like he claimed, this would have been the
perfect way to go about it. As far as the world's concerned, Aebischer is
just the most recent casualty of a boom-or-bust industry."

"Casualty?"

"Your old man's transition team at AgrInitiative began divesting
him within a week of taking over. AMDS, now a minority partner,

needed to distance itself from its association with Aebischer, too. Neither party could afford to simply walk away, and with its reputation having sustained significant damage, there was no chance of selling the company outright, so between them they reached a deal to divide the company into two units, equal in value to their ownership percentages, with the intention of marketing the assets to companies interested in investing in the intellectual properties and developmental potential, not the Aebischer name. AMDS held on to all properties specifically related to defense, which it turned around and sold directly to the U.S. government. AgrInitiative retained the biomedical and chemical units and had an offer on the table within two weeks. Looks like the sale will be finalized any day now."

"That was quick."

"Your dad's team must have received an offer they couldn't refuse. Either that or they took whatever they could get just to wash their hands of it."

"Who's the buyer?"

Mason realized he knew the answer before he even finished asking the question. Every aspect of the investigation had been leading to this revelation. And if he was right, not only did he know who'd hired the Scarecrow; he had his first concrete lead on a contemporary member of the Thirteen.

"Aegis Asset Management." Judging by the tone of Gunnar's voice, he wasn't surprised in the slightest, either. "A subsidiary of Royal Nautilus Petroleum."

"The same company that owns the apartment registered to Charles Raymond, the man who was killed in Central Park."

"If Nautilus is really a player here, why would it commission the murder of one of its own high-level executives?"

"It wouldn't," Mason said. "The murders are personal to the Scarecrow. Part of his own private agenda."

"You think he's playing both sides?"

"I think we're dealing with a man who doesn't have an exit strategy."

Gunnar performed one final, thorough search of the network for any other foreign holdings and downloaded the pertinent information to his laptop, just in case it might prove useful later.

Mason figured that since his father's team had already distanced him from Aebischer, it was probably best that he not say anything about what they'd learned, especially considering the kind of fallout he anticipated once this was all over. And it would be soon, one way or another. He could positively feel the inevitability of the coming confrontation, swelling like the pressure underneath the snowpack before an avalanche.

He and Gunnar descended the stairs into the parlor. The senator and Ariana were little more than wavering shapes through the glass fireplace in the dining room, but even then Mason could tell they were enjoying each other's company. He didn't want to disturb them any more than he already had. His father deserved a little bit of happiness in his life.

Mason closed the front door behind them with a soft click and headed back out into the cold.

52

As arranged, Gunnar's plane had been refueled and was waiting when they arrived. The pilot had filed their flight plan and was ready to take them to Fallston Airport, a small commercial airfield a short distance from the Edgewood Chemical Biological Center, where the command historian would be waiting for them at the Visitors Center. Mason's rear end had barely hit the seat when his phone alerted him to an incoming video call. He answered before the second ring.

"Tell me you found him."

"Roybal's in the wind," Ramses said.

"How can you be sure?"

Ramses turned around the camera and revealed a bedroom Mason didn't recognize. The bed was unmade and the blinds were drawn. Several dresser drawers had been pulled out and the clock from the nightstand rested upside down on the floor. The view shifted and focused on the walk-in closet, which swayed from side to side as Ramses walked closer. The clothes had been shoved to either side, revealing a wall safe. The open door granted a clear view of the empty steel interior.

"Are you inside his house?" Mason asked.

"No one answered the door. What was I supposed to do?"

"Where's Layne?"

"Waiting outside," Ramses said. "Probably still going on about this whole breaking-and-entering kick she's on. She can be a real downer, you know that?"

"You broke into his house?"

Ramses turned the camera back toward his face as he exited the master bedroom and passed through a dark hallway.

"See? That's where we have a difference of opinion. I didn't technically break anything. I just checked all the doors until I found one that opened."

"He left the door unlocked?"

"Not in the strictest sense. The guy didn't show up for work today. I was worried about him."

Mason glanced out the window as the Citation XLS taxied toward the runway.

"Any sign of where he might have gone?" he asked.

"Depending upon how much cash he had in that safe, he could be anywhere by now. What I *can* tell you, though, is that wherever he went, he won't be coming back."

"Damn it," Mason said. "Get out of there before someone sees you."

"No chance of that. This place is on, like, ten acres in the middle of nowhere. He couldn't have bought a place like this on a policeman's salary. This guy's been dirty from the start."

"Tell Layne to call in an anonymous tip."

"She's going to love that idea."

"She'll do it if it means someone will put out a BOLO on him."

"Too late," Gunnar said. "Roybal's passport was stamped at the Peace Bridge border crossing outside of Buffalo about four hours ago."

"Your guy at the impound lot must have tipped him off," Ramses said.

"Barrie wouldn't have said anything," Mason said. "Roybal had to know he was in serious trouble when the names of the guys who died out in the Pine Barrens hit the wire. Can you track the GPS in his car or cell phone?"

"Both are disabled," Gunnar said, "but their last known location was his home address."

"It doesn't matter now," Layne said. The image swiveled to show the kitchen, where she stood with her back to the camera as she carefully picked through a stack of mail on the eating bar with the end of her pen. "We're wasting our time here."

"I see someone decided to come in after all," Ramses said. "Does that mean we're friends again?"

"Roybal's last incoming call was more than twenty-four hours ago," Gunnar said. "His final outgoing call, however, was made roughly ten hours ago, the difference, if I'm not mistaken, is just about how long it would take to drive to Buffalo from there."

"Who'd he call?" Mason asked.

"Give me a second." Lines of code scrolled past on Gunnar's screen. "The number was assigned to a cell phone with a serial number that can be traced to a bulk purchase from a company called Discount Corporate Sales, LLC, which sold them to . . . What do you know? East Coast Transportation Services."

"The same company that paid him a quarter million to serve as a consultant," Layne said.

The plane lurched as it ascended into a bank of clouds. Mason yawned to equalize the pressure.

"Is the GPS still active?" he asked.

"No," Gunnar said. "But I can tell you its last geographical coordinates correspond to the East Coast Transportation Services hub in Newark."

"We'll hit it on our way back to the city," Ramses said.

The plane rose above the clouds. The black waters of the Atlantic intermittently appeared below them.

"What did you learn about Bern?" Layne asked.

"AgrAmerica acquired a Swiss company called Aebischer Pharma,"

Mason said. "It was the brainchild of some scientists from the Army Chemical Corps, who made a fortune selling antibiotics to the Department of Defense during the anthrax scare."

"That's the same time frame as when Chenhav and Mosche would have been there."

"Exactly."

"So what's the connection?" Layne asked.

"We're looking at two scientists with ties to the World Health Organization potentially being in bed with the same company that made billions from its recommendation to prescribe that company's proprietary drug. Discovering their bodies underneath a building where we found evidence of an engineered flu virus and the manufacture of a chemical weapon of mass destruction makes total sense in that context."

"Yeah, but only from the perspective of these guys outliving their usefulness and needing to be eliminated."

"Only five people were killed during the anthrax scare," Mason said. "Maybe they developed consciences when they realized that this was the real deal and millions of people were going to die."

"We need to get out of here," Layne said. "A commanding officer of a state police sector doesn't just blow off work without someone checking into it. Let me know what you find out at Edgewood."

She terminated the call and left Mason staring at the blank screen of his phone. He set it down on the table, furrowed his brow, and looked at Gunnar.

"So let's say Chenhav and Mosche were complicit in the plot to capitalize on the release of the anthrax back in '01," he said. "You can chalk that up to opportunism or greed, but there's a huge difference between using your position to secure a WHO recommendation for a specific antibiotic and faking your own death. They had to throw away their careers, abandon their families and friends, and sacrifice everything they'd worked their entire lives to achieve. That's an entirely different level of commitment."

"An ideological level," Gunnar said.

"Exactly."

Gunnar got up and checked in with the pilot, whose voice didn't carry from the cockpit. He grabbed a couple bottles of water from the mini refrigerator on his way back and tossed one to Mason.

"We're about twenty minutes out," he said. "He'll file the flight plans back to New York while we're at the base."

"You trust your pilot's discretion?"

"For what I pay him, he'd remain celibate in the Playboy Mansion."

"But there's more to life than money," Mason said. "Two scientists at the top of their respective fields had to be making a comfortable living. I can't see them throwing away the lives they'd created for themselves for any amount."

"Think about the pictures," Gunnar said. "From '89 to '91, they were involved with the Society of Clinical Microbiologists and Virologists and the Israeli Medical Association. Two fairly standard professional organizations. Then we get to the mid-nineties, when they're photographed at the Twentieth Assembly of the Society for Lasting International Peace and the Economic Strategy Conference of the US-Israel Science and Technology Alliance, and suddenly we're dealing with an added element of politics."

"So what happened between '91 and '94 that caused two scientists to step out of their labs and into the political arena?"

Gunnar lowered his eyes to his screen and his fingers buzzed on the keyboard.

"The Israeli-Palestinian peace process led to the Oslo Accords in '93, which allowed the Palestinian Liberation Organization to relocate from Tunisia to the West Bank and the Gaza Strip, paving the way for the establishment of the Palestinian National Authority."

"Was that a bad thing?"

"It was to organizations like Hamas and the Palestinian Islamic Jihad, who believed that nothing shy of the recognition of an autonomous Palestinian state was acceptable, and immediately launched attacks against Israel. The conflict escalated after the Philadelphia Conference, where the first President Bush outlined his new world order, which they interpreted as an assault on Islam itself and rededicated themselves to destroying Israel and promoting jihad throughout the region."

Mason had a sinking sensation in his stomach that had nothing to do with the plane starting its descent into Maryland.

"Who did they lose?" he asked.

Gunnar glanced up at him over the top of the monitor.

"On April sixth, 1994, Holocaust Memorial Day, a suicide bomber pulled up beside a city bus and detonated a homemade explosive device. It was the first terrorist attack against a civilian target. Eight were killed, among them Bayla Mosche and David Chenhav, aged thirteen and sixteen, respectively, and the only children of our dead scientists."

"Jesus," Mason said. "That would explain how they ended up at a UN summit on sustainable population growth and a World Congress on CBRN threat and terrorism."

"And it certainly checks the ideology box, but it doesn't tell us how they went from wanting to save the world to actively participating in a plot to destroy it."

Mason thought about the picture taken at the Twentieth Assembly of the Society for Lasting International Peace in Copenhagen, with Drs. Nitzan Chenhav and Yossi Mosche standing on either side of Andreas Mikkelson, managing director of Royal Nautilus Petroleum. And he thought about his wife, what her death had done to him and what he, in turn, had done to others.

"I think it just might."

53

Fallston Airport wasn't what one might consider a booming hub, which meant there wasn't a professional transportation service, so they opted to use a ride-sharing company. The drive to the Edgewood facility was only twelve miles but promised to take twenty minutes. Mason told the driver of the black Crown Victoria, a skinny man in his early fifties named Anthony, who both looked and smelled like a direct descendant of the Marlboro Man, that he'd double the fare if he could cut that time in half. The driver had been so committed to the proposition that he'd been forced to add the caveat "if you get us there without killing us first." How Gunnar managed to work with his laptop balanced on his thighs and the car seemingly hurtling toward certain doom was beyond Mason, who could barely keep up with the trees and fields whipping past.

"Royal Nautilus Petroleum is one of the oldest multinational corporations in the world, so its history is pretty well documented," Gunnar said. "Formed in 1907 in an effort to compete with Thomas Elliot Richter's Great American Oil. It's currently the largest company, by revenue, in Europe and the sixth largest in the world. It has interests in everything from petrochemicals to biofuels, a presence in nearly every country on the planet, and owns drilling rights to some of the most lucrative reserves in the entire world, including those in Iraq and the North Sea."

"How does a company like that end up working out of the Rocky Mountain Arsenal?"

"Nautilus Petroleum first entered the chemical business in 1929, when it formed a partnership with Centrum Steelworks, which produced commercial ammonia as a by-product of its steel-manufacturing process. Under the Nautilus Chemical Company banner, they commenced production of ammonia from natural gas and expanded into chemical solvents, synthetic rubber, liquid detergents, and, later, industrial pesticides, the foundation of what would become chemical weapons."

"What about this guy Mikkelson?"

"All right," Gunnar said. "Andreas Mikkelson served as managing director from 1978 to 1994, after which he assumed the role of deputy chairman of the board of directors, a position he still holds to this day, along with managing a handful of special projects."

"So he still has a large role in the company."

"Maybe not in its day-to-day operations, but he definitely helps shape the course of its future. He's the third-highest-ranking official, next to the chairman of the board and the CEO, and by far the most tenured among them."

"What puts him at the SLIP Assembly in Copenhagen and brings him into contact with Chenhav and Mosche?"

"Nautilus would have had a large stake in any energy-based economic reform, for starters, and while a petroleum company may sound like a strange bedfellow for any socialized-medicine initiative, you have to remember that most active pharmaceutical ingredients are produced by chemical synthesis. In fact, early antidepressants were actually by-products of the oil-refining process. A government-run single-payer model would allow it to lean on the elected officials it already owned to secure contracts and fix prices."

"That still doesn't explain what Mikkelson has in common with two Israeli scientists who'd just lost their children."

"Like I initially said, the picture looks like your standard PR photo op. As much as I loathe coincidence, we have to consider the possibility that there was no preexisting relationship between them."

An ornate sign composed of mortared slate and adorned with bronze placards featuring the logos of the U.S. Army, U.S. Army Materiel Command, and U.S. Army Installation Management Command blew past, announcing their arrival at the Aberdeen Proving Ground.

"What was Mikkelson's role prior to joining the executive council?" Mason asked.

"Give me a second," Gunnar said.

The driver pulled up to the security gate and rolled down his window. Two soldiers in camo fatigues and tan boots stepped out from behind the smoked glass of the guardhouse. The taller of the two approached the vehicle and asked to see their IDs, while the other walked a German shepherd around the car, allowing it to sniff for explosive materials underneath the carriage and inside the wheel wells.

"Here we go," Gunnar said. "Bachelor's degree in biochemistry and doctorate in cognitive neurosciences from Radboud University in the Netherlands. He was lured away from a neurosurgical residency at the university's medical center by Nautilus Chemical Company and sent to the Emeryville Research Center in Houston, where his team pioneered a class of materials called block copolymers, whose medical applications include artificial heart valves. He was rewarded with a more prominent role in the R and D department, which included supervisory duties at both the Rocky Mountain and Edgewood arsenals."

"And he leveraged whatever he did there into a promotion to managing director," Mason said.

The guard raised the gate and saluted them as they passed. Long industrial buildings with peaked aluminum roofs intermittently appeared through groves of barren trees. The driver wended through the forest and pulled up to the curb in front of the Visitors Center, a squat building with tinted glass and a corrugated roof.

"Thanks for the ride," Mason said, and handed a stack of twenties to the driver. "And for getting us here in one piece. Mind sticking around for a while? I don't think I'm going to be inside for very long, and we're going to need a ride back to the airport."

"Same deal?"

"Plus your time."

"You got it," the driver said. "And hey, I know they frown upon us eavesdropping on our passengers, but I couldn't help overhearing you guys talking about Royal Nautilus. You need to be careful dealing with those guys. They helped finance the rise of the Nazis before World War Two."

"Where'd you hear that?"

"I come from a military family. My granddad stormed the beaches of Normandy. Lost two brothers and a lot of friends that day. Said he'd sooner push his car ten miles through the desert than buy a single gallon of gas from people like them, who stirred up that shit in the first place, just to make a quick buck. And having personally dealt with those guys in the Iraqi oil fields during Desert Storm, I've got to say I wholeheartedly agree with him."

Mason turned to face Gunnar.

"Is that true?"

"I can vouch for Nautilus's picking up the drilling rights to most of Iraq following the war, but I'll have to look into the rest," Gunnar said.

Mason climbed out of the car and watched it swing around and park in the closest space. He was halfway up the front walk when a soldier wearing a Class B uniform with a navy skirt and a black cardigan emerged from the sliding glass doors and strode straight toward him. She had blue eyes, an abundance of freckles, and auburn hair drawn into a tight bun at the base of her skull. The insignia on her shoulder identified her as a specialist.

"Special Agent Mason?" she asked.

He held up his badge for her benefit. She scrutinized it for several seconds, nodded, and proffered her hand.

"Brenda Peele, public affairs specialist and command historian. I've assembled what I believe to be a solid collection of artifacts from the time frame you requested. I hope it will be of some use in your investigation. Now, if you'll come with me . . ."

Mason followed her inside and into a small museum, where she guided him through a veritable maze of displays featuring educational and historical signs, pictures, and relics.

"President Woodrow Wilson authorized the construction of the U.S. military's first large-scale chemical-production facility right here on the Gunpowder Neck Reservation on October sixteenth, 1917. It was renamed Edgewood Arsenal the following year and commissioned as the Gas Offense Production Division of the Chemical Warfare Service, under the command of Major General William Sibert. As you can see from the aerial photograph on your right, at that time there were four production plants for chlorine, chloropicrin, mustard, and phosgene, as well as three seventy-five-millimeter-shell filling plants, the testing of which occurred to the north at the Aberdeen Proving Ground."

They breezed past a banner celebrating the base's centennial anniversary, a detailed time line stenciled on the wall, and Lucite cases containing early gas masks, containment glove boxes, and field detectors.

"When we entered World War Two," she said, "we learned that our stockpiles of toxic gasses and chemical agents were woefully inadequate compared to the new stable of German nerve agents, which we officially tested here during the war. We determined that sarin, also known as GB, would be the best addition to our arsenal, although we didn't commence with the pilot program until 1952. Mass production was established at the Rocky Mountain Arsenal in Colorado two years later. The sixties brought extensive challenges for the Chemical Corps, which was forced to essentially justify its existence following wars fought in Europe and Korea without the aid of chemical weaponry. In response, we shifted our focus from production to research and development. We designed the M17 gas mask, the M8 automated gas detector, and the M11 decontamination sprayer and pioneered what was known as the Incapacitation Program, through which we attempted to produce an agent capable of rendering our adversaries inoperative without violating the tenets of the Geneva Protocol."

Peele led Mason through a closed door, down a ramp, and into a conference room with a podium and projector screen at the front. Several cardboard boxes with inset handles and lids had been stacked on one side of the long table, their contents spread across the polished wood.

"While we don't house personnel files on the premises, we do curate a fairly extensive library of photographs, memorabilia, and declassified research. You see, the history of an installation like this one is every bit as important as its future. The work performed here is critical to our understanding of modern warfare, the defense of our troops abroad, and, God forbid, the safety of our citizens at home."

"Thanks for preparing all of this for me," Mason said.

"It's no trouble at all," she said. "If this information can be of use to you in an investigation with national security ramifications, I'm only too happy to help. The time frame in question is what we consider the dawn of modern chemical warfare and, in my opinion, one of the most interesting times in our history. For nearly thirty years, we were primarily concerned with blister agents like mustard gas and lewisite, for which we developed antidotes and designed protective gear, and then all of a sudden we were faced with the possibility of the Nazis using nerve gasses against us. Our research here was not only integral to understanding the threat posed by these G-series agents but in developing the means of counteracting their effects in a very short period of time."

Mason walked the length of the table, studying the old black-and-white pictures as he went. There were men in lab coats, white shirts with black ties, traditional uniforms, and hospital gowns.

"You tested on your own people?"

"This was a different era, you must understand," she said. "Soliciting volunteers from within our own ranks was routine procedure. Even the chief of Clinical Research at the time, Dr. Tobin von der Nuell, understood how this might be perceived, and he subjected himself to all procedures before allowing them to be conducted on others. That's him right there."

She pointed at a picture of a heavyset man with bushy white hair in a hospital bed. He inhaled from a device held by a man in a white lab coat, while men with ties took notes in hardbound journals.

"What were these volunteers exposed to?"

"Low doses of G-series agents, V-series agents, experimental cures, and psychoactive drugs like BZ and LSD. All under the direct supervision of a highly trained medical staff."

"Speaking of the staff, do you happen to have any pictures of them?"

She walked around to the spread of photographs on the opposite side of the table. There was a group picture of men in uniform, seated in bleachers, all of them young and male, presumably the volunteers. There were nurses in crisp white uniforms and paper hats tending to patients, drawing liquid into syringes, and serving meals. Massive bare rooms filled with beds and primitive vital-signs monitors. Doctors with neckties and lab coats, interviewing test subjects, taking notes, and one of all of them posed as though for a class picture. She picked it up and handed it to Mason.

"This was our primary treatment staff," she said. "The majority of the doctors were civilians and wore lab coats to distinguish themselves from the other specialists."

Mason studied the fifteen young men, only a couple of whom could have been out of their twenties, searching their faces for any identifiable features. None of them looked familiar. He flipped over the picture and glanced at the back, where someone had written in pencil "A-Team Members, 1975." The names of each of the men were listed from left to right and by row. He recognized two of them right away.

He turned it over again and studied two of the men standing in the back row. With their flattops and baby faces, they were hardly reminiscent of the men they would become so many years later.

Charles Raymond and Andreas Mikkelson.

The current managing director of Research and Development and the deputy chairman of the board of directors of Royal Nautilus Petroleum.

54

"What role did Royal Nautilus Petroleum have to play in the human experimentation?" Mason asked.

"It had existing relationships with both the Chemical Corps and the Department of Defense through its work at the Rocky Mountain Arsenal," Peele said. "The testing here was an extension of what they were doing in Colorado, so it was only logical that their experts be integrated into our scientific team. Not only was it imperative that we understand the effects on the human body of the chemical weapons they were helping us manufacture but we also needed a partner with ready access to every existing chemical, an extensive research and development department, and the infrastructure to put our theoretical incapacitating agent into production at the drop of a hat."

"Were you able to produce it?"

"Regrettably, no. We learned that the reaction to psychoactive agents is completely independent of dose and subject to the individual's physiology, much like tolerance to alcohol."

"What about sarin?"

"It's a completely different animal." She looked away when she spoke. "As one would imagine, the subjects' reactions were entirely predictable, although the severity of symptoms varied by dose and body weight."

Mason removed the pictures Peele had found of the Nautilus contingent from a folder labeled "Human Volunteer Program, 1975." One showed Mikkelson monitoring the pressure on a tank of compressed gas while a soldier with electrodes attached to his head breathed through the mask attached to it. In another, Raymond was wearing thick rubber gloves while drawing a colorless liquid into a syringe. Mikkelson sedating a man in the throes of a seizure, saliva foaming from his mouth. The two men together in an office setting. Separately at the bedsides of men with sunken eyes and pallid skin, who didn't look like they were enjoying the experience. Men in khaki uniforms with black ties looked over their shoulders and took notes in just about every one of them.

"The men with the ties," Mason said. "Were they doctors, too?"

"They were army personnel," Peele said. "While some were physicians, the majority were engineers from the Chemical Corps."

"Do you have a staff photograph of them?"

Peele shuffled through the pictures until she found the one she was looking for and handed it to Mason. There were sixteen men in three uneven rows, all wearing khaki dress uniforms and long black ties. He recognized Mr. Ed right off the bat. Second Lieutenant Vance Edwards was seated in the middle row between a stocky man with thinning hair and thick-rimmed glasses and another with a thin face, long neck, and prominent Adam's apple. He flipped it over and saw the names written on the back. His heart raced as he read them.

They were all here. The three men O'Leary had remembered from the Rocky Mountain Arsenal and the man who'd owned the flatbeds used to transport the Novichok. Second Lieutenant Vance Edwards. Chief Warrant Officer Martin, not Milton, Bradley. Sergeants Jack Danvers and Peter Cavanaugh.

He turned it back over and looked at the faces again. A man in the back row caught his eye. He had dark eyes and a pale complexion. His smile revealed a golden incisor. The writing on the other side identified him as Cpl. Donald Helford.

Three of the dead men from the cornfield were in this picture. Quite possibly even all five of them. They represented the military contingent, and the man killed in Central Park the civilian. Six of what Behavioral believed to be a total of eight victims. Someone was missing, though, someone Mason was certain had to be here somewhere. And if he was right, it would confirm everything he thought he knew, including the names of the final two victims.

Something caught his eye. It took a second for his conscious mind to catch up with his unconscious. He grabbed one of the photographs and took a closer look at the group of men in the background. One of them was definitively of Asian origin, the first Mason had seen in any of the pictures, but he wasn't identified on the back. He tapped the man's face.

"Who's this?"

Peele leaned over his shoulder.

"I believe that's Dr. Nakamura." Mason immediately recognized the name from the interview with the woman who lived across the hall from the Scarecrow and the most-wanted board in Johan's archives. "He was chief of the Clinical Investigation Branch and the lone remaining hold-over from a team brought in from Japan in 1953 to help coordinate the launch of the Human Volunteer Program."

"He looks like he has to be in his thirties here. At least."

"I can't speak to that with any authority."

That meant he would be in his eighties by now. No matter how well he'd taken care of himself, there was no way anyone could have mistaken him for someone in his late forties or early fifties, but if he'd started a family, his child would be about that age now.

"What do you know about him?" Mason asked.

"Very little, I'm afraid," she said. "He was actually a pediatrician in Japan, believe it or not, but he was employed as a civilian contractor. Like all of the others, he left in 1975, when the program was terminated."

"Why wasn't he in the picture with the other doctors?"

"I have no idea."

"What about his first name?"

"Ichiro."

The Scarecrow had used that name so there'd be no mistaking his identity. It must have set off all sorts of alarm bells, which was why Marchment had usurped the investigation the second they learned the name of the occupant living in the apartment below Charles Raymond's. The deputy secretary of the DHS was connected to this place, somehow, and finding out how was critical to understanding what was happening now, nearly half a century later.

"I don't see any pictures of a man I believe was here during this time frame."

"If you know his name, perhaps I can help you locate him."

"Rand Marchment."

Peele's demeanor suddenly changed. Her smile faltered and her brow lowered.

"There are no pictures of him here."

It was a strange, oddly specific response.

"You know who I'm talking about, though," Mason said. "Don't you?"

"As I said, there are no pictures of him here."

"But he was stationed at Edgewood?"

"Yes, although he was only a private second class at the time."

"You're certain of it?"

"I'm not comfortable discussing this with you," she said.

"This information is crucial to my investigation," Mason said. "I'm not exaggerating when I say that millions of lives are potentially at stake."

She stared into his face for several seconds before nodding to herself.

"I received a call from the deputy secretary of Homeland Security himself asking me to personally remove all photographs of him from our collection."

"Didn't that strike you as an odd request?"

"It's not my place to say."

"But it did." Mason smiled. "Which was why you did as he asked but didn't dispose of them."

Peele's expression remained impassive.

"That would have been a slap in the face to someone charged with the curation of the history of a vaunted institution like this," he said.

"Like I said, the history of this installation is every bit as important as its future."

"So if you were to have removed the pictures from your archive . . ." he prompted.

"I would have probably placed them in a manila folder at the bottom of one of the boxes." She straightened her cardigan and fixed her stare on a random point in the distance. "Is there any way I can be of further assistance?"

"You've been a tremendous help."

"I'll be in the museum if you have any questions. Feel free to peruse the material at your leisure, although I insist that nothing leave this room."

And with that she strode out of the conference room and closed the door behind her.

Mason found the envelope underneath the inner flap of one of the boxes. There were only four pictures inside and, considering Marchment's rank at the time, he wasn't identified in any of them.

In the first picture, he wore a drab olive uniform and physically restrained a volunteer in a white undershirt. The man was in obvious physical distress, which presumably necessitated the injection Marchment jabbed into his shoulder.

The second showed him among a group at a cafeteria table, with the rest of the staff seated behind him by specialty. All of the doctors were together at a table beside that of the nurses, while the men in ties occupied another. Marchment sat at the end of the bench, ignoring his food and tablemates and staring at the men in lab coats.

In the third, he leaned over the side of a hospital bed and pinned down the shoulders of the man under the covers while Mikkelson administered a gaseous agent.

He wasn't the focus of the fourth image. In fact, he was barely visible at the edge, his face in profile and his mouth open in conversation with the man in the center, readily identifiable as Dr. Ichiro Nakamura. They'd been captured walking down a narrow corridor toward an open doorway, through which Mason could see a row of hospital beds. Dozens of shadows stretched across the tiled floor, elongated by the angle of the light that cast them. They almost looked like stars. A silhouette was visible through the crack near the hinges, as though someone were hiding behind the door.

Mason removed his cell phone from his pocket and took pictures of each of them, along with the group photographs, front and back, and forwarded them to Gunnar. That Marchment had been at Edgewood didn't surprise him; what did, however, was the deputy secretary's request to purge his likeness from the archives once he had the power to do so. Something terrible had happened here, something so awful that it created a monster like the Scarecrow and damned eight men to the worst deaths imaginable. He only hoped the key to unlocking the secret wasn't lost in the annals of time.

Peele was standing at attention beside the front doors when he left.

Doing what she had done had taken serious courage. He thanked her for her time and for the service she'd provided for her country.

The Crown Vic was in the same parking place, only Gunnar was now in the front seat, talking to the driver. He saw Mason coming down the walk and jumped out of the car.

"You are not going to believe what I just found."

55

"Sir Hendrick Langbroek was named the first chairman of Royal Nautilus Petroleum in 1907," Gunnar said. "He was knighted by the British Crown for ensuring the steady flow of oil during World War I, championed the company's expansion into the chemical business, and commissioned the construction of refineries throughout the world. Langbroek even negotiated the purchase of the Azerbaijan oil field in Baku, Russia, right by the Iranian border, which, at the time, was responsible for nearly half of the world's oil production. The acquisition ensured that Nautilus became the second-largest oil company in the world, extended its influence around the globe, and positioned it to save the Nazi party when it was on the brink of financial ruin."

Again, the driver sped across the countryside with an almost sadistic gleam in his eye. Were it not for the impending sense of disaster that seemed to intensify with each passing moment, Mason might have considered rescinding his offer, but there were only two victims left, and once they were dead, the Scarecrow would be free to deliver his professional coup de grâce.

"How did we get from Russian oil to Nazi Germany?" Mason asked.

"The October Revolution of 1917 was disastrous for the oil industry. Azerbaijan took advantage of the fall of the Russian Empire to declare its independence and establish a democratic republic, which didn't even last two years. The Bolsheviks dispatched the Soviet Red Army to reclaim the region, seize the oil fields, and nationalize the petroleum industry. The resultant fighting halted exports, stopped drilling, and caused extensive damage to storage facilities. Private companies were caught in the middle and incurred extensive losses. Needless to say, the Soviets won and shipped all output into the USSR. Exports dried up, causing a spike in the price of oil."

"They stole his oil wells? That must have pissed off Langbroek something fierce."

"I don't think he ever got over it. He hated the Bolsheviks with a fiery passion and cultivated that hatred throughout the twenties, during which time Nautilus expanded to become the largest oil company in the world, not to mention the near-exclusive provider to post–World War One Germany, where there was increasing anti-Communist sentiment, led by Adolf Hitler and his fledgling National Socialist German Workers' Party. Hendrick saw in Hitler an ally against the Soviets and a potential means by which to regain his oil fields in Azerbaijan. The problem was that in the early thirties the Nazi Party was in debt to the tune of twelve million marks and on the verge of collapse. Directly paying off the debt would have been perceived as, at best, a bribe of criminal proportions or, at worst, a treasonous attempt to circumvent the sanctions imposed by the Treaty of Versailles."

"That's two decades after the Bolsheviks seized his oil fields."

"What can I say? Langbroeks have long memories."

Again, Mason found himself looking back in time more than a century to find the origins of a modern plot to kill millions of people. Fields marked by rows of harvested corn and the occasional farmhouse blurred past. They passed a scarecrow with a faded Halloween mask and a raven sitting on its shoulder.

"So he devised a scheme by which he used ten million of his own money to buy excess food stores in the Netherlands," Gunnar continued, "which he then donated to a Nazi charity called *Winterhilfswerk,* or German Winter Relief, under the guise of a humanitarian effort to ease the suffering of Dutch farmers, whose crops rotted in the fields, and poor German families, who couldn't afford to eat. Donations were then solicited for that food. People gave as generously as they could to curry favor with the Nazis, while those who didn't found themselves victims of violence. It was in this way that the party paid off its creditors and positioned Hitler for his appointment as chancellor in 1933, setting the stage for what was to come."

"Linking the donation of food bought from struggling farmers to the rise of the Nazis and their subsequent atrocities is something of a stretch, don't you think?" Mason said.

"Not according to the International Military Tribunal, which presided over the Nuremberg trials. It released a statement saying that were it not for the direct financial contributions of German chemical giant IG Farben, the donations provided by Royal Nautilus, and the funds raised by *Winterhilfswerk,* Hitler wouldn't have been able to seize and consolidate power. Langbroek's support was so transparent that *The New York Times* suggested that Nautilus should be punished for helping the Nazis skirt the military restrictions mandate."

Mason had no trouble following the flow of money and the influence it undoubtedly bought, but he couldn't see how any of it was relevant.

"For the sake of argument, let's say you're right and the chairman of Royal Nautilus Petroleum contributed to the rise of Nazism in Germany," he said. "How does that have any bearing on what's happening now?"

"I freely admit that I initially approached this with an element of skepticism, too," Gunnar said. "The Nazi connection to both sarin and human experimentation is well documented, but I couldn't find any evidence that Nautilus knew about either, let alone participated in any of the atrocities. What I did find, however, was an opportunist who received a knighthood for profiteering during World War One, propped up a bankrupt foreign political party, and supported a questionable leader he hoped would foment war with the Soviets, just so he could regain the upper hand in Azerbaijan. Langbroek was a man determined to make money at all costs, no matter how much suffering he caused or how many people died in the process."

Mason suddenly realized where Gunnar was leading him. He was looking at the exact same MO as the plot to release the flu virus and, presumably, the Novichok, which was in play at that very moment.

"Let me show you something," Gunnar said. He swiveled his computer screen on his lap so Mason could see the series of pictures as he flipped through them. "Sir Hendrick died in 1939, before the start of World War Two. At the time, he was one of the richest and most powerful men in the world, a position inherited upon his death by his son, August. This is him right here." The formal portrait showed a handsome man who was a study in aristocracy, from his expensive suit to his severe profile. "He succeeded his father as chairman of Nautilus, helped establish and later sat on the board of the Bank for War Settlements and Repatriation, and was a charter member of the International Congruity Alliance and Society for Lasting International Peace. His eldest son, Douglas—his spitting image, as you can see—served as nonexecutive director of Nautilus and sat on the board of the investment firm Hart, Bradley, and Company until its merger with Lehman Brothers."

"How old is he by now?" Mason asked.

"He'd be in his eighties, if he were still alive," Gunnar said. "He died in 2018, leaving his son, Slate, a diverse portfolio worth approximately fifty billion dollars, not to mention the controlling shares of Royal Nautilus Petroleum and its subsidiaries, including Aegis Asset Management, the same company currently in the process of buying the biomedical and chemical intellectual assets of Aebischer Pharma, which, as I'm sure you'll be surprised to learn, recently patented a drug called Pyridocholinesterase, which combines pyridostigmine—used to treat muscle weakness—and a proprietary carbamate ester—a type of urethane produced exclusively by Nautilus Chemical Company—to create a drug designed to be taken prophylactically by troops at risk of exposure to nerve gasses."

And there it was. The trail he'd been following led to an oil and pharmaceuticals magnate descended from a Nazi collaborator. He was already one of the wealthiest and most powerful men in the world, and yet he was willing to kill millions of innocent people to run up the score.

Slate Langbroek was one of the Thirteen.

Mason leaned back in his seat and closed his eyes. He felt a sense of displacement he couldn't quite explain. How long had the Langbroeks been formulating this plot? They'd formed an alliance with the U.S. military and the men who worked at the Rocky Mountain and Edgewood arsenals half a century ago. They'd lured his brother-in-law, Victor, into the web of the Thirteen, who'd used him to enact its plan to release a deadly flu virus and make billions from the cure. It was undoubtedly through Nautilus that the Hoyl had been able to acquire the flesh-eating bacterium that so closely resembled the kind oil companies released to consume their spills, the deal for which had gone down in an abandoned building where the Scarecrow had wiped out Mason's SWAT team. Worst of all, they'd set into motion the series of events culminating in the murder of his wife, Angie.

And now, generations removed from the plan's inception, Slate Langbroek was on the brink of acquiring the rights to the medication designed to counteract the effects of the very chemical weapon he prepared to release.

"This is him," Gunnar said.

Mason opened his eyes and stared at the man on the screen, who couldn't have been much older than he was. Slate Langbroek was dapper and lithe, the kind of man who'd inherited physical beauty from women attracted to money and money from men who lusted for power, the living embodiment of a Greek god. The kind of man toward whom people instinctively gravitated, whose aura invited them to bask in its glow.

The photograph was captioned "Taschenbergpalais, Dresden, Germany, June 2016," and showed him emerging from the revolving door of an upscale hotel, beside which stood policemen in black uniforms. A concierge wearing a morning coat and top hat led the way, his white-gloved hand extended to deter the photographer from getting a clear shot of Langbroek, flanked by a bodyguard who appeared to be hailing a driver. A second bodyguard trailed his charge. He loomed over Langbroek from behind the glass partition of the revolving door, a hulking presence with a thick neck and tiny ears.

Mason recognized him immediately.

"Major Ashley Saddler," he said. The caption identified him as Marshall Saddler, chief of Langbroek's security team, who, unsurprisingly, went by his middle name. "The man who was incinerated in the flatbed to prevent us from learning his identity."

"And now we know why," Gunnar said.

Everything was finally falling into place.

"So where is Langbroek now?" Mason asked.

"He could be anywhere in the world," Gunnar said. "He personally owns properties in a dozen different countries, hundreds more all around the globe under the Nautilus banner, and has access to a private fleet of airplanes, cars, and ships, ranging from jets to bulk tankers and every other form of transportation in between."

"Are you telling me you can't find him?"

"Please. All I'm saying is that it's going to take a little time. Once I do, however, he's going to know we're looking for him and he'll be compelled to either go into hiding or make a move against us."

Mason nodded. He was rooting for the latter, as it would spare him the legwork and force a confrontation.

The driver returned them to the terminal where he'd originally picked them up. Gunnar handed him a small stack of hundred-dollar bills and thanked him sincerely for his help.

Mason climbed out, patted the roof of the car, and nodded his gratitude. He stared across the tarmac toward the western horizon, where a plane with twin propellers ascended diagonally through the bloodred stain of the setting sun. They now knew who was responsible for the Novichok threat, but they weren't any closer to finding where it was. Despite everything they'd learned, they still didn't know who the Scarecrow was or what had happened to him at Edgewood to turn him into a murderous psychopath with a penchant for deadly chemicals. And if Langbroek was truly behind the whole thing, why would he hire someone who'd been victimized by the early stages of his family's long game and wanted revenge against the parties involved? Was it possible he didn't know? Were the killings not personal to the Scarecrow after all and eliminating the potential witnesses had been his plan from the beginning?

There were too many contradictions, too many questions he couldn't answer.

But he was confident he knew someone who could.

"Get ahold of Johan for me," he said. "Tell him we need to have a candid conversation about the great-grandson of a Nazi collaborator. If we're right about Langbroek being one of the Thirteen and his involvement with the Scarecrow, then he should know exactly who you're talking about."

56

The flight time from Fallston, Maryland, to Republic Airport on Long Island was just over an hour, which put them touching down shortly after eight. They'd barely taken off when Mason's laptop had chimed to let him know that Johan had entered the secure virtual chat room.

"Sir Hendrick was no mere collaborator," the old man said. His eyes took on a faraway cast as he mentally traveled back in time. "He was a true believer. Perhaps his infatuation started as a means of wresting back his stolen oil fields from the Soviets and exacting a measure of revenge in the process, but it culminated in the implementation of anti-Semitic policies, the dismissal of Jewish directors, and even the swastika flying over Royal Nautilus's corporate offices in the Netherlands. It does not surprise me in the least to learn that one of his descendants was responsible for the horrific murders of two Israeli scientists after they had outlived their usefulness."

"Speaking of whom, what do you know about his great-grandson, Slate?" Mason asked.

"Apparently, I underestimated him. His father and grandfather were brazen men who flaunted their money and power, while he has masterfully hidden behind his executive boards and playboy lifestyle, deceiving me into believing he was not a threat. I failed to see through his public disavowal of his family's historical contributions to the rise of Nazism and recognize his personal adherence to the tenets that gave birth to it, beliefs closely held by the rest of his circle."

"The Thirteen."

"Assuming he is one of them and not merely a satellite in their orbit. Even I, for all of my resources, can only speculate as to their true identities, as I believe they would set the whole world ablaze before allowing themselves to be unmasked."

"I can't stop them if you don't tell me everything you know."

Johan leaned back in his armchair and sighed. The sound echoed

from his vast living room, the walls of which were mortared with a veritable puzzle of decorative moss rock.

"You must understand that these men are not motivated by money
or power," he said. "They are disciples of a cause passed down through
their bloodlines, devotees to an ideology to which they have dedicated
their entire lives. They do not consider themselves to be a master race as
much as a ruling class, a pantheon of men who have risen to the pinnacle
of their respective societies, who sit upon thrones above those of their
monarchs and elected officials, puppet masters controlling kings and
queens and presidents from the shadows. They understand that the key
to their dominion rests not merely in placating their unwitting subjects
but also in giving them a communal goal in which to invest their energies and a shared enemy against whom to direct their hatred, distrac-
tions to prevent them from realizing that they are being manipulated, a
system that worked to perfection for the Third Reich."

"Until Hitler tried to take over the entire world."

"Think of Nazi Germany as a trial run for the ultimate goals of
the Thirteen, who learned that power could most easily be maintained
over a finite number of subjects willing to accept a common rule. No
vanquished society will ever voluntarily pledge its allegiance to its con-
querors, and hatred dissipates once your enemy has been exterminated.
Thus, for the Thirteen to establish its new world order, it must cull the
population to a size that can be effectively ruled, present itself as the savior, rather than the oppressor, of the people, and channel their energies
in both positive and negative directions so they never suspect that the
means of their salvation is actually the mechanism of their enslavement."

The airplane emerged from the same thick layer of clouds through
which it had descended mere hours ago.

"The Hoyl's virus would have killed billions of people all around
the world," Mason said. "Wiping out nine million people in New York
City is a far cry from accomplishing that objective."

"Perhaps depopulation is not their sole motivation in this case,"
Johan said. "Three thousand people died in the terrorist attacks on nine/
eleven, and we sacrificed our Fourth Amendment rights in the hope that
giving the NSA permission to eavesdrop on our private conversations
would prevent the nightmare from happening again. Which rights would

we surrender, which freedoms would we forsake, in the wake of losing our most populous city? How much power would we willingly transfer directly into the hands of the Thirteen to keep us safe?"

"We can't afford not to treat the Novichok threat as though killing millions of people isn't Langbroek's primary goal."

"You are assuming, of course, that Slate Langbroek is in control of this plan. Does it not strike you as odd that he would work directly with someone like the Scarecrow or that so many key players are in the last place in the world they should be? Why would he independently implement his own plot when he is part of such a powerful organization?"

"Greed?" Mason said. And then it hit him. "Langbroek's not content with merely being one of the Thirteen. He wants to rule it."

Johan nodded and leaned forward in his chair. His eyes narrowed and radiated a light of otherness.

"And if you and I can figure this out, then surely the other twelve are well aware of what is transpiring. I have heard whispers of strife within the organization, hostilities on the brink of igniting into an internal war, one with potentially catastrophic consequences for the entire world. If this is truly the case, then I fear you might have stumbled right into the middle of it, in which case you must recognize that Langbroek is not your sole adversary. He is the enemy you can see, but he is far from the only one you face. Other players have yet to reveal themselves, and I believe the Scarecrow is the key to drawing them out. He is at the heart of the plot, and unraveling his motivations is essential to understanding his role. As Hitler showed us, hatred is a powerful emotion, one that can be easily weaponized."

"You think someone's using him against Langbroek?"

"What I think will be of no consequence if you fail to prevent the release of the Novichok," Johan said, and reached toward the screen. "I will be watching your progress with great interest."

He terminated the connection, leaving Mason to contemplate everything he'd said. The old man had offered insight into the nature of the Thirteen and essentially confirmed his suspicions about Langbroek, but their conversation had only served to amplify his growing unease about some of the contradictions he sensed within the plot. If Langbroek was truly on his own in the plan to release the Novichok and at odds with the remainder of the Thirteen, then Mason couldn't take anything for granted. Any one or all of the players involved, including Marchment and the Scarecrow, could be playing both sides at once and everything transpiring now was just for show, a distraction from the main event.

There was only one thing he knew for sure . . .

"We need to find Langbroek," he said, finishing his thought out loud.

"I'm still working on it," Gunnar said, "but I found Mikkelson. Believe it or not, he's staying at another corporate property in Manhattan."

"Why would two high-ranking Nautilus executives be in town at the same time when there isn't a corporate headquarters?"

"This is the holiday season. Maybe Nautilus arranged some sort of company function for its executive staff."

"Surely it would have put them up in hotels for something like that. Housing them in formal apartments implies they're planning on staying for some length of time."

"I'll find out when they arrived."

"That should at least help us narrow down—"

Mason's federal cell phone buzzed from the pocket of his jacket, which was draped over the back of the chair across the aisle. He grabbed it, glanced at the number, and answered on speaker.

"Tell me you found Roybal's contact," he said.

"East Coast Transportation's a dead end," Layne said. "This place is the size of a shopping mall and no one seems to have any idea what they're supposed to be doing. I couldn't find anyone who recognized the name Roybal, and the only person who seemed to know anything at all about Nautilus was the representative handling its account, and he was all but useless. He said half the time he doesn't have the slightest clue where the contracted trucks are, let alone where they're going, and I'm inclined to believe him."

The plane juddered as it passed through a wall of turbulence. Mason glanced out the window and saw the roiling black water of the Atlantic far below.

"What about someone in management? The consulting fee was paid from a corporate account."

"The owner's secretary said he didn't come in this morning, which isn't entirely out of character. We could try approaching him at home—"

"Don't waste your time," Gunnar said. "Ernest Winston—owner of East Coast Transportation Services—had his passport stamped in Puerto Vallarta eight hours ago."

"Of course," Mason said. "Have you heard from your guy at the army CIC about the older personnel records?"

"He got back to me maybe fifteen minutes ago," Layne said.

"Finally."

"Finally is right, but he didn't have the information we needed. He said he had a guy at the National Archives all morning and he couldn't find any of the personnel files we were looking for, so he contacted another guy he'd worked with before. The second guy was there for most of the afternoon and couldn't find them, either."

"How do you make official army records disappear from the National Archives?"

"That's pretty much exactly what he said, only with a few more four-letter words."

Mason clenched his fist in frustration.

"Here we go," Gunnar said. "Mikkelson and Raymond have both been in the city since early October. They arrived within twenty-four hours of each other. Raymond from Houston and Mikkelson from London."

"Any guesses as to why?" Mason asked.

"I don't see an immediate connection, but I'm working on it."

"What's the address for Mikkelson's place?"

"Seven sixty-five Park Ave. Penthouse A."

"Did you catch that, Layne?"

"What's the significance?" she asked.

"That's where Andreas Mikkelson, managing director of Royal Nautilus Petroleum, is staying. He's one of the Scarecrow's final victims and the easiest of the two to get to."

"If we're right about Marchment, he probably already has his people watching Mikkelson's place in case the Scarecrow shows."

"He would have anticipated surveillance and implemented a backup plan."

"We still don't know how the hell he got Raymond into Central Park without anyone seeing him," she said. "I followed up with Barbieri's digital forensics team. They'd already combed through the footage from the cameras both inside and surrounding the park, going back a full ten hours before the theoretical time of entry, but they didn't see anything out of the ordinary. Nor did they find anything on the cameras outside the Mayfair."

"Get to New York and scope out Mikkelson's place," Mason said. "We'll catch up with you there in about . . ." He glanced at Gunnar, who held up two fingers. "Two hours."

"Maybe less," Gunnar said. "It'll be after eight by then, so we will have missed the worst of the traffic."

"Call me the moment you get there and let me know what you find," Mason said.

"You said you'd tell me what you learned at Edgewood," Layne said.

The tone of her voice was sharp, as though she were convinced he was going to withhold the information from her. While there were still details of the investigation he was unprepared to share with her—namely, their identification of Langbroek as one of the Thirteen—she'd earned her place on the team.

"They were all there in 1975," he said. "Every single one of them. Edwards, Bradley, Danvers, Cavanaugh, Raymond, Mikkelson."

"Marchment?"

"He was little more than a kid at the time and all of the others outranked him, but he was there."

"And the Scarecrow?"

"There was a doctor named Ichiro Nakamura. He'd have to be in his eighties by now, though. No way the woman from the apartment across the hall from the Scarecrow's could have mistaken him for a man half his age, but a doctor with that name was definitely at Edgewood while they were conducting the experiments."

"The choice of aliases can't be coincidental," Layne said. "What do we know about this Dr. Nakamura?"

"I can't find anything on him," Gunnar said.

"Keep looking," Mason said. "There has to be something."

"No, Mace. I mean there's nothing to be found. This guy doesn't exist."

"Try running him through your facial-recognition program. Surely he's been captured on film at some point in his life."

"The only images we have of him are in the background of one picture and with his back to the camera in the other, but I can give it a try," Gunnar said. "You said he wasn't in any of the group photos, either, right?"

"What are you thinking?"

"I don't know. I get a weird feeling about this guy."

"He reminds you of the Hoyl."

"You talk about people adept at not being captured on film and he does spring to mind."

"The Scarecrow had to know that dropping Nakamura's name with someone like the lady across the hall meant it would eventually get back to us when we started asking questions."

"Precisely, so if he had a relationship with Nakamura, why would he leave just about the only clue that could help us discover his true identity?"

Gunnar was right. The Scarecrow had to know that by the time the investigators caught up with him in New York, the men he was hunting would already know exactly who he was, which meant that his use of the name hadn't been intended for their benefit, but, rather, for the benefit of the investigators.

"The Scarecrow wants us to know who he is," Mason said. "He used the Nakamura alias to solidify the connection to Edgewood."

"Why would he do that?" Layne asked. "By doing so, he'd be giving us the only possible means of finding and stopping him before he can release the Novichok."

Mason mulled it over. Allowing them to figure out who he was jeopardized the Scarecrow's entire plot, both the personal and the professional. Either there was no fail-safe and the plan would go off without a hitch, regardless of what they did, or he was willing to sacrifice his professional life in favor of his personal life.

And just like that, everything came into focus.

"He wants us to figure out what happened at Edgewood in 1975."

"Why?" Gunnar asked. "He couldn't have been more than a kid at the time."

Mason opened the photo gallery on his phone and swiped through the images until he found the picture of Marchment and Nakamura heading toward the room at the end of the hallway, where shadows reminiscent of stars stretched across the floor. He zoomed in through the crack and onto the silhouette hiding behind the open door. It was barely taller than the middle hinge.

Roughly the size of a child.

"Because he was there," Mason said.

57

ELSEWHERE

The Scarecrow looped the wire ligature over the man's head, tightened it just enough that he'd feel it when he awakened, and replaced the straw hat on his head. It took hold of the ends of the rope it had slung over the branches of the tree and pulled them with all of its strength, watching the wooden cross to which it had bound the man rise, inch after painful inch, until, with a lurch, the upright post slid into the ground and stood on its own. The process had gotten so much easier each time that it was almost a shame this would be the last cross it erected. It had struggled mightily raising its first victims back in Colorado, the men who'd helped create the chemicals to which it had been subjected, who'd stood there with their ties and clipboards, taking notes about its suffering as though it were an animal in a cage. And for as much as it had enjoyed returning the favor, it would revel in this man's fate even more.

It walked around in front of the post, untied the ropes from the crossbar, and tossed them into the bushes. There was no longer any reason to cover its tracks, especially after using Charles Raymond's murder to ensure that the forensic investigators sealed off Central Park to maintain the integrity of the previous crime scene, granting it all of the time, space, and privacy anyone could ever hope to find in the midst of millions of people. Besides, if the men hunting it didn't already know who it had once been, it was only a matter of time before they did. Either way, they wouldn't be able to stop it in time.

The wind kicked up from the southwest, rattling through the trees and assailing the Scarecrow with snowflakes. Were it not for the sound of car horns in the distance, it might have been able to forget that it was in the busiest metropolis in the country, at least for one more day, until the city that never sleeps commenced its eternal slumber.

The Scarecrow stared up into the face of the man bound to the post and momentarily wished it had dressed him in a white lab coat rather than flannel and overalls, that it could see the monster one last time through the eyes of the child that had hidden underneath its bed and prayed for death to take it before the monsters arrived. It wanted nothing more than to give that child the opportunity to bear witness to the moment when the man realized that he controlled the only means of ending his suffering, to watch him draw his last breath. The remote feed would have to suffice, though. It glanced at the camera affixed to the tree behind it to make sure the alignment was perfect before confirming as much with the live feed on its cell phone.

It appraised the man on the screen, who was beginning to stir.

Yes, this would work. This would work just fine.

The man groaned and tried to open his eyes, but he succeeded only in revealing white slivers between his lashes. He shivered against the cold, his fingers and toes already taking on a purple cast. Snow had begun to accumulate on the brim of his hat.

The Scarecrow shoved the travois through the manhole and listened to it clatter away into the depths. It retrieved its backpack from the shrub where it had stashed it and opened the top flap. Tapping sounds reminiscent of sleet against a windowpane greeted it. Carefully, it removed the container from the bag and watched the creatures inside attack the glass with mandibles and stingers.

A sharp intake of breath.

It looked up and met the stare of the man bound to the cross. His eyes were wide, his mouth a rictus of terror. He understood what was about to happen to him, realized that his entire life had been leading up to this moment. It was the execution of a sentence handed down for crimes he might have committed in someone else's name, but for which he'd always known he'd be judged, although perhaps not in this life. He must have thought no one would ever find out, clear up until the moment he'd gotten into the Town Car outside his apartment. Now, not only would he face damnation; those he left behind would learn that the man with whom they'd lived and worked, laughed and cried, had been a monster wearing the skin of a man they'd never really known.

"Don't," he whispered. "Please."

In response, the Scarecrow shook the container to agitate the creatures inside and raised it so he could better see.

"I was just doing my job."

That single phrase enraged the Scarecrow more than anything else he could have possibly said.

"You . . . had . . . a . . . choice," it said.

"I tried to protect you, to make the time between . . . treatments . . . bearable."

"You . . . enjoyed . . . it."

"I never enjoyed it, not like the others." His voice rose an octave and took on a tone of pleading. Tears streamed down his cheeks and quivered from his jawline. "Not like Marchment."

"His . . . time . . . will . . . come," the Scarecrow said. It unscrewed the lid and cast it aside. "Your . . . time . . . I'm . . . afraid . . . is . . . up."

It dumped the contents under the bib of the man's overalls and watched the creatures crawl through the gaps between the buttons of his shirt, seeking warmth. He thrashed against the sensation of tiny legs on his skin, which only served to trigger the inevitable. He screamed in a voice filled with fear and agony, mimicking those he'd summoned from the Scarecrow all those years ago.

It closed its eyes and savored the cries echoing off into the deserted park for several seconds before heading back down into the darkness.

Marchment would soon spring the trap it had laid for him.

And the final countdown would commence.

58

Mason arranged to meet Layne and Ramses near Mikkelson's apartment on the Upper East Side. The closest parking was in an underground lot on Seventy-second Street, across Fifth Avenue from Central Park. He backed the Escalade into a spot facing the street and left Gunnar, who needed more time for his program to work its magic on Dr. Nakamura, with the keys. He'd just struck off toward the rendezvous point when his old friend rolled down the passenger window and called after him.

"Alejandra's on the phone."

Mason knew exactly what that meant: Anomaly had made contact again. He jogged back to the car and climbed into the driver's seat.

"What did he say?"

"Hang on a second," Gunnar said, and put the call on speaker. "Okay, Allie. Mace is here. Tell him what you told me."

"Hello, James," she said. "Our anonymous friend wants to know what we learned about Rand Marchment."

"It sounds like he's fishing for information," Gunnar said, "but I got the impression from our earlier interactions that he was trying to lead us toward some kind of epiphany, not use us to do his research for him."

"I agree," Mason said. "He knew about FEMA's elevated activation levels and Marchment's involvement before we did. We have to assume he's trying to manipulate us and be careful not let on how much we've learned."

"Do you think he knows the Novichok is in New York City?" Alejandra asked.

"If he does, it essentially confirms our suspicions that he's in the upper echelons of the national security apparatus."

"Which would potentially put him in a position of helping us monitor Marchment's movements," Gunnar said.

Mason nodded. That was their play. The Scarecrow would eventually come for Marchment, and if they hoped to find the Novichok before it was too late, they needed to be there when he did.

"We did not reply fast enough," Alejandra said. "He sent the message again."

"He's getting nervous," Gunnar said. "Something must be happening behind the scenes."

"Type this," Mason said. "Marchment's been dirty since the army. He used the connections he made there to advance his career and now he's in a position to safeguard the current threat. We need assistance tracking him in real time if we're going to eliminate it."

"One moment," Alejandra said.

Mason glanced at the dashboard clock as she typed. He could positively feel the weight of time bearing down on him.

"Here is his reply," she said. "'Where he is matters less than why he is still there.'"

"Anomaly definitely knows the Novichok's in Manhattan," Gunnar said.

"Is he suggesting that Marchment doesn't?" Mason asked.

"If I'm interpreting him correctly, he's insinuating that either there's no threat of the Novichok being released here or Marchment's not in on the plan."

"There's no doubt in my mind he's in on it. He's been running interference from the start."

"That doesn't necessarily mean he's privy to all of the intricacies. He might be the deputy secretary of Homeland Security, but he's just a pawn to someone like Langbroek."

"The dialogue box closed," Alejandra said. "Anomaly is gone."

"Damn it," Mason said. "Try contacting him again. If there's even the slightest possibility that the Novichok is somewhere else, we need to know right now."

"The Scarecrow wouldn't be here if it wasn't," Gunnar said. "This is his show and, like you said, he's been planning the final act for years. As long as Marchment and Mikkelson are still alive, we have a chance of stopping him."

"Which means we need to keep them that way," Mason said, and hooked the Bluetooth device that would allow him to remain in contact with Gunnar over his ear. "Let me know if you hear anything else."

He climbed out of the car and hurried to meet up with Layne and Ramses, who were waiting in the dark courtyard of the Presbyterian church a block away on Seventy-third, which offered a view of Mikkelson's penthouse apartment through a gap between buildings. They'd sent him pictures of the federal vehicles surreptitiously parked around the apartment complex, a fourteen-story redbrick and limestone building with a twenty-four-hour doorman and an average unit price of fifteen million dollars.

"That guy in there is locked down tight," Ramses said. "No one's getting in or out of that building without passing through their net."

"The Scarecrow would have prepared for this contingency," Mason said. He thought of the pictures on the wall of the apartment underneath the one where the IED had been rigged in the telescope. "He studied Raymond's habits and routines for months before choosing the perfect moment to take him. He would have done the same for Mikkelson."

"Even if the Scarecrow knows where Mikkelson's going to be every second of the day," Layne said, "he has to realize there's no way Marchment's letting him go anywhere without an escort. Allowing him to leave the apartment at all is a huge risk."

"We should assume that Marchment hasn't told him."

"Hanging his own man out to dry?" Ramses said. "That's cold."

"Mikkelson would have heard about what happened to Raymond," Layne said. "There's no way he'd set foot outside that penthouse without being certain he was in the clear."

"Like I said, the Scarecrow would have anticipated this eventuality and had a fallback plan in place," Mason said.

"If you're this Mikkelson dude," Ramses said, "tell me you're just going to sit around waiting for this guy who's killed all of your old buddies to show up at your door. Not when you have enough money to hire your own personal security team. Either he's hiding out in a secure location on the other side of the world or he's already dead."

He was right and they all knew it.

"Damn it," Mason said. He tapped a button on his earpiece and opened the direct line to Gunnar. "I need you to access the security foot-age around Mikkelson's building and tell me when he was last here."

"What are you thinking?"

"The Scarecrow grabbed Mikkelson before he took Raymond."

"I'm on it," Gunnar said.

"They're surveilling an empty apartment?" Layne said.

"Marchment had to know that the only way to draw out the Scare-crow was to use Mikkelson as bait, but he couldn't afford to tell him and risk that he'd skip town," Mason said. "He'd dangle him out there like a worm on a hook, knowing full well the Scarecrow's victims have escalated in perceived value from the start and, after Raymond, Mik-kelson would be next."

"How can you be certain?"

"The men in the cornfield were all fairly low-ranking military members of the Edgewood staff. At second lieutenant, Edwards was the highest among them. Raymond and Mikkelson were on the medical staff and responsible for everything that happened there. They're the real prize."

"Marchment was just a private at the time," Gunnar said. "He ranked lower than all of them."

Mason recalled the photograph of Marchment leading Dr. Ichiro Nakamura down a hallway toward a room housing what he now be-lieved to be children, one of whom grew up to become the Scarecrow, an inhuman monster who used the name of the Japanese physician to force the investigators tracking him to look into the doctor's presence at Edgewood. In doing so, they'd found him with an enlisted eighteen-year-old who somehow orchestrated a meteoric rise to deputy secre-tary of the entire Department of Homeland Security, positioning him within striking distance of being in complete control of a quarter mil-lion skilled operatives already deployed on American soil. He'd used whatever he did at Edgewood to launch his career, but what could he have possibly done to the Scarecrow to make him the target of highest personal value?

And then it hit him.

"Marchment was the one who subjected them to the experimenta-tion," he said. "And not just the adult volunteers. The children, too."

The other pictures had shown him forcing one test subject to breathe a gaseous agent from an inhaler and physically restraining another while he stabbed him in the shoulder with a needle. If he'd done the same things to much younger patients, he would have become their personal bogeyman, the mere sound of his footsteps outside their room eliciting sheer terror and causing them to hide, but how could that trauma possibly be harnessed for use by Langbroek, the head of Nautilus, whose predecessors were directly responsible for inflicting that suffering?

"There's a security camera facing the front door of Mikkelson's apartment building," Gunnar said through Mason's earpiece. "I've got him leaving early in the morning three days ago, wearing a gray suit and charcoal overcoat. Switch to the camera on the building across the street and you can see the doorman hailing a driver, who pulls to the curb in a black Town Car and waits for the doorman to usher Mikkelson into the backseat. He returns four hours later, only this time on foot, wearing a gray fedora and carrying a leather satchel. A traffic cam picks him up on the opposite side of Seventy-second, reading a newspaper. He waits until the doorman is engaged helping an older woman into a limousine before slipping past him and entering the building. The brim of his hat is angled in such a way as to conceal his face from the camera, but it does little to hide the fact that he's about six inches shorter."

"You're telling me someone else returned to his apartment wearing his clothes?"

"No," Gunnar said, "wearing identical clothes. I probably wouldn't have noticed the difference in height at all had another man not passed him on the opposite side of the revolving door. He came back out fifteen minutes later in a black suit and fedora and disappeared into the foot traffic on Park Avenue."

"And he was able to hide his face the entire time?"

"Not quite. Check your email."

Mason opened the message on his phone and found a somewhat pixilated image of the lower portion of a man's face below the brim of his hat and above the top of a newspaper. Just enough to reveal the tip of a rounded nose, thin lips, and a weak chin.

He realized with a start that he was looking at the face of the Scarecrow.

A second picture from a broader angle showed a woman glancing back at him over her shoulder, an unguarded expression of revulsion on her face.

"I traced Mikkelson's movements using the GPS on his cell phone," Gunnar said. "Whoever that is brought his phone back and left it in the apartment."

"Where did they go in between?"

"According to GPS records, they made half a dozen stops. A coffee shop in Midtown. An office building on William Street downtown, near the New York Stock Exchange. A nearby Italian restaurant. A building at Eighty-fifth and Central Park West. A pharmacy a couple blocks away. And, finally, the parking structure underneath the apartment building across Seventy-second. You can see whoever's pretending to be Mikkelson emerging from the front door with his head lowered and the collar of his overcoat turned up."

"Are there any variations from his normal routine?" Mason asked.

"He hits the same coffee shop on the way to the same office building every day," Gunnar said.

"I didn't think Nautilus maintained an office here."

"It doesn't."

"So where does he go?"

"The building on William Street is thirty-two stories tall and houses as many companies. All I can tell you is that he goes inside and the beacon remains static until he leaves."

"Who are the tenants?"

"Your standard mix of real estate management firms, brokerages, and insurance companies. A law office, an executive recruitment agency, a couple of government contractors."

"What kind of contractors?"

"The New York City Housing Development Corporation and the Urban Development Corporation," Gunnar said. "I'm betting on one of those two entities. With as much time as Mikkelson spends there, I can't imagine he's hanging out with his brokers or lawyers."

"What about the building near Central Park?" Mason asked.

"It's an upscale apartment complex with street-level tenants, including a pediatric urgent care and medical wellness center."

"That's a holistic place, right?"

"It appears to be."

"And he goes from there directly to a pharmacy?"

"I don't see an oil company executive seeking treatment from a doctor who doesn't believe in pharmaceuticals any more than I buy a doctor of the holistic arts prescribing them."

"How close is that to where they found Raymond's body?" Mason asked.

"Not even a quarter mile."

"That's where the Scarecrow got Mikkelson out of the Town Car. Find out everything you can about the owners and tenants of the surrounding buildings. And check video surveillance from the corresponding time frame," he said, and turned to Ramses. "Where's your car?"

"In a garage about two blocks away. Why?"

"We found the Scarecrow."

59

"The building's called Rossleigh Court and it faces the Great Lawn across Central Park West," Gunnar said. "It abuts the building next to it, which is practically identical. Together, they form a backward C, inside of which is a small courtyard with limited patient parking, accessible by alley from both Eighty-fifth and Eighty-sixth. The only camera I can find covers the lot itself but neither of the alleys. You could park for a short amount of time in either and have access to the backyards of any of the adjacent properties with minimal exposure."

"The Scarecrow didn't drag Mikkelson up the stairwell of an upscale apartment complex in the middle of the day," Mason said.

"Especially not considering both are access-controlled and have doormen on duty."

The tires screamed as Ramses wove through the sluggish late-night traffic. Mason covered his free ear to tune out the horns blaring from all directions at once. Layne leaned over his shoulder from the backseat in an effort to hear Gunnar through the earpiece.

"What about the neighboring buildings?" Mason asked.

"They're all four-story row houses. Most of them divided into rental units."

Ramses slewed sideways onto Central Park West. The tires regained traction with a lurch and propelled the SUV toward Eighty-fifth Street.

"If you were planning an abduction in one of the most densely populated cities in the world and needed to get a body out of a car and into one of the buildings right there without any witnesses, which would it be?"

"The first of the row houses, right next to the alley. The backyard is contained by a retaining wall with an inset iron gate. You could almost pull right up to it, drag someone out of the trunk or the backseat, and only be visible to the uppermost levels of the surrounding apartment complexes for the amount of time it took to get the body across the yard."

"Then that's our place. Who owns it?"

"Next right," Layne said.

Ramses slammed the brakes and whipped the vehicle around the turn. Jerked the wheel to avoid a parked car. Skidded to the curb and nearly slammed into the back of a panel truck.

"A Manhattan-based real estate holding company called Integrity Group International," Gunnar said. "It owns a handful of other residential and commercial investment properties around the city, not to mention a couple dozen more overseas. The name on the lease is Verne Rasmussen, whose initial application lists him as an engineer with a nonexistent biotech firm and includes references with phone numbers no longer in service. His checks are drawn from a local account with a balance that never varies by more than fifty dollars from ten thousand. Seventy-five hundred goes out for rent, and the same amount comes right back in."

A frame composed of metal pipes supported a construction awning erected over the sidewalk. The banner hanging from it read THE FUTURE IS NOW and showed a picture of Times Square. It nearly concealed the mouth of the alley and the majority of the lower level of the adjacent row house, the first in a series that looked like the spines of so many books shoved unevenly onto a shelf.

Mason turned to Ramses.

"You stay here and keep an eye out. And watch the front door. If he's in there, we'll flush him right to you."

"He won't get past me," Ramses said.

Mason and Layne climbed out of the car and headed down the pitch-black alley. The few lighted windows on the back side of the complex produced just enough illumination to get a good look at the enclosed parking lot and the barrier separating it from the yard of the adjacent row house. The wrought-iron gate in the eight-foot brick wall was padlocked and reinforced with a sheet of plywood to prevent anyone from looking inside.

They were going to have to do this the hard way.

Mason ran straight at the wall. Jumped. Planted his right foot squarely against the bricks and used the leverage to propel himself higher. He braced his palms on top, drew his legs up underneath him, and perched like a gargoyle.

The yard below him was barren, the grass patchy and the slate path cracked. The lone elm tree was half-dead and surrounded by pots filled with sunbaked soil. Trash and debris had drifted into the corners. He glanced up at the buildings towering over him but neither saw nor sensed anyone watching him. It was a location as private as any in the heart of an urban center this concentrated.

"Gunnar," Mason said. "See if you can access the interior layout."

He dropped down on the other side. Drew his Glock. Advanced toward the shadowed back porch in a shooter's stance.

"The back door enters on the garden level," Gunnar said. "You'll pass through the dining room first, then the kitchen and a hallway. The stairs to your right lead to the basement. Past them, you'll find a bathroom, a bedroom, and the main staircase."

Layne alighted behind him with a thud and a whoosh of expelled air. She fell in behind him as he approached glass doors crisscrossed with wooden lattices. They were the kind designed to be carelessly thrown open on a hot summer's day, which meant the locking mechanism between them was inherently weak. A solid tug on both handles at once confirmed as much and they entered a completely empty dining room.

Mason switched on his mini Maglite and aligned the beam with his pistol. The hardwood floor creaked underneath him as he made his way into the kitchen. Layne's light bloomed behind him and stretched his shadow across the floor.

"There are three levels above you," Gunnar said. "You'll come up on the next level in the foyer, facing the front door. Behind you will be the living room, the study, and the stairs to the third level, which houses the master suite and bathroom. There are four smaller bedrooms on the top floor."

The kitchen was eerily silent. The refrigerator didn't hum and no heated air pinged through the ductwork. The appliances sat lifeless and neglected, the sink empty. A patina of dust had settled on the countertops.

"This is definitely the right place," Layne whispered. She shone her beam at the floor and revealed a smear of dried blood. There was another at the top of the staircase leading into the basement.

"You clear the upper levels," Mason whispered. "I'll go down."

"Not alone you won't."

"If anyone else is in the house, they'll have us both trapped down there."

She pursed her lips, reluctantly nodded, and turned her back on him.

Mason stood at the top of the staircase and shone his light down into the darkness. The landing at the bottom bent to the left and around a blind corner. He started down slowly, cautiously. The temperature dropped with each step, until a cloud of breath blossomed from his lips. He paused on the last stair and listened for any sound to betray the presence of someone waiting for him. He detected a faint whistling sound, like the movement of air through a hollow space. Smelled mildew and earth, the kind of dampness he equated with the aftermath of a rainstorm.

He went around the corner. Low and fast. Shone his beam from one side of the narrow hallway to the other, taking in his surroundings as quickly as possible. To his right: the utility room, the furnace and hot-water heater silent and nearly concealed behind a mountain of broken concrete. Straight ahead: the barren laundry room, ductwork and pipes protruding from walls connected to the ceiling by cobwebs as thick as ropes. To his left: a large room made small by the mound of fractured concrete and dirt in the center, and what looked like an animal cage in the corner. Tongue depressors tied together with yarn hung from the ceiling, casting star-shaped shadows he immediately recognized from the picture at Edgewood onto the back wall. He plucked one from the hook above him, tucked it into his jacket pocket, and followed a trail through the construction zone. A ragged hole had been cut through the foundation and the underlying soil had been excavated. There was a ladder inside, at the bottom of which was the dark mouth of a tunnel that ran horizontally away from the house and underneath the backyard.

"Talk to me, Mace," Gunnar said.

Mason tapped his Bluetooth microphone to let Gunnar know he was all right, but he remained silent, for fear the Scarecrow might be down there at that very moment, waiting for him in the darkness. He transferred his flashlight to his mouth, aimed his pistol down between his feet, and used his free hand to hold on to the ladder as he cautiously descended.

When he reached the third rung from the bottom, he let go and landed in a crouch, his weapon pointed straight into the tunnel.

There was no one inside.

Mason blew out his breath, slowly, quietly, and focused on slowing the thudding of his pulse in his ears. There was barely enough room for him to maneuver his body into the tunnel, which was snug against his shoulders and just high enough for him to enter on all fours. The packed earth was cold and hard and slanted downward at a steady rate. It had to be a good twenty degrees colder, and the dusty scent of age mingled with others he couldn't quite place, creating an almost industrial smell.

He was barely a dozen feet in when his beam limned the jagged edges of the end of the tunnel and diffused into the open space beyond. He saw bricks, discolored by time and stained by water, felt cold air caress his face.

"What runs underneath this block?" he whispered.

"Say . . . gain?" Gunnar's voice crackled in and out of the static.

"There's a structure down here."

The hiss of interference abruptly ceased with the complete loss of signal.

He crawled to the end of the earthen tunnel and found himself staring down into a man-made corridor that obviously predated the construction of the buildings overhead. Every surface was composed of mortared bricks, old and cracked, from the walls to the arched ceiling and floor, which cradled a pool of stagnant water as black as oil.

It took some doing, but he managed to contort his body in the tight space and lower himself into a tunnel that smelled of another era. He shone his light one way and then the other. The passage extended well beyond the limited range of his beam in both directions.

He stared off into the darkness and extrapolated the tunnel's course.

It led straight underneath Central Park.

60

"It's called the Croton Aqueduct," Gunnar said. The cell phone's speaker made his voice sound tinny and echoed inside the empty house, where Mason, Layne, and Ramses had gathered to plot their next course of action. "It was built during a five-year span from 1837 to 1842, with the intention of carrying potable water forty-one miles from the Croton Watershed in Westchester County to the Croton Receiving Reservoir in the middle of Central Park, in the hope of combating worsening sanitation conditions responsible for epidemics of yellow fever and cholera. It was considered a marvel of modern engineering at the time and stimulated construction of city sewers and indoor plumbing, but within a matter of years, it could no longer keep up with the demands imposed by exponential population growth. Cholera returned, uncontrollable fires raged, and the New Croton Aqueduct was commissioned in 1884. The city had grown too much to simply dig up and replace the old one, so the new line had to be run several miles to the east, where it fed Jerome Park Reservoir in the Bronx. It was much larger, buried deeper underground, and carried three times as much water as its predecessor. The former receiving reservoir was filled in to create the Turtle

Pond and the Great Lawn in 1940, while the old aqueduct remained in limited use until 1955."

"So they just left it?" Mason said.

"By then, the entirety of New York City as we know it had been built on top of it. Think of it as a forty-one-mile hallway with water running down the middle of the floor. It had to be constructed in such a way that it descended exactly a quarter of an inch per hundred feet, thirteen inches for every mile, to keep the water flowing at a steady rate from the source. Most of that hallway to the north was built above-ground, followed the topography, and had to be buried under mounds of dirt. By the time it reached the public water supply in Central Park, it was barely a dozen feet underground. Are you going to knock down apartments and skyscrapers just to collapse a tunnel to nowhere or invest tens of millions of dollars in dirt and labor to fill it in underneath buildings that are already structurally sound? Of course not. Instead, they tore down most of the gatehouses, put locks on the remaining entrances, and started prosecuting trespassers."

"You're saying there's still a forty-mile tunnel running underneath New York City."

"Forty-one, technically, but only a small portion of that is actually beneath the city."

"You know what we have to do," Layne said.

Mason nodded and glanced at Ramses, who was strangely quiet.

"What do you think?"

"This whole city's sitting on one great big man-made anthill. There are hundreds of miles of subway tunnels running underneath our feet, nearly all of which vent to the surface. You want to kill millions of people crammed into a small space? Try releasing an aerosolized weapon from trains moving through it at thirty miles an hour. The resulting cloud of gas would engulf the entire city within an hour. Think about the haze of dust that covered the entire island for days after the twin towers fell. Now imagine that as a lethal nerve agent."

"Christ," Layne whispered.

"The Japanese doomsday cult Aum Shinrikyo orchestrated a similar attack on the Tokyo subway system in 1995," Gunnar said. "They used sarin—albeit of lesser, homemade quality—and released it as a liquid instead of a gas, but the five men who carried out the poorly executed assault still managed to kill thirteen innocent people and send five thousand more to the hospital. Had they received the proper training and the financial backing of an organization like the Thirteen, they could have easily realized their own apocalyptic prophecy."

"It's classic misdirection," Ramses said. "You want freedom to move underground? Get everyone up top running around like chickens with their heads cut off."

"You're implying that the Scarecrow didn't murder Raymond, and quite possibly Mikkelson, in Central Park because we discovered the bodies in Colorado before he could finish his display in the cornfield," Mason said. "By your logic, this was his plan from the very beginning."

"There's a tunnel in the basement that would probably agree with me."

If that were the case, then the Scarecrow had used the design in the cornfield to either manipulate them into believing there were three more victims he'd never intended to take back to Colorado, or the pattern had been complete when they . . . found . . . it.

Mason removed the star from his pocket, only now that he looked at it more closely, its points were irregularly spaced. Four tongue depressors had been bound together with yarn in such a way that they almost looked like a gingerbread man with a long neck, a wide, triangular torso, and short knobby arms and legs.

He removed his mini Maglite from his pocket, held the creation at arm's length, and switched on the beam, projecting its shadow onto the wall.

The pattern had been staring them in the face since the beginning.

"It's a scarecrow," he said. "And look at the points formed by its hands, feet, and head."

"They make the same design as the bodies in the cornfield," Layne said. "We totally missed it."

It didn't matter now, though. Mikkelson was somewhere in the park, either dead or dying, and there was a madman out there with four thousand gallons of Novichok, access to an entire network of subterranean passageways, and a month's head start.

"We have to go down there," Mason said.

"What we need to do is call this in to Algren," Layne said. "Homeland's counterterrorism unit is far better equipped to handle this than we are. There's no way to potentially search all of the tunnels down there without their manpower."

"What makes you think she'll believe us?"

"If she finds Mikkelson's body in Central Park, she won't have much of a choice."

"And Marchment will make sure we're sidelined again."

"He does that and we die with the rest of the city," Ramses said.

"Do you really believe he'd be anywhere near this place if that was his goal?" Layne said. "A man motivated by power and greed wouldn't willingly sacrifice himself."

"But he doesn't have to be in the city when the Novichok's released. He just has to keep everyone trying to stop it away until it's too late to do anything about it."

"Even if we convince Algren to try, she can't override Marchment," Mason said. "The only thing she'll accomplish is letting him know that we're onto him and giving him a chance to stop us."

"I don't like this," Layne said, "but you're right. I don't see where we have any other choice."

Mason stared at her for a long moment. Sized her up. This was the point of no return.

"Once we go down there, we're on the wrong side of the equation," he said. "There'll be no talking our way out of it if they find us in that tunnel, and should anyone try to stand in our way . . ."

He let the implications hang between them. She needed to understand the ramifications of the course of action to which she was committing herself. They'd be going after the Scarecrow without any backup or support and deliberately placing themselves at odds with the Department of Homeland Security. In the strict eyes of the law, once they entered that tunnel, they became the bad guys.

"Nine million lives are at stake," she said. "That's more than ten percent of the world's population. I might be on the wrong side of the law, but I'll be damned if I'm not on the right side of history."

"*If* we succeed," Mason said. "We're running out of time."

"Then you'd better start trusting me."

"I trust you."

"With everything."

She looked deliberately from Mason to Ramses and back again.

"Bust his balls all you like," Ramses said, "but don't go bringing mine into this."

"I'll make you a deal," Mason said. "If we survive this, I'll tell you anything you want to know."

She stared him down for several seconds before nodding to herself, jacking a round into the chamber of her pistol, and heading for the stairs to the basement.

Mason grabbed his phone and switched it from speaker to Bluetooth.

"Are you still there, Gunnar?" Mason asked.

"I just sent maps of both the New York City waterworks and subway lines to your email," he said. "Ramses was right. The whole island is positively honeycombed with passages, including entire subway lines that haven't been used in decades."

"Thanks, man. We're going to need them."

"You obviously won't have a signal down there, so I won't be able to help you at all."

"Just mark my GPS and keep an eye on that satellite feed. If you can see us, so can they."

"Be careful down there, Mace." The note of concern in Gunnar's voice was unsettling. "You know what the Scarecrow is capable of."

Did they, though? Mason's biggest fear was that they'd only scratched the surface.

PART VI

By thus dividing the voters we can get them to expend their energies in fighting over questions of no importance to us except as teachers to lead the common herd.

—J. P. Morgan,
"Banker's Manifesto" (1892)

61

DECEMBER 31

Mason, Ramses, and Layne walked single file through a narrow brick aqueduct easily large enough to accommodate a procession of torpedolike, pressurized liquid containers, which could have been unloaded from the flatbeds at any of the remaining functional gatehouses north of the city and shuttled invisibly underground, assuming the Novichok hadn't already been transferred into smaller containers for ease of dispersion. And that was the problem; they didn't know what they were looking for any more than they knew where to find it.

Mason explored the tunnel with his flashlight beam, which seemed to dispel little more than the darkness in the immediate vicinity of the lens. He could barely hear a thing over the thunder of his pulse and the splashing of their footsteps in water that smelled like sewage. They had to be underneath Central Park by now, and yet they hadn't encountered a single surface-access chute or lateral branch.

"Keep your eyes open for trip wires and motion sensors," he said, his whispered voice echoing from the confines. "Watch for any kind of mechanism that requires movement or force to trigger it."

Ramses stayed right on his heels to take advantage of the faint glow. While he didn't have a flashlight, he'd miraculously procured a platinum-plated Sig P226 9mm semiautomatic pistol that shimmered in his grasp. Layne brought up the rear, alternately shining her beam behind them and casting their shadows ahead of them.

"You really think he rigged the tunnel?" Ramses asked.

"I'd be shocked if he didn't," Layne said. "If this guy's as smart as we think he is, he planned for someone to find this aqueduct and set up a way for us to kill ourselves."

"Wonderful. And here I thought the smell was the best part of this little field trip."

Mason traced the contours of the tunnel with his light. Sections of the ceiling had crumbled, exposing the rugged bedrock overhead and littering the ground with broken bricks and mortar. Someone had shoved them to the side to clear a path. The air was impossibly still. The sounds of their passage carried hundreds of feet ahead of them into the darkness. Their lights made them easy targets, but turning them off would make them even more vulnerable to whatever trap had been set for them. He brainstormed every possible container or dispersal device that could be used to vaporize chemicals or aerosolize liquids. Watched for any hoses or nozzles or reflections from metal. Listened for the hiss of pressurized gas that would signify it was already too late.

The mud and sediment preserved the smoothed trail of the travois-like contraption the Scarecrow had used to drag his victims into the park, erasing his own footprints in the process. Only smudged and partial impressions of work boots with a deep tread remained.

Mason's breathing was uncomfortably loud in his own ears. His pulse throbbed at the outer edges of his vision. His nerves were downed power lines. Each step brought him closer to setting off the trap he had yet to identify. There was no doubt in his mind that it was coming. He just prayed they recognized it before it was too—

He stopped mid-stride. There was an astringent smell. Chemicals of some kind.

Layne must have noticed it, too. Her light swept across his back and threw his shadow from one side of the tunnel to the other.

"I don't like this," she whispered.

"You were fine with everything up until now?" Ramses said.

"Chemical smells dissipate. This is too strong to have been here for very long."

She didn't need to remind them that the lack of circulation meant the source had to be nearby and they still hadn't seen anything out of the ordinary.

Mason slowly lowered himself to his chest in the shallow water and shone his beam across the surface. No shimmer of fishing line or infrared laser projectors.

Layne traced the arched ceiling with her light. There wasn't so much as a single cobweb. A section of bricks had fallen, creating a hollow filled with shadows at the farthest reaches of her beam.

Mason stood and shone his light straight down at the water, but he couldn't see anything through the disturbed sediment. He stepped to either side, straddled the water, and advanced in straight-legged scissor movements to avoid stepping anywhere he couldn't clearly see the ground.

The smell grew stronger by the second.

"We have to be missing something," Layne whispered.

Mason paused and studied his surroundings. Slowly. Carefully. No trip wires or pressure plates. No motion detectors or power sources. Nothing but a caustic scent that reminded him of bleach, only not exactly. Like bleach mixed with fuel oil.

"Smells like a pool," Ramses said.

"Chlorine," Mason whispered. "Definitely chlorine. But there's something else. Kerosene? Paint thinner?"

"Where is it?" Layne whispered. A note of panic crept into her voice. "I can't see a damn thing."

There was nowhere to hide a bottle or a bucket. No recesses in the walls. Nothing stood apart from the bricks or the darkness, and yet the smell continued to grow stronger.

The right combination of chemicals available in nearly every grocery or hardware store could produce noxious, potentially even toxic gasses from which they wouldn't be able to escape. Gasses strong enough to overcome them before they reached the nearest surface-access point.

Or worse.

"We've got to be right on top of it," Ramses said.

Mason inched close enough to shine his light into the shadowed recess where the fallen bricks had once been. Judging by the discoloration, the granite had been exposed for decades. Unlike the piles of rubble they'd passed previously, however, this one hadn't been shoved aside to make way for the transport the Scarecrow had used to move his victims. It sat right in the middle, forcing him to drag the travois out of the water, as evidenced by the sludge smeared up the sloped wall. There was something odd about the arrangement of bricks, too. Almost as though the pile had been deliberately stacked.

"One of us should hang back," Layne whispered. "Just in case. We can't afford to risk all of us dying at once."

Mason stopped and squatted as low as he could possibly go. He shone his light just above the surface of the water, from one side of the tunnel to the other, and noticed two things simultaneously.

A reflection from something buried under the bricks.

And a small black dome protruding from the top of the mound.

"Turn off your light," he said.

He took a mental snapshot and switched off his flashlight. Turned and snatched Layne's from her grasp. Extinguished it and prayed it wasn't already too late.

"Talk to me, Mace," Ramses said.

Mason closed his eyes, tuned out the metronomic dripping of condensation, and concentrated on the memory of what he'd seen in that fleeting moment before he killed the lights. He described every minuscule detail, as though to grant permanence to the mental photograph that was already starting to fade.

"There's an ornamental streetlight underneath the bricks," he said. "Like they have in London, only smaller. Black wrought-iron frame. Glass windows. A single inverted lightbulb with a hole drilled into it, near the fitting, which someone used to fill it with fluid. Two liquids, different densities. The one that settled to the bottom is yellow and oily. The upper is clear but sparkles with what looks like glitter. You can still see it, if you look hard enough. Little glowing dots, suspended in the fluid."

He remembered from a crash course on chemistry and terrorist applications at the Academy that substances that glowed in the dark contained some amount of phosphorous.

And with that realization, he suddenly understood exactly what the trap had been designed to do.

"The upper fluid is chlorine," he said. "The particles suspended in it are granules of oxidized phosphorus. The bottom layer is a sulfur-based industrial solvent, like thiodiglycol. Separate, they're stable, but catalyze the mixture of the three and you're looking at producing mustard gas. Throw in a large-enough electrical charge and you'd have a miniature napalm bomb that would shower us all with glass and flaming chemicals, even as the gas blisters our skin and shreds our lungs."

"Did you see the trigger?" Ramses asked.

"Exposed wires pass through the hole in the bulb, into the upper liquid. They're connected to a motion detector that barely sticks out of the top of the bricks. The domed kind with sensors that cover a full three hundred and sixty degrees. Not a very sensitive model. Battery-powered, little more than a toy. We could work around it in open space, if we could see it."

"So why can't we?" Layne asked.

Mason focused on the unmistakable rectangular reflection he'd seen.

"Because the lamp's been retrofitted with a solar cell. The kind you buy to charge your cell phone and that works even under indoor lighting conditions."

It was an ingenious trap. The Scarecrow had known that anyone pursuing him down here would have to use either night-vision goggles, which didn't have sharp enough resolution to discern the motion detector from the bricks until the wearer was well within its range, or flashlights, which would charge the photocells and send a current through the filament in the bulb. Setting off either one would create an electrical charge large enough to ignite the chemical bomb he'd created.

And they'd been shining their lights right at it.

There was no way of knowing how much charge had accumulated in the solar panel, so they couldn't risk turning on their lights again, even for a second, for fear of reaching the threshold charge and triggering the reaction, which meant they were going to have to beat the motion detector in total darkness.

They could only guess at its range, but even a three-foot radius was more than enough to cover the entire width of the aqueduct. The fact that the Scarecrow had lowered it into the bricks in an effort to conceal it just might work to their advantage, though. By doing so, he'd blocked off everything below the level of the rubble surrounding it.

"We go underneath the detector," Mason said. "That pile of bricks has to be at least a foot and a half high. We should be able to circumvent it if we keep our bodies pressed to the ground and don't knock over the lamp."

"Screw that," Ramses said.

"Then head back to the house. I won't hold it against you. We've got this from here."

"You think I'm scared of a little mustard gas and a fiery death? I'm just pissed I have to get down in that water. It smells like whatever died in it shit all over itself in the process."

Mason smiled in the darkness. There were worse people with whom to share an agonizing death than his old friend.

"I'll go first," he said. If he'd misremembered any of the details of what he'd seen, the remainder of their lives could very well be measured in seconds. "Don't follow too closely, in case something goes wrong."

"Like ten feet's going to make a big difference," Layne said.

Mason lowered himself to his chest and turned his face sideways, both to minimize his profile and to keep his mouth and nose above the vile water. He scooted sideways until he felt his shoulder rise up onto the slope, stretched his arms out in front of him, and planted his palms on the slimy bricks.

Deep breath in.

Long, slow exhalation.

He pushed with his toes, pulled with his hands, and managed to move about four inches.

Again, push with his toes, pull with his hands.

Four more inches.

The glow of the phosphorus faded. He could only guess as to where the lantern was now.

Push with his toes, pull with his hands.

Frigid water sloshed against his cheek, into his ear. The smell was so intense, he could taste it. His shoulders already burned from the exertion. He bumped something hard with his elbow—

A clattering sound, followed by a splash near his head.

He closed his eyes and listened for the electrical sizzle of current passing into the fluid.

Seconds passed.

Nothing.

He exhaled a breath he hadn't realized he'd been holding and scooted away from the bricks, careful how high he allowed his right shoulder to creep up the sloped wall.

Pushed with his toes, pulled with his hands.

Again and again.

He heard a faint clamoring sound behind him as Ramses knocked the fallen brick back against the pile, but he didn't even slow.

Push, pull.

"I'm past it," Layne whispered.

Mason tried to gauge the distance between them. Maybe a dozen feet. The length of his body plus Ramses'. There was no way the sensors reached that far, but he wasn't taking any chances. Another three feet and he eased to the side to allow Ramses to squeeze in beside him.

"We can't just crawl forever," Ramses said. "For all we know, this guy's standing right above us with night-vision goggles, having a good laugh at our expense."

"Surely we're out of range by now," Mason said. "Layne?"

"Just be ready to run if you're planning on doing what I think you are."

He closed the lens of his flashlight inside his fist and switched it on. A pale pinkish glow seeped out from between his fingers. He relaxed them just enough to allow a little more light to leak out, barely enough to see the impression of the pile of bricks behind them, at the farthest reaches of sight. It had to be a good twenty feet away, with the solar cell on the far side, facing the opposite direction.

The tunnel ahead of them was empty, save for the rusted rungs protruding from a flattened section of the wall. He slithered over to them and rolled onto his back. They led upward into a narrow, circular chute. His beam was just strong enough to reveal the hint of the iron disk sealing the top. He waited until Ramses and Layne were nearly on top of him before rising to a crouch.

"Stay here," he said, and scurried upward, the tapping sounds of his feet striking the sticky rungs echoing below him.

The manhole cover at the top was cold and solid, its edges sharp and uneven where someone had used an acetylene torch to cut through the welding that had once sealed it in place. He braced his feet and shoved the cover upward until he was able to slide it to the side with a screeching sound.

A column of moonlight, barely brighter than the tunnel itself, streaked past him and encircled Layne, who stood at the base of the ladder, silhouetted by the aura of light coming from deeper in the tunnel to her right. She must have given Ramses her flashlight, he realized.

"What do you see?" she whispered.

Juniper shrubs had grown over the manhole. He pushed them aside and found himself looking up into a dense canopy of deciduous trees, their skeletal branches intertwined to such an extent that he could barely see a handful of stars directly overhead. A gentle snow had started to fall, frosting their limbs.

"Nothing."

Mason transferred his flashlight to his mouth, drew his pistol, and crawled out through the vegetation. The manhole cover beside him was coated with a crust of dirt so thick, it would have been invisible even to someone standing right on top of it, assuming the person dug through the carpet of dead leaves first. A dusting of accumulation concealed a natural trail of stones that almost looked like a staircase ascending the hillside toward the granite formation at the top, above which he could see the outline of the crossbar to which Charles Raymond's arms had been tied.

The forensic team had packed up and moved on. There was no hint of movement through the surrounding trees, no aura of flashlights in the distance. No voices carried over the distant din of car horns and sirens. There wasn't a soul within the boundaries of the park.

His phone rang through on his Bluetooth. He tapped the button to connect.

"I've picked up your GPS beacon," Gunnar said, "but it doesn't appear as though anyone else has."

"Just poking my head out to get a look around and gather my bearings," Mason whispered.

"I sent you some more maps that might be of interest. Turns out there are a bunch of subway tunnels in various stages of completion and abandonment down there. And even more proposals that made it to some unknown stage in the drilling process. There's a lot of drama surrounding the early subway operators, especially during the twenties, with the Independent City-Owned line making an aggressive play to cut the Interborough Rapid Transit Company and Brooklyn Rapid Transit Company out of the East Side and bankrupt them in the process."

"Now's not the time for a history lesson, Gunnar."

"The moral of the story is that the mayor at the time, John Francis Hylan, hated that private interests controlled the subways, so he created his own public line to compete, which required a little creativity and a lot of secrecy. His early proposal for a Second Avenue line incorporated a shortcut under Central Park, some of which we know was actually built because it was incorporated into the Q line."

"How far is that from my current location?"

"Just under a half mile to the southeast."

"Guys," Ramses called from below. "You've got to see this."

"Heading back down," Mason said.

He slid back into the ground, dragged the manhole cover into place, and descended as fast as he could. The call dissociated into static halfway down. He killed the connection and let go of the rungs as soon as he was within range of the ground. Landed with a splash.

Ramses stood maybe fifty feet ahead of him, framed by mounds of broken bricks and granite. Curtains of roots cascaded from the exposed earth above him. He shone the beam at Layne and Mason as they approached, then to his left, into a gaping maw where the bricks had fallen. They caught up with him and followed the trajectory of the light down into the earth, to the point where it dissolved into the fathomless darkness.

Mason knelt and examined the mess of sludge that had been tracked up onto the rubble. The Scarecrow had definitely dragged Mikkelson's body through here.

"We're screwed," Layne said.

Mason could only nod. He stood, aligned his flashlight beam with the sight line of his pistol, and, without a word, ducked through the hole in the collapsed wall.

62

Mason skidded down the loose rocks to the edge of the hole, which overlooked a cavernous chamber bathed in darkness. The walls and ceiling were rugged, coarsely chiseled granite braced by a framework of ancient wooden cribbing so old and ravaged by water damage that entire sections had collapsed, including the one supporting the rubble upon which he now stood. Twin rail lines ran across the muddy ground, covered with so much loose talus, they disappeared in places. Murky puddles formed beneath weakened sections of the earthen roof, from which a steady drizzle of water fell. An ancient railcar protruded from the rocks below him, abandoned and forgotten. A mine cart overflowing with stones sat on the adjacent track, which vanished into the dark mouth of a tunnel leading deeper into the earth to the southeast.

Broken lengths of timber and boulders formed an uneven walkway down to the bottom. Mason descended cautiously, pausing every few steps to shine his beam into the crevices around him. There could have been motion sensors or pressure plates rigged all around him and he never would have seen them. The path where Mikkelson's body had been dragged was readily apparent. Unlike inside the aqueduct, no effort had been made to hide the trail.

Layne hopped down behind Mason and knelt over a footprint that couldn't have been more than a day old. She snapped a picture of it with her cell phone, then stepped in the dirt beside it to demonstrate scale. Her print wasn't all that much smaller.

"How does someone barely larger than I am haul a full-grown man down here by himself?"

"You think he had help?" Mason said.

Layne didn't answer. She walked past him and shone her light through the maze of wooden support posts, elongating their shadows into the tunnel. The brackets and bolts were rusted, the wood rotted in some places and nearly petrified in others. It was as though construction had simply ceased one day and never started back up, leaving the years and the elements to have their way with everything the workers had left behind.

Mason opened the file Gunnar had sent him. This tunnel wasn't on any of the modern maps, the hand-sketched blueprints of the BRT and IRT lines dating back more than a century, or even on the proposal for the mayor's Independent line, which passed diagonally through the park to the south. And yet here it was, a partially completed tunnel beneath one of the busiest metropolises on the planet, abandoned during the Great Depression.

"We can't be more than fifty feet down," Ramses said. His voice reverberated from the surrounding stone. "They're lucky the whole damn park hasn't collapsed."

Mason took a mental snapshot of each of the maps before returning his phone to its holster.

The scuffing sounds of their footsteps echoed ahead of them into the tunnel, which narrowed until it was barely wider than the twin tracks and maybe ten feet high. Wooden scaffolding was replaced by smooth granite. They passed stacks of rusted rails and decomposing railroad ties. Shovels, picks, and spades held together by rust and splinters. Kettle-like cement mixers and massive drums filled with rubble for removal. A wooden ladder scaled the wall into a chute drilled through the granite.

The trail left by Mikkelson's dragged body led straight to it.

"I guess we're going up," Layne said.

Mason shone his light toward the top of a ladder easily as old as the collapsed cribbing behind them and into shadows his beam couldn't penetrate.

"Ramses—" he began, but his old friend cut him off.

"No worries, Mace. I'm totally cool with waiting down here while you guys climb that totally stable and completely safe ladder."

"I knew I could count on you."

"Hey, what are friends for?"

Mason directed his beam at rectangular wooden rungs made from two-by-fours, the edges of which were scored where heavy objects had been repeatedly dragged across them. He climbed upward toward the shadowed recess in the earthen ceiling. As he neared, his light revealed the system of pulleys that had once been used to hoist equipment and excavated rock to the surface. It had been threaded with modern climbing ropes, presumably to help the Scarecrow raise Mikkelson's body to the ledge underneath the manhole, the welded seal of which had been cut in the same manner as the last one.

"You know what's up there, right?" Layne said from several rungs down.

"He could still be alive."

"You and I both know the odds of that."

Mason shoved aside the manhole cover, which supported a thick layer of dirt and weeds, and emerged into a thicket of evergreens and elms. Some distance behind him, across a walking path and beyond a wall of weeping willows, was the placid surface of the lake and a line of paddleboats tethered to a pier. To his right, Bethesda Terrace stood empty, its red bricks rapidly vanishing beneath the accumulating snow, which settled upon the outstretched wings of the bronze *Angel of the Waters* statue, posed as though emerging from the fountain, her heavenly form completely at odds with the one looming over Mason from behind.

He crawled out and reached back for Layne, who clasped his forearm and allowed him to pull her up beside him. They remained on all fours for several minutes, silently inspecting the ghastly tableau, until they were certain they were alone.

The post had been sunk directly into the earth, the victim bound to it in such a way that his toes grazed the detritus. Like the others, he wore overalls, a flannel shirt, and a straw hat, which had fallen down to the bridge of his nose, concealing his eyes. His face was swollen to such a degree that it appeared to have been molded from a paste of flour and water, the vessels in his cheeks and nose striking through it like black lightning. Open necrotic lesions ran upward from beneath his collar, across his neck, and onto his face, almost as though someone had splashed him with acid.

Mason barely recognized Andreas Mikkelson, who appeared to

have been dead for several hours. A wire ligature attached to the cross-bar was wrapped so tightly around his neck that it disappeared into the folds of skin. Faint scratching sounds emanated from beneath his clothes.

"They're coming from inside him," Layne said.

She took out her cell phone and started snapping pictures.

Mason glanced over his shoulder and searched the branches of a spruce for what he knew had to be there. The camouflaged camera was mounted about ten feet from the ground and directed straight at the victim's face. It was a remote-broadcasting model, the kind that could transmit for up to a mile, a radius that had to cover at least ten thousand apartments. He wondered if the Scarecrow had stopped watching after Mikkelson died or if the monster was staring back at him from the other end of the wireless connection at that very second.

"Oh God," Layne said.

He turned back to Mikkelson. She was right: The scratching sounds were definitely coming from inside of him. It almost sounded like he was trying to take a breath through his collapsed trachea, but he couldn't possibly still be alive, could he?

Mason brought his face to within inches of Mikkelson's, whose lips parted just far enough for a wasp nearly the size of his thumb to crawl out from between them. It had a red face, a black thorax, and a striped abdomen, with a stinger that had to be half an inch long. Someone had removed its wings. He snapped a quick picture of it and sent it to Gunnar, who called him back within a matter of seconds.

"It's called the Japanese giant hornet. *Vespa mandarinia japonica,* a subspecies of giant Asian hornets endemic—as I'm sure you surmised from the name—to the Japanese islands. It can be extraordinarily aggressive toward humans if provoked."

"Like by plucking off its wings?" Mason asked.

"I'd imagine that would do it," Gunnar said. "According to the *Journal of Immunology,* its venom is nearly as toxic as that of an Egyptian cobra. It eats through the skin and attacks the central nervous system. They don't lose their stingers, so they can inject you countless times."

There had to be at least fifty puncture wounds on Mikkelson's head and neck alone. The pain must have been excruciating, but the helpless feeling of being unable to prevent those horrifying creatures from turning him into a human pincushion would have been a thousand times worse. The Scarecrow hadn't been afforded the luxury of time to make Mikkelson suffer for days on end, which meant the agony needed to be so exquisite that he'd willingly thrust his head forward and strangle himself with the ligature before the venom took its toll.

"I count seven so far," Layne said. She lifted the bottom edge of the flannel shirt and a wasp came with it. "Make that eight."

"Be careful," Mason said.

The wail of sirens drifted across the deserted park.

"I'm picking up movement on the satellite," Gunnar said. "Multiple squad cars converging at the cordon along Terrace Drive. Get out of there before someone sees you."

Mason looked up at the camera in the tree.

"Someone already has." He turned to Layne. "Time to go."

"What's going on?"

"The Scarecrow's been watching us the entire time. He must have called in the discovery of the body himself."

Layne obviously understood the implications. They couldn't afford to be caught and sidelined. She lowered herself through the hole and Mason hurried down behind her.

"The police are entering the park on foot," Gunnar said.

"I need you to find Marchment," Mason said. He dragged the manhole cover back into place and mounted the ladder. "We have to get to him before the Scarecrow, who undoubtedly already knows where he is."

". . . try . . . going to know . . ."

"You're breaking up."

Mason lost the connection as he launched himself down the wooden ladder. Layne was already halfway down and moving at a rapid click. Ramses' light was so far to the south that it barely highlighted the walls of the tunnel in the distance.

They needed to be long gone by the time the responding officers discovered the manhole and came down here looking for Mikkelson's killer.

Mason hit the ground right behind Layne and ran as fast as he dared. The ground was covered with chunks of rock, sporadic puddles, and all kinds of wooden and metallic scrap, not to mention the enormous rusted rails and uneven railroad ties cutting straight down the middle.

Ramses heard them coming and shone his light into their faces. He'd just reached a point where the two tracks merged into one. The tunnel narrowed by half and the mortared slate and bare granite gave way to bricks.

"The police should be discovering Mikkelson's body at any second," Mason said. "We need to get out of the tunnels before they're overrun with cops. If we're taken off the board, there'll be no one left to stop the Scarecrow, who's preparing to make his move on Marchment as we speak."

He struck off deeper into the tunnel, jogging straight down the middle of the tracks. He felt, more than heard, the thrum of a train careening through the earth ahead of him. They had to be getting close.

Handmade red bricks gave way to commercial white ones, and finally to concrete. An elevated walkway appeared on the side of the tunnel, followed in short measure by rectangular pillars that supported a naked framework of iron girders. The passage curved to the left, charting a course to the east. He'd barely rounded the bend when his beam focused on a mountain of rubble that sealed off the tunnel. He pulled up short and swept his light across it. Massive chunks of granite had fallen from the ceiling, knocking down the horizontal girders and the support posts in the process.

"There has to be a way through," Layne said.

Mason crawled up onto the barricade and picked his way over the jagged, fractured edges of stone and concrete. A thick layer of dust clung to every surface, with the exception of a patch on the rock uphill to his right, where he saw a distinct palm print. Someone had gripped the edge and used it as leverage. He scooted laterally toward it and shone his light into a narrow gap nearly flush with the ceiling.

"Over here," he said, and squeezed inside. The passage was barely high enough to accommodate his chest and limited his depth of inspiration. For a moment, he feared he might get stuck, but he forced himself onward, squirming over broken concrete and under sharp protrusions from the roof. He wriggled out the other side, onto the end of an iron girder, and picked his way down the mountain of rubble, seemingly traveling from one century to the next in the process.

The pillars and girders were positively covered with graffiti, one layer on top of another. Trash and broken glass littered the ground, from which the tracks had been removed. The tunnel terminated against a concrete wall with an iron gate set into the lone doorway. The padlock on the latch had been broken, granting access to a narrow staircase leading down into an open space, from which the sound of his footsteps echoed.

He passed underneath an ornate brick arch and entered what must have been designed as an upscale station some fifty years ago. Mosaic tiles, most shattered or cracked, covered the walls beneath decades of accumulated spray paint. Fragments were scattered across the ground amid a modern midden of industrial refuse. The benches once bolted to the floor had been uprooted and smashed.

A tremor shivered through the ground.

The far wall was newer and utilitarian in design, a simple concrete barrier with a single inset metal door, the trim around which was buckled by the crowbar someone had used to pry it open from the other side. All Mason had to do was push it open—

A blinding light struck him a heartbeat before the train rocketed past on the far track, on the opposite side of a divider formed from girders sunken vertically into the ground every few feet. Subsequent cars thundered past at a staggering rate of speed, the faces of the passengers crammed inside a zoetropic blur. And then it was gone, stranding him once more in darkness.

Mason stepped out onto the concrete platform that ran beside the live rails.

"Was I right or was I right?" Ramses said.

While his theory about the tunnel beneath the row house on Eighty-fifth reaching the subway had borne out, it was physically impossible for anyone to have moved massive industrial canisters of Novichok along the route they'd taken to reach this point, let alone through either of the two nearly vertical surface-access hatches. Either it had been broken down into countless smaller vessels—a process that exponentially increased the chances of accidental release—and smuggled through here one container at a time or it had never been down here at all.

"Someone's coming," Layne said.

Mason followed her line of sight to where a light appeared in the far distance, faint at first, but growing brighter by the second. At the same moment he realized it wasn't moving fast enough to be a train, he recognized that it was swinging from side to side. A flashlight held in the hand of someone running toward them. The officers in the park must have discovered the manhole and dispatched backup from the nearest subway station.

"Damn it." He switched off his Maglite and sprinted in the direction the train had just gone. There were overhead lights every twenty feet, which meant they needed to round the coming bend first or they'd be caught out in the open. "There has to be a way to reach the street from the next station."

If they could get there first, they'd be able to blend into the early-morning crowds on the platform and merge into the flow of pedestrian traffic—

More lights materialized ahead, coming straight at them from the opposite direction.

They were trapped.

The ground trembled underfoot and he heard the distant rattle of an approaching train.

They had to find a way out before the officers converged on their position. To his left: a seamless concrete wall. To his right: the southbound track, four feet down, and the northbound track, a dozen feet farther away, on the other side of the divider. Steel I beams aligned with the support posts ran horizontally overhead, beneath the arched ceiling.

The headlights of a train brightened the tunnel at the farthest reaches of sight. In a matter of seconds, they'd be clearly visible to their pursuers from both directions.

Mason jumped down and hurdled the southbound track. Lunged. Planted his foot against one of the vertical girders and launched himself upward. Caught the bottom edge of the I beam. Pulled his legs up. Rolled his entire body on top, beneath the concrete ceiling.

Ramses was already hauling himself up onto the adjacent girder when Mason looked his way.

Layne was nearly a full foot shorter than either of them; there was no way she'd be able to make it on her own.

Mason leaned over the side. Squeezed his thighs around the steel. Let go with one hand and dangled upside down.

The rumble of the train bearing down on them made the entire world shake.

Layne recognized what he was doing. She sprinted toward the girder. Jumped and kicked it with her right foot. Turned as she propelled herself through the air toward his outstretched hand. Caught him just below his elbow with both hands, her momentum nearly wrenching her from his grasp before he secured a grip on her upper arm.

The headlights of the oncoming train struck her legs and stretched their shadows along the track.

She wasn't going to make it.

The rumble became a roar.

Mason shouted with the exertion and pulled with everything he had.

Layne screamed as the train raced toward her legs.

63

Layne released Mason's arm with her right hand and took hold of the beam. Drew her legs up. Transferred her weight to the steel. He wrapped his arm around her back and dragged her on top of him as the train screamed past mere inches below them.

Tha-thumpthumpthump. Tha-thumpthumpthump.

She reached around his chest and clung to the I beam to keep the slipstream from tearing them from their perch and hurling them out over the tracks.

The final car blew past below them and sped out of sight, its lights receding into the darkness with it.

Footsteps closed from both directions and converged underneath them. Mason caught a glimpse of navy blue uniforms and Kevlar vests bearing the words *Police DHS* and heard the voices of at least four men below him.

"Did you see anyone?"

"Negative. No one got past us."

"The suspect must still be in the tunnels."

"There's no way we're finding him if he is."

"Doesn't change the fact we're going in there after him."

"Radio ahead and let the units in the park know we're coming their way from the rails."

The officers might have been right about how the Scarecrow had entered the subway, but they were wrong about one crucial detail: He'd already gotten past them.

The chorus of running footsteps headed toward the closed platform leading back underneath Central Park.

Mason stared at Layne while he waited until he was certain the police were gone. She appeared so small and vulnerable, and yet possessed staggering inner strength belied by her size. He suddenly understood how someone as small as the Scarecrow could have overwhelmed and physically manhandled seven men larger than he was, even men with military training in their formative years. He must have spent his entire life stoking his hatred for them until it burned with the intensity of hellfire.

Layne released him and averted her eyes.

"What do you say we get out of here?" she said.

She shimmied backward down his legs until she had enough room to lower herself over the edge, then dropped to the ground with a muffled thump. By the time Mason joined her, Ramses was already up on the walkway and heading toward the next station in line, from which the second group of officers had appeared. Both teams must have already been at their respective stops when the officers in the park discovered Mikkelson's body and the underground tunnel, which meant that Marchment had deliberately posted them there. Was he preparing for a catastrophic event on the subway or just taking routine terrorism precautions in response to the Novichok threat?

They rounded a bend and a pinprick of light appeared in the

distance. It grew steadily brighter until it illuminated a subway platform lined with impatient people, all staring away from them and
toward where the next southbound train would burst from the dark
tunnel. The sign on the wall read: LEXINGTON AV-63 ST. They crouched
in the shadows and watched two NYPD officers in full tactical gear
work through the crowd on the northbound side as a train pulled into
the station, forming a barrier between them.

Mason seized the opportunity and emerged from the shadows onto
the platform, where he blended in with the other passengers, one of
whom, he could have sworn, looked like Johan's caretaker, Asher Ben-
Menachem, but he vanished into the throngs before Mason could get a
better look. He kept his head down to conceal his face from the security
cameras until he was through the turnstiles and making his way up the
stairs to the street. Cars honked and sirens wailed from some distance
away. His phone was already ringing when his first foot hit the sidewalk. He tapped his earpiece to connect.

"Park Avenue's a block to the west," Gunnar said. "Start walking
and try to look nonchalant. Turn right when you get there and keep
going. You'll pass a church. I'll meet you in the parking structure on the
next block up."

"How long do we have?"

"You hear those sirens? They're responding to a call for support at
the subway station you just left."

Police cruisers screamed toward them. One screeched to a halt
against the curb beside the stairwell access, while the other raced to
secure the main entrance to the station, across the street on the ground
level of a brown-brick apartment building.

"There were uniformed officers posted at both of the stations near
where we came out from under the park," Mason said.

"The city always bolsters its infrastructure security around the
holidays," Gunnar said. "They don't take any chances with two million people prepared to descend upon an open-air venue with inherent
security limitations like Times Square on New Year's Eve. There've been
officers at every station around the clock for the past two weeks."

"That's before we even knew the Scarecrow was here," Mason

said. "Posting four officers seems like overkill for what have to be fairly average stations, though."

"If they so much as suspected he was going to hit the city, the first thing they would have done is lock down the main transportation hubs."

"Which would have triggered a panic and impeded Homeland's movements, maybe even forced the Scarecrow's hand."

Mason turned right on Park Avenue, ducked under a construction awning, and wove through the foot traffic between support posts. Layne and Ramses followed, looking like they'd just crawled out of a Dumpster.

"What do you see on satellite?" Mason asked.

"Police converging on the subway stations at Fifty-seventh and Sixty-third and at least thirty guys in white jumpsuits and navy windbreakers surrounding the knoll where you found Mikkelson's body," Gunnar said. "And speaking of our good friend Andreas, he wasn't heading downtown every day for fun. He was working with the research and development arm of the New York City Urban Development Corporation on a project to help transition the city to renewable energy sources."

"That doesn't sound like it's in Nautilus's best interests."

"Fossil fuels will soon go the way of the dinosaurs. Literally. Green energy's the wave of the future. All of the major oil companies have bowed to pressure from shareholders and environmental interests and invested heavily in both clean and renewable sources. And not just out of the goodness of their hearts, either. Within the next twenty years, the renewable energy industry is projected to produce revenue surpassing Big Oil, even in its heyday."

"And in the meantime, Slate Langbroek gets a huge influx of pharmaceutical cash from Aebischer's nerve gas medication and takes a huge step toward achieving the genocidal goals of the Thirteen by killing over nine million people."

"Wiping out one of the world's largest cities is a big step in the right direction, but it's nowhere close to thinning the population to a level that can be more effectively ruled."

"Maybe New York City is just the first phase and only a small amount of the Novichok is here. The Scarecrow had plenty of time to divide it into smaller containers and ship it to every major port in the world."

"In which case, we're all fucked," Ramses said from behind him.

"Stands to reason," Gunnar said. "There's no way someone could have moved thousands of gallons of anything in massive containers into one of the busiest subway systems in the world without anyone noticing, especially during the holiday season. He really only needs a fraction of it anyway. If someone was smart enough, he could probably figure out a central location from which trains would be leaving in all different directions at once and rig them with remote devices to slowly release the gas. They'd be carrying a deadly cloud outward at thirty miles an hour, propelling gusts straight up from vents throughout the five boroughs."

Mason quickened his pace as more sirens joined the chorus. Cruisers streaked past on the other side of the median, which was metered by light poles adorned with banners advertising something called the Green Smart Grid at the Renaissance. The parking garage was an underground structure below a residential building. Gunnar had backed the Escalade into a space facing the entrance. He disconnected the call when he saw them descending the ramp, climbed out of the car, and tossed the keys to Ramses.

"And the Scarecrow's had his run of the entire subway system for the last month," Mason said. "For all we know, he's already installed those devices on half of the trains in town."

"He'd pick the busiest and most centralized hub he could find from which to launch the attack."

"So we need to get there first," Layne said.

"We don't know which station he's going to use and we don't have the manpower to cover them all, but we do know one place he's going to be for sure," Mason said, and turned to Gunnar. "We need to find Marchment. Tell me Alejandra heard back from Anomaly."

"Negative," Gunnar said. "He's gone dark."

"Then we're counting on you to locate him."

"I don't know where he is now," Gunnar said, "but I can tell you where he was."

64

The squeal of the SUV's tires echoed from the parking garage as Ramses ascended the ramp and pulled out onto Park Avenue, heading southeast toward Lower Manhattan. They needed to find Marchment and there was really only one way to do so. It was too risky for all of them to go to the federal building, so they'd agreed that Mason would go alone. If he was right, he had a pretty good idea of how he could get Algren to divulge the deputy secretary's location.

"Back up and start over," Layne said. "I thought Marchment and Mikkelson were at Edgewood in 1975."

"They were," Gunnar said. "With the exception of a short period of time in September. Records show that on August sixteenth, 1975, Andreas Mikkelson purchased four tickets on a commercial plane bound for Japan, by way of San Francisco and Honolulu, from an expense account established by Royal Nautilus Petroleum. Private Second Class Randall Marchment's passport was stamped three weeks later in Tokyo, alongside one belonging to a gentleman named Dr. Ichiro Nakamura, who promptly exited the airport and dropped off the face of the Earth."

"What do you mean?" Mason asked.

"Exactly what I said. His trail ends right there, but the trail of a man named Masao Matsuda picks up where his left off. This picture's from his obituary."

Gunnar swiveled his laptop so Mason could see the screen, a simple task made considerably more difficult by the stop-and-go traffic.

The picture was in black and white and appeared to have been scanned from a newspaper. The subject had a gray beard, thinning hair, and deep wrinkles around his eyes. He wore glasses with thick black rims and even thicker lenses. Mason stared at it for several seconds before determining that it was the same man he'd seen in the photographs at Edgewood.

"I would never have found him if I hadn't run his picture through age-progression software," Gunnar said, "and even then I only found a handful of images. This is the best one."

Layne turned around in the passenger seat and leaned as far back as she could. Gunner tilted the screen so she could see.

"Do you think someone tried to scrub him from the Internet?" she asked.

"I think he was a man who did everything in his power to avoid being captured on film."

"That would explain why he wasn't in any of the staff photos," Mason said.

"And for good reason," Ramses said. "If anyone made the connection between him and Unit 731, the Chinese and Russians would have been fighting over who got the first crack at him and we would have had an international incident on our hands."

"What do we know about the Matsuda identity?" Mason asked.

"Born 1913 in Tokyo, where he died in 1995. Earned his medical degree from Tokyo Imperial University in 1937. A prominent pediatric surgeon, he was commissioned as a lieutenant in the Japanese Imperial Army in 1940. Assigned to the Epidemic Prevention and Water Purification Department of the Kwantung Army in Manchuria, where he served under Dr. Shirō Ishii in Unit 731. There he performed invasive human experimentation resulting in the deaths of thousands of civilians and prisoners of war, most of them Chinese. Pardoned of charges of crimes against humanity in 1945. General Douglas MacArthur himself negotiated the deal exonerating Ishii, Matsuda, and a handful of others, in exchange for exclusive access to their research, which included amputations and vivisections, deliberate exposure to viral and bacterial warfare agents, and experimentation with lethal poisons and nerve agents. All on men, women, and even children."

Mason realized how much gaining access to that kind of medical knowledge, which would have been impossible to re-create under anything remotely resembling humane conditions, while simultaneously denying it to an adversary like the Soviet Union, would have been worth to the military, not to mention the field of medicine.

"Once I had his real name," Gunnar said, "I was able to find pictures facial recognition couldn't acquire."

He brought up a grainy black-and-white photo of a man wearing a surgical mask and smock and elbow-length gloves standing over a body whose abdomen had been opened from navel to sternum and its contents disgorged. In another, a man in a gas mask, raincoat, and rubber boots was hosing down a screaming girl with what looked like an industrial sprayer. One photo showed him in a surgical mask and butcher's apron, posing beside a pallet covered with human remains in various states of dismemberment. In the next, he was carrying a toddler by the front of his pants, the child's body folded limply backward.

There were more, but Mason couldn't bring himself to look. He'd seen enough to know what kind of savage this man had been, how he'd used Marchment to help conduct experimentation so sadistic, it had turned a little boy into a monster like the Scarecrow, and how Marchment had been able to use what he'd done to advance his career. Were it not for the fact that the Novichok was still out there, he would have been more than content to leave all of these wretched people to their own devices. As was always the case, though, it was innocents who ultimately suffered most at the hands of evil men.

"How did Matsuda end up at Edgewood?" he asked.

"According to an official release from the Department of Justice, a team of army scientists was sent from Camp Detrick to Manchuria in 1945 to authenticate the results of experimentation conducted by a group of Japanese medical professionals, who were offering the totality of their research in exchange for their freedom. This envoy concluded that American scientists could never independently amass such a comprehensive database of human medical knowledge because they had—and I quote—'scruples.' As Japanese physicians obviously didn't, the means by which they acquired this treasure trove of information was determined to be unethical rather than criminal, a semantic distinction that allowed the powers that be to feel good about cutting the deal, as not only did they reap the benefits; they were able to twist the knife in the back of the Soviets, who wanted blood—knowledge be damned—for the Russian prisoners of war killed by Unit 731."

Mason looked into the faces of the people they passed—in their cars, in Union Square Park, eating and drinking at outdoor tables—and wondered how many of them were capable of committing such atrocities. He thought of what he would have done to Matsuda if given the opportunity, and realized he wasn't a whole lot better.

"So we offered immunity," Gunnar said. "In exchange, we received the raw data, notes, and graphic documentation, which we brought back to Maryland. Along with the Japanese doctors themselves. There they served in an advisory capacity to our fledgling bioweapons program, the clinical arm of which was subsequently set up at—"

"The Edgewood Arsenal," Layne said.

"I can't find any records of how long Matsuda slash Nakamura was there or his role in the experimentation, though. The closest I can come is a peripheral mention of three pardoned Unit 731 members helping to implement testing protocols. There's no information on either identity between 1952 and 1975. His story picks back up again in 1976, when he founded Kenkō Pharmaceuticals. Takeo Tamiya, another pardoned physician, returned home and became president of the Japan Medical Association. Shirō Ishii, the Imperial Japanese version of Josef Mengele, remained underground until he popped up in South Korea right about the same time North Korea accused the United States of using biological weapons against it."

"You think these guys were brought over here as more than mere advisers?" Layne asked. "That they continued their experimentation under government supervision?"

"It wouldn't surprise me," Ramses said. "The powers that be don't give a shit about any of us."

"Why do you have such a hard-on for the army?"

"I find out it's been in bed with the Langbroeks since the fifties, that a private company like Nautilus was able to use its power and influence to infiltrate our country's defense and corrupt it for its own purposes, and you're asking why that might bother me? I did things for this country that still keep me awake at night. How am I supposed to feel knowing that I could have done so on the orders of the Thirteen?"

No one spoke for several minutes as cars and pedestrians blurred past beyond the windows.

"You said something about the emissaries from Camp Detrick drawing an ethical distinction between American and Japanese doctors," Mason said. "Do you think the same logic could be applied to test subjects?"

"Do you mean from the perspective that it would be unethical, rather than criminal, to allow experiments to be conducted on Japanese children?" Gunnar asked. "Or for unscrupulous Japanese physicians to experiment on children in general?"

"Take your pick," Mason said.

"You said the DoD bought four seats," Layne said. "Who occupied the other two?"

Gunnar was too busy typing to answer.

Ramses turned right on Leonard and pulled to the curb.

"You sure this is how you want to play it?" he asked.

"If you were Marchment, where would you go?"

"I'm not saying you're wrong, only that if they really want you sidelined, you're not coming back out of that building. And if they figure out you found Mikkelson and didn't call it in . . ."

He let the statement hang; the implications were clear.

"I should go with you," Layne said.

"We've been over this," Mason said. "If I'm detained, it's up to you guys to stop the Scarecrow."

He climbed out the rear door and was just about to close it behind him when Layne spoke.

"But what if we can't?"

There was an urgency in her voice.

"Then Ramses knows what to do from there."

Mason closed the door and stepped back from the curb. His old friend nodded his understanding before squeezing back into traffic. If their worst nightmares were realized, he had complete confidence in Ramses to get Gunnar and Layne out of the city or, failing that, to make sure they didn't suffer.

He turned to the south, where he could just barely see the top few floors of the Jacob K. Javits Federal Building over the complex across the street, and struck off to meet his fate.

65

Mason stopped at the drugstore on the corner, where he bought a cup of coffee, a stick of deodorant, and a Rangers T-shirt and windbreaker. He used the restroom to change and clean himself up and messaged Algren to let her know that he'd made a connection that might help her investigation. She promptly responded that she'd meet with him when he arrived.

He jogged across the street to the federal building and finished his coffee while waiting in line at security. An agent wearing an FBI lanyard was waiting for him on the other side of the metal detector. She greeted him with a firm handshake and ushered him into an elevator that took him directly to the twenty-third floor. The doors opened on an office far less chaotic than he'd expected. He turned to his left and saw Algren striding straight toward him in the same clothes she'd been wearing when he saw her last. If her eyes were any indication, she hadn't slept since then, either. Her expression suggested she'd nearly exhausted her limited supply of patience and wasn't about to waste what little remained on him.

She beckoned for him to follow her and headed back down the hallway to the tune of clicking heels. They forced their way through throngs of analysts and JTTF officers moving with an extreme sense of purpose on their way to the operations center. A riot of voices and tension spilled into the corridor when she opened the door.

Rows of massive desks spanned the width of the room, each of them equipped with a dozen stations, all of which had their own computers and networked telephones. Signs had been affixed to the top of the monitors to identify the dedicated operator's function for ease of identification at a glance. Each served as the central hub of communications for the various contributing parties, such as FEMA, SWAT, NYPD, FBI, DHS, FDNY, and the NJTTF—National Joint Terrorism Task Force—in Washington, D.C., which, presumably, coordinated the efforts here with those in Philadelphia and the District.

There were a dozen video screens mounted to the wall at the front of the room. All of them displayed different critical functions in real time. There was a map of the five boroughs with the locations of field teams represented by yellow beacons, satellite imagery from various elevations and of different areas, rolling surveillance-camera footage, and both local and national newscasts. Whiteboards had been wheeled in and positioned to either side of the rows of desks, leaving barely enough room to scoot between them. They were covered with photographs, maps, and handwritten notes. Crime-scene images from Colorado, New Jersey, and New York. Detail shots of victims and evidence marked with numbered placards.

Mason took in everything around him as fast as he could. They already had pictures of Mikkelson's body—including close-ups of the bruising from the ligature, the wasps, and the dark-rimmed holes where the venom had eaten through his flesh—on the board beside the photographs of Charles Raymond's body. They were only now beginning to put together the Nautilus connection. While they had a long way to go to catch up with him, they'd learned something that he hadn't. The majority of the executive committee was in town and at the top of the list of proposed interviews, along with Mikkelson's doorman, neighbors, and local business associates. A forensics team was already inside his penthouse, as evidenced by the live feed playing out on its liaison's screen.

He didn't see anything even peripherally related to the Rocky Mountain or Edgewood arsenals.

Algren's desk was at the front, beneath the central column of monitors, facing the madness. There were binders stacked on one side, notebooks on the other. Every line on her phone was flashing. She practically collapsed into her chair and looked up at him with raised eyebrows.

"You said you'd figured out something that might help us?" she said.

Mason glanced at the pictures of the Colorado crime scenes. He was looking for one in particular.

"Tell me you're not trying to use the promise of information to leverage your way back into the investigation," she said. "Because if you are, I swear to God—"

"Nothing like that," he said. "I was kind of hoping you'd offer, but I don't have any ulterior motives. I was just sitting around my hotel room, trying to keep my mind occupied, when I figured out the message in the cornfield."

She inclined her head to her right, toward where an aerial view of the Cavanaugh acreage was affixed to a different dry-erase board than he'd expected. He peeled it off and set it on her desk. The dead men on the crossbars stood apart from the corn. The angle wasn't quite right, so he turned it about fifteen degrees so the posts lined up for her. He grabbed a pen and drew a vertical line down the middle and a horizontal line intersecting it, connecting the top three victims to form the upper portion of a cross.

"Behavioral was right about the number of points, but not about the design," he said. "It was already complete when we arrived."

He drew the diagonal lines from what he considered the feet through the center of the circle and connected them to the crossbar.

"What's that supposed to be?" she asked.

"It's a scarecrow."

Algren picked up the photo and held it closer to her face.

"If you look at any number of points long enough, you'll eventually see a pattern."

She tossed the picture back onto her desk, but he could tell he'd set the hook.

"Sorry to have wasted your time," he said.

"I didn't mean for it to come out like that. I truly appreciate the effort. If you think of anything else that might be useful, please don't hesitate to call."

"I'm sure you have more than enough on your plate, what with this being New Year's Eve and everyone in town preparing to hit the streets."

"And a mayor who won't even entertain the notion of canceling the festivities."

"Can't you make him?"

"Even the DHS and JTTF are subject to politics. There've been credible threats on New Year's Eve before, none of which have come to pass. After the ISIS threat in 2015, they upgraded their security measures and claim you couldn't sneak a pocketknife into Times Square, let alone an explosive device. He insists they have the situation contained. The entire area's barricaded with sand trucks and concrete barriers. They have security checkpoints at every entrance, hundreds of camera drones overhead, thousands of uniformed and plainclothes officers on the ground, and fifty bomb-sniffing canine units."

"None of which will do them any good against the release of a chemical weapon."

"My point exactly, but you try convincing him."

"What about the subways?"

"Locked down tight. No one's getting on or off one of those trains without being subjected to facial-recognition software and passing through our security net."

"And the other cities?"

"They've raised the terrorism threat level to orange and are taking every conceivable precaution, but with the Scarecrow showing off his handiwork in Central Park, we have to figure we're sitting at ground zero here."

"You know I can help, right?"

"That's not my call, Special Agent Mason. Believe it or not, I actually did go to bat for you and your partner, but I agree with Deputy Secretary Marchment's assessment that our local assets are better trained and equipped to handle things here."

"Where's Marchment now?"

"In the field, conducting a sensitive interview. Like I said, there's always politics. Even at a time like this. As I'm sure you probably know that better than most."

"Unfortunately, I do," he said, and glanced at the list of interview candidates beside Mikkelson's honeycombed face. He had to concentrate on maintaining a neutral expression to keep from betraying his surprise at the sight of the last name on the list.

Slate Langbroek, chairman of the executive board of directors for Royal Nautilus Petroleum.

At this very moment, the deputy secretary of the Department of Homeland Security, who was seemingly helping the Scarecrow enact his professional agenda while trying to keep from finding himself mounted to a cross in the middle of Central Park, was preparing to interview the man responsible for the Novichok threat, quite possibly even leading the Scarecrow to him for the coup de grâce, which would signify the end of his personal vendetta and the enactment of his professional obligations.

Like Anomaly had intimated, however, there was an inherent flaw in that logic. If Marchment were an active participant in the plot to release the Novichok, why was he anywhere near New York City? And why was Langbroek here at all? Why in the world would he hire someone like the Scarecrow, who wanted to kill everyone responsible for his childhood trauma, when it was ultimately Langbroek's company that had caused it?

An agent pushed between them to get Algren's attention.

"I have the governor on his direct line again," she said. "What am I supposed to tell him?"

"The same thing you told the mayor. He's just going to have to cancel—"

"He said to tell you that in New York we don't knuckle under for anyone. He's not canceling anything. He'll bring the entire NYPD and the National Guard with him if he has to."

Algren groaned.

"I can see myself out," Mason said, and headed for the door.

He passed the agents coordinating directly with their sister task forces in Baltimore, D.C., and Philly and realized that, for better or worse, he'd put all of his eggs in one basket. With countless tourists in town and millions of celebrators preparing to flood the streets, the odds were definitely in his favor, but if he was wrong . . .

Mason closed the door to the operations center behind him and made his way to the elevator. He waited until he was outside the building before calling Gunnar.

"Did you get it?" he asked.

"Oh yeah," Gunnar said. "She must have called him about ten seconds after you left her office."

Mason smiled and hung up the phone. He'd known Algren wouldn't be able to resist taking credit for deciphering the scarecrow design in the cornfield. Not only had she just given them Marchment's phone number, which Gunnar could use to ascertain his GPS coordinates; she'd delivered a message to the deputy secretary of the Department of Homeland Security that they knew what had happened at Edgewood. So even if they couldn't use Marchment to lead them to the Scarecrow, they'd be able to count on Marchment to eventually lead the Scarecrow to them.

Ramses pulled to the curb just as Mason hit the sidewalk. He opened the door and climbed into the backseat beside Gunnar.

"What's with the Rangers getup?" Ramses asked.

"It was either this or the Giants."

"Not feeling the G-men right about now, are you?"

"You could say that."

Ramses smirked and hit the gas.

66

The bogeyman had come, as the Scarecrow had known he would. Obedient to the end. Willing to do whatever he was told, no questions asked. All it had taken was a strategically timed text message with the hotel's name, room number, and instructions to wait inside should the presumed sender not have arrived yet, and he'd come running. And, as expected, he'd come alone so that none of his underlings would suspect how completely he was owned by the man under whose name the room was registered.

Marchment knocked one final time before testing the knob and finding it unlocked. The Scarecrow sensed the bogeyman's indecision and prepared to improvise, but it relaxed when it heard the soft squeal of hinges and footsteps entering the suite. Even after all these years, it recognized those sounds and experienced the same ingrained physiological response. In that moment, it was once more a helpless child, its heart hammering in its chest, its pulse rushing in its ears. Its breathing accelerated, producing a rasping sound from the respirator of its gas mask and threatening to loosen the stoma cover on its neck. It battled the fear, forcing it down into the hollow core of its physical vessel, reminding itself that the child was dead. The Scarecrow had killed it and usurped its form, mercifully saving it from a lifetime of misery that could be traced back to the man on the other side of the wall.

This was the lone point of weakness in its plan. All Marchment had to do was turn around and leave and it would never be able to isolate him again. It had to trust that the bogeyman's fear and confusion would override his better judgment, that the message it had sent him using the bodies of the other surviving men from Edgewood would convince him to take just this one risk so he could find out why this was happening to someone like him, someone who was supposed to be untouchable. More important, he had to find out if the Novichok was really here and how quickly he needed to get out of the city.

Both Marchment and his master had come to this dreary metropolis for one reason and one reason alone: They'd known that this was one of the few places in the world where the Novichok wasn't. Or at least that was what they'd thought. Quintus didn't even suspect that his plan had been co-opted by another, who'd given the Scarecrow something far more valuable than money; he'd given it a collection of classified black-and-white films that showed what had happened to it as a child, not to mention the men responsible for its never-ending misery, men who, by the time the clock struck midnight, would all be dead. And of equal consequence to its new master, Tertius Decimus, the Langbroek name would be destroyed and he would ascend within the Thirteen on the deaths of nine million people, a fraction of the carnage Quintus had envisioned, but more than enough to allow the man known as Thirteenth to implement the machinations of the insurrection he'd started with his subversion of the release of Secundus's flu virus.

It was a double cross on an apocalyptic scale. Surely Langbroek was beginning to understand that he'd never had any control over the events he'd set in motion, that he'd been manipulated from the start by an adversary of his own creation. Neither he nor Marchment had so much as suspected who the Scarecrow truly was, at least not until they learned the identities of the victims it had left for them in the cornfield. Maybe they'd even dismissed the killings as coincidental clear up until they found Raymond in Central Park, and now, with Mikkelson's body undoubtedly being swarmed by investigators, there was no mistaking what was about to happen to them. Within a matter of hours, they would experience the same suffering they'd inflicted upon it.

And the coup of Tertius Decimus would begin in earnest.

The front door of the suite closed with a nearly inaudible click. The Scarecrow held its breath and listened. Several seconds passed before it heard footsteps in the interior hallway. It smiled beneath its mask, knowing with complete certainty that it had Marchment now.

In its mind, it envisioned not the aged man with the silver hair and expensive suit, but the younger version with the buzz cut and olive-colored uniform, walking down the sterile white corridor with its father. It imagined the bogeyman raising the mask he'd used to expose it to the chemicals, but rather than pinning it over the mouth and nose of a child, he affixed it to his own face. And instead of inhaling sarin, he was breathing diethyl ether halogenated with fluorine, oxygen, and nitrous oxide, a homemade anesthetic of its own design, which was currently diffusing into the main room from a vaporizer unit hidden behind a chair, an invisible gas that would render him unconscious in under three minutes.

The Scarecrow silently opened the closet door, stepped out into the bedroom, and crept down the hallway into the main room, where the bogeyman stood silhouetted against a circular window with red velvet curtains, his hands clasped behind his back. It was an irresistible view that people paid tens of thousands of dollars a night to see, one within mere feet of the source of the faintly sweet-smelling gas.

Marchment flickered before its eyes, as though projected from an eight-millimeter reel, only every other frame showed a different version of the bogeyman. Old man and then young. Suit and then uniform. Silver hair and then buzz cut. And yet the Scarecrow felt no corresponding change within itself. The child was dead and all that remained was a Frankenstein's monster cobbled together not from mismatched parts but from biomechanical components; rotted not by death but by disease; animated not by electricity but by hatred.

The bogeyman swayed ever so slightly and had to brace himself against the wall. He stiffened at the realization that something was terribly wrong and glanced to his left. His eyes met those of the Scarecrow in the reflection from the window and the bogeyman saw it—truly saw it—for the first time.

Marchment turned around, but by then it was already too late. His legs went out from underneath him and he collapsed to his knees. He grabbed onto the Scarecrow and tried to pull himself back to his feet.

"No . . ." he said. His voice was watery from the anesthesia, his eyes unfocused, his grip growing weaker by the second.

The sensation of his hands upon it ignited a fiery rage inside the Scarecrow. It grabbed the lamp from the end table and swung it with all of its might. The base struck Marchment squarely in the forehead, knocking him backward and spattering the window with a crimson arc. He folded in reverse, his body contorting awkwardly until his legs twisted out from underneath him and he collapsed onto his back. Blood trickled from his temple and dripped to the black-and-white patterned carpet.

The Scarecrow could have stayed there all day watching the bogeyman bleed, but it had so much more in store for him.

And so much more blood to shed.

67

"I've got a fix on Marchment's GPS," Gunnar said. "He's at the St. Regis Hotel."

Ramses wove through the congestion, braking and accelerating in sudden bursts, jerking the wheel to merge the SUV into gaps that hardly appeared large enough.

"I need an address," Ramses said.

"Two East Fifty-fifth Street." Gunnar's laptop bounced on his thighs, forcing him to hold it in place with one hand and type with the other. He minimized one window and maximized another. "Just off Fifth Ave."

"What the hell is he doing there?" Layne asked.

"Meeting with Slate Langbroek," Mason said.

Gunner turned to face him and did an almost comical double take.

"Langbroek's in town? Why in God's name would he be here when the entire city's about to be enveloped in a cloud of Novichok?"

"My thoughts exactly," Mason said. His phone vibrated and he answered it without checking the caller ID. "Mason."

"James?"

His father's voice caught him by surprise.

"Now's not a good time, Dad."

"Are you still in the District?"

"Not anymore."

Ramses locked up the brakes and the tires screamed.

"What was that?"

"Like I said, not the best time."

"Please tell me you aren't back in New York."

"I'm going to have to call you back."

"You need to get out of there, son. You're in over your head. I was just informed that we have verified intel of a possible terrorist threat in Manhattan."

"You're certain it's in New York City and not Philadelphia or D.C.?"

"Just get out of the city. Let counterterrorism handle it. From what I understand, you're not even supposed to be there."

"Turn left here," Gunnar said. "Two more blocks and it'll be on your left."

"Look, Dad. I—"

"Please, James," the senator said. Mason detected a note of pleading in his father's voice that he'd never heard there before. "For once in your life, do as I ask."

He felt a pang of guilt, but there was nothing he could do about it. Someone needed to stop the Scarecrow and he was the only one who could do it.

"I'll take it under consideration."

"You have to be the most exasperating—"

Mason terminated the call and stuffed the phone back into his jacket pocket.

"Like I said, Langbroek's movements are cloaked, so I can't tell you when he arrived," Gunnar said, "but there's definitely someone reg-istered in the Imperial Suite at the St. Regis under his name."

"Is Marchment with him?"

"All I can say is that his GPS beacon's static at that location."

"Drop me off at the front door," Mason said. "You guys make sure no one slips out the back."

"What are we supposed to do if they try?" Layne asked. "Arrest them?"

Mason didn't reply. Arresting Langbroek was the furthest thing from his mind. All he cared about was preventing the release of the Novichok, by any means necessary.

An eighteen-story Beaux Arts monolith rose above them, an opulent stone monument to the luxury and excess of early twentieth-century in-dustrialism. He craned his neck in an effort to see the top. Somewhere on the highest floor was a man he believed to be a member of the Thirteen.

Mason threw open the door and jumped out before Ramses had even stopped. He rounded the trunk and sprinted across the street toward the black-and-white awning above the entrance to the hotel. A porter in a green vest made a move to greet him, but Mason blew past him with a flash of his badge. He ran straight across the marble-tiled lobby to the elevator corridor and paced back and forth in front of four golden doors until one finally opened.

A man in a black jacket with platinum name tag strode toward him, wearing a forced smile and carrying a short-range transceiver.

Mason pressed the button for the top floor again and again until the golden panels whispered shut in the concierge's face. The floor shud-dered and he watched the numbers climb as he ascended.

His heart hammered against his rib cage. He clenched and un-clenched his fists. Felt the reassuring weight of his Glock in its holster.

The man registered in the Imperial Suite was one of the richest and most powerful men in the world. He was also directly responsible for the murder of Mason's wife and the subsequent annihilation of her family tree. He'd used the Thorntons to help modify a flu virus deadly enough to decimate the global population and thrown them away when he was done with them. He'd conspired with the Hoyl, and now the Scarecrow, to murder millions of people, and for what? Mason's former partner could romanticize it all he wanted, claim the Thirteen were saving the world from drowning in its own numbers, but when it came right down to it, Kane had been wrong. This was all about the money. Langbroek stood to make billions from a medication designed to counteract the symptoms of the very gas he intended to release.

The elevator dinged to announce Mason's arrival. The doors opened on a tan-carpeted hallway, at the end of which were the twin paneled doors of the Imperial Suite. On the other side was a monster the likes of which the world had never known. Or at least one of thirteen.

Mason knocked.

His stealth phone vibrated against his hip, but he silenced it.

Knocked again.

His pulse thumped so hard in his temples that the edges of his vision throbbed. He listened for voices on the other side. For the sound of approaching footsteps.

Again, his phone vibrated. He sent the call to voice mail with a swipe of his thumb.

All he had to do was reach underneath his jacket, draw his weapon, and with one bullet he could end the greatest threat to humanity that no one would ever know about.

He raised his fist and pounded on the door hard enough to make it rattle in its frame.

Only silence from the other side.

His phone vibrated again and he realized he'd been played. A man accustomed to hiding his movements wouldn't stay under his own name. The Scarecrow had already been waiting when Marchment arrived. He unholstered his phone and answered it.

"Goddamn it, Mason!" Layne said before he could utter a single syllable. "You need to get down to the parking garage. Right now!"

The ground seemed to fall out from beneath him.

He hooked his Bluetooth to his ear and transferred the call. Stepped back, braced himself, and landed a solid kick right between the handles. The doors parted with a loud crack and slammed into the walls to either side of the foyer. He drew his weapon and entered in a shooter's stance.

"There's a laundry cart down here," Layne said. "The cloth kind. With a lot of blood soaked into it. And it's still damp."

A table with fresh flowers was set in the entryway. The ornamental lighting reflected from black marble tile so glossy that it looked like an oil spill, save for the twin tire tracks running down the middle. To his left: a corridor terminating against a wall displaying original artwork, to either side of which was a doorway to a room outside his range of sight. Straight ahead was the master bedroom. To his right: the living room, where an end table rested on its side beside the lamp that had once stood upon it.

"It looks like someone wheeled the cart out of the service elevator and to a space reserved for delivery vehicles," Layne said.

There was a black-and-white-patterned area rug on the hardwood floor. A mahogany coffee table surrounded by formal furniture covered with decorative pillows. Red velvet drapes hung beside circular recessed windows that reminded him of rifle sights. The one straight ahead overlooked Fifty-fifth Street and seemingly the entire city to the north, while the one to his right revealed a view of the sky above Park Avenue, marred by a high-velocity blood spatter on the glass. An iPhone rested on the cushion of the window seat, its screen a crimson smear.

Marchment had been standing right where Mason was now when someone approached him from behind and waited for him to turn around before bludgeoning him upside the head.

"It's not a public garage, is it?" he asked.

"Valet parking only."

"So it's access-controlled. The Scarecrow had to have a code or key card to get in." He hurriedly checked the master bedroom. There were no suitcases or toiletries. He smelled something sweet, a scent that didn't mesh with his surroundings. "This was his plan all along."

"What?"

"We're being set up." Sirens erupted in the distance. "Get out of there, Layne. Langbroek was never here. The Scarecrow lured Marchment up to the suite and took him. And we walked right into the trap."

He remembered the expression on the face of the concierge in the lobby. He'd recognized that something was wrong and undoubtedly called security straight away. They'd probably been watching their cameras when he kicked in the front door of their twenty-grand-a-night Imperial Suite and were already on their way up.

Mason holstered his pistol and ran for the door. Bolted across the hall and into the open stairwell at the same time the elevator dinged at the far end of the corridor. The white marble stairs were ornamental, designed for aesthetics over functionality. They were surprisingly steep and narrow, the railings polished wood with elaborate gold banisters. He jumped to the landing. Grabbed the rail. Swung around the tight curve, past a curtained window. Hit the next set of stairs, going way too fast, and nearly went sprawling into the seventeenth-floor hallway. Regained his balance and propelled himself toward the next flight. Skipped down them as fast as could.

"We're out of time," he whispered. "Now that the Scarecrow has Marchment, he's free to release the Novichok."

He paused on the sixteenth floor. Pressed his back to the wall. Hoped the men on the top floor hadn't heard the echo of his footsteps from the marble stairs. Waited for them to pass the mouth of the stairwell on their way to the Imperial Suite, but they saw through his deception. A man with a broad chest and dark hair leaned over the railing.

"He's down there!"

Mason hurled himself to the next landing. Rebounded from the wall beside the window. Launched himself down the next flight.

A drumroll of footsteps overhead, coming down fast. Three men at least. One of them called for backup.

The wail of sirens grew closer. It wouldn't be long before the police had the building surrounded.

"You have to go without me," Mason whispered. "I'll call you if I make it out of here."

Around one bend, down the stairs, around another. And another and another.

The sixth-floor landing blew past beside him. It sounded like he was distancing himself from his pursuers, but he couldn't spare a glance up and risk giving up ground in the process.

A riot of voices flooded the stairwell from below.

He knew exactly what that meant.

A second security unit mounted the stairs from the main floor. They were going to attempt a pincer maneuver to catch him in the middle. Such a bold move undoubtedly meant they'd already disabled the elevators, so he'd find himself trapped if he attempted to elude the men on one of the few remaining floors between them. Even if there was a second stairwell on the far side, security was likely already rushing straight up it, with someone remotely coordinating their movements from a control center with a bank of monitors.

By the time he reached the third floor, he could see the hands of the men gripping the rails as they ascended. They couldn't have been more than twenty vertical feet down.

He maintained his pace. If a confrontation was inevitable, then he'd rather force the issue with the men coming up. With his momentum, he could easily take down two of them. Any more than that and he ran the risk of the team above him catching up. Maybe he could take them all, but not before the police had every exit covered.

At the same time he hit the second floor, the shadows of the men coming up the stairs fell upon the landing below him. A pair of men rounded the bend a heartbeat later. Their eyes widened at the sight of him and they reached for their weapons.

The footsteps from above grew ever closer. Someone shouted that they had him surrounded.

Two more men appeared on the landing below him. One of them raised his hands in a placating gesture.

Mason climbed up onto the railing. He was twenty feet up, twenty-five at the most. If he bent his knees on impact and rolled to dispel his momentum, he might not break his legs.

"Let's not make this any harder than it has to be."

"Too late for that," Mason said.

He stepped out over the nothingness and felt his stomach rise into his chest.

One of the security guards instinctively reached for him as he plummeted past.

Mason seized the opportunity and caught him by the wrist. Pulled him hard against the rail, nearly right over the edge. Used the momentum to swing to the first-floor landing. Barely cleared the railing. Let go and was airborne for a split second before he hit the ground on his side. Slid into the hallway. Popped up and ran down the remaining stairs. Past the lobby and through the door to the street. Darted left and dove behind a van parked against the curb as a police cruiser screamed past. Rolled over the curb and beneath the undercarriage. Scurried out the other side on the asphalt. Lunged to his feet and sprinted toward the opposite sidewalk, using the van to screen him from the exit as his pursuers burst from the door.

He'd barely rounded the corner when he heard shouting behind him. Row houses and leafless deciduous trees blew past to either side. Entire city blocks passed in a blur. The voices and sirens faded into the distance. He hurdled the wrought-iron fence enclosing the stoop of a five-story unit and landed in the recessed stairwell of the garden-level apartment.

Mason removed his stealth phone from its holster and called Gunnar, who answered on the first ring. He sighed in relief and slumped to his rear end on a crust of ice and dead leaves.

"I'm going to need a ride."

68

"We have to get off the street," Layne said. "The entire city is one great big camera."

"And what do you propose we do?" Ramses asked. "Take the subway?"

"They'll need time to check the security footage far enough back to find me getting out of this car," Mason said. "They'll deal with the blood in the suite first. The hotel's primary concern will be a potential murder generating negative publicity, and the NYPD's going to find itself embroiled in a turf war with the DHS once the name under which the room was registered crosses the wire and Algren can't get ahold of Marchment."

"They're going to assume you were responsible for whatever happened in that room," Ramses said. "Once they ID you, every cop in the city will be looking for this vehicle. If they find us, there'll be no one left to stop the Scarecrow."

He jerked the wheel to avoid hitting a cab that crossed into his lane without signaling.

"Would it be too much to ask you not to switch lanes for ten seconds?" Gunnar said. He was practically folded in half over his laptop in a futile attempt to hold it still while he typed. Ramses just chuckled and switched lanes again. "Real mature."

"The Scarecrow killed Mikkelson a lot faster than his previous victims," Mason said. "We don't have much time to find where he took Marchment before he finishes his personal vendetta and moves on to fulfilling his professional obligations."

"If we're right and he intends to release the Novichok on the subway, we don't have a prayer of finding it in time," Layne said. "There are more than six thousand individual cars servicing nearly five hundred stations on twenty-seven lines. Even if we knew exactly which cars he rigged, they're in constant motion all around the city."

"Then our only option is to find the Scarecrow."

"This is him right here," Gunnar said. He turned his laptop so Mason could see the screen. "I lifted this from the security system at the St. Regis."

The image had been acquired by a camera mounted near the ceiling and was time-stamped approximately five minutes before they'd arrived. It showed the back of a white van directly underneath it and a row of expensive vehicles parked on the other side of the narrow lane. The Scarecrow had been captured in the process of loading the body into the back of the van from the cart, toppling it in the process. He stood in profile to the camera, the brim of a white baseball cap concealing the upper half of his face. His oversized white uniform hung from his diminutive frame, as he struggled to manhandle the larger man into the vehicle.

"There has to be a better picture," Mason said.

"You're lucky to have this one," Gunnar said.

"Can you run his face?"

"Not a chance. I need a minimum of thirteen points of comparison."

"Damn it."

A beacon flashed in the upper right corner of the monitor. Gunnar furrowed his brow and buried his face in the screen again. He didn't speak for several minutes while he opened and closed windows with blinding speed.

"Here's something interesting," he finally said. "Nakamura slash Matsuda's obituary said he was survived by two children, but I can't find any record of them."

"Other than two empty seats on an airplane," Mason said.

"Precisely."

"He took two kids back with him from Edgewood?" Layne asked.

"I can't prove it, but I told you when Matsuda returned to Japan he founded a company called Kenkō Pharmaceuticals, right? He remained CEO until his passing, at which time the company was acquired by Kokoro Pharmaceuticals and absorbed into its corporate brand, effectively dissolving Kenkō and making his legal heirs, Kaemon and Kameko Matsuda, extraordinarily rich, after which they promptly disappeared. Assuming they'd ever been there at all. I can't find any record of their births or deaths, let alone where they are now."

"Twins?"

"Without access to anything resembling actual documentation, we can only speculate. Based on the names, though, I'd say we're looking at a boy and a girl."

"Kaemon Matsuda," Mason said, as though tasting the words. In his mind, the Scarecrow had become a larger-than-life, mythological construct. It was almost a letdown to learn that he was only human, and yet somehow that made his atrocities even worse.

"If the good doctor was experimenting on them at Edgewood in the seventies, why would they stay with him all the way into the nineties?" Layne asked.

"Because—for better or worse—he was their father," Mason said.

"Some of Unit 731's more reprehensible crimes included the rape and forced impregnation of female prisoners to test the vertical transmission of diseases," Gunnar said. "There's no record of how many children were conceived in such a manner or how many survived whatever experimentation was conducted on them after birth. It's possible he picked right back up where he'd left off at Edgewood."

"The military would never sanction rape," Layne said.

"True, but how hard would it be to secure the cooperation of a female volunteer being treated with experimental psychoactive drugs?"

"Even if they weren't biologically his," Mason said, "he could have raised them not only to think they were but to believe that he'd saved them from whatever cruelties they'd been subjected to. For all we know, they viewed him as the heroic father figure who rescued them from the monsters at Edgewood."

"Surely they would have learned about their father being a war criminal," Layne said. "That's not the kind of secret a guy can hide forever."

"The government of Japan has yet to even formally acknowledge the atrocities committed by Unit 731," Gunnar said. "Publicly outing the participants wouldn't serve the official narrative."

"Accusations, then. It's not like they lived in a vacuum."

"What if they weren't Matsudas?" Mason asked.

"They were at least long enough to inherit twenty million dollars each," Gunnar said.

"Maybe after his death, but what if up until that point they considered themselves Nakamuras? It makes sense to have given them the same last name as the man taking them out of the country. They would have needed some form of identification, right?"

"And the Department of Defense only records the names of its personnel. The identification of all nongovernment passengers are purged after a year. They'd be listed as—here we go—'minor children.'"

"Can you find anything on Kaemon and Kameko Nakamura?"

Even as he said it, he felt everything starting to come together, as though he were both a participant in and a witness to an event of historical magnitude, a moment of destiny.

"What do you know?" Gunnar said. "Dr. Kaemon Nakamura. Graduated from the University of Tokyo with a degree in biochemistry. Doctorate in biomedical engineering from Kyoto University. Worked at Tokyo Medical University Hospital. Sat on the board of Kokoro Pharmaceuticals through the acquisition of Kenkō. And that's where his trail ends."

"It can't be," Mason said. "What about his sister?"

"Dr. Kameko Nakamura earned her bachelor's in organic chemistry, followed by a medical degree. Both from the same schools her brother attended. Both the same years."

"What are they, Siamese twins?" Ramses said. "'Cause I've got to tell you, that would make for some seriously creepy shit."

"Obviously joined at the hip in some capacity, although all I can find about either of them are a handful of publication credits and mentions in professional societies."

"Which professional societies?" Mason asked.

"The Japan Medical and Hospital Associations. World Medical Association. The International Supplement and Pharmaceutical Standardization Organization—"

"The last two," Mason said. "Remember the picture of Mosche and Chenhav at the SLIP conference in Copenhagen? Those were the societies they were there to represent."

"Jesus. You're right."

Gunnar hammered the keys for several seconds, then flinched as though he'd been struck. Closed his eyes. His lips moved as though in silent debate with himself.

Mason leaned closer and tilted the laptop on his old friend's thighs to better see the image on the screen. It was from August 1994. The same Twentieth Assembly of the Society for Lasting International Peace where the Israeli scientists had been photographed with Andreas Mikkelson. None of them was in this picture, though. It was a group photo that showed a dozen men and women dressed in fancy suits and gowns, smiling for the camera. The caption read "Representatives of the international medical community," but the people were identified only by organization, not by name. The man and woman of Asian origin at the far left of the image represented the Japan Medical Association.

If they weren't twins, they could have easily passed as such. Kaemon was maybe an inch or two taller than Kameko, but both were of similar build. Her hair was longer and cut in a way meant to deemphasize her face, presumably in an attempt to downplay the vertical scars running down her cheeks from underneath her sunglasses.

Kaemon wore his bangs long, a tuxedo, and a blue tie that matched his sister's full-length gown. He'd been captured in that split second after allowing his smile to fade, when his true expression of discomfort was plainly evident. Not to mention the grafts covering his forehead and nose, which had a vaguely spiderweb appearance. His sister held the crook of his arm in an almost intimate manner. It took Mason a moment to realize it was because she was blind.

He used his thumb to cover the upper half of Kaemon's face. He couldn't be completely certain, but it looked an awful lot like the image capture of the Scarecrow standing on the street corner with the newspaper held up to his chin.

Gunnar swiveled his computer to face him and again started typing.

"Do you think—?" Mason started to ask, but Gunnar raised a finger to silence him.

"What did you find?" Layne asked.

"A picture of the Nakamuras at the same function where the dead men from behind the wall at the slaughterhouse were photographed with Andreas Mikkelson."

"You're sure it's them?"

"They aren't identified by name, but what are the odds?"

"One hundred percent," Gunnar said. "There's no record of either of them after they sold their father's company, but I can tell you that the majority of their inheritance was used as startup capital for a Swiss company called NexGen Biotech, which is currently one of the leading designers of implantable medical devices and prosthetics in the world. Listed among its subsidiaries are asset management groups for both its corporate facilities and global investment properties. NexGen Asset Management handles the former, while the latter is delegated to a real estate holding company called Integrity Group International, which just happens to own the row house on Fifty-third Street where we found the tunnel to the Old Croton Aqueduct."

"You said at the time that Integrity owned several other properties around town," Mason said.

"It does, although it's not what it owns that stands out, but, rather, what's underneath it."

69

The New York Office of Integrity Group International was little more than a pair of industrial doors behind the InterContinental Barclay New York and across the street from the side of the Waldorf-Astoria. They might have missed it entirely were it not for the discreet blue awning with the address in tiny white numbers and the security keypad beside the door. And the white van parked up on the sidewalk in front of it. Ramses drove past it once before finding an underground parking garage a few blocks away, where they left Gunnar with the engine running and his laptop propped on the steering wheel.

The late-afternoon shadows of the skyscrapers fell heavily upon Forty-ninth Street, especially in the block immediately east of Park Avenue, where there were no storefront windows or neon signs. The snow had turned to sleet that assailed them from behind on the gusting wind. There was no one else on the street, despite the bustle a couple hundred feet away.

"You ready to work your magic?" Mason asked.

"I'm already in the security system," Gunnar said through his earpiece. "Let me know when to open the door. I have satellite imagery of just about the entire area, but you're in something of a blind spot."

"There's a single security camera beside the awning. See what you can do about disrupting the feed just long enough for us to get inside."

"Now?"

"Give us about ten more seconds."

He was reaching for the handle when he heard the thud of the lock disengaging and a droning buzz behind the heavy steel door. He drew it open and held it for Ramses and Layne before ducking out of the storm and closing it behind him. They found themselves in a concrete corridor with electrical boxes on one side and a sliding pass-through window with the Integrity Group International logo on the other. He could see the entirety of the small office, which looked like every other he'd ever been in. The door was closed and displayed a placard labeled BY AP-POINTMENT ONLY.

"There's nothing here," he whispered.

"You'll find a staircase at the end of the hall," Gunnar said. "Just to the left of the rear entrance to the kitchen of the restaurant next to the Barclay."

The muffled clatter of plates and silverware and the scents of pasta sauce and kitchen trash radiated through the steel door. Plastic racks used for washing glassware were stacked on a dolly beside it, nearly concealing the mouth of the narrow corridor to the left.

Mason drew his weapon, crouched against the wall, and took a quick peek around the corner.

"I'm looking at it now."

He clicked on his flashlight and aligned it with his pistol. Gestured for the others to wait behind him. Descended slowly. One foot and then the other. Sweeping his light across the floor and the ceiling in search of trip wires and sensors.

"The hotel was built nearly a century ago on top of the under-ground tracks of what was once the New York Central Railroad," Gun-nar said. "It had its own station, which, like the tracks, is no longer in service."

Sporadic droplets of blood on the concrete stairs led him down into the darkness. There was no bulb in the overhead fixture. Pipes and conduits emerged from the ceiling and guided him toward an open ma-chine room, inside of which he could hear the thrum of flowing water. There was a second door to his right. Blood smeared on the knob. Solid steel with a digital keypad mounted beside it. Closed-circuit cameras facing it from every available angle.

"There's a second security door," Mason whispered.

"I'm on it."

A metallic thud echoed from inside.

"Can you tell if there are any counterincursion measures inside?"

"You mean like a security system or laser sensors?"

"If he was going to booby-trap one place, I'd have to believe it would be this one."

"I don't see anything, but it would have to be hardwired to the grid for me to be able to detect it."

Mason glanced up the stairs at Ramses and Layne, then back at the door. Quickly scanned the seams for trip wires. Turned the knob. Slowly. Nudged it open.

The smell that billowed from inside made his stomach clench. It was one he associated not with the dead, but with the dying. Sickness and ammonia. Chemicals consuming flesh. He forced himself to breathe through his mouth and shouldered the door inward, just wide enough to squeeze into the foyer.

A light flickered from somewhere ahead, limning the walls of an industrial corridor. Tongue-depressor scarecrows hung from the ceiling, all of them wrapped in yarn the deep red color of arterial blood. They turned ever so slightly with the air currents of his passage, their shadows creating the sensation of movement all around him. The floor was bare concrete, cracked and repeatedly patched, the walls little more than wooden frames covered with rice paper. They were just opaque enough to conceal the contents of what appeared to be four distinct rooms in a linear sequence, down the narrow hallway branching from the main living space, in the center of which was the source of the vile aroma.

A hospital bed surrounded by monitors, drip infusers, and warming units stocked with bags of saline and chemotherapy drugs dominated the space. The man underneath the covers was barely substantial enough to form a human-shaped bulge. His chest rose and fell slowly, in time with the clicking sound of the mechanical ventilator. His face was gaunt, his cheekbones prominent, and his closed eyes recessed. Tubes slithered from his mouth and nose, IVs from his arm. A bag of urine hung from the side of the bed, its contents a dark shade of yellow bordering on orange.

Mason turned at the sound of footsteps. Layne's light flashed across him and settled on the bed.

"What the hell is this?" Ramses said.

Mason glanced back at the body. Furrowed his brow. This was definitely the same man from the picture taken at the SLIP conference. He wore a wig that had been styled so that the bangs covered his scarred forehead and deformed nose, to which a delicate layer of makeup had been applied. He'd been dressed in a charcoal suit with a silk ascot and matching handkerchief, as though a mortician were in the midst of preparing him to be loaded into his coffin.

"Kaemon Nakamura," he said.

"Jesus," Layne whispered. "That means—"

"Kameko Nakamura is the Scarecrow."

They'd been wrong about everything from the start.

"Look at the monitor," Ramses said.

Squiggly colored lines crossed a screen displaying Kaemon's blood pressure, heart rate, pulse oxygenation, and EKG rhythm. The sine waves barely strayed from the horizontal, but that wasn't what had caught Ramses' eye so much as the oxygen tanks strapped to the wheeled post. Someone had removed the nozzles, bound them together with duct tape, and hardwired them to the monitor.

Mason recognized its function immediately.

It was an improvised explosive device, the monitor serving as the detonator.

Once the input flatlined, rather than sounding an alarm, the bomb would go off, cremating Kaemon and incinerating any evidence that he'd ever been here. And judging by the readings, it wouldn't be long before that happened. Arming it meant that wherever Kameko was now, she wasn't coming back.

The endgame had been set in motion.

70

There was no time to disarm the IED and they couldn't take the risk of inadvertently setting it off. Finding the Scarecrow before she released the Novichok was all that mattered now. They were just going to have to hope Kaemon survived a little while longer.

Mason raised his pistol and followed the lone corridor deeper into the darkness. He glanced into the first room, his light sweeping across an industrial washbasin under an exposed spigot, to which a shower-head on a rubber hose had been mounted. The smell emanating from the rusted drain suggested it also served a secondary purpose.

"How long do you think they've been living down here?" Layne asked.

Mason could only shake his head. He was having a hard time rationalizing the implications of what they'd found. Kameko had brought her brother down here and taken care of him for what had to have been years, knowing the whole time that he would never leave this place. She'd been sitting in the darkness, listening to her brother slowly dying, and doing nothing but plotting her vengeance against the men who had hurt them as children.

There was a glaring hole in the center of his theory, however. Kameko couldn't possibly be the Scarecrow. . . .

She was blind.

"Did you ever get the list of participants in the lawsuit against Edgewood?" Mason asked.

"Yeah," Gunnar said, "but I haven't even had time to look at the file."

"Do me a favor and open it now, okay?"

"What am I looking for?"

"Trust me," Mason said. "You'll know it when you see it."

Layne's light passed behind the adjacent paper wall, inside of which was a low wooden platform with a thin futon mattress. The walls were decorated with bamboo scrolls featuring traditional Japanese artwork ranging from koi and pagodas to samurais and mountain ranges. And a figure wearing a conical straw hat and hanging from a cross, the artistic representation of the yarn dolls hanging all around them.

Kuebiko.

The Scarecrow.

"Neither of them is listed," Gunnar said, "but the attorney's retainer was paid from a NexGen discretionary account."

"Why, exactly, are they suing?"

Mason entered the next room in the series. On his right was a wooden bench with a portable chemical fume hood, beneath which were a distilling flask, a stoppered vial, and a veritable apothecary of amber containers with handwritten labels: hexane, methanol, ammonia, sulfuric acid, and morning glory seeds. On his left was a stainless-steel table with an inset drain. It was covered with bloody gauze and sponges and a mess of surgical implements. If Marchment wasn't already dead, he was definitely well on his way.

"More than half of the complainants in the class-action suit reported some form of cancer," Gunnar said. "Most of them blood- or bone-related. Nearly all suffer from neurological disorders of varying severity, from tics to paralysis. Depression. Multiple sclerosis. The list goes on and on."

"There are chemo drugs down here," Mason said, "but it looks like Kaemon's been beyond their reach for a while."

"You think Kameko's sick, too?"

"That would explain the Scarecrow's lack of an exit strategy."

"And her desire to kill every last one of the men who did this to them."

The rice-paper wall of the next room glowed faintly purple from the black-light bulb illuminating a circular aquarium filled with tiny jellyfish, their tendrils dangling nearly to the rocks on the bottom. There were tanks with snakes, spiders, and flying insects crawling all over the inside of the glass.

"But then why would she be working for Langbroek when his family's company played a significant role in their suffering?" Mason asked.

"It's possible she doesn't know about Nautilus's involvement," Gunnar said.

"Or, more likely, Langbroek doesn't know about his family's." Mason felt a sudden tug of recognition from the back of his mind, a mental tip-of-the-tongue sensation, but the thought proved elusive. "He didn't take over the company until decades after everything that happened at Edgewood."

"Over here," Ramses said.

His old friend's voice came from the lone remaining room, at the far end of what had once been a railroad platform. The air grew noticeably colder with every step. The source of the flickering light he'd seen upon entering the apartment was back there, but neither the Scarecrow nor Marchment was. Five large flat-screen TVs had been mounted to the rear wall in three columns—two to either side and one in the middle—above a table of electrical components. The top row displayed footage from a local network of security cameras and every few seconds switched from one view to the next. The monitor on the left covered the outside of the building, the middle alternated views of the inside of the apartment, and the right showed various angles of what appeared to be a construction zone inside a large tunnel in the green-and-gray scale of night vision.

"In 1995, just prior to their disappearance, Kaemon and Kameko Nakamura each transferred five million dollars into the account of a Dr. Tatsuo Yamaguchi," Gunnar said.

"You think he's been treating them all this time?"

"I can't confirm as much, but it makes sense."

The other monitors featured imagery either hacked from remote security cameras or routed from live Internet feeds: Grand Central Station with its globe clock, vaulted windows, and constant stream of commuters and tourists, and Times Square, crammed full of revelers awash in flashing lights, preparing to count down the New Year. There wasn't another night during the year when so many people would be out of their homes and on the streets, completely unprepared for a chemical attack.

"Dr. Yamaguchi isn't an oncologist," Gunnar said. "He's a neurologist specializing in neuromuscular and neuro-opthalmologic disorders. That's not to say he wouldn't be able to prescribe the treatment for certain cancers, only that he's not qualified to cover the broader spectrum. What's most interesting about him, though, is that he was actually the specialist called in to treat the victims of the sarin attack on the Tokyo subway the same year the Nakamuras slash Matsudas dropped off the planet."

"He'd definitely be my first choice if I'd been exposed as a child and was exhibiting adverse effects in my early adulthood," Mason said. "After all, how much practical experience can any modern doctor have with sarin exposure?"

A flash of light from the corner of his eye.

He looked up at the top right monitor in time to see the light grow brighter and brighter, until it overwhelmed the night-vision apparatus. The feed switched to another angle, which revealed a silhouette wearing a broad conical hat staggering through the darkness, all details washed out by the bright light shining right at it.

"Where is this?" he asked, tapping the screen.

"It's a subway tunnel like any other," Ramses said. "She could be anywhere underneath the city, for all we know."

"It can't be any tunnel," Layne said. "She wouldn't be walking down the middle of a subway tunnel with an electrified third rail in the darkness like that."

Mason glanced at the video receiver on the table underneath the middle TV. It was a wireless system, which meant the source had to be nearby, and yet he hadn't heard the distant clatter of rails. The load-bearing walls were concrete and covered with what looked like acoustic padding, but that didn't explain why he hadn't felt so much as a single vibration from a passing train.

On the monitor, the Scarecrow rounded a bend and vanished from sight.

"What happened to the subway this platform used to service?" he asked.

"You're in what remains of the aboveground train station," Gunnar said. "They built this block on top of it, but not until after the new tracks were run underground."

"So you're saying there's still a tunnel down there?"

If Gunnar replied, Mason didn't hear him. He was too busy tearing the foam from the walls. It hadn't been put there to dampen the sound of the subway, but, rather, to insulate the apartment against the cold radiating from the hollow earth.

He exposed an iron door beneath padding that had been cut in such a way as to conceal its size and shape. Someone had chiseled away the concrete covering it and used an acetylene torch to cut through the welded seal around it.

"Where did the train run?" he asked.

"It was originally part of the line connecting Boston and New Haven, which they rerouted to make room for the subway."

Mason drew open the heavy door with a screech of metal. The air blowing into his face was even colder than it was outside and smelled of damp earth and dust. A rusted iron staircase led down into the darkness at a severe angle.

"So what's down there now?"

"I'm working on it."

Mason glanced at the monitor where the Scarecrow had been only seconds ago.

"It doesn't matter, Gunnar. We're going down there anyway."

71

Mason descended the staircase into a small concrete chamber with rusted pipes on the walls.

"... Track Sixty-one," Gunnar said. His voice cut in and out as the connection degenerated. "Originally designed ... connect Grand Central ... to an underground station at the Waldorf-Astoria, so ... rich and famous ... come and go without ... to rub elbows with the unwashed masses topside, but it ... never put into active service. It ... served as FDR's private station ... he was in town. He even ... his own custom railcar to help reach ... elevator that would take his armored limousine up ... the parking garage so no one ... see him using his wheelchair. It's rumored ... occasional president still uses ... but outside of that ... just collecting dust. Considering the only known surface access ... through the Waldorf, I'm surprised ... able to get in there at all."

A rough-edged hole opened onto a concrete pad surrounded by dirt and separated from the tracks by a wall with arched thresholds. Massive electrical boxes, now more rust than metal, clung to it. Conduits protruded from them but only reached as far as the exposed iron girders overhead, many of which were still braced by warped wooden posts. There were mounds of construction scraps and trash everywhere. Sheets of particle- and fiberboard had been left to disintegrate into soil that smelled like a combination of a root cellar and a latrine.

"Where does it go?" Mason asked. His voice echoed into the

distance, from which he heard the faint *thuck-thuck, thuck-thuck* of an approaching train.

He hopped down from the residual platform and swept his flashlight beam across twin rails supported by weathered ties.

"It's not . . . long track . . . connects track sixty and Grand Central . . ."

"Which would be the perfect location to trigger as many remote dispersal units as possible."

". . . since it's a terminal . . . every train has . . . stop there. She . . . easily arm fifty . . . same time . . . send them . . . back out . . . city . . . gas all . . . way."

"And she's somewhere ahead of us on the tracks at this very moment."

". . . breaking up . . . can't understand . . ."

"I'm about to lose my signal, Gunnar. I need you to get ahold of Algren at the New York Field Office. Tell her what's going on and have her dispatch units from Grand Central into the tunnel toward us. We'll trap the Scarecrow between us so she can't reach the station."

The only response was the crackle of static.

"Gunnar?"

"We have to keep going and hope he heard you," Ramses said. "She can't be too far ahead, and the three of us should be able to take her."

"What about Marchment?" Layne asked. "There was only one person on the screen and he wasn't in the apartment."

"He has to be down here somewhere," Mason said. "He's not our priority, though. We have to stop the Scarecrow from releasing the Novichok and hope Marchment's still alive when we find him."

"Or not," Ramses said. "He sounds like a real dick."

With the aid of their flashlights, they'd easily be able to outpace Kameko. Mason's best guess was that the cameras were set up near the junction of tracks 60 and 61, which meant that if they followed the sound of the incoming train, which grew louder by the second, they ought to be able to catch up with her. They could only assume Grand Central Station was her final destination and pray she hadn't figured out which combination of individual trains running nonstop throughout the city would be arriving at the terminal at the same time, armed and ready to be remotely triggered.

"We have to hurry," Mason said, and broke into a sprint. "Come on!"

The Scarecrow emerged from the underground to find itself surrounded by people. The press of bodies was overwhelming. It felt as though everyone was looking at it, and yet it knew that couldn't possibly be the case. No one ever saw it, or perhaps they merely chose to look the other way.

Its timing needed to be precise. There would be no second chances and either it succeeded and many people died or it failed and died alone. Either way, at long last, its life would soon be over, and it would make sure it took the last of those responsible for its torment with it.

And the fool didn't have the slightest clue.

The ground on both sides of the tracks was rocky and uneven, forcing Mason to run between the rails and try to hit the ties and not the spaces between them, slowing him to an uncomfortable extent. His light swinging ahead of him made the entire world seem to tilt from one side to the other. Walls covered with graffiti and soot blew past, bricks to one side and concrete to the other. The clapping sound of his footsteps echoed from dark alcoves on either side, inside of which any number of traps could have been rigged, but he was simply out of time and had to start taking chances. If the Scarecrow reached the terminal first, they'd all be dead soon enough anyway.

The rumble of the subway car faded and a deep red light materialized in the distance. It switched to yellow as he approached. By the time he reached the junction, the light was green and illuminated a concrete barrier with vertical rust and water stains. He recognized it from the surveillance footage. Kameko had been here less than ten minutes ago. They could still overtake her if they were fast enough.

Layne's flashlight cast Mason's shadow ahead of him onto the active tracks. He hit them going full speed and fell into stride on ground worn nearly level by decades of unrelenting use. The whole world seemed to shiver with the sheer volume of trains converging on and

departing from the station. The overhead lighting grew brighter, the fixtures closer together. Another track appeared to his right, a dozen feet
away, on the other side of a colonnade of iron girders.

A train roared behind him, its headlights bursting from the darkness.

He ducked from the tracks and glanced over his shoulder in time
to see Layne and Ramses silhouetted against the lights bearing down on
them. They lunged aside a split second before the train blew past.

Th-th-thuck. Th-th-thuck. Th-th-thuck.

The ferocious wind of its passage buffeted them with enough force
to knock them off stride.

Its brakes screeched as it slowed. Mason caught a glimpse of a
black box with an antenna affixed to the underside of the last car. And
then it was gone.

They were out of time.

The platform materialized in the distance, between the tracks. Yellow staircases leading upward. Massive electrical cables running down
the walls. Partitions made from squares of opaque glass.

Mason jumped up onto it and ran toward where the passengers
disgorged into the crowd waiting to board. Holstered his pistol before
he caused a panic. Fought upstream through the seething mass of humanity working its way against him.

They had to be getting close now. He hoped to God they weren't
already too late.

The sea of faces parted before the Scarecrow. No one so much as
looked in its direction, and the few who made that mistake quickly
averted their eyes and cleared its path. None of them had any idea what
was about to happen, let alone that the remainder of their lives could
be measured in minutes. They were simply in the wrong place at the
wrong time, which was neither its fault nor its concern. They knew
what they were. Humanity was a scourge upon the planet, and while
these people hadn't been party to its torture, they knew what monsters
did to children in the dark of night and condoned it with their silence.
They didn't care what happened to others behind closed doors, as long

as those monsters kept them safe. It had been easy to turn a blind eye because it wasn't happening to them.

But today it was.

Mason had to slow and turn sideways. Raised his arms and stood on his toes to see over the heads of everyone surrounding him.

"Out of the way!" he shouted.

He merged into the herd ascending the ramp toward the station. Found enough space to move and bolted away from the tracks. Through the dimly lit corridor connecting the lower platforms. Into a marble-tiled arcade with stores on either side. Nearly barreled through a janitor cleaning up a spill. The old man swore and threw his mop to the ground. Mason hurdled the wet patch without slowing.

The main concourse was directly ahead, framed by a domed entryway. He saw the globe clock and the arched windows over the heads of a riot of people.

And among them, a *sugegasa*. A broad conical straw hat.

He caught a glimpse of flannel and denim, and the startled expressions on the faces of the people who hurried to get out of the Scarecrow's way.

"Freeze!" Mason shouted.

He drew his weapon, sighted it squarely on the back of the Scarecrow's head, and prepared to end the threat right here and now.

Screams erupted all around him. Bodies ran in every direction. Uniformed officers fought through them. One shouted from the marble landing at the top of the twin staircases beyond the circular kiosk.

The Scarecrow swayed as she stood there. Cocked her head first one way, then the other. Slowly turned to face him.

"No," Mason whispered.

His heart sank.

The Scarecrow had outmaneuvered them again.

72

Rand Marchment stood before Mason, dressed as all of the other victims had been. The *sugegasa* had tipped back on his head, revealing eyes filled with terror. His pupils were dilated so wide, they nearly eclipsed his irises. Sweat glistened on his forehead. Tears ran down his cheeks. His lips moved in an attempt to speak, but no sound came out.

A uniformed agent wearing a helmet and a Kevlar vest assumed position on the landing of the marble staircase and shouted down at him.

"Drop the gun!"

"Federal officers!" Layne shouted.

Their voices were barely audible over the screams of those fleeing the main concourse.

The Scarecrow had used the chemicals in his workstation to create lysergic acid diethylamide—LSD—and given Marchment a massive dose, as he must have done to the volunteers at Edgewood. He probably didn't have any idea where he was or what he was doing.

Or even what was real and what wasn't.

Sirens wailed outside. Transit police in domed white electric carts sealed off the main exits. DHS and JTTF agents appeared as if from nowhere. Drew their weapons and aimed at the two of them, standing in the center of the concourse.

"Hold your fire!" Mason shouted.

Marchment held a black metal box in front of his chest. Antennas protruded from the top. There was a digital clock face on the front, only it didn't display the time. It counted down from 00:02:13 to 00:02:12 as Mason watched. The red wires attached to it passed above the bib of Marchment's overalls and through the gap between the top buttons of his shirt.

It was a remote detonator, and when the countdown reached zero, Novichok gas would be released from dispersal units affixed to the trains departing from the terminal.

"Hold still," Mason said.

He kept his pistol trained on Marchment and used his left hand to grab one side of the flannel shirt. Ripped it open to expose the deputy secretary's bare chest.

"Jesus," he whispered.

These were no mere electrical cords; they were blood-filled catheters exiting a gaping wound underneath the collar of Marchment's shirt. The skin had been retracted, exposing the muscles and tendons and blood vessels, which appeared to be the source of the lines.

The Scarecrow shoved through the hordes of revelers struggling to find anyplace to stand behind the rails to either side of the main walkway, where people were crammed so tightly together, there was hardly enough room to breathe. Banks of lights had been erected on fifty-foot poles and on elevated platforms where police monitored the bedlam through various surveillance devices. Digital billboards cast a carnival glow onto men and women wearing parkas and ponchos, party hats and novelty glasses, over whom lorded celebrities in private Plexiglas boxes, preening for the cameras.

The ball perched above the roofline of One Times Square, several blocks behind the Scarecrow, ready to make its 141-foot descent to the top of the seventeen-story column of billboards. In front of it, a wall of reporters and cameramen stood on the other side of a railed barricade, at the foot of the bronze statue of Father Duffy on his plinth, his back to a Celtic cross chiseled from green granite, their cameras directed up the ruby red stadium bleacher stairs ascending onto the roof of the TKTS ticket booth. A specially designed podium with the seal of New York City had been erected on the uppermost steps. Five men in suits stood behind it, flanked by a phalanx of NYPD officers in full crowd-control gear, basking in the glow of the spotlights directed down at them from the rooftops, where snipers and drone operators had taken up covert positions. Electric advertisements towered over them from the narrow side of the Renaissance Hotel.

"I Love New York" blared through the loudspeakers and the cameras started to roll. One of the men stepped up to the podium. The music faded and an expectant silence fell upon the crowd.

"It is with great pride that I announce the future has arrived," Peter Andrews, the governor of the state of New York, said. His voice boomed throughout Times Square, commanding the attention of the million-plus people stretching as far as the eye could see. "Today will go down in history as the day this great city declared its independence from fossil fuels. Our long-standing commitment to green energy demands more than lip service; it requires putting our money where our collective mouth is. It takes nearly two hundred megawatts of electricity—that's two hundred million watts—to light up this glorious square. This morning, we lit it with fossil fuels for the last time. Tonight, the ball will drop on the past and usher in the grand future all New Yorkers—nay, everyone in the entire world—deserve."

The crowd roared its approval. Cameramen jostled for the perfect shot of the five men, with the billboards scaling the Renaissance Hotel behind them and the statue of Father Duffy in the foreground, as Reuben Covington, the mayor of New York City, assumed the podium.

"On this night," he said, "we will cut Times Square, one of this great city's most recognizable landmarks, right out of the grid. From this moment forward, it will be serviced by the solar photovoltaic arrays on the surrounding rooftops, which will not only power the businesses and the billboards but will lead the charge in our citywide efforts to transition to sustainable clean energy and meet our goal of reducing greenhouse gas emissions eighty-five percent by the year 2050."

The thunder of applause was deafening. Covington raised his arms to better soak up the adoration. The policemen enforcing the barricade in front of the statue and ceremonial stairs turned to witness an event that would forever change the course of one of the grandest cities the world had ever known.

The Scarecrow forced its way right up against the rails.

"Evacuate the station!" Layne shouted.

She held up her badge like a shield and kept her body between Mason's and the agent with the gun aimed at him from the balcony.

"Listen to me," Mason said, but Marchment's eyes couldn't seem to focus on him. He holstered his weapon and took the deputy secretary's face between his hands. "I need you to listen to me very carefully.

That box you're carrying is designed to send a signal to remote devices on the trains arriving all around us at this very second. That signal will cause the remote devices to release Novichok gas, which the trains will then trail behind them and spread throughout the city, killing millions of people—including you—so it's important that you hold really, really still so I can figure out how to disarm it."

00:01:38.

00:01:37.

"Keep going," Marchment said. The inner workings of his neck moved and shifted in a manner that was both fascinating and horrifying. "Walk straight down the tunnel and keep going. Climb up onto the platform. Stand in the middle of the concourse. She said she'd take the stinger out of my neck if I did. Can you see it? Can you take the stinger out?" He gestured toward the flap of skin hanging from his open throat. "It feels like it's somewhere around here."

Mason took the box from him and turned around. Ramses stood behind him, his arms raised and his palms open in the least threatening manner possible. There had to be at least a dozen red dots swirling on his chest from as many laser sights.

"Help me, damn it!"

His old friend glanced down at his chest, then looked up at the officers and agents surrounding him. He hesitated only briefly before saying "Fuck it" and rushing to Mason's side.

"Hold this for me, okay?" Mason said.

He stretched the catheters as far as they'd go without putting strain on the vessels in Marchment's neck and passed the detonator to Ramses. It appeared as though one tube had been run from the internal jugular vein through a hole in the back of the box, from which another emerged and made the return trip to the external jugular vein.

00:01:06.

00:01:05.

"Do you have a good grip?" he asked.

Ramses nodded.

Mason carefully pried off the metal casing to reveal the inner workings. He identified the circuit boards corresponding to the antenna array and the clock. A flow-control valve on the main line. A series of small silver tubes that looked almost like batteries, only thicker. And what appeared to be a small hydraulic generator. Blood entered through one side and exited the other, creating the electricity to power the detonator in the process.

00:00:54.

00:00:53.

Brakes screeched outside. The sirens were just on the other side of the doors. Red and blue lights reflected from the marble floor.

"Tell me you know what you're doing," Ramses said.

Mason held up a hand to silence him. He needed to concentrate.

00:00:46.

00:00:45.

"Whatever you're going to do, you'd better do it in a hurry," Layne said.

JTTF agents swarmed the building. They burst through the doors, wearing bulletproof vests and gas masks, their assault rifles already seated against their shoulders, and took up position in the mouths of the various passageways and along the upper-level railings.

Layne pivoted between them, shouting her identification and demanding they hold their fire.

The Scarecrow had figured out a way to use a portable hydroelectric generator and Marchment's own circulation to power the detonator.

00:00:38.

00:00:37.

And the only way to shut if off was to stop the flow of blood.

73

"And we owe it all to the gentlemen behind me," the mayor said. "Allow me to introduce the innovators whose shared vision will help transform the city as we know it into the city we always dreamed it could be. Mr. Jonathan Feltman, director of the Department of City Planning. Mr. Aidan Dunham, president of the New York City Urban Development Corporation. And Mr. Slate Langbroek, chairman of the executive board of directors for Royal Nautilus Petroleum and its newest subsidiary, Nautilus Energy. Together, they designed and produced the miracle you're about to witness, which involved more than just slapping a bunch of solar panels on the rooftops surrounding us. They installed a fully integrated smart grid system with its own intelligent power-management system capable of diverting excess energy to on-site storage units and drawing from them during peak hours. A self-contained network capable of achieving total energy independence."

The three men waved to the packed square. Flashes strobed. People cheered.

"In conjunction with the U.S. Department of Energy, the state of New York has generously agreed to offer subsidies and tax incentives to any company willing to follow suit," the mayor continued. "It's only a matter of time before there are Green Smart Grids in every building in this great city. But those are just words, aren't they? Here in the Big Apple, we let our actions speak for us. What do you say we get a demonstration of the best New Year's present the Earth has ever received?" The ground positively trembled from the applause and stomping feet. "Mr. Langbroek, would you care to do the honors?"

Slate pumped his fist for the crowd, shook the mayor's hand, and assumed his place at the podium. He wore an overcoat with a scarf and gloves. His cheeks and nose were bright red from the cold. He was the last of a bloodline that needed to be purged from the world.

"I prepared a speech about the challenges of advancing a petroleum company into a clean energy future, but I'm just as excited as the rest of you, so what do you say we see what this baby can do?"

All eyes turned toward the opposite end of Times Square as the ball officially started its descent.

Langbroek and the other men on the top stair shielded their eyes from the spotlights to better see.

The buzz of the crowd made the air shiver.

The Scarecrow stared at Slate Langbroek, willing the man to see it. It wanted him to understand what was about to happen, to know who was responsible, to recognize that he'd been betrayed.

The ball reached the halfway mark.

Thirty seconds and counting.

The officers manning the perimeter looked past the crowds and up toward the glowing orb.

For the most fleeting of seconds.

Just long enough for the Scarecrow to climb over the barricade.

Marchment placed his hand on top of Mason's. The older man's chin quivered, but he steeled it long enough to offer a single firm nod.

"There has to be a way to disconnect it," Mason said.

00:00:29.

00:00:28.

Marchment wrapped the catheters in his fist and gave them a sharp tug.

Blood spurted from the ends of the tubes and flooded the open wound in his neck. He clapped his hand over it and dropped to his knees. Blood sluiced between his fingers and spattered the marble tiles.

"Call an ambulance!" Mason shouted.

He was just about to thrust his own hand into the blood in an effort to pinch off the vessels when he caught a glimpse of the timer from the corner of his eye.

It was still running.

00:00:23.

00:00:22.

The silver canisters that looked like batteries had to be capacitors, which stored enough charge that even if Marchment decided to be a hero, there would still be enough left to finish the countdown. The Scarecrow had completed both her personal and professional missions in one decisive stroke. Marchment would bleed out by his own hand and the aerosol units on the subway trains would still be activated.

They were all going to die.

00:00:16.

00:00:15.

Mason looked all around him. There had to be some way to stop it, but even if he managed to tear apart the detonator to get to the capacitors underneath the generator, there was no way of knowing how much residual current was already traveling through the circuits. It wouldn't take much juice to send out a signal, assuming there weren't other fail-safes already in place to prevent its disarmament.

00:00:14.

00:00:13.

He remembered the janitor he'd nearly run down on his way into the concourse. The mop clattering from his hands. The bucket of dirty water.

No matter how much power they possessed, no electrical components could conduct a charge large enough to deliver a signal if their circuit boards were fried.

00:00:12.

00:00:11.

Mason grabbed the device and sprinted toward the arcade, where a pair of JTTF agents had the corridor blocked off and the barrels of their rifles pointed right at him.

00:00:10.

00:00:09.

Their eyes widened in surprise. They hadn't expected him to run directly at them. He could only hope they wouldn't riddle him with bullets before he reached the mop bucket behind them.

00:00:08.

00:00:07.

"Don't shoot!" he shouted.

The agents leaned their cheeks against the stocks of their weapons. Drew a bead on center mass. Moved their index fingers from the sides of the barrels onto the triggers.

They were going to fire and there was nothing he could do about it.

00:00:06.

00:00:05.

Gunfire from behind him. Bullets struck the marble arch above the agents' heads. They instinctively hit the deck as marble fragments rained down on them.

Mason dove between them, slid across the wet floor toward the mop bucket.

00:00:04.

00:00:03.

Thrust the device into the filthy water. Felt a zap of current pass though his forearms.

He heard the rumble of footsteps behind him and turned in time to see agents converging at the center of the concourse from seemingly everywhere at once. Layne dropped her smoldering pistol and raised her hands. They tackled her into the puddle of blood on the ground beside Ramses, who struggled to keep his fingers clamped on the torn vein inside Marchment's neck with a knee between his shoulder blades and his other arm wrenched behind his back.

A heartbeat later, Mason was pinned under the weight of one man while another forced his face down into the water from the overturned mop bucket.

The device lay mere inches away, the face of the timer dark.

"Two!" the crowd roared.

The Scarecrow scaled the plinth and stood in front of the statue of Father Duffy, the cross at its back. It raised its arms out to either side. In each hand it held an electric vaporizer modified to hold canisters of a substance no e-cigarette manufacturer had ever imagined they'd be used to disperse.

"One!"

Kameko Nakamura experienced a moment of lucidity as she looked upon the sea of humanity staring up at the glowing crystal ball. She felt neither sorrow nor pity, for where had they been when the soldiers were exposing helpless children to chemical weapons and experimental cures? Where had they been when the tumor formed in her brother's brain, even as the muscular sclerosis ate through it? Where had they been when the cancer eroded her optic nerves and vocal cords, or later, when she developed Huntington's disease–like symptoms of a condition no doctor had ever seen before, one that robbed her of everything in her life that mattered?

The lights died with a thud that reverberated through the earth. Darkness filled the square, overwhelming the portable lights and raised cell phone cameras, which limned the scene with an ethereal glow, like a poorly developed photograph from a bygone era.

The whole world seemed to hold its breath.

Lights blossomed from everywhere at once. The billboards came to life. Music blared. Fireworks exploded. Confetti filled the air.

Kameko's rage exploded from the breathing stoma in her throat as a violent hiss, releasing all of the pain and the years of suffering, all of the anger for what they'd done to her brother and her, and all of her hatred in that one animalistic sound.

Colors flashed behind her, casting the shadow of the cross and her outstretched arms onto the unsuspecting onlookers below her.

She heard the voice of Slate Langbroek, the man she knew as Quintus, through the speakers. He had no idea the product he'd paid for would be the death of him. As far as he knew, it was thousands of miles away, not inside specially designed cartridges in the handheld vaporizer units and aerial-dispersal mechanisms affixed to the trains leaving Grand Central Station at that very moment. Quintus might have paid her a fortune, but Tertius Decimus, who had much to gain from Langbroek's death and the release of the Novichok, had given her information even she hadn't known about an oil company that had entered into a deal with the military to help produce and test chemical weapons. More important, he'd given her the opportunity to take what was rightfully hers.

Revenge.

All eyes looked in her direction. Cameras swung to face her. Focused on her.

Her *sugegasa* fell from her head, revealing the digital prosthetic lenses of her brother's design that served as her eyes, the hole in her neck through which she could speak only with the aid of a laryngophone, and the discolored patches where her hair had never regrown after the chemotherapy.

And in that fleeting moment, the entire world was forced to bear witness to what it had done to her.

The Scarecrow pressed the buttons on the vaporizers with her thumbs.

And released deadly, invisible clouds of Novichok A-234.

PART VII

*Where justice is denied, where poverty is enforced, where ig-
norance prevails, and where any one class is made to feel that
society is an organized conspiracy to oppress, rob and degrade
them, neither persons nor property will be safe.*

—Frederick Douglass,
speech given in Washington, D.C., on the twenty-fourth anniversary
of Emancipation (1886)

74

Mason had never been to Times Square, but he knew it well from countless pictures and movies and New Year's Eve celebrations. It was a place of magic and wonder, a monument to everything that was truly and rightly American, although now it was unrecognizable even to those who knew it best. And it would never be the same again.

He picked his way though the chaos in a CBRN suit, his respirations loud in his ears. He felt numb, disconnected from his physical being, as though merely a spectator watching through his own eyes. That things could have been infinitely worse was of little consolation to him, or to the families of the sixty-six men and women whose bodies were wrapped in military green blankets, or to the countless others crying in pain as they were triaged under the flashing lights. Had the wind been blowing in any other direction, the casualties could have easily been in the thousands.

A steady stream of ambulances struggled through the congestion of abandoned cars to get the worst-afflicted of the victims to whatever hospitals still had enough beds to take them, while those deemed in less severe condition received treatment right there on the sidewalk by nurses, doctors, firefighters, and emergency personnel. Volunteers who'd charged selflessly into action without thought or concern for their personal safety, only for that of the victims sprawled everywhere, screaming and sobbing and begging for help, a veritable war zone in the heart of a city that had never truly recovered from the last great act of terror, and while this one paled by comparison, it was somehow made worse by the fact that the perpetrator hadn't been a violent extremist who hated everything the country stood for, but, rather, a trained physician who'd embraced the monster within her, one that was neither her fault nor within her control. None of those details would ever be allowed to come out, though. The world needed to see Kameko Nakamura as the devil made flesh, if only so people would be able to sleep at night.

"We should have seen this coming," Layne said through the speaker in his left ear.

While he wanted to say something reassuring, he couldn't find the words. The truth of the matter was that she was right. They should have made the connection that the Nautilus contingent had been in New York City working on the Green Smart Grid project and recognized the implications when they saw the monitor displaying live footage from Times Square in the Scarecrow's apartment.

They found the evidence response team clustered around the statue of Father Duffy, which stood like a tombstone over an empty square filled with trash and confetti and awash with bodily fluids of all kinds, smeared where the trampled bodies had been dragged away. Those unfortunate enough to have been within a ten-foot radius had died within seconds, while those near the periphery of the hot zone probably wished they had. There would be many more deaths announced before the night was over.

Mason pushed through the cordon surrounding the lone body left untouched and stared down at the Scarecrow for the first time. Kameko Nakamura lay on her side, her body so small and fragile that Mason wondered how she'd ever been able to pull it all off. She was dressed like a samurai with a lamellar cuirass, or *dō*, made from hand-stitched rawhide strips, matching *kote* sleeves, and a skirtlike plated *haidate*. Her *sugegasa* rested against the base of the plinth near the wooden *geta* sandal she'd lost in the fall. She'd landed squarely on her face, breaking her jaw and her lower row of teeth. Blood leaked from the hole in her windpipe. Her eyes were obviously artificial. The irises were recessed and took up the entire space between the lids. The outer ring was composed of small titanium plates that appeared to function like the aperture of a camera, opening and closing in response to varying levels of light, while the inner sensors were concentric rings of what almost looked like solar cells, at the heart of which was a photosensitive array that reflected the bright lights shining down on her remains.

"Stars for eyes," Mason said.

"What?" Layne asked.

"Nothing." He stood and forced himself to look away. What a waste of a brilliant mind. "Just one last piece falling into place."

The podium had been knocked down the stairs and broken into a dozen pieces. There were spatters of blood on the top few rows, where an NYPD officer had tackled Jonathan Feltman, director of the Department of City Planning, in an attempt to shield him from the surprise attack. Unfortunately, despite his heroics, both of their names were listed among those of the deceased. As was that of Aidan Dunham, president of the New York City Urban Development Corporation. Governor Andrews had been evacuated on the first wave of medical choppers, while both Slate Langbroek and the mayor, Reuben Covington, had jumped over the railing and landed on the street below. While they'd presumably survived, their current locations had yet to be established.

Mason walked around behind the ruby red staircase, where harried nurses treated patients on blankets in front of the TKTS booth. There were patterns of blood underneath the overhang, where the men had struck the sidewalk. He hoped they belonged to Langbroek and that, wherever he was hiding, his wounds hurt. Very, very badly.

There was something about the whole situation that didn't sit right with him, though, something that had been troubling him since Mikkelson's abduction, but he hadn't quite been able to define it until after Marchment's. And now, with Langbroek being at ground zero, it simply made no sense.

"Why were they here?" he said. "If they knew the Novichok was in Manhattan and about to be released on the subway, why the hell were they anywhere within a thousand miles of this place?"

"Plausible deniability?" Layne said. "No one would ever suspect them if they were among the survivors."

"If the devices on the trains had been activated as planned, there wouldn't have been any survivors. At least not this close to Grand Central."

"You think they didn't know?"

Mason looked straight up at the lighted billboards reaching into the sky on the narrow face of the Renaissance Hotel. The Nautilus Energy logo flashed on the uppermost of the twenty-foot-tall screens. He recalled what Gunnar had said days ago.

Does this have anything to do with the sudden surge in energy futures trading?

"No," Mason said. "They weren't worried about an attack taking place here because they knew for a fact that the Novichok—or at least what they'd thought was all of the Novichok—was somewhere else."

75

For the first time in its storied history, not a single subway train sped through the underground tunnels beneath the city and wouldn't again until every one of its six thousand cars was cleared of remote dispersal devices. They'd already recovered sixteen of them within a three-block radius of Grand Central Terminal and were only now expanding their search to the surrounding stations, including Times Square–Forty-second Street, where there was one attached to the number 7 train, which sat lifeless on the platform when Mason and Layne arrived. The silver doors stood open, revealing vacant seats and empty walkways that glowed faintly green beneath the interior lights.

The MTA workers who'd found the device stood off to the side, about as far away from it as they could physically get without exiting the station. None of them had any desire to be there, but there was no one more qualified to determine if there were any foreign objects attached to the trains than they were, let alone in anything resembling an expeditious manner.

They'd made it clear, however, that they weren't touching the devices. That was someone else's problem, and the mayor, being currently indisposed, was in no position to object.

"Show me," Mason said.

A bearded man with a hard hat and an orange reflective vest broke away from the others. He approached as though preparing to proffer his hand, but thought better of it when he realized the implications of their isolation suits and veered toward the yellow tiles lining the edge of the platform. Dropped down onto the tracks behind the last car. Crouched and shone his flashlight up into the undercarriage.

"She could have easily leaned over the edge while everyone was boarding and slipped it right up underneath there," the man said.

Mason jumped down behind him and craned his neck to see the device. It was the same thing he'd seen on the train pulling into Grand Central Station when he arrived, and yet somehow it seemed even smaller up close. The homemade unit had been spray-painted black and affixed to the underside of the train with an electromagnet. Were it not for the antenna, it would have been indistinguishable from the other mechanical components. He recognized a battery pack, a remote transceiver, and a stainless-steel reservoir equipped with a high-pressure nozzle.

"Hold that light still for me, okay?" Mason said, and reached for the device.

"No freaking way." The man practically jumped straight up onto the platform. "You're on your own from here."

"I got it," Layne said.

She grabbed the flashlight and shone it upward from underneath so the shadows from Mason's hands wouldn't hide the unit as he disconnected the battery and released the magnet. He took it carefully in both hands and removed it from the train. The liquid Novichok sloshed inside the reservoir, which couldn't have been much larger than a whiskey flask.

"How much fluid do you think this holds?" he asked.

"I don't know. Maybe twelve ounces?"

"What's that? A can of Coke? If you figure a six-pack is roughly a half gallon, you could put one of these not just on every train but on every single car on every train and still only use a thousand gallons." Mason looked up and met her stare. He could tell she was thinking the exact same thing. "Where's the rest of it?"

76

By the time they made it back to the Scarecrow's apartment, Kaemon had been removed from his bed and taken to the nearest secure intensive care unit, where he was being treated under heavily armed guard. His early prognosis was grim, especially considering the doctors didn't have any idea what they were dealing with and no one seemed to have a clue how to track down Dr. Tatsuo Yamaguchi, assuming he was even still in the country. Considering even Kaemon's sister, who'd obviously been his primary caregiver for years, had written him off, the likelihood of his physician's having remained nearby was slim, especially if he'd known what Kameko intended to do. Mason looked forward to tracking him down and asking him in person.

The bomb squad had removed the IED from the monitor, which sat silent and dark beside the empty bed with its soiled sheets and veritable smorgasbord of DNA, seemingly all of which the ERT was hell-bent on collecting. They'd already confirmed that some amount of Novichok had been inside the apartment, having discovered residual traces in the workroom, but there was no way a single industrial canister would have made it down the narrow staircase, let alone the full load of two cargo containers. The biggest problem was they simply didn't know how much had been produced and the only person who could have told them had taken that knowledge to her grave, but no one needed two flatbed trucks to transport the minimal amounts they were still recovering from the subway.

The lead forensics agent was in the Scarecrow's workroom, watching over the shoulder of one of her specialists as he collected samples of blood and tissue from the drain at the end of the metal table. The equipment and ingredients used to make the LSD were already bagged and tagged and loaded into a plastic tub overflowing with evidence.

Mason cleared his throat and she turned around. It was the same freckled officer from Central Park, the one with the Puerto Rican accent. She acknowledged them with a nod and gestured for them to follow her down the hallway.

"We found it in the closet of what we're calling the AV room," she said. "I need to ask how you knew it would be there."

"Educated guess," Mason said.

"You're going to need to come up with a better answer than that."

She led them into the room at the end of the hall, where the surveillance monitors showed a steady stream of agents flowing in and out of the building, like ants from an anthill. The live feeds from both Grand Central Station and Times Square had been terminated in an effort to limit the amount of carnage broadcast around the clock on every network and cable news channel.

There was an old reel-to-reel projector on the floor amid stacks of circular metal canisters. It didn't take a genius to realize they had to be around here somewhere. The human mind was designed with the most perfect bleach bit, the kind of mental defense that could wipe the hard drive clean in the event of trauma beyond its ability to cope. The fact that a woman in her early fifties hadn't been able to repress the horrors she'd survived at Edgewood meant that either she didn't want to forget or she'd been subjected to constant reminders beyond her physical deterioration and her brother's slow demise.

Mason sat on the floor behind it and switched on the power.

"You sure you want to do this?" the lead investigator said. "I've only seen a few minutes and that was more than enough for me."

He nodded as he perused the faded labels.

"We're going to need a little time," Layne said.

"Take all you need," the criminalist said. "We have enough down here to keep us busy for the next week, and that's without getting any sleep."

She left them alone in the cold room. They could see straight into the hole in the wall and hear the voices of another overwhelmed team trying to understand how the Scarecrow had done everything she had right under their noses.

It took Mason a minute to figure out how to work the archaic machine, which made a loud buzzing sound as it projected the film onto the wall. The images were black and white and the way the frames jumped from side to side was disorienting, but there was no mistaking what was happening in the sterile white room with small beds lining the wall. It would have been completely bare if not for the tongue-depressor scarecrows hanging by paper clips from the brackets between the ceiling tiles. A little girl in the bed nearest the camera clung to one of them like a doll and pressed herself flat against the mattress as though in an attempt to merge with it. She couldn't have been more than three or four years old.

A man in a white lab coat was seated beside her. Dr. Ichiro Nakamura, the monster from Unit 731, whose real name was Masao Matsuda. He said something in Japanese and the girl stopped her thrashing and stared at him through tear-drenched eyes. He held up a small canister with a clear mask attached to it, one just large enough to cover her tiny mouth and nose. She shook her head violently back and forth until the doctor barked a command and Marchment, little more than a teenager himself, rushed to the other side of the bed. He pinned her down and held her head to immobilize it.

A shrill scream from off-camera.

Marchment turned toward the source in time to see a young boy charging at him. He raised his forearm to ward off the flailing fists until he was able to get a grip on the boy's upper arms and lift him from the ground. The child kicked at the much larger man's knees, to no avail.

Nakamura spoke softly in Japanese and the boy immediately ceased struggling. Marchment looked warily at the doctor, who nodded for him to proceed, and set the boy back down on his feet.

The boy straightened his shirt, climbed onto the bed, and hugged the little girl, who looked just like him. She sobbed and clung to him, but he patiently pushed her away and scooted to the edge of the bed beside the doctor. He thrust out his chin and closed his eyes as tightly as he could.

The doctor slipped the elastic strap over the boy's head, affixed the mask to the lower half of his face, and pressed the button to release the gas.

The boy's eyes opened wide. His shoulders bucked. Tears streamed down his cheeks. He released a muffled scream that speckled the inside of the mask with blood.

Mason had to turn away. He recalled the initial briefing of the Dodge-Hill Strike Force, when Algren listed off the symptoms of sarin exposure and the lethal doses by injection, skin contact, and inhalation. Layne had commented that the information was awfully specific considering they were dealing with a banned chemical weapon of mass destruction.

So how did we get this information? she'd asked.

The army conducted its own experimentation with sarin in the fifties, Algren had said, *but that's neither here nor there.*

But it was. It was here and it was now. It had been the process of ascertaining that information that had brought them to this singular, catastrophic moment in time, which had resulted in the deaths of innocent people in Times Square. They'd been right about the Scarecrow's having personal and professional agendas, but they'd been dead wrong about one thing: The two had never been in opposition. They'd been aligned from the very beginning. And while she might have fulfilled her professional obligations to a large extent, she'd failed to tie off all of her personal loose ends. Lucky for her, Mason was on the case. He fully intended to make sure that Marchment was held accountable for his actions and that Langbroek paid for his family's contributions to the nightmare experimentation at Edgewood, his personal involvement with the production of the Novichok, and the massacre in Times Square. More important, he was going to use him to track down the rest of the Thirteen.

And then he was going to make every single one of them pay.

77

Marchment had been airlifted to New York–Presbyterian, where he'd passed straight through the emergency room and into a surgical suite. The surgeon had repaired the damaged vessels in his neck and was optimistic about his recovery. Despite saving his life, Ramses had been remanded into federal custody and taken to the twenty-third floor of the Javits Federal Building, at least until they sorted out the nature of his involvement.

Algren had been generous enough to let Mason and Layne see him, although she'd given them only five minutes to do so and demanded they report to her office for their debriefings the moment they were done. She might not have known everything that had transpired, but the fact that they weren't in cuffs was a positive sign. Ramses, on the other hand, was shackled to the arm of a chair facing the maze of cubicles. He sat silently, a contented smile on his face and his eyes closed. He opened one at the sound of their approach, then closed it again.

"What's the saying?" he said. "Let no good deed go unpunished?"

"The doctors think Marchment will pull through," Layne said. "You saved his life."

"Don't sign me up for sainthood just yet. I only did it because he has information we need. I'd have been fine letting him bleed out on the floor."

Mason smirked. His old friend talked a good game, but when it came right down to it, he was full of shit. He'd acted on instinct, without conscious thought or deliberation, and in doing so had saved the life of a man who would have been at peace with the release of the Novichok. In fact, his heroics were probably the only reason they hadn't all been gunned down where they stood by the DHS agents surrounding them in the terminal. Ramses might have been a lot of things, most of them not even remotely endearing, but he was also the bravest person Mason had ever met and one of the few people he knew would lay down his life for him, and one of even fewer for whom he would do the same.

"I'll see what I can do about getting you out of here," he said.

"Take your time, Mace. This is the most rest I've had in days. And, truth be told, the boss lady back there's totally rocking the whole cougar vibe. I'm thinking that might require further investigation. You should have seen the way she was looking at me, like she wanted to devour me."

He was undoubtedly right about Algren, although for entirely different reasons than he thought.

Mason followed Layne down the hall toward the command center, which currently resembled the floor of the New York Stock Exchange. There were agents everywhere. Shouting into their phones, studying monitors, nearly trampling one another in their hurry to get to wherever they needed to go. Algren saw them coming through the bedlam and diverted them into an interrogation room on the other side of the corridor. She closed the door behind them and gestured for them to take the seats across the table from her.

"You both know the drill," she said. Her voice was hoarse and her hands shook from too much caffeine. "This room is wired for video and sound and everything you say will be recorded."

The door opened behind her with an explosion of noise and three men in suits entered the room. None of them needed an introduction. Mason recognized Thomas Wallace, director of the FBI; Susanne Clavenger, the U.S. attorney general; and Derek Archer, secretary of the Department of Homeland Security. They pulled chairs up to the table and hung their jackets over the backs.

Mason sighed and settled in.

This was definitely going to take a while.

78

By the time Mason left the Federal Building, the sun was preparing to set once more. The exhaustion was a physical entity inside his body. His cell phone let him know that he had fifteen missed calls but only three messages. He listened to them as he and Layne walked without a destination in mind. Traffic across the entire city was in gridlock, so they weren't getting out of there anytime soon.

"James?" his father said. "I just wanted to call to make sure you were okay. I heard that you were right there when . . . you know, when everything happened. I'm sure you have your hands full, but just . . . just call me back when you can, okay? Or text me. Either way, I need to know you're safe."

The second call was from Gunnar, who was already talking when the recording started.

". . . to talk to you pronto. I figured out something you're definitely going to want to hear."

His phone vibrated in his hand. He recognized the number right away.

"I was just listening to your message—"

"It doesn't matter. Just shut your mouth and listen, okay?"

Gunnar had his undivided attention.

"Give me a second, okay?" Mason said, and put the call on speaker so Layne could hear. "What did you find?"

"So I was sitting there in the car, waiting for your GPS signal to pop back online, when it hit me that Novichok gas could come up through the grates in the sidewalk at any moment and that the car windows wouldn't be able to keep it out. Not that I didn't have complete faith in your ability to stop the attack on the subway, but it's only natural for a man sitting on enough Novichok to wipe out the population of the entire eastern seaboard to at least consider the idea of saving his own skin, which brought to mind Major Delvin Roybal, who's got to be so deep in the Canadian Rockies by now that he's probably speaking French."

"You found Roybal?" Layne said.

"Just listen, okay? So that got me thinking about the company that paid him to dispose of the flatbeds, which he would have done had that trooper not recognized the significance of the trucks and had them hauled to impound. But here's the thing. That's not a quarter-of-a-million-dollar job. Not by a long shot. The guys who actually started the fire and tried to kill you to cover it up? They only received ten grand apiece and they took all the risks. What could Roybal have possibly done for these guys that was worth twenty-five times as much? And then it hit me."

"He was in charge of the Hazardous Material Transportation Unit," Mason said.

"And special operations for Homeland Security, don't forget. So I hacked into the computer network of East Coast Transportation Services—you know, the guys who paid him for his consultation—and did a little poking around. And guess what I found? A contract signed on November eighth for the lease of two flatbed trucks. That's not out of the ordinary at all. In fact, they leased a dozen others that same day. What is, however, is the fact that they were paid half a million dollars for those trucks."

Mason nodded toward a plaza with an odd maze of benches beside the Federal Building, where they found seats away from the handful of other people braving the cold.

"There's the source of the money," Layne said. "Who signed the check?"

"Aegis Asset Management," Gunnar said. "The same company that owned the apartment where Charles Raymond was living."

"Do you know where the trucks were heading?" Mason asked.

"Not very far at all. In fact, they never even left Newark."

"How do you know?"

"The license plates of the vehicles were listed on the lease, as were the numbers of the RFID tags the Port Authority registers to commercial vehicles for automated entry through the marine terminal gates. I was able to confirm both passed through security at the Port Newark Container Terminal that same day."

"Roybal was in charge of Marine Services. That's where he earned his money."

"There's no record of the containers being dropped off, though, let alone where they might have been shipped. Assuming they were even shipped at all."

"Langbroek wouldn't have been anywhere near the city if they were still sitting on the docks. Any kind of accident and a gust of wind could carry a cloud of deadly gas across the Hudson."

"So where did it go?"

Mason closed his eyes and tried to imagine where someone like Slate Langbroek would ship thousands of gallons of Novichok. He felt as though they'd tied off just about every loose end except the one Gunnar had brought up on the night he and Layne were nearly killed in the Pine Barrens. When he opened his eyes again, he felt everything falling into place around him.

"Energy futures," he said.

"What are energy futures?" Layne asked.

"The name's something of a misnomer," Gunnar said. "They aren't like stocks, where you're investing in the future of a business or industry. They're essentially deals between a buyer and a seller that a certain amount of a product—in this case, crude oil—will be delivered by a certain date and will be purchased for a prearranged price. Not only does such an agreement reduce the risk in a market where the cost of a barrel of oil changes by the hour; it provides both the producer and the consumer with the price certainty they require for daily operations. Speculators make a killing buying futures. The producer is guaranteed the negotiated price for the oil, but if the market rises, the investor can then turn around and sell it for more than he paid."

"The higher the price of oil climbs, the more money the futures are ultimately worth," Mason said. "And there are really only two basic factors that influence that price: supply and demand. So if someone wanted to increase the price, he'd either need to decrease the availability or create an artificial demand."

He was reminded of something Gunnar had said earlier, in the back of the car on the way to Edgewood.

What can I say? Langbroeks have long memories.

Mason smiled and looked directly at Layne.

"I know where the Novichok is."

EPILOGUE

Whoever controls the volume of money in any country is absolute master of all industry and commerce.

—James A. Garfield,
Inaugural Address (1881)

SHELTER ISLAND, NEW YORK
January 2

Mason sprinted to the edge of the tree line and crouched in the deep shadows, his respirations harsh inside his gas mask. His black CBRN suit was nearly indistinguishable from the darkness thanks to the sparse moonlight permeating the dense cloud cover. Waves thundered inland and crashed against the dock on the far side of the estate, inside of which their thermal-equipped drone had detected two distinct heat signatures. His heart raced at the prospect of one of them belonging to Slate Langbroek.

"We go in on my mark," he whispered into his inset microphone. "You know your assignments."

They'd been unable to track the head of Royal Nautilus Petroleum through the chaos in Times Square, and an exhaustive search of every hospital within a hundred miles confirmed that he hadn't been admitted under his or any other name, but he couldn't have gone far. A single street-level camera had captured him rising from the sidewalk in front of the TKTS booth, his visibly broken arm cradled to his chest and his face covered with blood. Fortunately, they'd discovered a Queen Anne–style mansion on five acres overlooking Peconic Bay among Aegis Asset Management's holdings, and it looked like the perfect location for an extended convalescence.

Layne crept along the front of the wraparound porch and assumed position within striking distance of the side door, while the FBI SWAT agents crawling through the mist that had settled upon the pasture and clung to the oak trees prepared to penetrate the back door and take up containment positions around the house. Langbroek's token security force had provided no resistance whatsoever and seemed resigned to the fact that it had backed the wrong horse.

"Boathouse and dock secure," a voice whispered through Mason's earpiece.

"I need him taken alive," Mason whispered. He advanced beneath the overhanging branches to the edge of the porch. Raised his M4 to his shoulder. Prepared to switch on the laser sight. Forced all other thoughts out of his head and focused on the moment. The world around him slowed to a crawl. "Now."

He cleared the railing and raced across the deck. Another agent converged upon the main entrance at the exact same time. A swing of a handheld battering ram and the door burst inward with a booming crack and an explosion of splinters. He heard the same sound from elsewhere in the house as he switched on his sight and swept the interior with the crimson beam. Polished hardwood floors. Crown and wall-frame molding. Nautical theme with mounted brass sextants and looking glasses. A pair of bare feet descended the ornate staircase from the second level.

"Don't move!" the SWAT agent shouted. "Get down on the ground!"

Mason caught a glimpse of an older woman in a nightgown, holding out her trembling hands as she lowered herself to the landing.

"*Husholderske,*" she said, and then in heavily accented English: "Housekeeper."

The other agent moved to secure her while Mason veered to his right, through a living room with leather furniture and an antique wooden hearth, and into a hallway adorned with black-and-white photographs of angry seas and ice floes and rocky fjords. He needed to find Langbroek before anyone else to make sure nothing happened to him, although the irony of protecting the man ultimately responsible for the production of the Novichok and the death of his wife from potentially comprised agents within his own agency wasn't lost on him.

Layne emerged from his peripheral vision, her sight slicing past him in the darkness.

"We caught someone trying to slip out the back," a voice said.

"Tell me it's Langbroek," Mason said.

"Negative. He claims to be the caretaker."

"Damn it," Layne said. "We're too late."

Mason burst into the master bedroom with his partner at his heels and absorbed everything around him at a glance. A massive bureau and a nightstand, upon which rested overturned prescription bottles and a stack of single-use emesis bags. The bed was unmade, the sheets discolored by some kind of salve. The wastebasket overflowed with soiled gauze and bandages. Clothes littered the floor of the closet. It looked like Langbroek had torn practically everything from the hangers in his hurry to pack.

"Someone must have tipped him off," Layne said.

Mason's federal cell phone vibrated from the outer pouch of his isolation suit. He removed it and noticed that the number of the incoming call had been blocked. He realized, right then and there, that not only was Langbroek gone; he was never coming back.

He pressed the speaker button and answered before the call could be routed to voice mail.

"Slate Langbroek, I presume," he said.

"Special Agent James Mason." The voice on the other end spoke in an accent that was an amalgam of Nordic and British and sounded pained, as though the mere act of speaking caused considerable discomfort. A motor thrummed in the background, metered by the thumping of waves against the hull of a seafaring vessel. "I regret that we are unable to have this conversation in person, but surely you understand the circumstances well enough to realize why we cannot."

There was no point in asking how he knew Mason's name or how he'd gotten his number; Langbroek wasn't about to give up his asset inside the Bureau, the agent who'd betrayed their operation.

"I need an ID on every AIS transponder within satellite range," Mason said into his comlink.

"Do not waste what little time we have together," Langbroek said. "You must realize the first thing we would do is disable our maritime automated identification system. And believe me when I say we are already well outside your reach."

"Then why are you calling?"

"There are many aspects of what happened that are a mystery to me. Perhaps you'll be able to help solve at least a few of them."

"Why would I want to help you?"

"Because you are every bit as curious as I am. There are simply too many questions for which there are no answers."

Layne stepped out of earshot while she attempted to coordinate a trace of the call. She gestured for Mason to keep Langbroek talking.

"You've seen the stills from the live broadcast, haven't you?" Mason said. "Five men in suits, standing behind a podium, flanked by security. Four of them staring in shock at the scene unfolding before them, while the fifth is already halfway over the back railing. Strange that he'd be able to recognize what's about to happen when all he could possibly see from his vantage point were two outstretched arms from the other side of the statue. And the brim of a conical straw hat."

Langbroek said nothing.

"You didn't know who she really was, did you?" Mason said. "Maybe you knew her background, just not the nature of your company's involvement at Edgewood, certainly not that she blamed your family for everything that happened to her there. You wouldn't have hired her if you had, or at least you would have taken precautions. There's no way you would have been in New York City after she killed two of your top executives if you'd thought for a single second that the Novichok was there. And you didn't, because you knew for a fact that your stockpiles were somewhere else."

"It was a banner day for Nautilus Energy," Langbroek said. His voice was strangely distant, hollow. "I wouldn't have missed the grand unveiling of the Green Smart Grid system for anything in the world. Do you have any idea what it means to my company, let alone the future of the planet?"

"Speaking of futures, how much do you personally stand to make if the price of oil suddenly spikes?"

"Fossil fuels are killing the Earth. It's up to people like me to save us from ourselves."

"You're a regular humanitarian."

"Mock me all you want, but the world will see it that way once I am able to clear my name."

"Why don't you come in and we'll see how that goes?"

"My location must remain a secret," Langbroek said. "At least for now."

"We'll find you, wherever you go," Mason said. "Assuming the other twelve don't find you first."

"Are you trying to threaten me?"

"I'm trying to help you."

"One does not reach my station in life without being able to differentiate between the two."

Mason's phone vibrated, alerting him to the arrival of the email he'd been waiting for. He knew what the attached photographs would show, but he had yet to see them with his own eyes. Not only would they prove Langbroek's involvement; they were the whole reason this operation had been green-lighted in the first place. He brought up the images and scrolled through them with a smile on his face.

"You think you'll ever be able to return to the Thirteen's good graces?" he said. "Surely they don't take kindly to one of their number stepping out of the shadows. They'll need to make an example of you, if only to keep the others in line."

"I have no idea what you are talking about, I assure you," Langbroek said. "And I fear you are wasting valuable time looking at me while the party truly responsible is still out there."

"So you're innocent?"

"I am guilty of many things, Special Agent, but what happened in Times Square is not one of them."

"Are you telling me you had nothing to do with the mass production of thousands of gallons of chemical weapons?"

"You are not listening to me."

"Perhaps you'd be surprised to learn that mere hours ago, a SEAL team raided a Nautilus tanker bound for the Port of Baku in Azerbaijan. Do you know what they found?"

Langbroek fell deathly silent.

"A drone with a remote aerial-dispersion unit bearing Russian military markings, armed with a hundred gallons of the same Novichok that was released in New York City. We traced the ship's origin to the Port of Newark, where we discovered two bulk shipping containers filled with empty liquid holding tanks, plus several of the exact same modified drones that we're in the process of removing from Nautilus vessels bound for dozens of ports all around the world, primarily throughout the Mediterranean, Arabian, and Caspian seas, where the release of the gas would not only kill hundreds of millions of people in Europe, North Africa, Western Asia, and the Middle East; it would also cripple the entire oil business, making someone heavily invested in energy futures and alternative energies, not to mention the patent holder of the only known prophylactic treatment, the richest and most powerful man in the entire world."

"They know who you are," Langbroek said. "They will come for you, too. Your wife was a warning. No one will be able to protect you this time. They will annihilate everyone and everything you hold dear."

"You'd better hope they find you first or I'll make you wish to God they had."

"Give my regards to your father."

"Don't you dare threaten—" Mason started to say.

But Langbroek was already gone.

DENVER, COLORADO
January 4

"What are you waiting for, an invitation?" Special Agent in Charge Gabriel Christensen said. "Get in here and shut the door."

Mason entered the conference room, where he found Chris seated at the head of the table. The blinds on the windows were drawn and there was a black box bristling with antennas in the middle of the table. He was just about to ask why they needed an electromagnetic frequency jammer when the door at the back of the room opened and a man he recognized from his debriefing in New York entered. Derek Archer hovered for several seconds before assuming the seat across from Chris. He gestured for Mason to take the chair between them, at the head of the table.

"I understand you two have already met," Chris said, "so let's not waste time with formalities."

Mason nodded warily to the secretary of the Department of Homeland Security, who had treated his debriefing in the Scarecrow case like a holy inquest. To say he was surprised to see him again was an understatement.

Archer checked the device positioned between them to make sure it was on and pulled out his cell phone to confirm it had neither a signal nor a functional GPS beacon before proceeding.

"I'm not going to beat around the bush," he said. "It's my understanding that both of our organizations have been infiltrated by hostile actors."

"Some more than others," Chris said.

Archer glared at him.

"Be that as it may, it happened on my watch, which makes it my responsibility. Through acts of subversion and outright treason, my second in command compromised a federal task force, derailed a manhunt, and was responsible for allowing chemical weapons to be released on American soil. He also facilitated their shipment to foreign ports, specifically in the Middle East and along the Russian border, where its dispersal would have caused an international incident that could very well have precipitated World War Three. I need not only to figure out how it happened but also the extent to which my department's been compromised. And I think you know a hell of a lot more than you let on during your debriefing."

Mason glanced at his SAC from the corner of his eye.

"Don't look at me," Chris said. "I know you're full of shit, but like I told him, I question your forthrightness, not your loyalty."

"Your statements were riddled with half-truths and convenient lapses in judgment, but they were always consistent," Archer said. "You told us just enough to satisfy our inquiries, and not one iota more. Maybe the others couldn't see through you, but don't think you had me fooled for a second. You knew Marchment had been co-opted and didn't tell anyone, and you stopped the terror plot on the subway without calling for backup. Now those are either the actions of a self-righteous glory hound or someone who genuinely doesn't know whom he can trust. I called your SAC here the moment I left that debriefing and he and I agreed it was the latter."

"You have to trust someone," Chris said, "and now's as good a time to start as any."

Mason watched the light flash on the electromagnetic frequency jammer and said nothing.

"I'm in charge of one of the most powerful agencies in the world," Archer said. "I answer directly to the president of the United States and have a sworn duty to protect the people of this great nation. A quarter of a million agents—good men and women who've devoted their lives to this country—count on me to maintain the integrity of that organization, and I failed them. I won't let it happen again."

"Then ask yourself a question," Mason said. "What would have happened had the Novichok been released on the subway?"

"Millions of people would have died," Chris said.

"A tragedy of unequaled proportions, to be sure, but look past that. The bodies of innocent people fill the streets. Pictures of the carnage play nonstop on TV. No one feels safe, even at home. What happens next?"

"The president declares a state of national emergency," Archer said. He furrowed his brow and looked down at his hands. "The National Guard is deployed. The entire country panics. Martial law goes into effect. There's rioting in the streets."

"And twenty thousand troops with specialized training in urban conflict and civil unrest are deployed under the command of USNORTH-COM, establishing a military presence in the streets of the United States of America."

Chris cocked his head and stared him down.

"What aren't you telling us?"

"There are some bad people out there, Chris."

"And we need your help to stop them," Archer said.

"What do you propose?"

"I'm offering you a job."

"I already have one."

"What I'm offering is off the books. A special operations unit with a discretionary budget and minimal oversight. You would answer solely to me, and all I ask for in return is the truth."

Mason studied the secretary's face for any hint of deception. Checked his phone to make sure the EMF jammer was working. He couldn't even make his voice recorder work.

"I told you that would be the deal breaker," Chris said.

"And I'd have control over personnel?" Mason asked.

"Yes."

"And autonomy."

"Within reason."

"No one outside this room could ever know. If even a single person found out, the entire operation would be compromised. You need to understand what kind of power we're up against."

"Fair enough," Archer said. "Why don't you tell us?"

Mason looked from one to the other. He wanted desperately to trust both of them, but the consequences of being wrong would be catastrophic.

"Let me think about it."

DOWNTOWN DENVER

"You told him what?" Ramses said. "I'll bet no one's ever told him that before. Did he have a coronary right there?"

"What should I have said?"

"How about 'Yes'?" Gunnar said. "Imagine what we could do with unrestricted access to Homeland's network."

He unconsciously swiveled in circles on the chair in the center of the room that Mason had commandeered in Ramses' penthouse, his laptop open on his thighs, while he worked on several projects at once, chief among them scouring the globe for Slate Langbroek, who might have eluded them so far, but wouldn't be able to hide forever. Eventually, he'd have to come up for air, and when he did, they'd be waiting.

In the meantime, Gunnar had to continue rebuilding his business as a corporate raider, which was back on track thanks to some inside knowledge about the vulnerabilities of one of the world's largest oil companies. Royal Nautilus Petroleum's competition was already pecking at its still-living carcass, but with federal investigators scrutinizing every facet of its business, its chief executive in the wind, and the cloak of national security concealing its involvement in what could very well have been the greatest disaster in the history of mankind, its governing board was more than happy to let them have it.

Unfortunately, its assets—including those of subsidiaries like Aegis—had been frozen before the sale of Aebischer Pharma's biomedical and chemical properties went through, preventing Mason's father from formally distancing himself from the pharmaceutical conspiracy among his in-laws, the Hoyl, and the Thirteen. The only consolation was that the senator now controlled the rights to Pyridocholinesterase, the prophylactic treatment for exposure to nerve agents, which he'd already begun shipping to the military to protect the troops disarming the drones on Nautilus's shipping fleet. It was almost too bad no one would ever know the service he'd provided for the men and women in uniform.

"We're doing just fine on our own," Ramses said. He grabbed a bottle from the six-pack on the small table, popped the cap on his belt buckle, and caught it in his free hand. "Besides, I don't trust him."

"You do not trust anyone," Alejandra said. She'd probably meant for it to sound more flippant than it came out, but it was likely part of the reason she'd decided to return to Mexico and her special forces unit. The main factor being how useless she'd felt babysitting the computers while they'd been off tracking the Scarecrow. She needed to get back to fighting the battles on her own terms, which was undoubtedly the only part of her decision that Ramses understood. "And yet in this case, I agree with you. Promise me you will be careful with these men."

"It doesn't have to be an all-or-nothing proposition," Layne said. She was only beginning to grasp the enormity of the Thirteen, but she'd already contributed to the organizational charts hanging on the walls surrounding them. She'd mapped the tentacles of influence radiating from the Langbroek family to dozens of foreign governments and international corporations, one of whose most powerful officers was likely plotting a way to take Slate's place in the hierarchy at that very moment. "Surely there's a way to hedge our bets and work from both inside and outside the system at the same time."

"Trust me," Mason said. "That's a hard tightrope to walk."

Archer's offer held a certain appeal to him, though. He was tired of trying to rationalize his actions in relation to the law and wished he could go back to a time when the bad guys wore black. The Thirteen had become so inextricably woven into the fabric of society that it was impossible to tell his friends from his enemies.

"There are still things I do not understand," Alejandra said.

"Join the club," Layne said. She stood before a section of the wall devoted to Slate Langbroek and the network he'd built, one created with the intention of murdering countless innocents and starting a war that would have killed even more. "These guys are like hair stuck in a drain; no matter how much you pull out, even more just keeps on coming."

"Remind me not to shower at your house," Ramses said.

Beneath Langbroek's photograph was a picture of Rand Marchment, who was still recovering from surgery and a stroke caused by the sudden and acute loss of blood, and one of the Scarecrow, Kameko Nakamura, whose autopsy demonstrated countless lesions in the parts of her brain traditionally associated with aggression, personal identity, and moral judgment: the ability to distinguish right from wrong. Layne had yet to formally slot the pictures of the other men responsible for the atrocities committed at Edgewood, including Charles Raymond and Andreas Mikkelson, who might not have been active participants in the plot to release the Novichok but who had played a pivotal role in its inception. There was also a picture of Dr. Tatsuo Yamaguchi, who'd served as the private physician to the Scarecrow and her brother. He was potentially the only living link between the Nakamuras and the Langbroeks, one that just might be able to connect them to the Thirteen, which meant they needed to find him first.

"I still can't wrap my head around the idea that we're dealing with an overarching plot spanning four generations," Layne said. "How can anyone dedicate his life to implementing a plan that he'll never see come to fruition?"

"That's what makes these guys so dangerous," Mason said. "We're only now stumbling upon plots hatched in the early twentieth century. I don't even want to imagine how many more we haven't exposed yet."

"I don't understand why Langbroek would need to paralyze the oil industry, reclaim the wells stolen from his family a century ago, and drive up the cost of crude when his own green building management system is poised to take over the renewable energy market. It's a risk he didn't have to take."

"You have to understand that the oil field in Baku isn't the only one at stake," Gunnar said. "Think of what happened in Iraq following the Gulf War. We not only usurped their drilling operations; we privatized them. Nautilus itself assumed control of nearly fifty percent of them. Langbroek could have literally monopolized the industry by slaughtering his competition."

"And blaming it on the Russians," Ramses said. "Between the use of a Soviet chemical weapon, the federation's insignia on the drones, and the fact that the catastrophe would serve the country's financial interests as the third-leading oil producer in the world, it wouldn't have been a hard sell in the media, which already has us primed to hate all things Russian."

"What better revenge could Langbroek hope for than the start of a war that would likely destroy the entire former Soviet Union?" Gunnar said.

Alejandra slowly paced the room, surveying the pictures on the walls like they were pieces of a puzzle. Her expression was one of confusion, as though no matter how she turned them, she simply couldn't make them fit together.

"Even if Nautilus took over all of the oil wells in the Middle East, it would not have been able to resume operations until the chemicals were cleaned up," she said. "It would have sacrificed its income, as well as the men responsible for its shipping and drilling operations."

"Thanks to the medication from Aebischer, they would have been able to start right back up the very next day," Ramses said. "Or at least once they'd cleared out the bodies."

"A medication they wouldn't have been able to manufacture had it not been for the experiments at Edgewood," Mason said.

"You're all missing the big picture," Gunnar said. "The petroleum fields in that area are also rich in natural gas, which is considered a 'clean' energy and is easily converted into liquid form for rapid transport. Between oil, LNG, and renewables, Nautilus would have controlled nearly all of the world's energy, giving Langbroek the ability to fix prices and destroy his competition, a single corporate entity capable of siphoning the wealth from the Middle East. He'd be a modern-day tycoon like Thomas Elliot Richter, making him the richest man on the planet and allowing him to stage a coup within the ranks of the Thirteen. And should the global economy ever transition from the International Dollar Standard to a commodity-backed currency, one using energy like we once used gold, he would literally become the most powerful person in the history of mankind."

"That's a hell of a long game," Layne said.

"The culmination of which was decided by a chance meeting of the principal players at a convention for, of all things, the Society for Lasting International Peace."

Mason stood beside Layne and stared at the faces tacked to the walls. The ties binding them were so convoluted, he wasn't sure they'd ever be able to unravel them all.

"There's still one detail that doesn't fit, though," she said. "I understand the Scarecrow's personal agenda and, truth be told, don't really care. Those men got what they deserved. But why rig the Novichok in the subway? Why release it in Times Square? Neither makes sense in the context of Langbroek's plan. In fact, both work against it in some way."

"Not least of which being the risk of the lone surviving Langbroek heir being killed along with millions of New Yorkers," Gunnar said.

"Releasing the Novichok in Times Square guaranteed we'd track the remaining stockpiles to the ends of the Earth if we had to," Mason said.

"And deploying the Third Infantry on American soil only complicates domestic operations for an international company," Ramses said. "Martial law can't possibly be good for business."

"So if Langbroek didn't pay the Scarecrow to orchestrate the attack on the subway and the massacre in Times Square, who did?"

Gunnar abruptly stopped spinning and set his laptop on the table.

"I'm detecting an attempted cyber intrusion," Gunnar said. "Someone's trying to hack into our system."

Mason leaned over his shoulder just in time to see a dialogue box open on the screen. The message consisted of four words.

GET OUT OF THERE.

"Is that Anomaly?" Mason asked.

"I can't imagine who else it could be. You don't think—"

The message vanished and another appeared.

NOW!

Mason realized with sudden clarity that not only did Anomaly know who and where they were, something terrible was about to happen.

"Go!" he shouted.

He dragged Gunnar out of the chair and shoved him into the hallway. Sprinted down the corridor toward the kitchen. He caught a glimpse of red and green flashing lights through the window, heard a sound like mechanical thunder in the distance. Ushered the others past him and down the staircase to the lower level of the suite. Ramses led them to the elevator and hit the call button.

The floor thrummed beneath their feet.

A spotlight burst through the wall of windows on the western side of the building and swept across the booths and reptile cages on the forty-first floor.

It was a helicopter. Coming in too way fast. There was no way it would be able to pull up in time.

A chime announced the elevator's arrival. Ramses practically pried the doors open.

"Get in," he said. "Hurry!"

The light struck them from behind, casting their shadows ahead of them onto the back wall of the car. Alejandra was already pushing the button for the lobby when Mason ducked inside. He turned around and watched the flashing lights grow larger and brighter as they neared the building. The spotlight pinned him through the closing doors, like an ant under a magnifying glass. The *thupp-thupp-thupp* of the rotors metamorphosed from a sound into a physical sensation he felt in his chest.

And then it was gone, sealed off by the reinforced elevator as it commenced its descent. Red numbers counted down the floors. Far too slowly.

40. 39. 38.

"Hold on to the rail," Mason said.

37. 36. 35.

The elevator shook with the impact above them, dropped several stories. Stopped hard, driving Mason to his knees. Superheated air raced down the shaft and washed over them.

"What the hell was that?" Layne asked. "Did that chopper just fly right into the—?"

The lights died, the readout went black, and the car plummeted straight down.

Mason clung to the rail with both hands as his feet left the floor. He rose weightlessly toward the ceiling. Collided with someone in the darkness. Air screamed past as they accelerated toward the unforgiving earth.

The brakes engaged with a metallic scream that trailed them on a slipstream of sparks. The elevator came to a sudden stop and they collapsed to the floor. The buttons on the panel flickered before the emergency light kicked on, bathing them in its red glare.

"Is everyone all right?" Mason asked.

"No time for that," Ramses said. "We need to get out before the whole building comes down."

He turned his back on them and jimmied the doors, admitting the wail of an alarm. The elevator was trapped between levels, leaving just enough room for them to crawl out onto the floor above them. Sprinklers sprayed from the ceiling in response to the burning debris raining down the shaft. The stairwell was across the hallway, its door clearly marked with the number 4.

Their footsteps echoed from the concrete walls as they rounded flight after flight until they reached the bottom and shouldered through the door into the lobby, where the security guards helped evacuate the few employees who'd still been in their offices this late at night.

They exited through the revolving door onto a sidewalk riddled with shattered glass, chunks of concrete, and metallic shrapnel. A haze of dust and smoke filled the street. A single warped rotor blade stood from the asphalt near the remains of the helicopter's tail assembly. Cars had pulled to the curb and crowds were beginning to gather.

Mason shielded his eyes, leaned back, and stared straight up the face of the building, toward where the upper floors were engulfed in flames, billowing thick black smoke into the night sky. He pulled Gunnar closer so his old friend would be able to hear him over the sirens converging from seemingly everywhere at once.

"How did Anomaly know . . . ?" he started to ask, but the answer hit him before he even finished asking the question. The anonymous hacker had alerted them to the elevation of FEMA's activation levels, guided them to the revelation of Marchment's involvement at Edgewood, and confirmed the Novichok was in New York City, when even Slate Langbroek, the man ostensibly in charge of the plot to release it, hadn't known. "He's not inside the national security apparatus; he's inside the Thirteen."

"Then why did he save us?" Gunnar asked.

"Because he's using us as pawns in the Thirteen's civil war."

Ramses stood several feet away, his expression unreadable in the flickering glow of the flames, his jaw muscles flexing and unflexing.

"I don't give a shit about their civil war," he said. "And I don't take kindly to being used."

"We'll find them," Gunnar said.

"And when we do," Mason said, "we'll burn every last one of them to the ground."

ACKNOWLEDGMENTS

As an author, I'd like to think that I have a decent grasp of the language, but I struggle to find the words to properly express my gratitude to all of the generous and dedicated individuals who've contributed to this book, not to mention how fortunate I am to have them in my life.

My undying appreciation to my team at St. Martin's Press/ Macmillan: Pete Wolverton, my friend and ingenious editor, with whom working these past few years has been the highlight of my professional career; Hannah O'Grady and Lily Cronig, who keep the wheels turning behind the scenes; Carol Edwards, copy editor extraordinaire (and then some); Michelle Cashman and Sarah Bonamino, marketing and PR wizards; Ken Silver, who's responsible for the beautiful product you hold in your hands; and Young Jin Lim, who perfectly captured my vision.

To my amazing support system at Trident Media Group: Alex Slater, who's so much more than just my agent (I'd be lost without you, my friend); Nicole Robson, who's given so selflessly of her time and expertise; Caitlin O'Beirne, queen of graphic design; and Robert Gottlieb, the man behind the curtain.

To my home team: my wife, Danielle (who needs sleep?), and my brood, who make life worth living; my mom, for her unwavering support; my dad, whom I miss every day; Jane Gauthier; and the Bannigans.

Special thanks to: the Bedard family; David Bell; Richard Chizmar;

Colorado Humanities & Center for the Book; Liza Fleissig; Mark Greaney; Michael Patrick Hicks; Gus Isuani; Michael Koryta; Jennie Levesque; Jonathan Maberry; Jim Marrs; Tom Monteleone; Andi Rawson; James Rollins; Michael Marshall Smith; Jeff Strand; Team TPMI; The Tattered Cover; Thomas Tessier; Paul Wilson; Kimmy Yerina; and to everyone else who's contributed to my success on a personal level: You know who you are and how much you mean to me.

My most sincere admiration and respect to all booksellers and librarians, who keep the torch of literacy burning.

And, most important, to all of you, my readers, without whom this book wouldn't exist.